GLIMMER IN THE ASHES

A Novel by D.S. Newman

Written by

D.S. Newman

Cover by

Amanda Demigod

Glimmer In The Ashes

A Novel by D.S. Newman

Cover by Amanda Demigod

Edited by Nandita Naik

First Edition, Paperback – published 2013

D.S. Newman Publishing

ISBN: 978-0-9911089-0-9

LCCN: 2013921159

10 9 8 7 6 5 4 3 2 1

This is a work of fiction. Names, characters, businesses, places, events and incidents are either the products of the author's imagination or used in a fictitious manner. Any resemblance to actual persons, living or dead, or actual events is purely coincidental.

Do what you love!

In Loving Memory of my Great-Grandmother,
Bessie Moore, who lived through 2 World Wars and
the Great Depression. (1912-2012)

Introduction from the Author

First of all, I'd like to thank you for purchasing my book and stepping into the world I created. This is my first dead serious shot at writing a book and I've put a lot of time and effort into it. I've also put a lot of my personal inspirations into it. I paid homage to some of my favorite works of fiction and even made some of their concepts my own. I'd like to challenge readers to discover which parts of this novel are inspired from my favorite works of fiction. It will be fun to see what my readers spot. You may even notice things that I didn't while writing it. The story is kind of an intended "hodgepodge" of different ideas that appeal to me. Although many of the ideas have deep meaning and are thought provoking, I want to remind people that this *is* a work of fiction. So please, nobody take any of the themes here too serious. Anyhow, be sure to check out the Afterword of the book for information on my other works. But for now, enjoy!

Prologue

Jon Peters is a man who has reached a pinnacle in his life. At age 29, just three years out of graduate school, he teaches archaeology at a university in Southern California. In the realm of academia, there are few as well versed in their field as Jon. Also in his repertoire is a vast knowledge of conspiracy theory and conspiracy fact. Although Jon feels he knows much about secret societies and related areas, nothing can prepare him for the journey he is soon to embark upon.

In the last few years, Jon has felt that things have gotten stale for him. Although he is a relatively attractive man, with dark hair, coal black eyes, and medium build, he is lonely. He thinks that things are the best they can possibly be, that his best days are behind him, and life cannot get better. He is soon to discover that this thinking is false. Although his motivation is not the highest, he is a champion in his arena, the classroom. On this particular day, Jon is shining rather brightly in the classroom setting.

Chapter 1:

Voices from the Past

Standing in front of a class of college students, Jon is explaining why he feels known history is only a fragment of the truth. "We really can't know anything outside of 100 hundred years within our lifetimes," says Jon profoundly. "It's really all one big guessing game. Sure, we have documentation of events and people, but that only goes so far. I mean, how do we really know it's true if we weren't there to witness it ourselves?"

Jon surveys the room, looking at all the intrigued yet semi confused faces. He continues, "I myself believe we may only know less than half of the true story, and I'm an educator."

Just then a student interrupts. "That's ridiculous," he says. "There's no reason to not trust the written word of those before us. It's all been passed down by the greatest minds throughout the centuries." As the student argues with Jon about his lecture, a bald, white-bearded man appears at the doorway of the classroom. An older and more experienced colleague of Jon's, Professor Gray sees great potential in him.

As the professor watches, Jon begins to prove that there may be more evidence to what he's teaching than mere opinion. "Yes, but what if some of these great minds didn't know all the answers?" Jon proclaims. "Or what if they didn't want all the truth known? Wouldn't their great minds be capable of generating a great illusion?" The student settles back in his seat to hear Jon out. Jon continues, "But perhaps it simply is just a construction made in favor of not knowing. It's widely taught that the first American flag was sewn by Betsy Ross. But this story was manufactured by descendants of hers in order to make a quick buck. Somewhere along the way, it became historical fact." The other students, as well as Professor Gray, look on and listen. "Columbus is another one," Jon says. "It is said that he had a harsh three-month trip where the crew was near mutiny by the time they reached the Americas. In actuality, the trip took about one month and the ship's logs state nearly perfect weather the entire voyage." Jon surveys the room once more before continuing. "Oh, and how about World War I?" He asks. "No one seems to be able to give a good reason why it happened. Sure, something about Archduke Franz Ferdinand's assassination, but what does that have to do with the majority of the powers that were involved in the conflict?"

The student, taken aback by Jon's quick account of shady historical "facts," begins to nod his head in agreement. Jon smiles and says, "I hope this gets some gears turning for you all, knowing that even a trained professional like me has to question everything. Class is dismissed."

As the students begin grabbing their things and scurrying out of the room, Jon notices Professor Gray standing in the doorway.

After several students come up and thank Jon for the lecture, he heads over to the exit with Professor Gray. "Another fine lecture, Jon," Gray asserts. "I couldn't have stated it better as a history professor."

Jon smiles and says, "Thank you sir." The two head to the teachers' lounge together.

Once in the lounge, the two sit down and enjoy some coffee and conversation. "You know what, Jon?" Professor Gray asks. "What are you doing?"

Jon looks up abruptly and replies, "What do you mean?" Gray reiterates, "I mean, what are you doing with yourself? You come here every day. You give these amazing lectures. Then you go home and eat Ramen like you're still in college. You never go on dates. You don't take your research into the mainstream or produce any publications. You haven't gone on any excavations since you left grad school. You just all around seem unnecessarily stagnant." Jon sighs and nods his head slowly. Professor Gray asks, "What's holding you back, son? You have great potential."

Jon, agreeing halfheartedly says, "I suppose."

Gray sighs and hands Jon a newspaper before leaving the room. "Here," he says. "Enjoy something before rushing off to nothing." Jon looks at the paper for a while before finally heading home to his lonely apartment.

The next day when Jon arrives back at the university, the secretary of his department stops him and says, "Oh, Jon, you have a package."

Jon turns and asks, "Really, who from?"

The secretary responds, "Well, it's anonymous, but judging by all its postage it seems to have made a tour of Europe."

Jon, curious, takes the package into his office and opens it. Inside he finds an old journal written in Greek, which seems to be from the early 1900s.

There's a letter with the journal. Jon looks at it and on reading the heading says, "Rachel." His heart sinks as he remembers his old girlfriend, whom he hasn't seen in three years. The letter reads:

"Jon, I found this old journal behind a loose stone in the museum's basement. It seemed like it might be something that's up your alley. I translated the first few pages into English for you. If you're interested in where it came from, contact me. Rachel."

After Jon reminisces a bit more about Rachel, he looks into the pages of the journal. Just as Rachel said, he finds notes tucked into the first several pages, translating the Greek into English. Jon wastes no time and begins reading the journal. The journal begins:

"Cyrus Methena, Museum Archives Curator, 1911..."

As Jon continues to read, he discovers that this man, Cyrus Methena, knew of a terrible truth. As a Great War reigns rampant throughout the world, a mysterious force is moving about, wiping out all records of known history. Methena seems to be afraid that his museum will eventually become a target. The journal reads, "There are strange reports, all across Europe, of men dressed from head to toe in black battle fatigues, wearing gas masks, with weapons emitting fire and destroying museums and libraries. Accompanying these men are large airships that drop liquid fire on buildings, leaving only burnt ash."

"What Great War can he be talking about?" Jon thinks. "Surely he's not talking about World War I. It won't start for another three years from the time of this journal, although it *was* called the Great War in its day." As Jon reads further, the mystery deepens.

"It's been said that the United States will be making its way back into this conflict here in Europe. I'm not sure what good they can do. It's only been 12 years since they started their reconstruction." This makes no sense to Jon, in the late 1800s the US was just fine, immigration was at an all-time high, and the industrial era was in full swing.

That night, after investigating the journal a little more, he decides to give Rachel a call. Since it is 11 PM in California, he estimates it must be 1 PM for her. Jon waits a few moments for the overseas call to go through, and then Rachel picks up. "Hello," she says.

Jon hesitates a moment then says, "Hey, Rachel. It's Jon."

Enthusiastically, Rachel responds, "Oh, hey! So I guess you are interested in my little find. I mean, I knew you would be."

Jon chuckles and says, "Yeah."

Rachel switches to a more serious tone. "Odd, isn't it? The dates and events just don't add up. I mean, unless it's a complete work of fiction, I don't know what to make of it."

Jon replies, "The thought crossed my mind. We have to be sure it wasn't just some fantasy manuscript dreamed up by a bored curator."

Rachel says, "I agree, but there's more to the story. This museum had a fire several years before World War I started. Because of the war, it wasn't able to be rebuilt and the archives weren't replenished until after the war was over. But according to some entries, it could have burned down during the war, which makes no sense."

Jon goes on to say, "Hmmm, I'd like to see the place where you found it."

Quickly, Rachel suggests, "Great, then you can come on a research leave to Greece and investigate this."

Jon, stunned, hesitates even more. He stumbles over his words, saying, "Well, ummm, ya see. I'd like it too. But…"

Rachel breathes deeply and interjects, "But what Jon? What could you possibly be doing that's more important than this? This could be a real find, and I sent it to you because you're *you*, and I know you can figure it out if there's anything to it." Jon goes quiet. Rachel sighs and says, "It's okay, Jon. I understand. It probably is just a work of literary fiction anyway. I'm sorry that I got my hopes up."

Suddenly, Jon speaks up. "I'll do it. I'll come. I'll put in for field research, and then I'll get a substitute to cover my classes for the rest of the semester."

Rachel, now excited again, says, "Great! I'll meet you in Athens and bring you here myself. This may very well be the adventure you've always wanted Jon."

Jon chuckling slightly responds, "Could be."

Before getting off the phone, Rachel says, "It will be good to see you again, Jon."

Jon replies, "You too Rach."

The following day, Jon takes this prospective field research to his department head. While discussing with the dean about his research project, they are overheard by Winston Drake III, a much older archaeologist and past critic of Jon's abrasive teaching style and questioning of procedure. Winston seems overly interested in Jon's choice of going to Greece and wants to know what the journal says. Jon, who is quite intimidated by Drake, doesn't offer much information.

The dean says, "Winston, would you mind covering Jon's courses for the next six weeks, while he carries out this research?"

Winston answers, not taking his eyes off Jon, "Sure. But I would like to review this find once he returns."

"Great," says the dean. "Then you may leave for Europe by the end of the week."

Jon thanks both of them, then goes about his day.

Later on in the week, Jon makes his way to Athens. Getting off the plane, he begins looking around. There, at the end of the terminal, he sees someone he thought he would never see again. Rachel. As she comes toward him, he recalls the last time they saw each other. Her long dark hair, soft white skin, and always cheery smile, is something Jon has all but forgotten. Before he gets too deep into thought, she calls out to him, "Jon!" Making her way over to him, she hugs him. "Great to see you. Come on; let's get right down to business. I'll take you to the museum and show you where I found the journal." Jon is amazed at Rachel's eagerness about the find.

Once at the museum, Rachel takes Jon down to the basement. "Right over here," she says. "This is where I found it. This stone was loose. It's part of the original museum that was used as a foundation to build the current one on."

Jon sees a crevice in the stone wall. "Have you read the rest of the journal, besides the part you translated for me?"

Rachel's eyes widen as she answers. "Yes," she says. "It gets really wild toward the end. Let's go look at it and I'll tell you what it says."

Upstairs, the two sit down and begin reviewing the journal. As Rachel reads on and translates from Greek what the journal says, Jon realizes that this is much deeper than he originally thought. Cyrus, in his journal, writes about the widespread destruction of knowledge throughout the world. Amidst the chaos of the war, these incinerator troops are sweeping the globe. Cyrus' final entry recounts how he is having his assistant travel to Cameroon in order to preserve his personal collection of records so that they may survive the war. The journal ends with a cryptic entry that suggests the incinerators have made their way to his museum. After reviewing the journal, Rachel looks up at Jon and says, "We need a while to reflect on this. Care for some dinner?"

That night, as Jon and Rachel enjoy dinner together and discuss the day's discoveries, a tough topic arises. Rachel asks, "So how have the last three years been?"

Jon answers, "Well, I made it I guess."

Rachel laughs and says, "You guess?"

Jon pauses a moment before continuing, "It's just... I teach, I lecture, and I continue my studies. But I haven't really done anything with my credentials. This is my first field research since grad school. Since you left."

Rachel frowns and gives Jon a look. "Jon. You know I had to take that opportunity. I needed it for me. You're the one who didn't think we could last apart from each other."

Jon, remembering that it was he who called off their relationship when Rachel accepted an internship at this very Greek museum she works at now, bows his head.

Rachel adds, "Jon, you didn't need me to do what you do best. And besides, we're here now, and you've got a serious chance of making a find that will far exceed anything you could have achieved all this time."

Jon replies, "About that. What do you think we should do now?"

Rachel's eyes light up. "Well. Go to Cameroon, of course. What else?" she chuckles.

Jon responds, "You can't be serious?"

Rachel retorts, "And why wouldn't I be? We've got a good lead here, and I wanna know what that assistant had with him."

Chapter 2:

A Great Secret Revealed

Leaving by plane the next day, they fly to the northern part of Cameroon, just off the border of Nigeria, which according to the journal, is the site to which Cyrus' assistant escaped by boat during the attack on the museum. Going in rather blindly, the two follow the instructions that were left in the journal as if following in the very footsteps of the terrified assistant trying to save whatever precious information he was carrying. Rachel notes, "During World War I, this entire area was a German colony. Greece was an enemy of Germany during the war. If they were trying to escape, why would they go directly to where the enemy was?"

Jon comments, "Maybe it wasn't Germany who attacked the museum in the first place." Rachel and Jon decide it is best to hire a guide to take them to a village near the area where Cyrus' assistant may have gone. While riding with the guide through the jungles of western Africa, Jon turns to Rachel and tells her, "Hey. I'm really glad you convinced me to do this. I feel like I'm finally getting into my element." Rachel just smiles and looks at the scenery.

Having no more leads to follow from the journal, Rachel asks, "Now what?" Jon says, "Now we ask the locals."

After an afternoon of inquiring, the pair discovers a local legend about a European man, not a German, who came to the village and bartered for a piece of land. Nothing was ever built on this land, so not much was thought of it other than that the man was crazy for taking such a small piece of land so prestigiously. When they are shown the land, they find nothing, just as the legend says. Now is when Jon's archaeologist instincts kick in, telling him to dig. For two days they dig for what seems an aimless endeavor.

Finally, Rachel says, "Jon, it's over. It was fun giving it a shot and seeing you again, but at this point I think we're on a wild goose chase."

Jon says, "Rachel, please give it a little more time, my gut says we are still on to something." Rachel nods and agrees to try some more. The moment her shovel breaks ground again she hits something. Sifting through the dirt, they dig up a medium-sized steel chest. Once unearthed, they take it back to their hut. Inside the chest, they find a plethora of documents and journals, all records from before the time of Cyrus' journal.

Upon investigating the contents of the chest, they discover uncanny amounts of proof as to the alteration of history. According to these records, the war had actually begun in North America in 1881 following a series of wars such as the Indian wars and the civil war among others. All of this information has been dated to before 1911, three years before what we believe was World War I had started. The entries go on to say that the United States was obliterated and only about 35% of the population survived. Typhus was actually a manmade disease developed in a lab as a form of germ warfare that escaped its test tubes and ran rampant. Although it's believed to have been developed by the Ottoman Empire, its true origin is unknown. Creatures thought to be extinct much earlier, such as the wooly mammoth and the Moa bird were used early on in the war.

Experimental weapons such as steam powered planes and tanks, as well as weapons utilizing ice and electricity were also used early on. Nikola Tesla, who was Serbian, had actually developed his fabled death ray to be used by the Ottoman-Austrian Alliance to destroy enemy aircraft, but when he realized its destructive capabilities could wipe out whole cities, he destroyed it and defected to the allies. Being one of the prominent people to have survived the war, he was permitted to live because of his contribution but his name was demonized so his story would never be believed.

Jon realizes that other campaigns that preceded the war such as the Spanish American war and the Russo-Japanese war were not independent conflicts, but extensions of the same war, only fragmented by history. The immigrants coming to Ellis Island at the turn of the century came as refugees to escape the war as it heated in Europe. They were put through a reeducation process before being allowed to mix with the survivors from North America, from 1899 once they helped to rebuild the United States and Canada.

The two read on about a shadowy group known as the Cabal whose purpose was to destroy history as we know it and restructure society. Jon, already well versed in conspiracy theory, realizes this may be the focal point of all the supposed rumors or secret societies bent on world domination.

In the midst of all the chaos of the war, another factor remains. Horrible gas masked cloaked soldiers known only as incinerators. They are usually accompanied by firebombing dirigibles, capable of spraying kerosene and butane down on targets for maximum efficiency. Wherever they go, they leave a trail of ashes behind them in an attempt to destroy known history. They attack libraries and museums as well as homes of intellectuals and private collectors. It is unknown who these soldiers are and where they came from but Cyrus (and Jon at this point) suspects the Cabal. Cyrus got wird of these and was preparing to escape Greece and hide in a time capsule when his museum was attacked by the perpetrators.

They then read the diary of a disillusioned trooper. According to his writing, the man was 20 years old in 1910. This would have made him so young, that all he would have known his entire life was the war. Jon notes, "If this journal is accurate, and everything we have read is true, then it's no wonder that people have been so ready to accept this mass cover up. They were so sick of war; they didn't want the next generation to keep thinking about the atrocities of the last three decades."

After reading this, Rachel and Jon take a moment to assimilate all the new information. They determine that what they are reading may very well be true considering Jon's already well versed knowledge in the attempts to destroy history in the past. His lesson to his students flashes into his mind and he tells Rachel, "If this is true, then the Cabal could very well still be around in one form or another."

Rachel responds, "Well, if they were, I don't suppose they would want this knowledge out there. What should we do?"

Jon answers, "I'm not sure. But for now we should head back to Greece and think it over."

On their flight back to Greece, Rachel suggests, "I think we should take this information to others in our field for further review. This may very well be the largest archival find since the Rosetta Stone."

Jon says, "Yes, this time capsule appears to be a glimmer in the ashes, of a world we never knew." Jon then notes, "Cyrus must have left no record of his assistant's name in the journal for fear that he'd be discovered. This information was of the utmost importance, and may very well be so even today."

When they arrive back at the museum, someone unexpected is waiting for them – Winston Drake III.

"What are you doing here?" Jon asks.

Winston, with his pompous attitude says, "I have been sent here to notify you that you are being charged with plagiarism, malpractice as an instructor, and now forgery of historical evidence by the university. You are to cease any further investigation and return to California for official review."

Jon, surprised responds, "What? That's absurd! I've done none of those things."

Winston smirks vilely and simply says, "Well, you can take it up with the education board."

As Drake walks away, Rachel stands next to Jon and says, "Don't worry, I'll go back to California with you and vouch for you. I know the truth."

On arriving at the university in California, Jon says to Rachel, "You know what? If anyone's part of some secret Cabal set out to cover up history, Drake is."

Rachel smiles, nods and says, "That's too funny, but let's hope it's not true."

Jon continues, "I've always had a bad feeling about that guy. But I never thought he'd try to end my career though."

Rachel says, "Hmmm, tell you what. I'm gonna go try and research him to see if I can find anything weird. If I find anything at all, I'll bring it to the board."

Jon smiles at her and says, "Thank you Rachel, you're the best. You always have been."

Chapter 3:

Apples that Fall from the Same Tree

A few minutes after parting from Rachel, Jon walks into the room where the board is waiting to assess his charges. Soon after, Drake enters the room. He makes eye contact with Jon before he walks over to the board and whispers a bit. After a moment of quiet, the speaker of the board stands up and says, "Jon Peters, you are here to face charges that may result in the loss of your teaching and research license. Are you prepared to defend yourself?"

Jon nods his head and says, "Yes. I am."

The speaker announces, "Very well, the floor then goes to Winston Drake. Professor Drake, you may begin your indictment."

Drake stands up and begins with, "Professor Peters, do you consider yourself an educator with an unconventional teaching style?"

Jon answers, "You could say that."

Drake goes on, "Do you or do you not teach your students an overly zealous belief of opinionated history?" Right out the gate, Drake comes in with guns blazing with accusations.

Jon defends himself by stating, "I merely show them the frailty of the evidence we have of the past."

Drake laughs and says, "And have you conducted research to support this?"

Jon responds, "Well, I haven't done field research in some time. But I assure the board that my new find will back up everything I've taught and then some."

In a very charismatic way, Drake tears apart Jon's research saying, "After three years of no field work, Jon Peters has now taken it upon himself to make up a wild find with little or no leads to make himself look good. He has also abused the use of his Archaeological Excavation License to take a lavish vacation in the Mediterranean." Jon feels like this is the end of his career.

Meanwhile, as Rachel is sitting at a computer in the research lab, Professor Gray comes in. As he approaches, he asks, "You wouldn't happen to be Rachel Lynn would you?"

Rachel responds, "Yes, and who might you be?"

The Professor answers with, "I'm Professor Gray. I like to think of Jon as a friend of mine and I would like to do anything I can to clear his name. I assume that's what you're doing here, research to try and prove something?"

Rachel says, "Well, yes actually, and I do have a few interesting things I've discovered. But I have to ask. How did you know my name? I haven't been here in years."

Gray smiles at Rachel and chuckles, "You don't hang around Jon Peters these last few years and not hear about Rachel Lynn a time or two." Rachel blushes before looking back at the computer screen.

Back in front of the board, Jon is taking all sorts of blame of misleading his students. When the onslaught from Drake is over, the board says they will take a 15-minute break for deliberation before deciding Jon's fate. Just before the group breaks for recess, Rachel and Professor Gray barge into the room.

"Wait!" Rachel shouts. "We have new evidence regarding this matter."

Drake, discouraged, looks at Rachel and snaps, "Young lady, this is not the time for this."

Rachel quips back, "Oh, I think it is."

The speaker of the board stands and says, "Professor Gray, you are a respected member of this institute. I hope you have a good reason to back your intrusion."

Gray answers, "Yes, the girl is right. This new knowledge will shed some light on this wrongful accusation against Professor Peters."

Rachel holds up the printout of her and Professor Gray's research and says, "I have documentation that Drake's grandfather, a young archaeologist at the turn of the century, was very close to Woodrow Wilson. During the close of World War I, Drake's grandfather with Woodrow's help shut down many prominent voices in the history and archival world of education, accusing many of them of plagiarism, false finds, and misconduct of teaching."

Drake splutters, "This is preposterous."

Rachel goes on, "Also, in the 1950s, Drake's father shut down an excavation in Cambodia not far from the Angkor Wat ruins. These were later destroyed during the Vietnam War, ruining any chance of a major discovery about that civilization's past."

Drake interrupts again, "This is an outrage. Tearing apart my family will not change this board's mind. Even if these statements were true, what does it have to do with me?"

Rachel adds, "Conveniently, Drake himself was a filter of the artifacts and evidence brought in from the Iraq war excavations of Babylon."

The board members start whispering among themselves.

"Furthermore," Professor Gray adds, "We have a student here who is willing to testify against Drake that he bribed him to create unnecessary opposition in Jon's class. Come on in, son." Gray motions toward the doorway, where the student who challenged Jon's theory the previous week in class is standing.

Winston's jaw drops just before he says, "What? This is ridiculous!"

As the student approaches, the board asks the student if this is true. He confesses, "Yes, he paid several of us. But I'm the only one to come forward about it."

After a few moments of deliberation, finally the speaker of the board stands up and says, "We have decided to acquit Professor Peters of the charges and allow him to continue his investigation in any way he chooses. However, in light of new evidence concerning Professor Drake, we are now opening an investigation into him and his family.

Drake sinks back into his seat, not knowing what to think.

Back in the teachers' lounge, Jon thanks Rachel and Professor Gray for saving his skin. He says, "I knew something was fishy about Drake, ever since I first met him. But how did you find out about him bribing the students?"

Professor Gray in a smirky fashion tells Jon, "Well, that's not exactly true. I remembered this boy and his peers' reactions to your teaching style. So when I approached him and asked what he thought of you, he said he was skeptical at the beginning of the semester but you've changed his whole perspective on how he views the world. So naturally when I told him you were in trouble he wanted to help."

Jon looks questioningly at Professor Gray.

Gray then says, "It was all there. We just needed a little white lie to ice the cake." The trio then laughs and goes on about their afternoon.

The following day Jon goes to Rachel's hotel to discuss their next move. He asks her, "How invested are you in this project?"

Rachel answers laughingly, "Trust me Jon. I'm in this for the long haul. After all, I'm the one who found the journal in the first place. And if it wasn't for me, you'd never have escaped that board. Besides, all I've been doing is maintaining archives at a Greek museum that may not even be factual."

Relieved that Rachel wants to go on with him, he reveals what he plans to do. "Okay, Rach. Here's what I wanna do. I want to take the discovery to Tokyo, where it can be shown to other academics. The UN's think tank is at the University of Tokyo. If enough of us show it to them, this may get global attention. Maybe then, the truth can be more widely explored as to what happened and why it did at the turn of the previous century."

Rachel starts getting excited and says, "Okay, I'm in."

Jon says, "Good. We'll leave tomorrow night."

Chapter 4:

A Radical Change

On their flight to Japan, Rachel says, "This is genius Jon. There's no way you won't get scholarlysupport for this. Especially since that board found your research to have merit."

Jon smiles and says, "I certainly hope so. My gut feeling says that things are going to change drastically for us here in Japan."

Rachel adds, "And your gut feeling means a lot. You've always had fantastic intuition."

Just then, Jon's cell phone rings. He looks at it and says, "Hmmm, it's Professor Gray. I wonder what's up." He answers the phone, "What's going on Professor?" Rachel looks on as she sees Jon's expression get serious. "You're kidding," Jon says. Jon's jaw drops. "I understand. Okay professor. Thank you for telling me this. I'll let you know what happens after our presentation. Goodbye."

Rachel looks at Jon and asks, "What happened?"

Jon, looks stunned as he turns to her. "It's Drake. He killed himself."

Rachel shudders and gasps, "Oh my God! How?"

Jon replies, "He overdosed himself. The authorities have stated that he probably wasn't able to cope with the disgrace to him and his family, so he did himself in."

For the rest of their flight, the two studiously avoid the subject. Although they did not like Winston Drake III, they still viewed him as a human. Jon can only feel how unfortunate it is that he took the path he did.

After arriving in Tokyo, the pair makes their way to the university. There, Jon submits a formal request to have his find reviewed. If the review commission deems the find worthy, Jon and his supporters will be allowed to present to the UN think tanks, academic sector. From there, Jon can only hope it makes its way around the world into the proper hands.

Their second night in Tokyo, the two relax at their high rise hotel suite. Rachel, standing across the room, looks at Jon as he gazes out the window at the endless city lights and teeming perpetual motion of the Tokyo nightlife. "Ya know what? Things are different now Jon," she says. Jon turns around as she continues. "When we were together before, we were still in college. I hadn't experienced the things I had wanted to yet, because I spent so much time working and studying. But now, I'm 30 years old, and I got the experience I wanted in that world. And now, together, we may have come across something huge."

Jon slowly walks across the suite toward Rachel and says, "Together?"

The two begin to fall into one another's embrace, for a kiss. But before they can rekindle what they once threw away, an explosion rocks the building. Glass bursts all around them. The impact throws them to the other side of the room, along with a couch and coffee table. As they gather their wits about them, a nightmarish scene confronts them. They see a metallic figure silhouetted against the moonlight streaming through the remains of the blown out window. With expressionless glowing emerald eyes and a sleek body design, the figure appears to be some sort of robotic ninja. Out of the shadows, Jon is able to get a good look at it. The humanoid robot is silver with green markings all over it. The two crouch quietly and watch as it walks around the room appearing to be looking for something – probably for them.

Jon realizes it's only a matter of time before they are discovered. He grabs Rachel by the arm and makes a dart for the door. With a *Snick* sound, the cyborg releases three blades from the top of its right wrist and moves toward them. Gaining momentum, the robot with its claw extended closes in on the two. Just before it reaches them, the door Jon and Rachel are heading toward bursts open. A Japanese man standing in the hall shouts, "Run!" As the two run out the door and past him, the man tosses a sticky bomb at the robot. The tiny goo covered explosive sticks to the droid's chest. After a moment it explodes, blasting the terrifying killing machine backwards.

As the pair run into the hall, they see two more men outside the door. Both are carrying submachine guns. The man who threw the bomb joins the group running toward the elevator. Joined by the other two men, the group enters the elevator. As the elevator goes down, the first man draws a gold plated pistol and looks up, as they hear what appears to be the cyborg climbing down the elevator shaft toward them. The three Japanese men aim up and fire relentlessly through the ceiling. Rachel and Jon crouch down on the elevator floor.

Once they reach the lobby floor, the lead man takes Jon and Rachel out of the elevator and out front to a car waiting with a driver. As they run, they hear the sounds of combat inside the lobby between the other two men and the droid. Jon and Rachel get in the back seat as the other man gets in on the passenger side. As the car speeds away, a second car follows with three more Japanese men. The man who helped them out turns around in his seat and says, "My name is Shigeru. I'm Lieutenant of the Hogo-sha Clan."

Jon looks at Rachel and whispers, "Yakuza."

Before they can ask questions, Shigeru looks back at the other car following them. Speeding through the streets of Tokyo, the rear car is being attacked by a mildly tattered cyborg that they *thought* had been destroyed. The men in the car fire at it as it jumps from hood to hood of vehicles in pursuit of them, like a frog leaping from lily pad to lily pad. As it lands on the back of the car, one of the Yakuza leans out of the rear window, aims his TEC-9 submachine gun at the droid, and fires off several rounds, grazing it across the shoulder and rib area. The robot grabs the man by the back of his shirt and pulls him up out of the car, impaling him with the metallic claw protruding from its wrist. It then flings the man like a rag doll on to the street. The cyborg, now gripping the top of the car, opens a small port on its chest, from which a small sphere-like explosive drops onto the roof of the car. As the mechanized terror leaps off the vehicle toward a skyscraper, the car and its passengers are destroyed in a fiery explosion.

Jon asks, "What is that thing?"

Shigeru answers, "It's a Cybernetic Shinobi, built by a Japanese advanced robotics company owned by the Cabal."

Jon, shocked at this enlightening information, replies, "So the Cabal *is* still around today. But why is it after us?"

Shigeru responds, "Same reason the Cabal took out your academic friend, except they must have really wanted you gone to send this thing." Shigeru punches out a text message on his phone and barks orders in

Japanese at the driver as they race aggressively through the streets of Tokyo.

Jon looks puzzled as he realizes Shigeru is referring to Drake who supposedly committed suicide.

Jon, with his hand on Rachel's shoulder asks Shigeru, "What are we going to do to escape?"

Shigeru answers, "We are heading to an alley in Yakuza territory. Some reinforcements will be waiting there for us." Abruptly, Shigeru hangs out the window, firing several shots back at the Shinobi.

As the car pulls into an alley where seven Japanese men armed to the teeth are waiting, Jon guides Rachel out to take cover behind some skids and a dumpster. Together, Shigeru and his eight men prepare to open fire. A moment of silence sets in before the hydraulics of the droid can be heard coming around the corner. The Shinobi, claws extended, comes into view only for a second before realizing that it's outnumbered. It aims its fist and fires its claws at the Yakuza just left of center, piercing his chest.

"Why?!" the fellow shrieks.

A clap of gunfire bursts out as the Shinobi lunges toward the wall firing two ninja stars from a mechanism under its left wrist into the arm of one of the shotgun-wielding men, bringing him to one knee. The droid now draws a very futuristic looking Samurai sword about a foot and a half in length, from a built-in scabbard on its back. The blade looks so shiny and solid it seems as if it could survive an atomic blast. As a few of the men run to different points of cover, the robot cuts down the man nearest to Shigeru. Now taking a direct combat stance, Shigeru and two of his men fight the thing close quarters. Slicing the blade through another man's chest, the Shinobi takes a small leap back. As the man breathes his last, Shigeru and the other Yakuza run for cover with the remaining four men and they all begin fire relentlessly once more. Taking severe damage, the cyborg stands swaying from side to side as the last shell casings are heard hitting the ground from the men's guns. Silence holds as everyone reloads and the droid stumbles a few short steps toward some of the group. Some lights flicker on the Shinobi's chest and a few seconds later a whining sound is heard before the robot self-destructs in a fiery explosion throwing everyone back. Only burnt scrap metal and a large black mark on the floor of the alley remain.

When everyone catches their breath, two of the men tend to the injured arm of the man hit with the ninja stars. Shigeru looks around to assess the location of Jon and Rachel. When he sees them, he takes a step in their direction as Jon exclaims, "We need to have a serious talk."

Chapter 5:

An Age-Old Struggle

Now relaxing back at the Yakuza safe house, Jon and Rachel are about to be enlightened about a great many things. The safe house is in the basement of a nightclub and appears like a luxurious club itself, where the Yakuza enjoy a fully stocked bar and pool table among other amenities.

The group turns on the news to find the explosion at the hotel being reported. Jon states, "They're reporting it as a terrorist attack, well it was, just not as they're saying it is."

Rachel concurs by adding, "Yeah, that certainly wasn't the work of Islamic Extremists."

Shigeru agrees, "Yes, the Cabal will use it to manipulate countries that adhere to the UN to further their agenda. That's what they always do. Whether it's something they manufactured or not, they exploit it through the might of their media outlets the way they see fit to enact weapon and possession laws. If it's something they didn't do, it makes their job easier. If they need someone like you gone, whether they succeed or not, they still benefit from it. They probably just had some CIA MK-Ultra sleeper agent, give a suicide shot to your friend Mr. Drake."

As Jon takes all of this in, he raises the point. "But people were all over those streets, and there were security cameras. Surely someone else got a tape or a picture of that thing with how many cameras and cellphones there are, especially here in Japan."

Shigeru replies, "Even though many eyewitnesses saw something, maybe even had cameras out, they will be called nuts because they have no evidence. The Shinobi are equipped with a device embedded in them that blots out visual recording devices. A prototype of them was used to take out Princess Diana, that's why all the security cameras in the tunnel weren't working when she was killed."

Jon and Rachel listen with curiosity as Shigeru continues, "They wanted you gone and since you escaped them the legal way, they had to get you the hard way."

Jon says, "So then they must have taken out Drake because he failed them."

Shigeru chuckles a little and replies, "You really are quite the detective, no wonder you became an archaeologist, and no wonder they want you gone. You've snooped too much."

Rachel stands up with a startled look on her face and asks, "So how do Yakuza play into this? How do you know all this and why did you come for us in the first place?"

Shigeru laughs and says, "I thought you'd never ask. Our clan goes back to the pre feudal era, in a time before the Cabal had as much power as they do now. Mystery schools of thought cropped up all over the world, such as Freemason guilds and temples of Kabbalah study. Everything was studied and taught. From numerology on up to alchemy, the arcane was embraced the world over, as well as various forms of spiritual and esoteric wisdom. My clan was one here in Japan. Later, when forces sought to destroy such studies to darken them from the world, orders were formed to eliminate them, such as the Jesuits and the Templars. Secret societies were formed in each culture to maintain that knowledge. Some evil, like the ones that integrated into the upper echelons such as the Cabal, and others benevolent, like the Ninja guild and Ronins that my clan originates from. In modern times we act among the Yakuza clans to stay active in a world that's full of secret knowledge and unlimited possibilities. Possibilities can be philanthropic, like some of the work you've seen the Peace Corps do. Other possibilities can be dark, like that assassin droid you saw earlier."

As an image of that horrible machine flashes across Jon's mind, he says, "I'm very well versed in history and even things macabre like the occult, but why are they doing what they are doing and how are they benefiting from all this?"

Shigeru answers. "I'm afraid I've exhausted my limited perception of what's truly going on. All I know is that you have stumbled on to a huge piece of evidence suggesting to the world that things were different before the Great War. But I do know where you can find out the truth."

Rachel asks, "Where?"

Shigeru replies, "There is a Native American tribe that has the ability to record history in a very peculiar way

35

I am told, and has done a wonderful job keeping it intact from before the time of the war. I can offer you safe passage and even personally accompany you back to America to find them."

Rachel asks, "Why go so far to help us?"

Shigeru responds, "Well for one, it's my job, and secondly, I am also interested in uncovering the truth."

Several days later, the couple along with Shigeru and three of his men take a Yakuza private jet from Tokyo to Chicago. Shigeru suggests not landing near the coast since it's expected that Jon would make his way back to California. On the plane ride, Rachel asks Jon, "Do you trust what is happening? I mean, being with the Yakuza and everything."

Jon answers, "I do. Not only because they helped us this far, but because my instinct says they can be trusted."

Rachel smiles and squeezes Jon's arm. "That's all I needed to know, because your instincts are always right Jon."

Shigeru walks toward the two and sits down in front of them, saying, "We have several hours before we arrive."

Rachel tells Shigeru, "Thank you for everything you've done for us. But I'm curious, how can you speak English so well?"

He responds, "I was originally a bridge piece between the American Yakuza and the mainland organization. So I learned it there. This also influenced the decision to go to Chicago, since I know the area."

Rachel nods and says, "Oh wow. And by the way, you never fully answered my question. How did you know about us and how to find us when you did?"

He responds, "Well it's like this. Our order is part one of the light secret societies. We light ones, like the dark; have a connection around the planet and network information to each other. Just as things are done in conspiracy for evil, the same is done for good. Like Iraq, the public was told there were weapons of mass destruction, nukes, and mobile weapons facilities on the highways throughout the country. Well there were, but they were put there by agents of the Cabal. Our people moved in before they were 'uncovered' by American forces, and were swiftly removed. This move was done to make those who supported the Iraqi slander look like idiots when nothing was found there. But anyway, to finish your question, we were notified that you were coming to Tokyo to blow the lid on a major find you had. And that you beat out that board that was trying to destroy you."

Jon looks at Rachel and exclaims, "Well, that that was more her doing than mine!"

Rachel smiles.

Shigeru goes on to say, "People in high places wanted someone like you not only to survive but to be enlightened on the goings on of what's behind the scenes. They want you to join us. I was actually on my way up to get you two out when the building was rocked by the explosion in your room. I thought I was too late when I got there but thankfully you were still alive. The fact that you survived that thing alone shows that your spirit melds with destiny very well."

Jon looks searchingly at Shigeru, wondering what he means. The trio relaxes and enjoys the rest of their flight to Chicago.

Chapter 6:

Friend or Foe?

On arriving in Chicago, Shigeru and his men take the couple downtown to the Chicago based Yakuza headquarters. The building has a large neon sign that says Miyagi's. It appears to be a high class Hibachi Grill Restaurant. Once around back, the two realize the restaurant is not unlike the nightclub in Tokyo. The rear entrance leads down to a basement, fitted for the local Yakuza.

Once inside, Shigeru urges the two to make themselves at home. "Just relax for a while," he says. "I'm having one of my men do some research on the exact location of the tribe I told you about. There are very few members left, so it may take a few days. But once they are found, transportation will be arranged to go to them."

Jon suggests, "Maybe I can be of some help. After all, it is my specialty finding things that are thought to be lost."

Shigeru, with a look of alarm, says, "I don't think that's a very good idea. It might be best to lay low for a while after that attack, especially now that you're back in the US."

Jon, feeling quite discouraged by this notion, accepts that it's the best course of action for him and Rachel to take for now.

"I assure you," Shigeru says. "We have everything covered."

That night, the two are having a discussion with Shigeru about their upcoming trip, and what they may be up against in the near future.

"It's a good thing we were in Japan when they attacked us, Shigeru," Rachel says. "I don't know what we'd have done without you."

Shigeru responds, "If we hadn't, other groups that weren't as friendly as the Yakuza could have gotten to you. And where you were in the world would determine how dense or shallow the presence of positive forces would have been. Destiny always plays its hand as well."

Jon's curiosity on the subject awakens once again and he asks, "Yeah, about that. What did you mean when you said some people's souls meld with destiny well?"

Shigeru then explains, "In esoteric circles, the concept of destiny is widely explored and it's thought that certain people's souls can magnetize to a streamline of destiny more fluidly than others. Some just fall into the cracks, such as some of my men who were killed by the Shinobi. They were part of destiny, but theirs was less of a conscious act in the grand scheme of things."

Jon and Rachel both receive this new concept lightly and with skepticism. After winding down the conversation, the group decides to get some sleep. The next day they will set out to find the tribe Shigeru spoke of.

The following day, Shigeru explains the current status of their mission. "Our sources found that the tribe we're seeking is in Northern Texas. We've arranged a ride to the train station. The train will take us quite close to the tribe's location."

Jon shrugs his shoulders and says, "That's fine by me. Just as long as we make some sort of progress once we get there."

Shigeru gestures toward the door and says, "After you."

As Jon and Rachel along with Shigeru and his men exit the restaurant into the alley, they see a group of people walk around the corner. It appears to be a squad of thugs in suits lead by a small light skinned African American woman. The thugs seem to be heading to the restaurant. After a brief stare down both sides begin to draw their weapons. Jon and Rachel ease themselves behind Shigeru who is standing next to two of his men, aiming intently at the woman and her five thugs who have their weapons aimed right back. After a few moments of silence in this sort of 'Mexican standoff' between rival groups, Jon asks in a whisper, "Ummm, Shigeru. Who are these people?"

Shigeru replies, "Italian Mafia. I don't know who the girlie is, but she sticks out like a sore thumb among these guys."

The woman responds, "My name is Keena, not girlie you Yakuza scumbag. I'm leader of this outfit. We're enforcers for the Turoni family and we've heard you've got someone special in your possession; my boys and I are here to relieve you of them."

Shigeru spouts back, "They're not going anywhere with you girlie."

Rachel asks, "Shigeru, how could they possibly know about us?"

He responds, "Mafia are grunts to the Jesuit order and they probably caught wind that we brought you here, spies on both sides are everywhere."

"Enough!" Keena shouts. "They don't need a history lesson now. Just hand them over quietly. I'd rather not have this get bloody, but I'll do what I have to."

Shigeru asserts, "Look, Yakuza aren't exactly allies to the Mafia, but we stayed out of the affair between you and the Triads. We could have easily sided with them to rid you from both of our territories."

Keena snaps back with, "Yeah, and you could have easily sided with us. Don't use your neutrality as a bargaining chip with me."

Jon then steps forward between the two groups aiming toward one another and says, "Gentlemen. And lady," as he nods to Keena. "Violence is not necessary to solve this problem." Jon looks back toward the Yakuza and says, "Guys, Keena doesn't seem to be evil here. Surely you can explain to her how taking me to her superiors is detrimental to the larger scheme of things."

Without taking his eyes off Keena, Shigeru says, "She's not going to understand that Jon. Those controlled by the Jesuits always think they are doing the right thing. Remember the crusades and Templars, the inquisition, and Black Ships."

Keena snaps once more, "Again, stop with the history lesson, I'm tired of playing!" She points her gun toward Shigeru, causing him to tense up.

Rachel steps up and says, "Yes, but Jon's right. Look at her. She's not the same as them, or anywhere near like that thing that attacked us. Let's try and reason here people."

Quiet fills the air for a moment. Then nervously, Keena says, "I didn't come here thinking it would be like this, but something tells me it's not worth it. I don't want to die, nor do I want my men killed. I couldn't care less for the Yakuza, but something tells me I've been led astray in coming here to get you Jon. I'll let you go, but I'd appreciate if the Yakuza didn't retaliate against us for embarrassing them. I know how honor means so much to them."

Jon assures her. "They won't. Right, Shigeru?"

Shigeru, still looking intently at Keena, gun in hand answers, "No, we won't."

"Thank you, both of you," Jon says, as he looks back and forth between the two gang leaders. The suited men start to back up. The Italians and their petite yet feisty leader back away as they leave the alley. The sound of their footsteps turns into a jog after they disappear around the corner.

The Yakuza all lower their weapons in relief as Shigeru says, "I don't know who she was, but I have a feeling if you hadn't intervened, this would have gotten bloody.

Jon adds, "Yes, she was determined to do her duty, a lot like you. But I knew she had the ability to do the right thing. That's why I knew she could be reasoned with."

Rachel says to Shigeru, "You'll find that Jon's intuition is what makes him good at basically everything he does, even trusting you Shigeru."

The group then moves to get into the car. Once in, Shigeru announces, "Change of plans. I'm not gonna risk taking a train ride through the country with so much attention on us. We have less of a chance getting spotted with me taking you myself by car to Texas, than having a half a dozen of my men protect you on a train. As long as we take the back roads and get off to a stealthy start, they won't be able to lock onto us with one of their drone planes or something."

Jon looks worried as he realizes the true capabilities of the Cabal.

Shigeru makes a call in Japanese to his men, telling them to get an off-road vehicle to the rendezvous point but make no mention of its model or make over the phone.

Chapter 7:

Home Will Never Be Home Again

Once away from the restaurant, the group takes the long way to their destination to ensure they are not being followed. After about an hour, they arrive at a warehouse on the industrial side of town. Waiting for them there is a small group of Yakuza and a yellow Jeep.

After being briefed by his informant, Shigeru offers a satellite phone to Jon and Rachel. "If you want, you can make a call to any loved ones before heading out. This is a secure line that the Cabal can't track. If anyone's worried about you this would be a good time to update them."

Rachel answers, "Jon's parents died when he was very young, and my father is no longer alive. But I would like to call my mother."

Shigeru hands her the phone. Rachel places the call and after a few rings, Rachel's mother answers. When she discovers that it's her daughter, she becomes frantic.

"Mom, what's wrong?" Rachel asks.

After listening for a few moments, Rachel tells the others what her mom said. "She says that a several days ago, two men wearing black suits and sunglasses came to the house asking all kinds of questions about me. She told them that even though she keeps up with her me, she hasn't seen me in a few years. Since that day, those men, as well as a few others, have been parked outside the house. It's as if to watch for me to arrive."

Rachel then tells her mom, "Don't panic. I'll be there soon, okay? Alright, I love you mom. Bye."

After getting off the phone, Rachel asks Shigeru, "Who could those people be?"

Shigeru explains, "It's agents of the Cabal, commonly referred to as the Men in Black. They probably want to use her as bait to catch you two. We can go to help her, but we have to be careful. The line may be secure enough to prevent us being located, but it won't stop a phone tap from the other end, which I'm sure they have done to your mother's phone. So that means they know we'll be coming."

Jon nods and says, "Right, but what can we do to help her?"

Shigeru asks, "Where does your mother reside?"

Rachel answers, "Evansville, Indiana. It's where I was raised."

Shigeru replies, "Good, then it's not terribly far from here and not too far out of the way heading to Texas. I'll contact my sources and find out if we have any allies in that area that can help us."

Loading up into the Jeep, the gang then heads out toward Southern Indiana.

On the road, Shigeru receives a call from his contact. After a brief conversation, Shigeru hangs up and fills the others in, "We may have an ally after all. A small faction known as The Order of the Square and Compass is an arcane study group that has made an alliance with the Yakuza in Japan by a man simply known as X. He is the Order's 'Ambassador to the Hemispheres' and now resides in Japan. He's going to patch me through to someone named M. He's the 'Master Scribe and Keeper of the Archives' of the order. If we can get your mother out, they may be able to give her some asylum until things blow over."

Later that night, the group arrives on the north side of Evansville in Rachel's mother's neighborhood. Shigeru points out the car with the two Men in Black sitting in it out front, he drives casually and comes out back. Shigeru then comments, "It's best if we pull around back and come in through a back door. When I spoke with M earlier, he said that the he himself could take us to a safe house. When I asked how we could find him he told me not worry as they'll find us."

The trio drives the jeep into an alley around back and parks it. They begin walking up to Rachel's mother's backyard ever so cautiously. As soon as they reach the screen door, Rachel taps it lightly. Her mother answers the door, pleased to see them, and has them come in. She hugs Rachel and says, "I'm so glad to see you. I just wish it wasn't under these circumstances." She then turns to Jon and says, "Oh my, Jon, it's wonderful to see you with Rachel again."

Rachel's mother hugs him as he says, "Nice to see you again too Mrs. Lynn."

She corrects Jon right there, saying, "Please Jon. I told you before, call me Karen." She then turns her attention to Shigeru. Wearing his brightly colored club jacket, bell-bottom pants, and shiny silver belt buckle, he sticks out like a sore thumb. It's not every day you see a Japanese man dressed like that walking around in a neighborhood at night in Southern Indiana. She asks, "And who is this?"

Rachel introduces Shigeru and explains that he's been the one helping them. He extends his hand to her and says, "Pleased to meet you Mrs. Lynn."

Karen shakes Shigeru's hand and says, "You may call me Karen as well. A friend of Rachel and Jon's is a friend of mine." She steps back and gives a traditional bow to Shigeru to make him feel more welcome by using one of his greeting customs.

After the introduction, Shigeru notes, "It's not safe to stay here. We should leave soon."

Jon agrees, saying, "Right."

But before making a move, he is interrupted by Shigeru. "Before we go, I would like to use the restroom."

Karen gives him directions to the bathroom. But as Shigeru heads down the hall he is attacked by one of the agents who is hidden inside the house. Although taken unawares, Shigeru disposes of him easily with his skill, but before he can draw his pistol, another agent crashes through the window in a shower of broken glass and attacks him. Jon and the women come rushing in to see what's going on just as another agent bursts through the window and immediately attacks Jon.

Amidst the chaos, Jon attempts to engage the man as Shigeru is busy with his own problems. The first man is now on his feet and has a gun drawn on the group. As the man who was tangling with Shigeru draws his gun, the man in front of Jon gets on his earpiece to a fourth man outside. "We've got them. Come on in so we can detain them," he says.

The front door opens, and instead of the fourth man walking in, he is pushed in and slammed against the nearest agent. Frantically, the other two agents turn to see what has just happened. Shigeru attacks the other agent with a gun, as Jon notices the large man with glasses standing in the doorway. "This must be the man who threw the agent into the house," Jon thinks to himself.

The large man attacks the other agent fiercely and knocks him out just as Shigeru finishes off his opponent.

The group looks at the large man. Jon asks, "Who are you?"

The man responds, "I'm 'Sergeant-at-arms' of the Order of the Square and Compass, and I'm here to help you. You can call me J. Come on, M is parked out front."

Rachel and Karen dash for the gray car parked out front. There is a bearded man sitting in the driver's seat and he has the engine running. Jon and Shigeru run out back to the Jeep. Once in the Jeep, the gray sedan comes around the corner. M shouts out to them, "Follow me. I'll take you to the safe house." Shigeru follows.

The men drive them to a house in historic downtown Evansville near the river front. In front of the house, a gas powered torch is burning. The gates open up to let them in to the large driveway. It's a large tri-level house with a fence around the rooftop, large porch, three car garages, and a brick wall blocking off the alley.

As they pull up into the drive behind M's car, Jon says, "Well it's a good thing everything turned out okay, despite that little scuffle."

Shigeru turns off the ignition and responds, "Speak for yourself. I still haven't got a chance to pee."

Jon snickers as he gets out of the jeep.

Once parked, the group goes into the house. They are in awe at the vast library the lodge house boasts of, and the cozy décor. A man greets them and introduces himself, "My name is D. I'm the 'Grandmaster Viceroy of the Order.' I trust my associates took good care of you?"

Shigeru answers, "Yes. They are good. We are indebted to you for saving us."

D says, "I'm not sure what exactly prompted the Cabal to disperse their agents and go after someone like Mrs. Lynn and her daughter, but I trust you can enlighten me."

Karen concurs, "Yes. I'd like to know what's going on myself."

After explanations, the Order offers that Karen and Rachel stay there until things settle down. Karen accepts the offer. "Yes, I don't mind staying here. This place seems lovely, and apparently I have a lot to learn."

Jon says, "Good, then the two of you will be safe while Shigeru and I find this mystery tribe."

Rachel then protests. "No! Remember, I told you I'm in all the way. Nothing has changed with that. I'm going with you guys no matter what."

Jon smiles and says, "I'm glad to hear that."

After resting for a while, farewells are said to Rachel's mother and the 'Order of the Square and Compass.' The trio then gets back up into the Jeep and continues their trek across country to Texas in hopes of finding the mysterious tribe that may very well hold the secrets of the past as well as the secret purpose behind the Cabal's nefarious activities.

Chapter 8:

The Mysterious Crowfeather

Part 1

After nearly two full days of driving the back roads of North America, and bedding down in sleeping bags, the group finally reaches the small Indian reservation they have been looking for. Arriving in the waning hours as the sun goes down; the streets of the small town seem quite empty. As the uncovered jeep pulls up to a man on the side of the road, Jon says, "Excuse me sir, are we in the right place to find Chief Crowfeather?"

The man, around the same age as Jon, with a dark native skin, glasses, and black hair pulled into a small ponytail, answers, "Yes, Crowfeather is the elder of our tribe. What business do you have with him?"

From the driver's seat, Shigeru says, "Your tribe is a friend of my clan. I wish to speak with the chief on a very important matter."

The man says, "I'm sure he will be glad to speak with you, but he doesn't reside here in town. I can take you to him though, if you could give me a ride in your jeep."

Jon answers, "Of course," as he hops in the back with Rachel, letting the man get into the passenger seat.

The group introduces themselves all around as they begin to drive. The man returns the introduction with, "My name is Bear."

With only 20 minutes or so of daylight remaining, the group makes their way out of town.

Arriving at a small clearing in the woods, the night sky is filled with stars and a near full but slightly crescent moon. A small fire is burning with a circle of stones around it, and an older Native American man, probably in his early- to mid-sixties, sits tending to it. As the group gets out of the Jeep, Bear approaches the man by the fire and says, "Chief Crowfeather, these people have traveled a great distance to seek an audience with you."

The chief looks up from the fire and asks, "And who do I have the pleasure of addressing?"

Shigeru proclaims, "My name is Shigeru, of the Hogo-sha Clan. If I'm not mistaken, you are friendly and sympathetic to our cause."

Crowfeather, still tending the fire, replies, "That's right. I am familiar with your clan, and you are welcome to my circle. May I ask who your comrades are, and what is their purpose in coming here as well?"

Shigeru says, "This is Jon and Rachel, and they share a common enemy with us. They were attacked when they made an effort to understand the truth about the past. If I'm correct, you may have answers to their questions."

Crowfeather asks, "And what answers do you seek?"

Jon says, "I wish to know the truth. "

Crowfeather responds, "I shall answer your question by asking you another. What truth do you wish to know? All things have depth to them. The wealth of knowledge is immense among the cosmos. Simply knowing the truth can mean a multitude of things beneath the stars."

Jon takes in what Crowfeather has said and rethinks his question. This time he asks, "What is the truth about the past, before the Great War? And what is the truth about the Cabal? Why are they still around, and what do they want?"

The chief sits quiet for a moment before beginning his long-winded tale. "Many, many moons ago, the search for knowledge and wisdom was highly regarded by all cultures, and it was used as a form of peace to bridge together different nations. Those who sided with light were predominant in the global community and were responsible for many great things. Those on the side of darkness coveted knowledge. So they formed societies in secret and conspired in the shadows to corrupt the light so that they could use the knowledge for themselves and only themselves and become extremely powerful. They learned that through the manifestation of fear they could draw dark power from people. They also learned that their many symbols could be used as beacons to harness the power of fear. In every culture these groups would form and infiltrate the powers that be of their societies. And once they did, they would begin using this dark power to open gateways to the nether world and allow demons to come out in to their aid. What they didn't know was that these demons would only use what the evil men had established to rule themselves. These demons were recorded and written about in many cultures in ancient times.

In Europe, these demons were portrayed in renaissance art. In the Middle East, they were recorded in literature as fallen angels and Jinns. In Shigeru's culture, the Japanese painted them in beautiful swift brushstrokes, as gods. In Africa, they were told of through oral traditions, as well as by our people."

Jon asks, "Is this why the Aztecs had records of a lizard-like God, Quetzalcoatl?"

The chief answers, "Yes, and like all demons who ruled a culture, he too was brought down by the forces of light. Every attempt to rule was thwarted the world over. In Europe they were driven into caves and tunnels where it took over a century to root them all out. This is why it was believed that hell was underground, because people knew that those evil beings dwelled there. The Israelites of the Bible fought a demon brought through from the nether world by the Sumerians, who were able to interbreed with humans. Because of this, many hybrids were created. These hybrids were finally ousted by Alexander the Great. Since these hybrids were not of this world, when they were killed, their souls could not return to the nether world. So they roamed the planet, seeking to latch on to susceptible hosts. The forces of light learned of ways to banish these beings and in modern day, few remain. But the ones who do are subordinate to the Cabal. For everything that is established by the forces of light, a counterfeit is made by darkness. This is why the churches of the world were corrupted and gained so much power through conquering. When the Great War started, most of the world was part of a global community. It was then that for the first time, a united effort was made by the forces of evil to rule the planet. Due to the power that was caused by the fear and destruction, they came dangerously close to opening a gateway to the nether world again. In the aftermath of the war, the Cabal was formed and those in power who didn't agree with them were eliminated or became the enemies of our modern world."

Jon adds, "Hence the cold war and those wars in the Far East."

Rachel interjects, "Forgive me, Chief Crowfeather. I don't mean to be rude, just curious. I understand how your tribe was able to preserve local history so well and have such a deep understanding of the situation, but how is it that you know so much about the global scene?"

The chief, smiles and answers, "That question is not without merit. In my younger years, I too traveled the world in the search for truth, only taking with me what knowledge I imbibed from my ancestors. After I found what I sought, I returned here to assume the leadership duties of my tribe, and to protect the secrets of the light."

Crowfeather goes on to say, "Leading up to the war, many other conflicts had already been under way, such as the Civil War here in the United States. But the historical records of that, as you have already discovered, have been fragmented. To make a better story and to fill in the gaps for the next generation, a new history was written. The wedding of the rails was done originally to support the war effort, but after the United States was left in shambles, it became desolate and was only used in select areas. When the nation was rebuilt decades later, it was rediscovered in full and the story of how it came to be was fabricated to give it a more patriotic and less dark origin. The remaining tribes of our indigenous people had a much larger part in the war than recorded by the United States. We fought in both the Civil War as well as the Great War on the side of the Allies. That was before they were corrupted by evil."

The chief pauses for a moment so the others can take all of this in, before stating, "If the Cabal had gained enough power, this world could have been flooded from all corners of the globe with wickedness. By the end of the war, everyone was so ready for change, they accepted anything. The roaring 20s saw what seemed like an endless celebration, which served as a distraction while the Cabal got much accomplished. The Great Depression of the 30s brought people back to a state of survival which only hastened the changing of history. The 1940s had World War II, which in itself was a rehashing of the change in leadership of the new order. By the mid-1950s, the Cabal had installed a system of education for the masses that swept away any remaining knowledge of the old world."

Crowfeather pauses momentarily to let it sink in. "A lot has changed since before the Great War. Now that the world is as small as it is, and with all of the things in place by the Cabal to create and draw fear from people, it could be a serious threat. Every time a great civilization is corrupted by darkness, the old world's legacy is attempted to be destroyed or at the very least fragmented. This was attempted by the Third Reich and again by Mao Zedong, but both were foiled. 'Operation Paper clip,' carried out by the OSS, served as unification between the Cabal's branches here in the west and its post war toppled leadership in Europe. Mao attempted to destroy the knowledge of Taoism by killing its priesthood and destroying its temples. But a fraction of them survived thanks to Chiang Kai Shek's retreat to Taiwan during the Chinese revolution. This has been done over and over again many times through history, but never has it been so close a struggle with such power and resources at the hands of the dark ones."

Shigeru asks, "What can we do then? I know that destiny has brought me and Jon together. And his skills at figuring things out have proven to be of great importance."

Jon says, "I want to know more, and I want to do what I can to help stop all of this."

The chief replies, "If you wish, you may partake of my tribe's ancient elixir, memory water. It will show you the past so clearly that you will know all of this to be true and you will understand the way things were. As a side effect, it will show you an image of the present relative to the situation, and a glimpse of the future."

Jon, slightly skeptical still, says, "Hmmm. Memory water, huh? I'll try anything once. If what you've told me is true, then this certainly would be too. So it's definitely worth trying to get to the bottom of all this."

Chief Crowfeather offers, "Very well then, I shall prepare the memory water drinking ritual."

Chapter 9:

Once Upon a Time...in the Past

As the moon nears its highest point in the sky, a wolf is heard howling off in the distance. Chief Crowfeather, with the assistance of Bear, has gone off to prepare a batch of memory water. Sitting by the fire, Rachel asks Jon, "Are you sure you're ready for this?"

Jon answers, "As long as I've got you to make sure nothing happens to me, I'll be okay. I've never done hallucinogens before."

The chief and Bear return with the memory water. The Chief is carrying it in a medium sized gourd and the substance appears to be just plain stream water. As Jon begins to drink, he asks, "How does it work?'

Crowfeather responds, "As the fluid runs through your body, it opens up a connection to the unified consciousness that connects all things. It will then show you what you need to see – no more, no less. Those souls who are tied close to destiny are now committed to it, and what is needed to be done shall be prepared to be done by the beholder."

Once Jon has fully consumed the liquid, he looks at Shigeru and Rachel on either side of him and begins to sway a little. His vision starts to blur, and the crackle of the fire begins to be drowned out by what sounds like a soft song played by harp and flute. Darkness then sets in and Jon feels as though he's floating in a peaceful abyss. He speaks out into the darkness. "Hello." But only an echo is returned. "Wow, so this must be what the unified consciousness of the cosmos is, huh?"

A moment or two passes as he floats. The next thing he knows, he's suddenly in a physical form again. Only now, he finds himself in a body, not his own, marching through a no man's land in battle fatigues with a rifle on his shoulder. All around him are soldiers heading in the same direction. As wonder starts to flee from Jon's eyes, he figures there's no telling how long this might last so he'd better inquire to learn what it is he's supposed to be shown. He asks a trooper near him, "What year is it?"

The man responds, "Huh?"

Jon says again, "What year is this?"

The trooper says, "Geez buddy, you haven't even been in the foxhole yet and you're already shell shocked, it is 1911.

Jon realizes this is the same year Cyrus Methena wrote in his journal that the museum was attacked.

Noticing up ahead what basically appears to be now a desert, Jon starts paying more attention to his surroundings. Debris of machinery and junk is strewn all about as if action had already taken place here. The ground is blasted apart, and very little vegetation is to be found except some brown malnourished weeds and thorn bushes. As the group approaches a system of trenches, Jon notices more debris and war-torn skeletons littering the innards of the divide. The company appears to be hunkering itself down in the tomb of a battlefield. Jon notes that whatever battle has happened here has not been fought in a very long time, possibly years.

After questioning a few more soldiers, Jon discovers that he is in Northern Bulgaria on the border of Romania. Afterwards, Jon gets comfortable, as comfortable as one can be in a muddy trench, wearing battle fatigues, and surrounded by skeletons. Jon looks up at the sound of a voice coming from atop the trench. An officer is yelling, "Everyone, get ready! The colonel is about to address us."

Jon and the other troopers' attention turns to a man Jon presumes is the colonel. The man shouts, "Alright men, as you know, you've been assigned to this special unit to aid our allies as best we can until the US is able get back into this war full time."

Jon recalls from the journal that the US was destroyed rather early on and our historically recorded account of joining the war must have actually been our return to it in Europe.

The colonel continues shouting, "Now our buddies in Greece have reported that an anonymous brigade of pyromaniacs has moved north after firebombing their way up the coast into Bulgaria. We're gonna attempt to ambush them here by letting 'em head right toward us before engaging them. Word has it that a firefight broke out between them and the Ottomans a couple nights ago. They managed to take out all of their dirigibles, so this should be a pretty fair fight. We outnumber them 4 to 1. So this shouldn't be a problem. Remember men, these aren't Turks or Krauts we're fightin here. No one knows who they are, and they're ruthless so don't expect any prisoners."

A chill hits Jon as he remembers the horrific writing of Cyrus about what the Incinerators have done.

A few hours go by as Jon sits waiting patiently for whatever may happen next. His rifle is lying across his lap, and he has his back against the trench wall. Suddenly, he hears a shout. "They're here!" Two scouts come rushing in from atop the wall of the ditch, as everyone scuffles to bring themselves into positions of readiness. Then silence sets in. Jon's trench is one of the larger ones just inside the outer perimeter. A smaller trench is located about 35 yards ahead of his. A few moments pass, then gunfire breaks out from the other trench. The sound of men yelling and flames erupting soon follows. As the fighting seems to be drawing closer, the officer who earlier called the men to attention signals to a group of men to get ready and yells, "Get those halocarbon canisters ready!"

Jon thinks to himself, "Halocarbon? That's a refrigerant; they must be using it as some kind of experimental weapon. Pretty fitting considering the enemy is using fire."

Right then, the men fire one of the canisters out of the trench from a small but wide mouthed mortar. As the burst hits, what sounds like glass shattering followed by snarling and roaring is heard about 15 yards away from the trench. Jon leans up to take a peak. In the background he sees a full-blown firefight between soldiers and the menacing incinerators as well as hand-to-hand combat. In the foreground is the site where the canister exploded. Fragments of frozen chips are lying on the ground and two of the faceless, gas masked incinerators are sprawled stone dead, half covered in icy refrigerant. After observing for a brief moment, he realizes three incinerators are heading his way and are only 10 feet from the trench. He ducks down back behind the wall as he sees the men preparing another round for the mortar. By the time the men have it ready, a burst of flames encircle them from just above where Jon is sitting in the trench. An incinerator is right above him, discharging his flame thrower. The officer, who already has his pistol drawn, begins firing at the incinerator. It takes several shots before the flames stop and several more before the masked fiend finally drops. A second masked trooper now comes hurtling over the trench wall and attacks the officer melee style. Falling backwards, the officer's gun fires straight into the mortar, exploding frozen particles all over the inside of the trench. Jon turns to shield his eyes from the icy shrapnel heading his way. The trooper, with his left shoulder covered in ice and snarling, wildly turns toward Jon holding his shoulder, moving like an injured deer. Right about that time he notices Jon. Jon uses his rifle to fire a few rounds into the trooper's chest, ceasing his random flailing. It's at that moment that Jon realizes, he fired his first gun. And of all things, it is through the eyes of another person over a hundred years in the past, who he didn't know existed until now. As the shock of what just happened wears off, and the chaos all around him comes back into focus, Jon stands up and begins fitting his bayonet. Just then, another trooper drops down right next to him. As it aims its torch toward him preparing to fire, Jon swings the butt of his gun into it turning the weapon off to the side before it fires. He swings again, this time knocking it out of the trooper's hand. Again he swings, this time hitting the trooper across the side of his head. He stops for a second to regain his balance and so does the trooper. The trooper stumbles toward him as Jon swings his rifle again, this time in an uppercut fashion knocking the gas mask off the trooper. Jon gets a good look at the trooper without a mask for the first time and notices that it's actually a monstrous creature. Underneath the mask is what seems no different than Frankenstein's monster, stitched and sewn together. The creature roars as it moves toward Jon once again. He hits it again and after a brief scuffle, sends his rifle's bayonet directly through its chest. Fighting around in the trench, the monster is at the opposite end of Jon's rifle, reaching out toward him from across the bayonet. It manages to grab Jon's shoulders. Jon fires his rifle into the creature until the gun is empty. Moving against the trench wall, he finishes it off with a slamming blow to the wall and pulls the rifle out of the monster.

Shaken once again by the vicious attacks, Jon decides it's time to leave the area of the trench he's in; it is far too vulnerable to attack. Moving down through the trench caverns, he sees members of his fragmented unit preparing to retreat back through the system of trenches as well. As he approaches them, two more incinerator troopers drop down over the wall and begin spraying their liquid fire. Jon aims and fires, but nothing happens. He realizes that he forgot to reload. One of the troopers turns and runs toward him as he fights his own vest for ammo to reload his weapon. Right as the creature gets near him, a soldier standing up on the other side of the wall fires his rifle down at the monster's back, hitting his fuel tank. The impact causes a massive explosion that encompasses him as well as Jon. As the blast hits Jon, everything ceases. No noise, no vision, no light, just black again, as if nothing had happened.

Jon immediately finds himself floating back in the abyss. He realizes his experience is now over, but then remembers that there would be a side effect of seeing an image of the present. As light starts to appear, he sees a dark room decorated in all things macabre. There is a circle of men dressed in black robes chanting, performing some kind of occult Luciferian ritual. It looks like something right out of a horror movie. Not that what Jon experienced in the trenches was anything less of a horror movie.

After only a few brief flashes of this event, Jon floats back to the abyss once again. A moment passes, and then the light comes again. Another vision appears, this time of the future. First, he sees a desert, with small rocky formations and cacti. Next, he sees soldiers in uniforms that are neither of America nor of any known nation. They are occupying city streets. Another flash hits. It's a US Army Unit encamped somewhere in the countryside. Abruptly, the images stop and Jon fades back into the current reality.

Chapter 10:

The Mysterious Crowfeather

Part 2

Waking up, Jon discovers he is lying sideways with his head in Rachel's lap. He looks up and sees everyone still sitting around the fire, as if nothing had happened at all. He wipes his eyes and sits up. Rachel's hands are resting on his shoulders. He asks, "How long was I out?"

Shigeru answers, "About 40 minutes or so."

Jon, shocked, says, "What I experienced lasted several hours." He tells them what he saw in his journey into the past.

Jon asks, "What was the purpose of being shown that?"

The chief explains, "That was the universe's way of clearing up any remaining doubt you had about all of this being true. You needed to be 100% sure that what you were learning was fact."

Jon agrees, saying, "Yes, after that experience I have no doubts as to the validity of what you told me."

He then tells the group about his vision of the cloaked men.

Crowfeather says, "Those were members of the Cabal. They were performing a ritual that gathers the fear energy they are honing in on from their many symbolic beacons that draw negative energy from people. It is how they harness it for themselves."

Jon then goes on to tell of his vision of the various soldiers.

"What do you make of that chief?" Jon asks.

Crowfeather replies, "I cannot determine what is meant for only you to discover. But, if you wish to know more about your own personal quest, you can drink Personal Memory Water. It's a far less potent elixir that will just show you a glimpse of your own past, present, and future."

Jon agrees and rests while the chief prepares the new tonic. When Crowfeather returns, he lets Jon know, "This won't be nearly as long an endeavor and won't take as much out of you."

As Jon drinks the new water, white puffy light starts to form around the periphery of his vision. The light starts to consume all that he sees from the outside in, until everything is white. Soon, the vision of the past sets in. Jon sees himself as a child living with his parents, then as a young teen when his parents passed away, and being sent to the boys' home. He then sees a time when he and Rachel were together. It was when they lived together in grad school. Things were very pleasant, and neither of them could ask for more than what they had. Then he sees the point at which Rachel was asked to intern in Greece for her last year of grad school. Next, he sees the conflict they had over the separation, and her storming out of their apartment. Finally, he sees himself meeting Professor Gray his first day at his new job at the university. Then, suddenly, the image of his past ends.

The image begins to fade and suddenly he sees the world from his current perspective. Spiraling from the night sky, he has a bird's eye view of himself sitting by the campfire across from Crowfeather and Bear, with Shigeru and Rachel on either side. This image of the present only lasts a few moments, and then he begins to see the future.

First he sees a desert, with small rocky formations and cacti. Afterwards, there is a vision of another one of those Shinobis like before, this one with yellow markings and bright yellow eyes. Then again, the vision changes quickly to Rachel. She's in danger, but he can't see from what. Before he can grasp it, the image flashes again, now to a small group of soldiers like he saw before. Finally, he sees a woman in a white lab coat, with glasses and strawberry blonde hair pulled into a bun. With her image in the backdrop, the vision fades into black as Jon comes out of it. Then once again, he's back into reality as with the previous session.

When he explains what he saw, he seems rather shaken up, especially at the danger Rachel could fall into. The chief interjects, "I know of a place in New Mexico where the Cabal may have built an underground base cloaked by the desert. That could be the place in your vision."

Jon states, "Since that was the first thing in my vision, maybe it's the next place we should go."

Shigeru says, "Could you give us directions?"

Crowfeather explains the route so that they can go investigate it themselves. He says, "You must have been shown for a purpose. Your destiny wants you to find this place for some reason."

Jon says, "Thank you Chief Crowfeather, your help is much appreciated."

The chief responds, "Thank you, Jon Peters, for your willingness to participate in such matters."

As Jon and Shigeru prepare to get on the road, Rachel says to the chief, "Thank you for letting me in on this experience."

Chief Crowfeather acknowledges her gratitude and takes her aside while Jon and Shigeru are talking to Bear. He whispers to her, "You have obviously been a huge motivational force for Jon. When a soul has been sewn to a pattern of destiny, sometimes it takes such motivation to bring it to the right path. Such intuition as Jon has can be used for good or for evil. The Cabal knows this as well. Stay close to Jon, and everything will work out the way it should. Oh, and about his vision, don't be afraid. Things will turn out as they should, if you realize that you yourself can align your own personal destiny with the universe."

She nods and thanks him again.

Meanwhile, Bear tells Shigeru and Jon, "Don't bother taking me back into town. I wish to stay and talk to Chief Crowfeather awhile longer." He gives the duo directions back to the highway heading north to put them on their way to New Mexico and then bids them farewell.

As the team drives off into the waning hours just before sunrise, Bear sits with Chief Crowfeather and asks, "What could that ragtag little band do to sway the shift of things?"

Crowfeather answers, "Jon has an incredible ability to find things and figure them out. Rachel has a level head and her skepticism at times helps keep things in perspective. Shigeru's loyalty to our cause and his newfound friends combined with his skills will drive them through many more obstacles. Also, I feel as though the three of them will not be alone on the remainder of their journey."

Chapter 11:

Revelation

After the group spends the night at a hotel on the Texas border, they cross over into New Mexico. Around mid afternoon, they reach Dulce, New Mexico, exactly where Crowfeather described. Pulling up in an area that seems to be a good place to make camp, Shigeru suggests, "Why don't I go into town to ask the locals what information they can give about the area and any anomalies that could allude to some strange activity? You two stay here and make camp."

Jon and Rachel agree and start to set up camp as Shigeru heads into town. Once finished, they decide to go walking around the rock formations that are nearby to see what they might find. After a few minutes, Jon stops and says, "Wait a minute; this is exactly what I saw in my vision, cactus and everything."

After further investigation, the couple stumbles across what appear to be faux rocks made out of drywall. Inside are ventilation shafts. The phony rocks are positioned in a way that makes them look like randomly strewn rocks from the highway, but actually block the view of the vents.

Rachel says, "This is rather odd."

Suddenly the ground beneath their feet begins going down.

"This is *really* odd!" Jon exclaims. The two then realize they are on a square shaped platform lowering into the sand, like an elevator. Once about 40 feet down, the elevator stops with a large garage door-sized opening showing what appears to be some sort of underground facility. The wide hallway leading from the elevator lift is shiny and silver with white light emanating from the ceiling and wall panels. Jon states, "Well, I guess this is what we're supposed to see. We might as well investigate, that okay with you Rach?"

Though a bit spooked, she agrees.

The two begin moving down the hall. Finally, after walking down the hallway for a minute or two, they come across a large window about eight feet tall and thirty feet wide. Through the window they see a vast amount of vegetation, trees, bushes, and various other plant life all over. After a moment of gazing, the couple notices something moving in the shrubbery. Suddenly, from out of the vegetation, they see something quite unexpected. Astonishingly, a tall carnivorous dinosaur darts by the window and then back into the woods. Rachel steps back. Stunned she says, "What in the hell is going on."

Jon replies, "My God, that was a raptor. What is the purpose of this?"

The two hear a voice behind them, "To show that we can create whatever we want."

Whirling around, they see a suited man who looks about 60, standing there with his hands in his pockets.

"Somehow, I expected your arrival Jon Peters." the man says.

Jon asks him, "Who are you and how do you know me?"

The suited man answers, "As for the 'how do I know you part' I think you can figure that out. But as for me, I'm the administrator of this facility. You can simply call me Ben T." Walking around the two, the man goes on to say, "I'd like to show you around. After all, you came all this way to see something didn't you? Don't worry, I assure you, you are safe for now, and so's your little girlfriend."

The two reluctantly follow Ben T. as he begins telling them the purpose of this facility. He says, "We built this place, one of several, in the late 40s and early 50s. Area 51, as you may know, was used to build experimental aircraft and stealth technology. None of that alien hodgepodge we spit out as disinformation to make people think there was some sort of threat from space. This installation's focus, however, became genetics testing. When the OSS conducted Operation Paperclip after World War II, Nazi Germany's Ubermensch project was brought here and needed a suitable location to conduct research. What better place than the vastness of the desert, right?"

Jon asks, "So there *was* a super soldier project then, it's not all myth?"

Ben T. replies, "Oh wow, I didn't realize one needed an archaeology degree to figure that one out." Laughing sarcastically, he goes on to say, "We had a much earlier project before the Third Reich started trying to make Uber Soldats in laboratories on live subjects. They thought experimental drugs were a better alternative to the reanimated corpses used to make our incinerators in the Great War."

Jon remembers both the diaries of Cyrus Methena and his own personal experience seeing the Frankenstein's monster-like creatures hidden beneath the gas masks of the incinerators.

Ben T. continues, "They were slow and tough to make, created from stitching various body parts from different subjects and giving them life through electric charge. Mary Shelly's work was not a complete fiction.

71

We, however, used her 'Dr. Frankenstein' persona to slander Tesla when he didn't want to continue his work for us. That's how the perception of the mad scientist was born, through propaganda."

Finally, the group reaches another larger window through which they see hundreds of large glass cylinders filled with liquid and men floating in suspended animation within them. After noticing that they all look the same, Jon exclaims, "They're clones!"

Ben T. corrects him, saying, "Human replicates actually. We call them HRTs. Totally subordinate, genetically modified to only require four hours of sleep at a time, and can survive on a special nutrient paste we developed for them. Since they are grown in those tubes in under a year, their vocal chords don't develop properly so they can't speak, but they can understand orders. Sounds like something from a blockbuster sci-fi fantasy movie, doesn't it?" Laughing once more, and noticing Jon and Rachel don't share his humor on the matter, he continues explaining. "We modeled them on the genetic structure of a Marine who fought in Vietnam, he was one hell of a fighter. His comrades called him 'Maddogg'."

Rachel asks, "What do you plan on doing with them?"

Ben T. smiles and says, "Martial Law is going to be declared in this country very soon. Insurrection is inevitable, even from our very own military. If this happens and we are unable to sustain order by our men and women in uniform, we shall do so by other means. We have nearly 800,000 HRTs ready to deploy, with an order for 5 million more in the next two years to come. With this might, we can replace UN and NATO forces with our Human Replicate Troopers and put down any nation that attempts rebellion."

Jon curiously asks, "Why are you telling us this, and why are you allowing us to see it?"

Ben T. answers, "Because Jon, you've proven yourself to be quite the problem solver. You discovered the truth about the past, survived the education board, escaped the cyborgs and our agents, and you even found your way to our facility here without any help from us. We could use a man like you, on our side, to help us solve problems and come to conclusions. Really Jon, do you think that after all that has transpired in your life lately that you could really go back to being an archaeologist and a teacher. You should join us."

Showing the two into a smaller elevator than the one they came in on, Ben T. implores, "Take a few days to think about it, go back to your Yakuza, watch the unfolding of things from the outside looking in, *then* make your decision. We'll come to you for your answer."

Jon asks, "What if I say no? Why let us go, knowing what we know? Why not kill us?"

Ben T. responds, "We don't need to kill you, Jon. We'd simply demonize your name, the same as we did with Nikola Tesla. He served his purpose, but we left the door open for him if he ever wanted to assist us again. But, until then, we simply desecrated his name so that no one would believe anything he said. Don't do what he did, Jon. Surely you have more dignity than that.

The door closes, and the elevator begins to rise. When the door opens the two find themselves at the foot of the rocky area just on the other side of the formation where they found the entrance. Heading back to camp, Jon and Rachel are unsure of what to make of things. A few minutes after returning to camp, Shigeru pulls up in the Jeep with a look of disgust.

"I didn't find out much, just some local legend about reptilians and time travelling Nazis seen in the area, but maybe we can find something tomorrow," Shigeru says with a sigh.

Jon stands up and says, "Never mind, we're leaving."

Holding his hands up in confusion, Shigeru says, "Huh?"

Rachel adds, "Yeah, we've already found out everything we need to here."

Resting his hands on his hips and looking confused, Shigeru asks, "What in the hell happened while I was gone?"

Rachel, while helping Jon get the rest of the camping stuff loaded answers, "Come on, get back in the jeep."

Jon says, "Yeah, I'll explain on the way back to Chicago."

Still confused, but now interested, Shigeru gets back in the vehicle.

Chapter 12:

Keena's Revenge

After explaining to Shigeru the events that took place while he was asking around for information, the group arrives back in Chicago. Within the stronghold of the Yakuza's Hibachi restaurant, Rachel sits at the computer. She begins researching things about the facility they were just shown. They agree it is best if they find out as much as they can as evidence and try to take matters to the UN building in New York City to make one final attempt at blowing the lid on the Cabal publicly.

The next night while researching, one of Shigeru's men comes rushing downstairs shouting, "We got trouble out back."

The group rushes upstairs where they find two more Yakuza helping Keena and her men. Some of them are injured, including Keena herself. The group starts helping the frantic bunch into the back door.

Taking stock of the situation, they see one of Keena's five men with a shoulder wound, probably caused by a bullet, and another man with several gunshot wounds to the chest and gut. Keena is grazed in the upper hip by a bullet and her white tank top is stained with blood, both from her wound and from helping her injured man.

Shigeru asks, "What happened?"

Keena responds, "We didn't know where else to go. After we stood down in our standoff with you, I was scolded for letting you go. After I refused a second order to retrieve Jon, they put a hit on me and my men's heads. We were attacked at our hideout, never saw it coming. Shit's real fucked up!"

Shigeru tells his men in Japanese to get the badly wounded man to the basement. The ponytailed gangster is quite the largest of the entire group, over 6 feet tall and 320 lb.; he is difficult to move downstairs in his state.

Lying on the table, the man begins coughing up blood as two of the other mobsters and one of Shigeru's men try and help bandage the wound. The man with the wounded shoulder is sat down in a chair on the other side of the room and tended to. Keena, while not concerned about her own wound starts bandaging the wounded hand of the other mobster.

As Keena gazes back at her man on the table, she sees him breathe his last. Silence hangs heavy. She slowly approaches him saying, "He was one of my best men. I handpicked him first to be a part of my team of enforcers. I can't believe we were betrayed the way we were."

She turns to Shigeru and says, "My men and I are in shambles. I know we don't deserve your help, but I must ask. Can you help me to exact revenge?

Shigeru looks over at the man on the table, and back to Keena as a tear drops from her eye. She says again, "Please?"

He looks back at her and nods.

Jon walks up and puts his hand on her shoulder. "Come on," he says. "We need to dress your wound."

She sniffles and then goes with him.

Later that evening, Keena explains the location of the Turoni family headquarters. "It's a mansion just outside of the city. It's very well-guarded. I think its best I lead the strike team to take out Don Turoni."

Her other men veto this suggestion. One man says, "Lady no, you're already hurt. We can do this."

Disagreeing, she tells her men, "No. Stay out of it. I don't want any more of you to be involved. This is between me and Turoni, no other mobsters. I only need Shigeru's men to get me onto the grounds and into the house."

The next night, after preparing three of his best men, Shigeru, Keena, and the Yakuza dress from head to toe in black with only their faces exposed. Outside, they scale the walls of the mansion's perimeter. Armed only with Katanas and Sais, the Yakuza silently move into the grounds of the mansion. Keena and Shigeru are the only ones carrying firearms. One of Shigeru's men eliminates a guard silently while the other two secure and open the gate to allow Keena in, since her injury doesn't allow her to climb.

Approaching the house, they wait for a patrol of two men with guns to pass the window before cutting the glass and entering silently. As they leap in through the window, one of Shigeru's men runs stealthily down the hall to distract any men who may be around while the group goes up the staircase. At the top of the stairs, a guard is encountered and executed silently by one of Shigeru's men before he is able to alert the other guards.

Just before approaching the door to the Don's office, the two cloaked Yakuza take out two more mobsters before securing the door. They take a watchdog stance outside the office while Keena and Shigeru enter. Taken by surprise, Don Turoni looks up from his desk as he sits in his office chair. Keena draws her silence pistol as Shigeru closes the door with his men keeping watch outside. Keena declares to the Don, "You son of a bitch,

I've worked for you my entire life. This mob family is all I've ever known."

Don Turoni raises his hands and begins to stand up. "Keena," he says, "I only did what I was told to do from above; you know that's how loyalty is. You were loyal to me, and I'm loyal to the Archbishop. That's how this works. It was nothing personal."

Keena, now with tears in her eyes says, "Don't try and weasel out of this."

Turoni states, "Keena, don't do this. I've raised you from a small girl, and let you in on many secrets of the Mafia. Come back to us. Let's forget this whole thing ever happened."

"Yes, lets!" Keena replies as she fires a shot right through Don Turoni's forehead.

She lowers the gun to her side and continues to cry as she turns away. Shigeru rests his hand on her back and says, "Come on, let's go."

After collecting the man downstairs who has been giving the guards on the bottom floor the run around, the Ninja-like team accompanied by Keena leaves the Mob house and return to the Yakuza stronghold.

On returning to the restaurant, they find Jon and Rachel watching the news. "Due to national security concerns, martial law is being declared. The government has issued a travel restriction. We advise everyone to abide by the curfew and wait patiently."

The screen cuts to a Congressman stating, "We have everything under control. The 'Bill of Rights' is being amended, and the Constitution is subject to 'revision' as well. Once we assure that order is maintained, a census will be called to the property of all citizens."

Cutting back to the news anchor, "US troops have been deployed for the first time on US soil in an attempt to keep down resistance."

Appalled by all of this happening so soon, Jon realizes that what Ben T. told Rachel and him is very real.

Shigeru says, "We really should leave the city. Being in Chicago under martial law would make us an easy target for the Cabal."

Jon responds. "I agree. As soon as Keena and her men are able to leave the city, we should go. But before we leave, we should try to find more info on Ben T."

Rachel says, "It wouldn't be hard if we could access a list of classified government IDs. Surely he's had one at some point, being in the position he's in."

Keena steps up and says, "Well, I'm a real tech person. It was one of my assets in the Mafia. I could hack a government site and get you that list."

Jon replies, "That's awesome. Rachel, pull up that page you found on eugenics testing here in the US."

After pulling it up, Rachel allows Keena to sit down and work her magic.

Chapter 13:

A Bargaining Chip

Through the wee hours of the night, Keena works to hack the site. Late that night, Shigeru goes in to see how she is progressing. Keena stops and stretches saying, "I've had to get through a lot of firewalls but I'm sure I'm on to something."

Sitting down next to Keena, Shigeru says, "I know we got off to a bad start, but I hope after helping you and taking you and your men in, you trust me."

Keena responds, "You don't even have to ask. I've already dedicated myself to helping your cause. Once I help Jon figure out who this guy is, I'm gonna go with you to help blow the lid on this whole thing."

Jon, waking from sleep, gets up to check on the project himself. One of the Yakuza goes over to turn on the news again to see any updates. Several of Keena's men are on the couch across the room watching as well. The group realizes that if things have ever been serious, they are now. The news reader is now reporting, "Several rogue factions of the military have broken off in rebellion at the martial law declaration. Their commanders are assuming their own leadership. Also, many Army Reserve and National Guard enlistees have not answered their call to arms. Among the vast resistance, many active military have abandoned their ranks and have fled their units."

Jon shakes his head and says, "This is all happening so fast. I don't think even the Cabal planned for things to escalate this quickly."

Shigeru turns to Keena and says, "If you and your men are ready, we'll leave tomorrow night."

"I think we can manage," she responds.

Finally, Keena in her search discovers a match to the name Ben T. When Jon sees his picture, he recognizes him instantly.

Keena skims through the file, "Benjamin Thomas Washington. Former stem cell researcher working in the private sector. Picked up in 1982 by a government contract to head up a black project."

Jon interrupts Keena's reading, "Right there, that's all we need. Print this file up and let's take it with us as proof of what he and the Cabal are doing."

Suddenly, the lights flicker and the power goes out. Everyone goes silent as they hear a noise upstairs. On the restaurant level, they hear the sound of glass breaking and footsteps scurrying about.

Several more of Shigeru's men and the rest of Keena's men enter the room to see what's going on. Upstairs a fight can be heard between nearly a dozen Yakuza and a group of unknown assailants.

After a few minutes of violent yelling and scuffling, silence sets in. The door to the room that Rachel is sleeping in opens and she stumbles out to find out what the commotion is. "Jon," she says irritably, "What's going on out here?"

Before he can even take a step toward her, an explosion emanates from the ceiling. Smoke bombs and bits of debris are lobbed in the direction of those standing in a semicircle around the room. As the group coughs wildly and attempts to clear their eyes, Jon sees the silhouettes of three figures standing around Rachel.

As the smoke clears, he begins to make out the figures. It is three more Cybernetic Shinobis, just like the one that attacked them in Tokyo. The two standing on either side of Rachel have red and blue glowing eyes and markings respectively. The one right in front facing Jon and the others has bright yellow eyes and yellow markings. This is precisely the robot he saw in his vision.

Lunging forward at any attempt to approach them, the yellow one takes on a defensive stance. The other droids extend telescopic whips from the wrists of their right hands. They each lash forward in an attempt to lasso Rachel. Once impacted, the whips begin igniting with lightning like electrical pulses, like that of a Taser. Rachel lets out a cry of pain and collapses to her knees before the two terrifying machines. Her voice, now very shrill, shouts, "Let me go."

The blue Shinobi leans in and releases a chloroform gas from a tube protruding from the top part of its left wrist. Rachel, now unconscious, is hoisted up by the red Shinobi. Once the smoke clears, everyone draws their weapons and aims them toward the Shinobi. Shigeru shouts, "Don't shoot, you could hit Rachel!"

The yellow cyborg abandons his battle-ready stance and stands up straight. From the droid's collar a hologram is projected on to the floor. It's an image of Ben T. He says, "Your time to make a decision is up Jon."

The blue and red Shinobis leap upward, carrying Rachel up through the ceiling. Ben T. continues, "I'll be 'taking care' of Rachel until you give yourself up to me."

Just as quickly as the hologram appears, it fades away. The Shinobi then kneels down on one knee. From the opening of the adjacent knee, another smoke bomb is fired like a mortar, screening the Shinobi from everyone in the room. The yellow Shinobi then leaps up through the ceiling, following the other two.

Jon anxiously says, "We have to get her back."

Shigeru, understanding of Jon's agitation, tells him, "Hang on man. You need to think with a cool mind before taking off in pursuit." Shigeru orders one of his men to turn on the basement generator. "Remember, we have to get that info Jon. We can get Rachel back and bring him down, but we need to get that info out first."

Sitting down, Jon agrees, "You're right. We have to stick to the plan."

When the lights come back on, Keena turns the computer back on. A notification runs across the screen, 'Due to security reasons, the internet will be blacked out until further notice.'

"Shit!" Shigeru shouts. "They must have used the IP address from our search to find us. Now that they've got what they wanted, they can move on to the next phase of their agenda."

Jon sits and thinks for a moment before he makes a realization, then says, "Wait, before the power went out I saw something else on the page. It was a part of Ben T.'s background. Something that said he started his work in a lab outside of his hometown in Brooks Lake, Wyoming. I've studied conspiracy theories and supposed stories about an entrance to an underground tunnel system near there. If it's anything like what I've read, I could find it."

Keena says, "But how do you know that's where they've taken her?"

Jon answers, "I don't, but it's the next most likely place. He wouldn't take her to the desert facility; he'd know that's where we'd try to go. Do you guys trust me that this is the move we need to make?"

Shigeru replies, "You've been right so far."

Keena answers, "I owe you one for helping me get away from my Stockholm syndrome type of lifestyle, so I'm in."

Some of Keena and Shigeru's men nod and mumble in agreement.

Jon says, "Okay, then we leave the city tomorrow night."

Shigeru adds, "Come on, let's take all we need and move to a safer location. Too much attention has been drawn here."

The group heads to a Yakuza owned loft apartment downtown.

Chapter 14:

The Face of the New Order

The following day, the team realizes that the news has now been shut off as well, probably blacked out like the internet. As night begins to fall, Jon, Keena, Shigeru, the four former mobsters, one of whom has his arm in a sling, and the six surviving Yakuza set out to a parking garage down the road to leave by car. The group has no idea about the condition of the outer city or their chances of making a safe exit. Not knowing if they will be met by the police or military resistance, the group decides to take a chance.

Just before reaching the entrance to the garage, one of the Yakuza points to the sky. The rest of the group turns, noticing a bright purple and blue light rocketing over the city like a comet. The light explodes in the atmosphere above, and an electrical charge is seen flowing overhead in all directions. The group feels a rush of wind and in an instant all of the lights of the city cease to shine.

Looking around at what seems like a citywide power outage, Shigeru proclaims, "Dammit, they must have launched an EMP."

One of Keena's men says, "EMP? You mean like an electromagnetic pulse?"

Shigeru nods.

Keena says, "But that would mean not just the city power going out. All the alternators in any vehicle in the area will also be defunct."

Jon says, "Well then, we'll have to leave on foot. Maybe once we get out of town, we can find some working vehicles, or even a ride maybe."

Shigeru looks up and says, "Yeah, or the military. If we walk, we have to be even more careful, they're gonna wonder why people are moving around on foot in the way we are. We can't just say we're going on a skiing vacation in Wyoming."

Keena adds, "Well, we have to get going now, or we'll get nowhere fast."

The group begins walking toward the outskirts of town. They see slightly panicked crowds, a lot of looting, and doors being shut and locked. As they near the edge of town, the moon is overhead and the group realizes that it's almost midnight.

Out of the blue, they hear screams. Then they see a handful of people running toward them from the end of the street. A large crowd soon follows and runs past them. In the midst of all the fleeing, Jon says, "I wonder what's going on."

Gunshots are then heard, first from pistols and semi-automatic weapons. In return they hear shots from machine guns and full auto rifles. The armed members of the group draw their weapons that consist of pistols and submachine guns. They hunker down behind a group of parked cars, and just around the corner they hear a shotgun bursting off several rounds. Moments later they hear a semi-auto burst, and the shotgun sound ceases. Soon after, a man with a hunting rifle darts down the street and turns the corner.

Alfonso, the mobster with his arm in a sling asks, "What could he be running from?"

Shigeru says, "I don't know, but let's try to go by it quietly."

As the group sneaks by, they see a small congregation of soldiers wearing all gray uniforms. The men are large, standing over seven feet tall, bald, and upon closer examination, all have the same face. Keena exclaims, "What in hell?!"

Jon says, "Those are the HRTs. The human replicate troopers Ben T. showed Rachel and me. Things must have really gotten out of hand for the Cabal faster than they expected. They probably deployed them to make up for all the insubordination from the military."

Just then a grenade lands by the HRTs feet and detonates, blowing away three of them. The other two kneel and run for cover, firing in the direction of the tossed grenade. A silver truck, unlike anything the group has seen, pulls up from around the corner behind the two. Its doors open on the back like a garage door on either side, and four more troops jump out. A group of three men charge, fire, and hit one of the HRTs. Soon after they are cut down by gunfire coming from a turret mounted in the center of the truck. Jon and the others realize that it is time to keep moving, and hopefully under cover. Just outside of town, it starts to rain. The team uses this as an advantage to keep moving under the cover of the elements. A mile or so out of the city, they come across a National guard camp and a large concentration of the replicates. They appear to be working in coordination with each other. Jon says, "These must be soldiers who stayed and attempted to keep order, they probably have been forced into working with the replicates."

Over the hill in the distance, they see six more trucks like the one they saw in town earlier, coming to join the others at the camp. Shigeru suggests, "Come on, we have to get as far as possible from here."

After walking all night, the group finally sees a sign saying they are 55 miles from the border of Iowa. With the sun having been up for several hours now, it is decided that the best thing to do is make camp and use the daylight to catch up on their sleep. Several times throughout the night, they took cover off the road as not to be seen by passing vehicles on the highway. Keena suggests they do the same for their camp.

When the group rests, turns are taken to keep watch. While the others are sleeping, Jon is woken up by one of the former mobsters who is acting as a lookout. The man whispers, "Look, over the ridge. It's six of those things and one of their trucks. They must be scouting to see if they can find anyone on the roads."

Jon says, "Maybe we can take them by surprise and get their truck."

When Jon wakes the others up, he tells them about the scouts and how they should try to get the truck.

Keena asks, "How could we do that?"

Shigeru, says, "Well, we might be able to pull that off easily if we can separate them. If Alfonso shows his sling and pretends to be wounded, Jon can yell to them for help. Maybe some of them will come over here. Keena, you, your men and mine can get the jump on them from all the sides of the clearing up there. I'll go with three of my men and take the truck from behind."

Jon agrees, "This just might work."

Shigeru picks three of his men and says, "Once you get them over here, wait for my signal before attacking."

Keena asks, "What's the signal?"

Shigeru answers, "You'll know."

Keena smirks at him as he and his men disappear into the woods.

Jon, with Alfonso braced over his shoulder, asks, "Are you ready?"

He replies, "As ready as one can be in this situation. To think, last week at this time, I was eating spaghetti in my best suit down at Luigi Brothers. Now I'm all banged up in a field with a bunch of drones running around."

Jon chuckles and says, "Alright, let's do this then."

The two stumble out into the clearing making themselves visible. The six replicates off in the distance are standing next to their truck. They don't notice Jon and Alfonso, so Jon gives a shout out to them. "Help! We need some help over here, please!"

Attention turned toward them, four of the replicates come running over into the clearing. As they come to a stop with their weapons drawn, Jon looks down into the bushes at Keena. Pretending to be frightened, he says, "Oh, we surrender."

Suddenly, Shigeru and his three men spring out and ambush the two remaining replicates near the truck. Confused, the other four look back at the truck. Before they can even make a move, Keena and her six men open fire into the group of HRTs. The replicates barely have a chance to rattle off a shot.

Before the final shot is fired, one of the Yakuza with Shigeru is hit by a seventh trooper, unknown to the others, that comes out of the woods. Firing his last two rounds at the replicate, Shigeru runs in a rage toward him. Moving to hand-to-hand combat, Shigeru leaps into the air, taking a roundhouse wind kick to the head of the trooper. The trooper, shot in the chest and disoriented by the kick, falls to one knee and leans to the right. Shigeru reloads his pistol, and fires a shot to the HRTs face, killing it.

Running to the truck and the aid of his fallen comrade, he notices that Keena and the others too were successful with their part of the plan. Shigeru kneels over his mortally wounded man and thanks him in Japanese for his service. The man says as he dies, "It was an honor to serve you."

Keena approaches Shigeru and consoles him saying, "I understand. I'm not the only one to have taken a loss. You've had many of your men fall recently. I'm sorry."

Shigeru says, "We should get moving, there could be more out there."

Jon interjects, "No, we'll bury him first."

The men prepare a makeshift funeral service and say a few words to honor all the Yakuza who have been killed lately. Loading up into the truck, the group begins driving toward Iowa.

Once over the border, the group tries to get their bearings and plot the rest of their course into Wyoming. As late afternoon approaches, the team has made their way well into the state of Iowa. While driving, a voice suddenly comes from a speaker in the dash of the truck. Keena, driving, stops the vehicle. "What is that?" she asks.

The voice comes on again. "DSN-423, report in...DSN-423 why aren't you at your post? Dial in your compliance code into the com panel."

The group sits in silence. Then the voice says, "DSN-423, your positioning shows you far off designated course." Afterwards, the radio goes silent.

Shigeru says, "Wait a minute. Everyone out, everyone away from the truck, RUN!"

The group flees following Shigeru's example.

BOOM!

In a fiery explosion, the truck is destroyed and the blast rocks its fleeing occupants.

Jon comments, "They must have tracker devices on every one of their vehicles to prevent theft."

Keena asserts, "Well the sun will be going down soon, looks like we're on foot again. Might as well make camp."

Shigeru adds, "Yeah, but let's do it down the way a bit. They may send a detachment or a drone to find out if we're still alive."

That night, around the campfire, the group talks about how the world may change forever from this. Jon hypothesizes, "This attack is probably only on the face of North America for now. The Cabal wasn't fully ready to use the HRTs globally. If they can be stopped, this may not spread any further."

When Keena begins to speak, Shigeru silences her. "Wait!" he says, "Do you hear that?"

Jon asks, "What?"

All of the men around the fire begin looking around. All that's heard is crickets and owls in the distance. They wait a moment more. Then without warning, from all directions a group of soldiers storm out of the woods with guns drawn, capturing the group before they can even reach a pistol.

"Freeze," one of the soldiers says, "Hands in the air."

Jon says, "Okay, we give up."

Out of the woods comes a short, blonde haired female Army officer. She breaks through the crowd of her men and approaches Jon and company. "Take their weapons boys. They're civilians," she commands. "When we first heard you, we thought you were those things. We found a truck down the road blown out with no bodies in it."

Jon says, "Wait a second. You're not on their side either? You must be one of those rogue military units the news reported."

The woman turns to Jon and says, "We're the *real* military. We, unlike a lot of the others, didn't bow down to tyranny and support the transition to a totalitarian state. What brings you all the way out here anyway?" she asks.

Jon responds, "I'm an archaeologist, and I've uncovered the truth about what's going on. I was trying to get the word out before something happened, but I wasn't able to in time."

The woman says, "Archaeologist, huh? How many of those run around with a bunch of Asian guys, some suited thugs who look like they've seen better days, and a petite black woman?"

Jon scrambles up and offers his hand. "My name is Jon Peters."

"Major Emily Morgan of the United States Army, pleased to meet you Jon Peters," she says as she shakes his hand.

Jon begins introducing the others. "This is Shigeru and Keena, they and their men have been helping me. Before all this happened, the powers that be attacked where we were staying and kidnapped my girlfriend Rachel. In an attempt to kill two birds with one stone, we're heading to Wyoming to get her back and stop the one responsible for the HRTs."

Emily asks, "Wyoming? Why there?"

Jon says, "We have a lot to fill you in on."

After sitting around the fire and filling Major Morgan in on everything that has happened from the time Jon first received the letter from Rachel to the second attack from the Shinobis, Emily agrees to use her forces and army vehicles to escort them to Brooks Lake.

Now it is Emily's turn to tell her story. "When martial law was declared, my reserve unit was deployed to help maintain order just outside of Des Moines. When we got word about how much was being done on the political spectrum, my commander decided not to follow protocol and to defend the country in the way we swore we would. Some men chose not to follow; several others fled and went home. But the rest of us stuck with him. A few days later, we were attacked by those things. A lot of my men were killed, including my CO. There're only 23 of us left. Jon, not only do I want to help you, I *have* to help you. This so called Cabal is not what I have declared my allegiance to."

"How soon do you think we can reach Brooks Lake?" Jon asks.

Morgan responds with, "We'll head out at sunrise. With a little luck we won't meet any resistance and can make it through South Dakota by tomorrow morning. Then another day for Wyoming, maybe a day and a half."

Shigeru asks, How many vehicles do you have?"

She answers, "Two troop transports, three Humvees, and a supply truck. It'll be a bit crammed, but we can squeeze you guys in."

After the pleasantries end and the conversation winds down, the group gets some much needed rest. At dawn, the group sets off into South Dakota.

Chapter 15:

A Terrible Truth...and the Rockets' Red Glare

Riding in the second Humvee with Emily and two of her men, Jon, Shigeru, and Keena enjoy the ride as best they can. Major Morgan, in her dark aviator glasses, turns to say. "We'll be coming up on Sioux Falls soon. If we encounter any resistance before Wyoming, it will be there. We'll stop a few miles outside of the city until my scouts report what the city is like. It's a decent sized city, but there's little military presence there. The city would have fallen easily to the HRTs."

After waiting some time, the scouts return with their report that there is in fact an HRT presence in the city. The group decides to move on foot under the cover of night to see if they can liberate the town or if they should just move around it. Looking through binoculars, Emily acknowledges, "Just as I thought, they've got a road block through the center of town. We may have to just go around."

Shigeru takes a look. "Wait, look down there. It's a human commanding them," he says.

"Let me see," Emily says, as she takes back the binoculars. "Yes, yes, see that thing on his arm? That device sends out a signal that shows the HRTs where to take the commands from. It's what stops them from just listening to anyone."

Keena says, "Yes, we heard that signal coming out of the dash of the truck we hijacked."

Emily says, "If we can take him out, all the troops in the area won't know who to take orders from anymore and after a while their current orders will just dissipate and they walk around confused. I saw it when my unit engaged them before, it's how we were able to beat them."

Jon says, "Good, but how are we gonna get down to them?"

Emily counters with, "Easy, watch this." She signals a soldier come over. The soldier with an M203 grenade launcher attached to his M16 comes up and sits on the ledge to take aim.

The group all begins smiling. "Yes," they all exclaim.

The soldier hones in on the man walking around with the metallic wrist band as he oversees the city's barricade. After a moment, he fires. The grenade lands somewhere just off from the feet of the commander, blowing away a couple of the replicates near him and injuring a few others. The commander himself, though badly injured, survives and orders the replicates to attack up the hill toward them.

"Dammit!" Emily shouts. Standing up, she yells to her men, "Assault the blockade!" as she begins firing shots down at them before running herself.

Shigeru and Keena follow suit with their men. Jon makes a run for it alongside them. Now with every HRT in the area coming at them, the quiet, prairie like entrance to the city is engulfed in a full scale war zone.

After clearing the area of replicates, Emily runs up to the commander and ignoring his pleas for mercy, shoots him, killing him instantly. After a while the battle winds down. Some armed locals have now come out of the woodwork to help. Emily explains to them, "The remaining HRTs will be leaderless and can be disposed of easily even after my soldiers and I leave."

This is one town in Middle America that is now liberated of the Cabal, for now. All thanks to our quick witted heroes and the armed citizens that were brave enough to stand up to them.

Surveying the battlefield, Jon finds the commander's body and notices his wrist band. He takes it off and starts to put it on. Emily shouts, "Jon, don't! If a person who's not supposed to be wearing it puts it on, it will kill him. It detects the DNA of the wearer and if it doesn't match, it releases a toxic injection that kills the unmerited host within a half hour."

"How do you know this?" Jon asks.

Emily hesitantly responds, "Because my commander tried to do what you had in mind. Wear the band to control the replicates. When it pricked him, he realized it could kill him, so in his final conversation, he entrusted the unit to me. Twenty minutes later, after promoting me in front of the men, he died."

Keena takes the band from Jon's hand and says, "I'm really good with my hands. Maybe I can rewire it."

Major Morgan, with a tear in eye, turns and says, "You're wasting your time," before turning to her men arriving, with the trucks that were left behind.

That night, the group stays at a motel the people of Sioux Falls provided for the band of heroes. Down in the lobby, Jon tells Keena. "That commander seemed awful familiar to me."

Keena, working on the armband, states, "Yeah, he did seem familiar. Seems like I've seen him in a commercial or something."

Just then, Jon's memory flashes back to the newspaper Professor Gray handed to him the day he lectured him in the teachers' lounge. The cover had an article with the HRT commander on it. He was the CEO of a big-time fast food chain based out of South Dakota that has recently been gaining popularity across the nation. "My God," Jon exclaims, "They must be assigning the replicates to corporate leaders who support their cause."

Emily overhearing from the hall, comes in with a cup of coffee in hand. "Yes," she says, "And leaders of various paramilitary organizations. The commander of the replicates my CO killed was a prominent leader of a paramilitary organization called Dark Stream. They went to military school together and when he found out my CO was rebelling, he was sent to negotiate surrender. When it didn't work, a firefight broke out and my CO killed him."

Right about this time, Shigeru steps in. With a sad look on his face and his hands in his pockets he says, "We have the casualty report. I lost two more men, and you're down to 17."

Emily lets out a sigh and says, "We may have won the day, but the cost was heavy. Tomorrow at noon we're heading out toward Wyoming."

With nothing left to say, the group heads off to their rooms to retire before taking on the long road ahead.

Chapter 16:

Home of the Brave

After the group is seen off by the remaining citizens of Sioux Falls, they start down the road toward the border of Wyoming. Jon starts thinking of Rachel. He knows she's still alive. The Cabal wouldn't kill her if they wanted any chance of him joining them at all. But still, he wonders if she's being treated well. Several hours pass before they reach the state line. Emily assures the group, "We're making great time and the only city between us and Brooks Lake is Casper, Wyoming."

Time passes fairly quickly and the group can't help but notice the beautiful landscape and how peaceful it is away from all the fighting. Emily wonders how other units are faring and whether or not the whole country is as bad as the Midwest is.

Finally, the caravan reaches Casper. When they roll into town they discover from the locals that a battle had taken place two days before. But no one was around other than townsfolk. No soldiers or replicates. They learn that some soldiers had been here but most of the battle was fought by a group of survivalists living in a fortress they constructed on their piece of land outside of town. Emily insists they be given directions to the fortress.

Once they have the directions, our heroes drive out of town to the modern-day concrete fortress. Just off the road, a fence is seen all around the property and the fortress can be seen just up ahead about two hundred yards away. On the gate, there is a device used to call in to the main property. Before even using it, the speaker goes off. It says, "We have you in our sniper scopes. Please state your business and your affiliations."

Emily responds, "I'm Major Emily Morgan of the US Army. I have important people in toe regarding the survival of the nation and possibly the civilized world."

After a brief moment of quiet from the other end, a second voice comes on. It says, "Emily, Emily Morgan, hang on. I'll have 'em open the gate and let you and your party in."

Jon asks, "Friend of yours?"

Looking back at the group stunned, Emily shrugs her shoulders. The gate opens and the group enters half cautiously. At the entrance to the fort, several men armed to the teeth and wearing homemade battle fatigues, along with an Army officer, come out to greet the team. "Emily?" the officer questions, "It is you."

"Kyle? Kyle Mathews?!" Emily says excitedly.

Kyle answers, "Lieutenant Kyle Mathews now. Oh and look at you, Major now."

Emily's smile fades. "Not by good circumstances I'm afraid. Major Riggs was killed but promoted me before he died," she states.

Kyle frowns. "I'm sorry to hear that."

Emily brightens back up and says, "Guys, this is Kyle. He and I went to basic together before he transferred to another unit."

The group expresses pleasure in their hellos. Kyle turns and introduces a man and a woman, both in fatigues. "This is Jeff and Bridgette Carls. They started this little survivalist community. It started as a family thing and now it's 40 strong."

"Forty-one strong," Jeff corrects him, "After our losses in the battle. We had 53 to start with." Jeff invites everyone in.

Over dinner, Kyle says, "We have a lot to catch up on."

After explaining the situation with her Jon, and the others, Emily asks, "What happened to you and how did you end up here in Casper?"

Kyle explains, "When the orders went out, most of my unit disbanded or went rogue. Only me and less than a platoon's worth are still around. Yep, me and seven of my boys are all that's left. Who would have thought that a week's worth of fighting would hit us so hard."

"All is fair in love and war," Emily says.

"Anyway," Kyle continues, "We came here to Casper after the battle of Denver and that's where we met Jeff and Bridgette. They already had a plan underway to liberate the city and we helped them execute it."

Jeff interjects, saying, "We want to liberate the whole state but we just don't have the numbers. We would like to assist you in any way we can with your attack on this mystery lab at Brooks Lake, but I'm afraid that's as far as we can go."

Jon says, "Thanks, we appreciate any help."

Jeff stands up from the table and heads over to Jon. Resting his hand on Jon's shoulder he says, "Don't worry, we'll get your woman back. After that, you'll have to teach her how to shoot so she doesn't get caught again," nodding and smiling over to Bridgette.

Shigeru and Keena laugh.

"Well you'd have to teach Jon to shoot before he can teach her," Shigeru says.

"What?!" Jeff exclaims, "You've never used a gun?"

Jon replies, "Well, I have, but umm, well not in this body, it's really tough to explain."

Bridgette stands up from the table and says, "We'll fix that. Let's take him out and let him fire a few rounds."

Jon, timid but understanding the need to learn at this point, agrees and goes out to the shooting range with them.

Jeff puts a very large revolver in his hand and has him aim at a dead HRT the survivalists have strung up at the end of the shooting range. He fires a few times and misses. Jeff chuckles, "Let me show you."

Shigeru interrupts, "No, let me."

Drawing his pistol, Shigeru fires three shots one after another into the chest and head of the dead replicate.

"Hot damn, that Jap can shoot. Marine style even," Jeff expresses in admiration.

Jon says, "Let me try again."

Thinking of Rachel and remembering the words of both Shigeru and Chief Crowfeather about a soul being tied to destiny and how a person's will, can manipulate it, Jon prepares to fire. Accurately, he puts a bullet right into the HRT's forehead and three bull's eyes next to it.

"Nice!" Bridgette exclaims.

"There ya go Jon," Keena congratulates him.

Shigeru smiles, glad to see Jon taking a step out of his comfort zone.

"Well," Emily says, "We had better sleep so that we can take this show on the road tomorrow."

Jeff and Bridgette show the group to some cots.

The following day, the unified force of freedom fighters sets out to engage the laboratory of Benjamin Thomas Washington.

On the way out, Emily asks, "What's our head count for this operation Kyle?"

Kyle responds, "Well, we have your sixteen men, my seven, Shigeru and his three men, Jon, Keena, and the four mobsters. Jeff and Bridgette are coming themselves but they can only spare fifteen of their men."

"Kind of a skeleton crew, considering what's waiting for us," Emily states, "If Jon's right and this is an entrance to a tunnel system as well as a laboratory, there's no telling how many we'll be up against. Not to mention the fact that that the town probably has some sort of occupancy."

Keena, understanding that Emily doesn't see eye to eye with her about the HRT control band, has reengineered it and is now able to wear it without being harmed. She decides to show it to Jon.

"How does it work?" He asks.

She proceeds to explain, "When not active, the light is red. When you turn it on to search, the light turns yellow. I assume that means its seeking nearby HRTs to hone in on. Once active, the light turns green and commands can be issued."

"Wow," Jon says, "Not only are you tough, you're smart too."

Keena smiles, and says, "Thanks."

About this time, Shigeru comes in and says, "Okay, we're loading up and moving out. Kyle asked if me if I could round up some scouts to go ahead of us. I volunteered my men and I to do it."

No," Keena says, "My men and I will. Alfonso can ride with you since his arm is still pretty banged up."

"Okay," Shigeru says, "Whatever you say."

So Keena and her men set off ahead of the group in a truck provided by Jeff to scout the way to Brooks

Lake. Jon, choosing to ride with Jeff and Bridgette, explains to them, "From what I understand, it may be possible that supernatural forces are behind all of this. If so, then HRTs might not be the worst thing the Cabal can throw at us."

Jeff, looking in the rearview mirror at Jon says, "I've never believed in hocus-pocus stuff. But, after everything I saw last week, I figure I didn't think clone soldiers were real either. So, demonic beings may very well be real. I suppose if that's what we're up against, then we'll throw whatever we have at them and hope that's enough."

Bridgette smiles and rests her hand on Jeff's knee.

"Let's hope you won't have to," Jon replies.

Just after sunset, the group catches up to Keena's camp. She and her men have set up a house tent about 10 miles away from Brooks Lake. The crew gets out and begins setting up their own camp. Keena greets the team saying, "I have something to show you, but I want to show Jon and Shigeru first."

Entering the tent, the two are startled by what they find. Sitting in the corner with hands tied behind his back and his bald head looking down at the ground is none other than a human replicate captured by Keena's men. She explains, "We they found him scouting just outside of town."

Jon states, "I take it you're gonna test the device on him then, right?"

She responds, "Right. His tags read MSC-1138," so let's try some individual commands. "MSC-1138, stand up." The replicate abides and stands up. "Walk to the other side of the tent." Sure enough he walks. "MSC-1138, do you have a way to bring your detachment to your location." Yes, he nods.

Excited, the group devises a plan to capture a whole squad and use it as a diversion to get into the lab. They show Kyle, Emily and the others Keena's bounty.

After approval from the others, although with hesitation from Emily, Keena has the HRT touch the com pad on his wrist. This sends a signal that tells his squad to come to his location.

Keena says, "I don't wanna risk trying to control all of them, as they may have an override for the individual command bands, and we don't wanna be in the middle of all the replicates turning on us."

When the squad of six replicates arrives, Keena easily takes over their command. Kyle and Emily devise a plan.

Emily explains, "Keena's replicates are going to go just outside of town and start a ruckus, causing a response from any other HRTs in the area. Kyle's men, along with Jeff's, will go into town and get any help they can to help liberate it. I'll head up the strike team to attack the lab entrance. Jon, Shigeru, Keena, and their men make up the team."

Jeff asserts, "Count me and Bridgette in. We'll take five of our boys and go in with you, our guys can handle themselves."

Kyle adds, "Count me in too. No way am I going to miss this lab."

Keena assures the others, "My men and I will hang back and guard the door so you don't get boxed in down there."

Jeff says, "Okay, so we have a plan, but how do we know where to find the entrance to the lab?"

Jon steps up and says, "If I remember correctly, the story goes that an access road goes off the highway but has a road closed blockade. A few miles down the road it leads to a tunnel that goes into the underground system."

Bridgette states, "It's a big hunch, but worth a try."

Kyle says, "We'll go on and have our guys in place outside the city. Once the distraction kicks in they can move in."

Emily claps her hands together and says, "Alright, let's do this then. Let's find that lab entrance."

Jeff adds, "We attack at dawn."

Chapter 17:

Who Has Who Cornered?

As the crew drives down the highway, sure enough, they find the blocked road off to the side. Following the access road, they see a mountain ahead. Bridgette says to Jon, "It doesn't look like there's any cave entrance or anything, maybe it's hidden."

Approaching the mountainside, the team feels a sense of hopelessness fall on them. The road leads straight into the wall of the mountain. Shigeru says, "Well, it was a good try, I guess. We can still liberate the town, maybe they know about the lab and its location."

Emily says, "Or maybe, she's not even here. She could be anywhere in the world for all we know."

Jon interjects, "Hold on."

He starts walking toward the mountainside. As the others look on, they see his hand disappear into the wall as he touches it. Jon steps forward and walks right through.

"Well, I'll be," says Jeff, as he looks on in amazement.

Jon steps back out. "It's a hologram," he says, "There's a huge tunnel in here. Big enough for trucks and everything else to come through."

Keena says, "This must be how they were able to mobilize all over the country the way they did."

The team begins to move in. Several hundred yards into the tunnel they come up against a giant steel door. Bridgette says, "Well too bad we don't have a giant garage door opener on hand."

Jeff replies, "Now hunny, don't reduce things so quickly. The pipe bombs that Major Morgan's men are carrying are more than capable of blowin this old thing open. Look at it, its rusty."

Keena says, "Alright, I'm gonna start the distraction. My men and I will be right outside keeping watch. Good luck everyone. And Jon, I hope Rachel's in there, and she's okay."

Jon nods his thanks to Keena.

Keena commands her HRTs to move down to the valley just outside of town and start firing down from the hillside. It works like a charm and replicates begin moving out of town to engage them. Following the diversion, the survivalists and Kyle's men rush in to secure the town.

Back inside the tunnel, the team prepares to blow the door down using explosives. Standing on either side of the steel wall, Kyle and Emily detonate the pipe bombs in place. The blast creates a huge hole in the iron wall.

When the smoke clears, the team goes rushing in. Emily, Kyle, Jeff, and Bridgette first, followed by Emily and Jeff's men. Shigeru and Jon follow swiftly. Inside the door they find a fork in the tunnel, one heading due south and sloping into the ground and the other going northward. A monitor turns on above the north entrance. It's Ben T. "I knew you would probably find this place Jon, but I didn't expect you to come here with such a powerful force. Nonetheless, you are all still outmatched," he says.

"Where's Rachel?" Jon asks.

"Here, in my lab," Ben replies, "Come get her if you can, but you may be having company soon."

Just then the group hears footsteps from the south entrance. "It's replicates, they're coming from the tunnel!" shouts Emily.

Emily divides her troops to hold them off while the rest move on into the lab. Going straight into the lab, the group immediately faces resistance. One of the soldiers and a survivalist is shot instantly. Up ahead, the group notices two descending stairwells separated by a wall. "Which way?" Emily asks.

Jeff suggests, "Let's split up. Jon you come with me and Bridgette this way. Emily, Kyle, take your men down that way. Shigeru you and your boys go with them."

"Right," Shigeru says in agreement.

Heading down the stairwell behind Jeff and Bridgette, Jon shields himself from the gunfire spraying upward toward them. Jon says, "I think we chose the wrong direction. This seems to be where Ben T.'s soldiers are coming from."

Jeff replies, "Maybe, but either way we have to fight our way down to stop them from pinning the others in upstairs."

Just then, a rogue bullet hits Bridgette in the chest. "No!" Jeff shouts, rushing to her aid. Jon runs up beside her as well, as the other survivalists continue firing downward.

Bridgette, with a dazed look on her face tells Jeff, "Be sure and get those sons of bitches."

Closing her eyes, in her husband's arms, she dies.

Jon says to Jeff, "I'm sorry."

Jeff, holding his emotions in check in the midst of the battle replies, "No time for sorry, only revenge. Let's get to it."

Picking his rifle back up and firing, Jeff rejoins the team. Moving on down, the group finds an open elevator shaft. Three HRTs, coming up, fire and kill another of Jeff's men. The others return fire to stop them.

After the replicates are disposed of, Jon says, "If we take this lift down, the only thing we're sure of finding are more replicates, no telling how many."

Jeff states, "We have some explosives. We could go down and blow whatever's there."

Jon responds, "But that could mean destroying the lift. There may not be any other way out."

Jeff smiles at Jon and says, "Go on back and join the others. Get your girlfriend back." Putting his hand on Jon's shoulder, he continues, "I lost my woman today. I don't want someone else to lose theirs."

Jon replies, "Thank you for all you've done, Jeff."

Jeff and his two remaining men then descend in the lift. As Jon starts walking back up the stairs he hears gunfire down the shaft and Jeff shouting 'yahoo' as an explosion rocks the stairwell. Jon, in deference to Jeff's sacrifice, bows his head as he moves up the steps. His attention then turns back to finding Rachel and getting back to the others.

Meanwhile, outside, Keena realizes her distraction has run out and her HRTs have been killed. She and her men prepare to defend the entrance from the remaining HRTs summoned back to the tunnel. They don't want the team inside to get flanked. The HRTs who aren't on the march back to the lab are being fended off by the resistance in town led by Kyle's men and the remaining survivalists.

Keena and her men get ready as the replicates within range begin firing. Instantly one of the mobsters goes down, leaving Keena and the other three to fight off the rest. It doesn't take much. Keena and her men eliminate the HRTs quickly.

After finishing them off, she decides it's best to move into the tunnel to assess what's going on. She starts to worry that Jon and Shigeru are in trouble. Arriving at the tunnel fork she finds five surviving army soldiers, two wounded. She asks, "What happened?"

One of the soldiers explains the trap and how the others moved down into the lab. Just then the group hears the sound of more replicates moving down the tunnel toward them. They all take a stance, preparing to fight once again.

Jon, now catching up with Shigeru and the other soldiers, finds them at the bottom of the stairwell that they took. They are trying to shoot their way into the hall, but it's protected rather heavily by replicates.

Shigeru asks, "What happened? Why did you come this way?"

Jon answers, "We definitely weren't going the right way."

"And Jeff?" Shigeru asks.

Jon replies sadly, "He didn't make it. He and his men blew the entrance so no replicates could get behind us."

"Damn, I liked that Yankee," Shigeru says.

Jon asks, "What are we gonna do now?"

Before Shigeru can muster an answer, he is grazed in the arm by a bullet.

Jon shouts, "Are you all right?"

Shigeru responds, "I'm fine. Just a flesh wound."

At the front of the group are Emily and Kyle. Emily looks back at them and shouts over the gunfire, "We're gonna have to retreat, there's just too many of them, and they are too tough one on one."

The world spinning around him, many thoughts flash across Jon's mind in the heat of the chaos – his wounded friend beside him, the sacrifice of Jeff, Bridgette and the other survivalists, and then Rachel. Jon flies into a rage and grabbing the rifle nearest to him from a fallen soldier, he flips into 'rock and roll mode'. Running up to the front of the team, he begins firing. He takes out two replicates himself immediately. With his body fully exposed to gunfire he moves on into the hall killing another replicate. Emily gives the order to move in and the rest of the team follow up on him, covering him from behind. Out of ammunition, Jon disposes the assault rifle off to the side and draws the revolver Jeff gave him. His mind flips back to target practice and how he remembered Crowfeather's words about destiny, then Shigeru's words. Now at the end of the metal hallway, Jon fires right into the face of the last two replicates in the way, killing them both. Clear of fire, the rest of the team moves forward.

Jon, pistol still in hand says, "Ben T. is just beyond this door in front of us, I feel it."

"Yeah, but how many more replicates?" Emily asks.

Kyle says, "We don't have the numbers to keep this up."

The group then hears movement behind them, coming down the metal stairwell. They prepare to be attacked from the rear. Fear begins to set in at thoughts of the cost of this next skirmish. Suddenly, they notice it's Keena, her men, and the rest of the soldiers. They are leading a group of about 20 replicates down the stairs. Keena says, "We got hung up and I realized if ever was a time to really use this armband, it is now."

Jon opens the door. On the other side is a very large room with a high ceiling. In the room there is a big circular platform in the center with a railing around it. Standing at the top is Ben T. Dozens of HRTs are at his feet, ready to finish off the pitiful little band of rebels about to enter. As the door opens, to Ben's surprise it's not the heroes, but a large group of HRTs funneling into the room. "What?!" He exclaims, "How can this be?"

The replicates begin firing at one another and a big battle unfolds. The team comes running in behind them to assist their captured replicates in winning the day. With the push of a button, the small room-sized platform raises Ben T. 10 more feet into the air, away from the line of fire.

In an attempt to stop him, Jon, Emily, and Kyle climb up only to discover Ben T. wearing thick silver cufflinks and a metallic band around his head. Holding his hands out in front of him, the metal rings begin vibrating as Jon and the others fire at him. Their bullets are stopped mid-stream and with a flip of his hands to the side, Emily and Kyle gripping their rifles are thrown to the side. Another move of his hands to the side and Jon's pistol is thrown away.

"Huh?" Jon thinks, "Wow, he can manipulate metal magnetically. That must be some sort of experimental weapon of his."

Ben T. says, "I can't believe you have made it this far. You would have been a magnificent member of the Cabal, Jon Peters. We didn't think America had the heart to revolt in the way it did. Yet we didn't expect the military to break down as quickly as *they* did. I will make an example of these pathetic rebels," says Ben, as he walks past Jon over to Emily and Kyle, lying on the ground over at the edge of the platform.

The last of Keena's replicates has been killed and the rest of the team is busy fighting what's left of Ben's.

Ben T. continues, "Even if you survive here, it's not over. The Cabal is far more powerful than just mere human replication."

Holding his hands up, Ben T. causes Emily and Kyle's rifles to levitate above them. Just before Ben magnetically squeezes the triggers of their weapons to finish them off, Keena climbs up onto the platform behind him. She now has control of his HRTs and gives them the command to turn on Ben T. The five remaining replicates scale the platform and just before assaulting him, Ben T. turns the levitating rifles on them and fires them off. The rifle clips empty, spraying out all the shells into the replicates, killing them off.

Dropping the empty rifles from the air, Ben T turns to Keena and before she can draw her pistol again, he throws her magnetically against the wall, crushing her HRT control band. "I don't know where you came from missy, but you have been quite the nuisance with your reprograming skills."

Just then, Shigeru, with his slightly wounded shoulder climbs up and attempts to shoot Ben T. Shigeru, gripping his custom gold plated pistol, is thrown off to the side as well when Ben T. manipulates it like the others.

Ben T., laughing and seeming invincible and impervious to anyone holding a gun, presses a button on his control pad. A glass cylinder with Rachel inside lowers from the ceiling. It is set down beside Jon and the robotic arm that lowered it is released and returns to the ceiling from whence it came.

Jon rushes to the cylinder and bangs the glass in an attempt to get Rachel out. The other soldiers, along with the Yakuza and mobsters, now trying to get Emily and Kyle to their feet, are helpless.

Ben T. says. "You came all the way here for her. So I'm going to give her to you. And give her to you, and give her to you..." He repeats while laughing maniacally as he manipulates the cylinder Rachel is contained in with his magnetic wrist bands and starts crashing it into Jon.

Rachel is thrown around on the inside like a rag doll. Laughing hysterically, Ben T. continuously throws the cylinder into Jon, taking a little out of him with each blow. With Ben T. humorously distracted by his crude execution of Jon, Keena manages to get back onto her feet. Pistol in hand, she approaches Ben T. from the rear. Unbeknownst to the laughing Ben, she aims with the barrel of her gun straight at the back of Ben's head and in a very anticlimactic fashion, pulls the trigger. Ben T. is killed instantly.

With Ben no longer manipulating the cylinder with his arm bands, it falls to the ground, jolting Rachel harshly. Jon rushes over to find a way to release her and once he does, the two embrace each other.

Rachel says sweetly, "The whole time he had me, I kept remembering what Chief Crowfeather told me when you and Shigeru were talking to Bear. He said that sometimes, a soul that is tied to destiny can be super charged by a motivation. He also told me I was that motivation for you, and that when geared right, you can do amazing things. The Cabal must have known this too. I won't ever leave you Jon, not like I did in college. I promise. I'll be your inspiration to do what's right."

"I love you Rach," Jon says as he leans forward and kisses Rachel passionately.

"Uh guys," says Shigeru, holding his wounded shoulder. "I don't mean to interrupt, but we should blow this place and see how the guys in town are doing."

Emily comes up and proclaims, "Alright troops, let's move out."

Chapter 18:

When One Door Closes...

After destroying the laboratory and returning to Brooks Lake to discover it's been liberated by Kyle's men and the survivalists, the group gets some much needed rest. That night, the team, the soldiers and the remaining survivalists along with the townspeople mourn the loss of the heroes. Among the dead are Jeff and Bridgette, several of their men, Keena's enforcer Tony, and several of Emily Morgan's company.

Kyle asks, "So where are you going now Jon?"

Jon answers, "We're going to head to the coast. We need to leave the country in order to plan our next move against the Cabal. Hopefully, we can find a boat or something."

Emily adds, "Me and my boys are gonna escort him. I figure Portland, Oregon is a good place to try and find a boat."

Kyle says, "I wish I could go and help you Emily, but my men and the survivalists are needed to help here."

"I understand, Kyle," replies Emily, "But I'm glad you made the right decision when everything went to hell."

"I'll say the same to you," says Kyle, as he looks in appreciation at Emily.

After resting and bandaging the group's wounds, Emily and her nine remaining men leave with Jon and his party. Rachel, now brought up to date and introduced to their new friends is the first to thank them before leaving.

By the time the team drives through Idaho and crosses the border into Oregon, Emily realizes that they won't have enough fuel to complete the trip. Examining the map, they realize that a railroad track nearby will lead straight into Portland, so if they are forced to walk, at least they have some sort of guide to go by.

After driving up to the track, they decide to make camp for the night, as Shigeru and his men scout the perimeter.

That night at the campfire, Keena and Emily have a heart-to-heart discussion.

Emily says, "I owe you an apology. I never thought your plan with the HRT controller would work, and I was wrong. It's just that the Major's death really shook me up. This whole thing is so crazy. I feel so betrayed by my country. I know that Jon is on to this so called Cabal and Shigeru is well aware of it, even you weren't oblivious to it before all that's taken place. I just feel left out, probably like most of the world. I just don't see how we could have been so expendable. We signed up to defend our country, not act as jailers for it."

Keena replies, "Look, I understand, I was betrayed by my superiors too. I was orphaned at a very young age. My parents were taken out by the Turoni family when my father couldn't pay their outstanding debt. The Don's son was a top enforcer for the family. He led the hit. Afterwards they found me. He took me in and raised me, telling me the entire time that I was better than my parents and not weak like they were. As he became the new Don when I was a young girl, he educated me on the Mafia's secrets and their connection to the Cabal. He trained me to be an enforcer. When I disobeyed a second attempt to capture Jon, he turned on me. I didn't even know my last name. I mean, it's been Turoni as long as I can remember. But how many black women do you know with an Italian last name."

Emily consoles her, "I'm so sorry. If it's any consolation, I know my parents, but I might as well not, that's why I joined the reserve."

Keena smiles and says, "Thanks for letting me vent to you."

Emily replies, "No problem and thank *you*."

Jon and Rachel, sitting at another fire across from the others begin to talk as they observe Keena and Emily.

Jon says, "I'm glad Keena can talk to Emily. I can relate to her to some degree being orphaned and all, but at least I knew my parents."

Rachel adds, "Yeah, dad's been gone a long time but at least I knew him."

Jon asks, "What about Shigeru? He never has spoken to us about his background."

Rachel answers, "If he feels the need to, he will. You should know him by now."

Jon laughs, "Yeah, it's funny how well you get to know someone in such a short time under such dire circumstances. Like Emily – we met her just a few days after you went missing, and I feel like I've known her for years. She is definitely a valued member of this team, and she and her men have sacrificed so much to help us get where we're going."

Rachel replies, "Yeah, I hope she and I can become friends. After all, she helped rescue me. Geez, I hate being a damsel in distress when there's bad ass tough women like her and Keena running around."

"Hey now," John says, "You're not totally helpless. I wouldn't even have left my Ramen noodles if it wasn't for you convincing me to go. And you sure weren't afraid to get your hands dirty when we dug up that chest in Cameroon."

Rachel just smiles as she leans on Jon's shoulder. The group enjoys the night and the fire. Tomorrow they will begin the long walk to Portland in hopes of finding a boat.

Getting up rather late, the group heads out from camp just before noon, abandoning their fuel-less vehicles.

After several hours of walking, the group comes across what seems like a godsend to them. Up ahead is train yard, switch track and all. As the team investigates and finds no one around, Jon suggests they use the train there in the yard to take them the rest of the way to Portland.

Shigeru asks, "Are you sure that's a good idea?'

Jon exclaims, "It's not like the trains are running, we won't run into another one, the whole country's infrastructure is down."

Emily turns to one of her men, "Sergeant, secure the engine and prepare for mobility," she commands."

"Yes, ma'am," The young sergeant responds as he moves to the front of the train.

"Corporal," she continues, "Take two men down the line and uncouple the train separating the third boxcar from the fourth. The rest of you, secure the area."

Keena says, "My men and I will check out the boxcars, make sure there are no surprises."

Jon and Rachel hop aboard the first boxcar behind the engine.

After starting the train and loading what little supplies the group has, they start their way down the track. Emily, on board the engine with a few of her men, assesses the map.

"Just 30 more miles until we hit Portland," she says. "What the hell?" she questions as she notices a shadow of something in the air running across the ground next to the train. Looking up, she sees it. It's a drone plane and it appears to be locking on to them. "Prepare for impact!" she shouts. A rocket propels itself down toward the ground bursting just in front of the train diagonal to the track and engine. The train rocks from the blast. "Precision targeting my ass," Emily mutters to herself. "We can't stop or we're sitting ducks," she shouts, "We have to find a way to take that thing down."

Meanwhile, back in the boxcar behind her, Jon and Rachel, curious as to what's going on, take a peek. In fear, the duo quickly closes the door to the car after seeing the drone whiz by. In the second car, Keena and Shigeru opt to help. They and their men start shooting at the drone as it passes, but they are unsuccessful. The third car carrying the soldiers begins firing from the door as well and three of the men start climbing to the roof of the train. Keena and Shigeru's group follow suit and climb aboard their roof. As Shigeru helps one of his men climb up, a second rocket hits just below their car onto the ground, rocking the train once again. The jolt sends the Yakuza hurling toward the ground, killing him on impact. Coming around for another pass, the drone, now out of rockets, aims a suicide mission into the engine of the train. Emily and her men consider this pattern and just before climbing over to Rachel and Jon's boxcar to escape, they detach the engine from the rest of the train causing it to drift slightly behind it.

Moments after crossing the threshold between engine and boxcar, the drone plane collides with the front part of the engine causing a fiery explosion and an impending wreck with the momentum of the boxcars catching up to the crash site. The cars collide just as Emily and her two men drop from the skylight of the train in with Rachel and Jon. Holding on for dear life, Keena, Shigeru and the others take a slightly less, but still rough, blow during the impact.

Exiting the crash, Emily and Jon go out to check on the others. Everyone's a little banged up, but no one's seriously hurt, and with the exception of Shigeru's man, no one is killed.

After regrouping they realize that they are only about 10 miles from city limits and decide to use nightfall as cover to get into the shipyard.

Once night has fallen, the team sneaks into the port and begins looking for a powerful boat to hijack. Jon points at a boat not very far away and suggests. "We should take that one."

After looking and realizing it's an old fishing trawler, Rachel says, "Ummm, maybe not." She points at large high tech luxury yacht. "How bout that one?" she says.

Shigeru concurs, "Alright Rachel! That thing's awesome. You could house three families on that thing, and I bet it's fast too."

Jon says, "What? Don't look at me. I'm an archaeologist, not an expert on maritime exploration."

As the group gets closer to the dock, the moon can be seen reflected on the ocean. A squad of HRTs is patrolling the boardwalk.

"Looks like we just have to get past *them*," one of the mobsters suggests.

As the patrol moves on, the team darts for the edge of the dock. Just before turning the corner, gunfire comes their way. Another squad that they were unaware of has spotted them. Attention is drawn to them and the patrol that passed earlier is now on its way back to assist.

Jon yells, "Run for it!"

And with Keena, Shigeru, and Rachel leading the race, the mobsters and Yakuza follow. Emily and her men start to engage the replicates.

Jon turns and says, "Come on Emily, we have to go now."

With no hesitation, she replies, "No Jon. My men and I are going to stay and make sure you get away."

Ducking down next to her behind her cover of crates and sea equipment, Jon implores, "No, Emily. Please come with us."

Emily, still firing, stops to reload. "I'm sorry, Jon, but my destiny lies on a different path than yours. I swore to defend this country and I'm gonna keep trying."

Jon's mind goes back to what Shigeru said about everyone's soul having a part of destiny, and how some of them just fall into the cracks and do their part in the greater scheme before fading away. He realizes now that Emily and her men fall in those cracks. Standing up and moving backward toward the yacht, Jon says, "Goodbye Major Emily Morgan. Thank you for everything, I'll never forget you."

Emily turns and says, "Goodbye Jon Peters and you're welcome."

When Jon reaches the ship, Shigeru and one of the mobsters are there to remove the gang plank.

"Where's Major Morgan?" Shigeru asks.

Jon answers, "She's not coming Shigeru. She's doing her duty."

Looking back as the ship sets out to sea, they see Emily and the last of her men charge the replicates. Just before going out of sight, they see her swept up into a hail of gunfire, giving the others just enough time to leave the harbor. Just like that, in a blaze of glory, one of the last true American heroes passes on into the night. Thus ends the legacy of Major Emily Morgan.

Chapter 19:

The Island Paradise

Once out to sea, Jon realizes that due to the massive upheaval, the navy is probably no threat to them as of now.

Jon asks Shigeru, "Where should we go from here?"

He answers, "We shouldn't go back to Japan because the Cabal would expect us to. Europe and Australia are most likely to be the next targets once North America is secure. We have no friendly place available in the rest of Asia, and no allies to speak of in Africa. My satellite phone was disabled by the EMP in Chicago, and until I can get some components for it I'm out of contact with my sources. Right now we just have ourselves to depend on."

Rachel states, "Four former members of the mob, three Yakuza, and two scholars."

Shigeru continues, "Wherever we choose, we're going to need to refuel eventually. I say we head to Fiji for now until we can better assess our situation. The inhabitants are very peaceful and they are far from the reach of the Cabal."

Keena agrees, saying, "That sounds like a plan."

So the newly christened seafarers set out to Fiji to refuel and reassess their predicament. Out at sea, the group relaxes in the luxurious accommodations of the very expensive yacht. Down in the mess hall, a non-English speaking Yakuza brings a vanilla cappuccino to

Rachel. He bows to her and she returns the bow saying, "Thank you, Hiei."

The group has now gotten very personal with one another. The mobsters, after all they have been through together, now get along very well with the Yakuza as well as with Jon and Rachel. Enough technical knowledge exists among the crew to navigate the yacht safely against the vagaries of the Pacific Ocean.

Shigeru enters the room, preferring a bottle of champagne over coffee. He states, "At the rate we are going we should be in Fiji after only a few more days. This boat peaks out at just over 50 knots which is very impressive. Whoever built this thing must have been loaded. We have it *all* on board."

Jon interjects, "Yeah, but how long can we live on caviar," he jokes.

One of the mobsters responds, "I couldn't care less, just as long as we're not eating any more of those military rations."

Keena adds, "Yeah, or getting shot at and running."

Jon changes the subject. "Ya know, I've been thinking. Ben T. said that the Cabal was more powerful than even his operation showed. I mean, I know they have massive political and corporate pull, and incredible espionage abilities. Their genetics experiments seem to be quite on par. But what else could they have? Ben T. knew what we were aware of. Why did he have to state the obvious, unless there was something more?"

Shigeru now sitting with the champagne bottle in hand asks, "What are you getting at?"

Jon goes on, "I mean, what if the Cabal is closer to opening up a vortex to the nether world that Chief Crowfeather told us about than we thought?"

Everyone in the room looks around at each other silently.

Jon continues, "How would we even fight something like that? Guns can surely only do so much to forces from another world. Am I right? And obviously the world would never be the same with that kind of presence."

Rachel says, "Well, maybe we can stop them before it gets to that point."

Keena reaches over to take the bottle from Shigeru to take a drink herself. He passes it to her.

"Maybe," she says. "But right now, let's just relax while we can. I mean, there's nothing more that we can do right now out here on the ocean. Things will happen as they must."

Jon nods in agreement and says, "Yeah, let's just enjoy the ride for a while."

A few days at sea pass and then one morning, the islands of Fiji come into view. As the crew gets close to the port they see the locals coming out to greet the approaching yacht. After docking, Jon goes out first to introduce himself and the modernized islanders greet them cheerfully. The group is put up for the night and there is much discussion about what has happened in America.

At a local island gathering, Jon and company are introduced to a couple in their mid-to-late fifties who expatriated themselves from the US over a year ago. They explain to the group that they knew something big was bound to happen and once they were able to retire, they left the country.

The older man says, "Folks called me an old conspiracy theorist for years, and I had no clue about this Cabal you speak of. But there has to be a group like that behind such a massive covert operation. The rest of the world is being told that the HRTs were ordered to be created to subvert a crisis."

Jon responds, "Well, from a certain point of view, that's true, but the crisis was manufactured. It was result of the people not wanting to give up their rights. The Cabal had the HRTs to protect their interests using security of the nation and rebellion as a disguise to cover their real intentions."

"Where are you off to when you leave the island?" the man asks.

Jon says, "We're not sure about our next move. We only know we need to connect with someone who can help us strike at the Cabal directly. Shigeru needs parts for his satellite phone in order to contact his sources."

Shigeru says, "One thing's for sure, we can't stay here. It's nice and all and we're glad some part of the world is safe. But we're going to have to leave soon."

After bidding each other goodnight, the group goes their separate ways for the night. Shigeru meditates in his room before bed. Keena finds a hot spring to relax in. As she relaxes in the water, she begins thinking about Emily Morgan, and then her mind returns to her rocky past. She begins to cry as she realizes how much things have changed. The three mobsters and two yakuza head to the local casino to have a nostalgic night of what their lives use to be like.

Meanwhile, Jon and Rachel go for a relaxing walk along the beach. Stars fill the sky, and the waves, crash lightly against the shore.

Rachel says, "Jon, I realize the importance of finding help to take down the Cabal. But where are we going to go? I mean, it's nice here and we don't have a clue as to where we should start. Don't get me wrong, I'm not saying we should abandon the mission. I meant it when I said I was with you all the way. But it's not wise for us to just take off into the ocean, sailing off into the blue and hoping we find something."

Jon responds, "Rachel, I know. I know we can't do that, but what *can* we do?"

"I don't know," Rachel answers, "Maybe wait here until Shigeru's people come to us."

"But in that case the Cabal could find us too," Jon rebuts. "I'm sure the forces of light are scattered right now, they may not even be looking for Shigeru. They may even assume we're dead. The only ones who *know* we are alive is the Cabal." Jon walks toward the water by himself. "I know I can come up with something," he says, "I'm better than this. I can figure it out."

Rachel walks up behind him and puts her arms around him. "You always do figure it out Jon," she says, "I have faith that this will be no different."

Looking down at the dunes on the beach, the gears of Jon's mind start to turn. He starts thinking back to his knowledge of geography and the political unfolding of history.

"That's it!" he says, "I know where we can go to find help. The Middle East!"

"Huh?" Rachel asks.

"Think about it," Jon says. "Who has had the most tumultuous relationship with the west since the end of World War II? The Middle East! Oil and greed on both sides is all that have kept us at peace with most of those countries. I'm sure we can make some kind of alliance with enemies of the Cabal there."

"Jon, that's a long shot," Rachel says.

Jon shakes his head. "No, trust me. I know you do Rachel. The fear of the west has stopped them from taking any action and many places have been a volatile defensive war zone for them. With the US in chaos and the info we have about the location of the HRT facility, they may be more likely to make a move."

"Okay Jon. Let's tell the others," Rachel says.

After returning to their lodging, Jon explains his plan to Shigeru. Keena, coming back from the hot springs, hears them agree with each other.

Okay, we're leaving tomorrow," Jon states.

Keena asks, "What's going on? Where are we going?"

Jon turns to Keena and says, "Tomorrow, we set sail for the Middle East."

Chapter 20:

Sand Ho!

Following the goodbyes and the gracious refueling provided by the amiable residents of Fiji, the group's yacht leaves the harbor on its course past Indonesia and toward the Arabian Sea.

Several weeks pass in the long, and at times treacherous, journey the team endures. After turning north up and around the Indian peninsula, Rachel comments, "All these years, we've been told how bad the Middle East is, and now it's the safest place in the world for us."

Realizing that the ports of the Persian Gulf will not be very accepting of their unregistered charter, the group is forced to run ashore off the coast of Saudi Arabia. Treading lightly in the shallows, the team takes all that they can carry as supplies on to the beach, abandoning their luxury cruise vessel.

Keena says, "We've been spoiled by that ship. There's no telling how far we have to go before finding someone."

Shigeru says, "If we stay along the coast, we should eventually reach a port city."

Jon replies, "Yes, but that's also where the border patrol is going to be if we are to encounter any. I say we head straight into the mainland. We'll come across something eventually."

"Okay," Shigeru submits.

After a few days, the group finds themselves deep in the notorious desert land that Arabia is.

Hours go by and the sun beats down hard on the adventurers as they walk aimlessly through the Rub- al Khali desert of southern Arabia. Realizing that they are less than a week into the country and they seem to be destined to die at the rate they are going, Shigeru begins to be annoyed.

Sarcastically he states, "Head straight into the mainland, right Jon?"

Jon laments, "I'm sorry, I wasn't thinking."

"Oh that's right. You're an archaeologist, not a maritime explorer, or survivalist, or a soldier are you, Jon? Apparently you're not a navigator either!" Shigeru shouts in sudden anger.

Just then Keena hushes the group. "Wait," she says, "Do you hear that?"

Everyone in company starts looking around and straining their ears. One of Keena's men says, "What? I don't hear anything."

Rachel chimes in saying, "Ssshhhh, I hear it too."

Listening intently, the group all begins hearing a slightly faint whooshing sound.

Jon says, "Sounds like its coming toward us."

Then suddenly the sound stops. Everyone looks at one another. Then, without warning, *Wham!* Shigeru is thrown backward against the dunes as if hit he were hit by a truck.

The others rush to his side. One of the Yakuza speaks to him in Japanese.

He responds in Japanese first, then in English to the others. "I felt something hit me, right in the chest."

Rachel asks, "Are you gonna be ok?"

"Yeah," he says sitting up, "I feel fine. I don't know *what* that was."

Startled but concerned and realizing that they had better keep moving, the group trudges on.

Night falls, and the coolness of the desert feels like a blessing to the team. As stars encompass the sky, Rachel can't help but romanticize the desert in her mind.

Sitting away from the group as to not be further agitated; Shigeru stares out into the sea of dunes.

"He gonna be okay?" Jon asks Keena as she walks toward him and the others away from Shigeru.

"He's fine. He just doesn't want to snap at you again or anything."

Jon states, "Really, it was foolish of me to decide to come this way. It's really not what I had in mind for the group when I thought of all this. I just didn't want us to get arrested and separated from each other. "

Keena comforts Jon by saying, "Don't worry Jon. You can't be right all the time, and besides, I'm sure something good will come of this."

"Yeah Jon, I still trust your judgment," Alfonso says in agreement.

Keena goes on, "Whether we trust each other or not, the fact that we don't have any water past tomorrow morning still remains."

With Keena's words echoing in their minds, the group quietly calls it a night.

Starting out before the heat of the sun fully sets in, the team tries to make as much headway as possible before finishing off their last canteen of water.

Shigeru, on the verge of flying into a rage, lashes out again, "I can't believe I'm in this predicament because of you, and for what? We can't stop the Cabal. They've been around this long; they have to be unstoppable by now."

Jon asks, "Shigeru, why the sudden change of heart? You have been the most adamant from day one about doing what's right and helping us."

"Yeah, that was before I was in a fucking desert Jon," Shigeru shoots back.

Rachel cuts in, "Shigeru, please calm down."

"No!" he shouts, "You're as much to blame. We rescue you and what do you do? You convince him that he's right. Like some messiah to bring us all the way out here to die. I'm the one who has kept this group together *and* kept what's left of us alive."

Jon jumps back in, "Shigeru, I only have your best interests in mind. I've always had your back in this, just like you've had mine."

"Oh yeah," Shigeru asserts, "Just how much have you had my back? Did you have my back like you had Jeff and Bridgette Carls' backs? How about Emily's back? Guess what? They're all dead Jon. And we're gonna be soon too."

Keena cuts in, "Enough Shigeru!" she says.

"No, that's not enough," Shigeru says, turning on Keena now. "The only reason you're even part of this group is because your own people didn't want you. Oh wait, that's because you didn't follow your orders. And you wanna attack me for my loyalties. Who saved you from the Shinobi? Who saved your mother, Rachel? Whose contacts found the tribe?" Looking at Keena, he says, "Who helped you get Don Turoni? I've been shot, lost men, and disrespected. You didn't even pick up a gun until your little girlfriend needed help did you Jon? Yeah, you've got my back. Watch it as I take on this desert by myself, like I should have done with this whole escapade."

"I don't believe this," Rachel says, shaking her head in disbelief.

"Oh believe it," Shigeru snaps, as he shakes off the hand on his shoulder of one of his men trying to comfort him.

Then off in the distance, just over the farthest dune, one of the mobsters notices something.

"Look!" he shouts.

Their attention turns to a string of men on camels and horses. There appear to be about a dozen of them.

Jon shouts and waves his arms, "Over here!"

With the exception of Shigeru, the whole team begins shouting with him.

Having gotten their attention, the group awaits their approach. The men, all armed with automatic weapons, appear very well kept for desert folk. An English speaking member of the desert dwellers drops off his mount and moves toward the team.

"If you give us your weapons for a time, we will be more than happy to take you in to our residence."

Jon says, "I think we're all in agreement on that."

Rolling his eyes, Shigeru takes out his pistol and unloads the chamber, handing it over.

"What brings you to our desert?" the man asks.

Jon replies, "We're refugees from a war raging in the Americas and we shipwrecked here."

"You are welcome to take refuge with us. We are a neighborly folk." the man says.

Water is given to the group and they are all doubled on to mounts and taken in by the apparent desert dwellers.

Chapter 21:

The Great Tent City

On the ride to the presumed homestead of the Arabs, the group is curious as to who their new hosts are.

Jon asks, "Who exactly are you?"

The response from the man amazes Jon and the others.

The man recounts, "We are of an ancient Nomadic tribe. Our people, even though they allied themselves with the British during World War I, did not agree with the formation of a unified Arab kingdom, and wished to remain nomadic. A large piece of land here in the desert was granted to us and we move our great tent city around from time to time to hide our numbers. We were scouting the area for the next move when we found you."

Jon asks, "How is this not known outside of Arabia?"

The man responds, "Although peace exists between us and the kingdom of Arabia and trade exists too, the royal family wishes to keep our existence secret outside of the country so as to not show signs of weakness and lack of unity."

Jon, amazed, asks, "And who is your leader?"

The man responds, "The Sheik. He has kept us very wealthy with his business skills and knowledge of our land. You will find we have many modern conveniences."

After traveling over the next few ridges in the desert, a valley with a rocky crevice around it comes into view. At the center, there is a large concentration of red tents glowing with lights. In the middle of the great tent city is the largest tent Jon or any of the others have ever seen.

As the men approach, Jon's new friend addresses the guards of the large tent in Arabic. The three men allow the outsiders to come in. Entering the giant tent, our heroes are blown away by what they see. A rush of air conditioning slams them upon entry. The room appears like a palace court full of vibrancy and people carrying on in a seemingly happy state. The smell of flavored tobacco hits their senses. Looking around, they observe that the aroma is coming from various hookahs being smoked by what appears to be dignitaries of the nomads. Brightly colored, yet revealing outfits are worn by veiled dancing girls at the center of the room. They are moving to the tune of what sounds to be electronica mixed with local ethnic based music. The ground at their feet is covered by soft, deep rugs.

A man with a long white beard, carrying a wooden staff with a large ruby atop it, approaches. His clothes seem very fine in tune with the rest of their surroundings. In English, he is introduced to the group.

"Ah," the nomad scout says, "Grand Vizier, I found our new friends lost in the desert. They were shipwrecked here in Arabia. They are escaping a crisis in America."

Turning toward Shigeru, his attention goes back to Jon and the others. "Pleased to meet you," he says, "I hope your stay with us is pleasant and I'm sure the Sheik will be glad to meet you."

Still unapologetic to Jon, despite the fact that he was right about the direction they took, Shigeru, now quite pale, moves with the group on in toward the court area. The group is seated on very comfortable pillows toward the center of the room. They are told to wait there until admitted to see the Sheik.

Further down the line, they see a congregation around a large throne with a well groomed man who looks about 40, sitting on it. All around him are dignitaries and beautiful women laughing girlishly at each other's jokes. The Grand Vizier is whispering to the Sheik. The Sheik nods in agreement with whatever he is saying and the Vizier stands back. The scout who helped the group is now called forward and the Sheik makes a simple statement to him. The man then bows and returns to the group sitting on the pillows.

He says to Jon and the others, "The Sheik will see you, but he requests only one of you for the moment."

The group, of course, elects Jon, with no vocal vote from Shigeru. Jon is taken up to the Sheik and the Vizier.

He bows and says, "Your highness, I am most grateful for your people's hospitality to my party."

The Sheik nods, "And we are more than happy to continue to accommodate you on one condition."

"Anything, sire," Jon replies.

The Sheik continues, "It has been brought to my attention that a member of your entourage is..." looking over to the Vizier then back to Jon, he finishes, "...possessed."

"What?!" Jon exclaims.

The Vizier interjects, "Yes, the Asian man with the attitude. I sensed the demon upon your arrival. That's why I went to the entrance to greet you myself."

"How can this be?" Jon asks.

The Vizier explains, "They attach themselves when they happen across people who are vulnerable to things such as depression or self-worth issues. If caught in a moment of weakness, something as petty as sarcastic anger can be latched on to. From pent up rage and deep-seated issues, it can thrive and grow."

Jon recalls the impact from thin air Shigeru had in the desert the day before. He explains this to the Arabs and says, "He was a bit hysterical at the time, and not without reason. We thought we were going to die."

"We would like to exorcise him with your permission." the Vizier says.

"You need my permission?" Jon asks.

"Yes, or his," The Vizier explains, "A family member or close friend will suffice. You are a good friend of his, are you not?"

Jon answers, "Well yeah. At least I was, and I'd like to be again. But don't you think we need to assess him a little more to make sure we are doing the right thing."

Looking over Jon's shoulder, the Sheik states, "I believe he is displaying the necessary signs."

Turning around, Jon sees Shigeru away from the rest of the group knocking end tables over and shouting, "Where's my gun?! I'm sick of waiting here!"

Running behind a huge tapestry hanging from the tent wall, Shigeru searches for an exit. The group begins to stand up in pursuit of him. The dancing girls scream and run for cover as Shigeru shows signs of absolute hostility and near feral behavior.

Now joining the pursuit are several Arab guards. Raising his AK-47, a veiled Arab prepares to shoot Shigeru, but is stopped by an order from the Sheik. Closing in on him, Jon and the others see a yellow tint in Shigeru's eyes.

Tackled by two of the mobsters and one of his fellow Yakuza, Shigeru shouts, "No! I hate all of you! Let me go!"

Jon says, "Shigeru, you need help."

"No I don't Jon. You don't know what's best for me. I hate *you* most of all," Shigeru reiterates, his eyes now bright yellow.

Several Arabs manage to secure him and take him away with much resistance on his part.

After about an hour or so, the Vizier approaches the group standing outside in the shade of a tent covered in symbols that appear to be an older form of Arabic calligraphy.

The Vizier says, "If he has the will to participate midway through, we can save him."

Jon asks, "Can you explain how you know exorcism?"

"Yes," the Vizier states, "My priests and I are the descendants of an ancient Zoroastrian priesthood. We were some of the first to learn the banishment of Genies and Jinn's. Those markings on the walls of the tent are containment spells to prevent the spirit from leaving once out of your friend's body. The ceremony will involve chants from my priests, spoken in a long forgotten language and a series of motions from me represent the exit from his body of the spirit. Assistance from one of you to coach him would be a great help in the process. It will aid his will to be released from it."

Jon says, "I'll do what I can."

Keena interjects, "No, let me do it. I care about Shigeru, and I owe him the same favor I fulfilled by helping you. He helped me get away from the mob just as much as you did."

Rachel agrees, "Yeah, and at this point Jon's presence may only aggravate the situation."

Jon nods and says, "Okay."

Entering the tent with the Vizier, Keena instantly smells incense. Six priests draped in elegant silk robes surround the cushioned table Shigeru is strapped to with his head propped slightly up facing the entrance. Without wasting time, the Vizier begins the ritual. The chants start off.

Keena crouches next to Shigeru and places her hand on his head. With her other hand she begins dipping a cloth into a pot of water next to them and starts stroking his forehead with the dampness of the cloth.

Shigeru, eyes now a mix of red and yellow says, "What do you want? Just leave me be."

Keena asks, "Is this the demon or is it Shigeru?'

Shigeru replies, "I don't even know myself at this point."

"Well, we need to fix that," Keena declares.

"Why do you wanna help me?" Shigeru asks.

Keena pauses, and then answers, "Because you're my friend. You're a friend to all of us. And I know you are better than this. Your loyalty is to a great cause. Probably one of the most loyal Yakuza that ever lived. You have never given up on those that you are trying to help. Including me, which you didn't have to do. You helped complete strangers in the Midwest, not because you felt you had to, but because it was the right thing to do. It was you, just as much as Jon that helped me realize I was on the wrong side of the fence. Where's all that loyalty now? Don't tell me some stupid demon can just erase it all. I *know* you are not that weak. Start fighting, and get back to your old self. We have a mission to carry out. Make your clan proud."

Shigeru, with his face now softer and his eyes lightened up says, "You're right. I am ready to go on. I want freedom from all of this. Once and for all."

Outside the tent, the others begin hearing Shigeru screaming out in force trying to rid the demonic presence from his body and away from his mortal soul.

A few minutes later, he feels a great pressure release from his chest and his breathing returns to normal. A silhouette rushes out of his body and into the air. Not being able to escape the confines of the protected tent, the spirit bounces around rapidly. The Vizier turns his staff and points its ruby up toward the corner of the room. The ruby begins glowing bright red and lighting charges around the ceiling. Suddenly, a spiral in the very fabric of reality opens up and consumes the silhouette of the spirit, now exposed by the light. The spiral and all the ruckus surrounding it suddenly snaps out of existence and things return to normal.

Untying Shigeru, together, the Vizier and Keena welcome him back to his old self as he thanks them. Exiting the tent, the rest of the group greets Shigeru asking how he feels.

He says, "Well a little dehydrated from sweating, but I'll be okay. I owe you all an apology for the things I said, especially you Jon. I won't doubt your intuition again. I swear it."

Jon shakes his hand and the two share a brotherly hug.

Jon says, "It is okay man, just glad to have you back on the team."

Rachel comes up and hugs Shigeru herself. "Welcome back!" she exclaims.

Shigeru starts shaking hands with the mobsters and his fellow Yakuza, then wraps his arm over Keena's shoulders and says, "I owe her a lot guys. She reminded me of where my true loyalties lie."

The team is invited by a short attractive Arab woman to return to the main tent to enjoy some festivities once more before getting their next audience with the Sheik. The group follows her cheerfully.

Chapter 22:

Shigeru's Past

Now back in the main tent, sitting off to the side from the rest of the group in the enjoyable atmosphere of the festive tent, Keena continues her conversation with Shigeru.

Away from the pressure of the demonic deliverance that occurred minutes earlier, Shigeru says, "I realize that a lot of the stress I've been feeling isn't even from the battles we've been in, or lack of feeling appreciated. It stems from my insecurities."

"And what are those?" Keena asks, "If you don't mind telling me?"

Shigeru, hesitant, says, "I'm afraid to talk about it because I avoid it. And I know you have a past that rivals mine."

"Come on now, we're both cold blooded 'gangstafied' killers," Keena assures him.

"It's not that Keena. It's about my family," Shigeru explains. "I know you don't really remember your family and I don't want to bitch since your story is harsher."

"Don't feel that way. That's the kind of thinking that led you to pen it up in the first place. You can tell me," Keena says encouragingly.

Shigeru says, "My mother was the daughter of a big time Yakuza boss, so I inherited the knowledge I have. My father was a Yakuza too. His romance with my mother led to an alliance between two clans. When I was very young, eight I think, he walked out on us. We never got a reason. I started thugging at age 12 for lower members of the clan. But by the time I was 14, my mother taught me not to use our power like that. She gave me this gold plated custom pistol I always carry. It was the one thing my father left. So by the time I was 18 years old I had become a central piece to the more respectful circles of our organization. It was then that I transferred to Chicago the first time as a connection to the mainland organization. While I was away, our headquarters was hit by a rival clan and my mother was killed in the crossfire. I feel like I should have been there to help instead of being overseas conducting mere business. I also feel like my father could have protected her if he hadn't walked out on us."

"I'm sorry to hear this," Keena consoles him, "I understand how hard it is. We can sympathize with each other's situations."

"Yeah," he carries on, "I do feel better for expressing it. But one thing still bothers me."

"What's that?" Keena inquires.

Shigeru says, "You saved my life several times, Keena. Back at Ben T.'s lab, and various other times fighting the replicates. I've never been able to save your life. I just turned on you when that demon got me."

"That's not true Shigeru," Keena rebukes him, "You've done a lot for me. You didn't send your men to retaliate after that first encounter in Chicago. You took me in and tended to mine and my men's wounds. You helped me take down Don Turoni. You saved us all from that explosion in the HRT truck. Look, you and I have to stick together. We both know what it's like to lead people and be tough. But, until we met each other, we've had no one else to rely on. You talk all this destiny stuff but you don't factor yourself into that. We were supposed to team up. Rachel has Jon, but who do I have?"

Shigeru then looks up at Keena in a way he hasn't looked at her before.

Sitting across the room, Rachel observes the conversation between Shigeru and Keena. "I think it's wonderful that they are connecting so well," Rachel says smiling.

Jon replies, "Yeah, pretty nice how things turned out for them considering when we first met her, they almost killed one another."

Rachel changes the subject, "So what happens next?"

Jon answers, "We wait to speak with the Sheik and find out if there's any way we can form some kind of alliance against the Cabal. Maybe Shigeru can get the parts he needs to get his satellite phone working again. Then he can contact his sources again. For now, we relax and enjoy the atmosphere."

Not long after the team gets a chance to relax, they are graced once more by the Sheik. Sitting on his throne in front of the group of foreigners, he asks them, "What brings you to our region of the world of all places, in escaping the crisis in the west?"

Jon explains their situation and Shigeru's connection to the forces of light.

The Sheik says, "I am familiar with both the Cabal and the forces of light."

Jon goes on to explain how he got the intuition to come to the Middle East. He then asks if there is any way their tribe could help the group's effort.

The Sheik responds, "Although we are not allied with the unified forces of light, we are definitely no friend of the Cabal either. We will help you in any way we can. There is an ally of ours in Russia who has been an enemy of the Cabal since its inception. Relax at our encampment for a few days while I make contact with them. I'm sure I can make arrangements for you to meet."

Shigeru says, "That's wonderful! By any chance could I get some components to fix my satellite phone? I need it to contact my sources."

The Sheik answers, "I am sorry, but we do not have anything on hand that would suit you. I would gladly send for the items if you were staying longer."

Shigeru replies, "Don't bother. We won't be here long enough to wait for them. But thank you for the offer."

After concluding their meeting with the Sheik, the group is shown to their quarters in a handful of guest tents.

The next morning, Shigeru and Jon are called up by the Sheik. The duo is introduced to an Arab man about Shigeru's age, who is dressed in modern clothes.

"This is Sahib Al-Nashmi," the Sheik says, "He is the most educated man in our tribe. He has traveled the world and studied history and the occult, as well as the workings of the Cabal while attending several prominent universities in Europe. Also, he has relations with our Russian friends. I'm assigning him to take you to meet them when you are ready. But the only condition is; only part of your party may take the trip. The Russians won't want a large group of outsiders coming in."

Jon responds, "We'll make some sort of arrangement. Thank you for your assistance, your highness. We'll ready ourselves to leave as soon as possible."

Later on, after talking with Rachel and Keena about the new plan, Keena and Shigeru approach their men. The three surviving mobsters and two yakuza are playing a game taught to them by the Arabs at one end of the main tent.

Alfonso asks, "What's goin on guys?"

Shigeru answers, "Keena and I have been talking and we've decided that the time has come to relieve you men of your service to us."

The men start to protest. "No, come on," Alfonso replies, "We're dedicated."

"Yeah, and we've been through so much with you," One of the other mobsters adds.

Keena responds, "Guys, it's okay. It's not that we don't want you around. You have been very loyal. But only Shigeru and I are able to do this next mission. We just felt that you've done so much, and this is far away now from being your fight anymore. So we figured it's time we relieve you."

The men all start to reluctantly agree.

Shigeru adds, "The Sheik says that you guys are welcome to stay here until things start smoothing out on the world scene, then he will charter you back to Japan and the US so you can return to your families."

The men brighten up a little knowing that they will be taken care of by their new Arab friends. They thank Shigeru and Keena for being great leaders to them and wish them luck on their unknown journeys ahead.

Walking away from the group of former gangsters, Keena says, "There it is. We just have each other to be responsible for now.

Smiling, Shigeru says, "We still have to take care of Jon and Rachel though."

Keena laughs as the two exit the tent and return to their quarters.

Chapter 23:

Ah...Nostalgia!

The next day, on the outskirts of the tent city, Sahib and another Arab prepare a Humvee to begin the journey. The group says their goodbyes to their now former comrades. Handshakes are exchanged and Rachel hugs all the ex-gangsters. Jon personally thanks the Sheik once more, and Shigeru thanks the Vizier for helping him get rid of the demon that plagued him a few days earlier.

After the team loads up in the Humvee, they begin driving into the desert toward a large rock formation off in the distance.

Jon asks, "Where are we headed to, to leave the country from?"

With the other Arab driving, Sahib answers from the passenger seat, "On the other side of that small mountain is a hangar that was abandoned by the Allies after World War II. Since it was permitted by the Sheik at the time to be built on our tribe's land, we've maintained it from time to time in case of an emergency. We'll use one of the larger planes to transfer us to Russia."

Shigeru asks, "Are you sure it will be able to fly us?"

Sahib responds, "The planes are in mint condition. No different than they were at the height of the war."

After arriving at the far end of the rock formation, the driver takes the group into a small tunnel with the entrance to the hangar about 50 yards in. Once parked, the group gets out and moves to open the old doors.

Inside the hangar, the group sees an assortment of about 15 planes, mostly fighter planes, some equipped with water landing gear, and three large bombers. The room appears to be in nearly pristine condition, fitting the era from whence it came. Only a few traces of objects from the modern era are seen in the mostly retro atmosphere of the large room, mostly lighting and maintenance equipment.

At the far end of the hangar, the large bay doors can be seen.

Keena asks, "Which one do we take?"

Sahib replies, "Let's take a closer look and decide which seems most fitting."

Walking across the room, Rachel with her arms crossed across her chest looks around in awe at the nostalgia she is in the midst of. All of a sudden, the group hears a noise, like a metal object being dropped on the ground behind some crates near one of the bombers. The whole group stops at once and turns their attention to where the noise came from.

Out from behind the crates, something unlike anything the team has ever seen before comes strolling out into the open. A short olive colored creature with pointy ears and sharp teeth trots along slowly and stops on noticing the team standing there. It has scrawny lanky arms with talon-like claws protruding from its fingers. Standing just over two feet tall, the creature doesn't even come up to the waist line of its human parallels standing about 35 feet away, absolutely stunned by what they are witnessing.

Jon exclaims, "What in the hell?!"

The creature appearing to be just as shocked at running into the group, as they are of him, gives out a snarly, "Uh Oh!"

Without another word being said, Shigeru draws his pistol and fires at the monster before it gets a chance to run away. It runs back only a few feet before taking three shots from Shigeru's gun. The midget sized creature is blown back against a set of adjacently stacked barrels behind it.

After confirming that the monster has been killed, the team rushes over to assess it more closely.

Rachel asks, "What in the blue blazes is that thing?"

Sahib says, "It's an Imp demon or Gremlin if you will."

Jon asks, "You mean Gremlins, as from World War II pilot folklore?"

Sahib goes on to explain, "Yes. The Third Reich opened up a portal just large enough to let several of them through to our world. With their size and technical precision, they were used to sabotage allied aircraft."

The other Arab reaches into his coat and pulls out a small MAC-10 submachine gun.

Sahib adds, "Let's have a look around. There may be more of them."

Keena draws her pistol as well. Just then another Gremlin comes out from behind one of the small planes about 10 feet away from Keena and Shigeru. The two fire their pistols seamlessly, eliminating the creature before it becomes a threat to the group.

In an effort to secure the hangar, the group pans out away from each other slightly to better cover the hangar in search of the Gremlins. Rachel moves behind Jon, who has just picked up a three foot steel rod. Placing one hand on his shoulder, she picks up a large crescent wrench from a toolbox.

She asks, "How did they find us here?"

Sahib, walking near the Arab with the submachine gun in hand responds, "The demon that possessed Shigeru must have been scouting for the Cabal. Knowing that he was located in the area, the Cabal must have sent them to disable any aircraft in the area so you couldn't escape."

Walking slowly, Rachel follows Jon under the belly of the next nearest bomber. Suddenly, a third Gremlin drops from an access panel beneath the plane and reaches out to her. Rachel swings back and strikes out at the creature with the large wrench, knocking it out of sight behind a stack of oil cans and tool boxes. A moment passes and the little monster makes a run for the crates stacked against the wall of the hangar. As the creature moves, the other Arab fires his submachine gun at it but misses before it disappears behind the wall of crates. The team closes in on the crates to try and surround the creature. Another creature pops out from a crate next to Jon and he swings at it wildly with the metal rod. Hitting the creature twice, Jon rears back as it attempts swiping at him with its gruesome claws. After reloading, Sahib's comrade fires off a burst from the machine gun, annihilating the little demon. Just then, the creature that ran over to the crates pops back up and lunges toward Shigeru. Simultaneously, a fifth Gremlin jumps out from the belly of one of the water landing fighter planes. Shigeru fires at the monster near him as Keena and the Arab blast away at the new Gremlin.

Having disposed of all the apparent threats, the team quickly surveys the rest of the hangar, discovering no more Gremlins than the five they already encountered. Upon further investigation, they find that only one of the three bombers has yet to have been tampered with by the Gremlins.

Shigeru and Keena go over to open the hangar bay doors while Sahib and the other Arab prep for flight. Jon and Rachel at the back of the plane get comfortable in hopes that the plane will function properly after minimal use in the past seven decades.

After Keena and Shigeru open the hangar bay doors, they rush back quickly to the plane. Once everyone is aboard, Sahib in the copilot seat looks back and asks, "Is everyone ready?"

The whole group nods.

The other Arab, now sitting in the pilot's seat, turns the ignition of the plane. Running like it did in its prime, the bomber's engine purrs like a kitten. The pilot pulls the plane into flight position and taxis toward the exit of the hangar. Making its way down the tarmac, the old-time bomber trundles along toward liftoff.

Once in the air, Rachel gives a sigh of relief.

Jon says, "Well, we've made it this far."

Sahib turns and says, "We'll be flying for a while. It's best that you all make yourselves comfortable."

While the pilot and Sahib concentrate on manning the archaic aircraft, the others head back to the rear of the plane. Slightly cramped, but roomy enough for the band of four, the back of the plane has several benches and a navigator's chair. Keena walks up and takes a seat at the navigation chair while Jon and Rachel grab a seat on the bench across from her. Shigeru walks toward the back of the plan resting his hands on a metal bar extending across the plane above his head.

Rachel asks, "When we meet these Russians, what are we even going to tell them?"

Shigeru answers, "Well, we already know that they're not friendly with the Cabal, so not much need for pleasantries. I suppose we'll just inquire about their knowledge of the Cabal."

Jon adds, "And then we can find out what they can bring to the table in terms of taking action against them. Hopefully, the info we have about the HRTs will help them."

Keena, sitting with her hands cupped together between her knees jumps up. "Did you hear that?" she asks.

The others, looking confused, say they didn't hear anything.

Keena says, "Wait, listen."

Just then the group hears a slight clanking underneath the floorboards. Shigeru steps forward and reaches down to lift up a floor panel in the center of the plane. As he lifts it, he sees another gremlin dart off down the shaft underneath the walkway. "Shit!" Shigeru says. "It must have been hiding down in the cargo hold."

Jon hops up. "We have to stop it before it chews on the wiring or something," he says.

When Shigeru gets to the next panel, he moves to open it with gun in hand.

Rachel shouts, "Wait!"

Shigeru turns around.

Rachel goes on, "Isn't it dangerous to fire a gun in a plane?"

Jon responds, "Only in a pressurized cabin at high altitude. This plane won't have that issue."

Shigeru turns back down toward the panel. When he opens it, the Gremlin jumps out past him and grabs the cabinet door on the right wall of the plane. Before he can turn around, the Gremlin makes his way into the cabinet and continues through the cavern of the wall toward the front of the plane. The group moves toward the cockpit.

Jon and Rachel rush in to warn Sahib and the pilot. Meanwhile, Shigeru and Keena start opening cabinets and wall panels frantically searching for the creature. Keena, standing near the center of the plane opens a door, only to have the Gremlin pounce on her, knocking her pistol out of her hand. She lets out a slight shriek.

Sahib, hearing her shout, turns around saying, "What's going on?!"

Shigeru who is just outside the cockpit door, turns as well. He sees the little monster swing around Keena's neck, landing on her back. She reaches up behind her to grab it, but the creature is fighting and swiping at her so rapidly she can't shake it. The claws dig into her neck and the tops of her shoulders as well as forearms as she reaches toward it. Shigeru, hesitating, aims his gun. Afraid to fire for fear of hitting Keena, he waits for an opportune chance. The Gremlin then reaches down and bites her on the neck. Keena's screams now turn even more bloodcurdling as she fights harder to get the Gremlin off of her. Finally, Shigeru, unable to watch the creature mutilate Keena anymore, takes the first good shot he gets. The bullet whizzes right by Keena's head, straight into the face of the Gremlin, throwing it off of her and back down on to the floor of the plane. Shigeru and Jon rush to Keena's side to assess her wounds.

"Are you alight?" Shigeru asks.

"I've fared better, but I'm okay," Keena responds.

Rachel takes Keena back to the rear of the plane to get a first aid kit and dress her wounds. Shigeru picks up the body of the Gremlin to dispose of it via the bomb doors. Afterwards, he joins Jon in the cockpit where he is explaining to the others that everything is under control.

Sahib says, "Well this hasn't exactly been a steady flight, but hopefully things will be smooth once we land in Russia."

Jon asks, "Who exactly are these Russians we're going to see anyway?"

Sahib replies, "Some of them are followers of idealists that have been in hiding since Vladimir Lenin passed away and Stalin took over. Others are experimental scientists that didn't want their technology being used by the Cabal or the USSR. They are protected and housed by a remnant of the KGB that went rogue after it was officially disbanded. The location we are going to is just outside of Chernobyl. They chose it because no one would dare look for them there."

"Except us, right?" Shigeru adds, "Anyway, I'm gonna go back and check on Keena."

Walking into the back room of the plane he finds Rachel finishing up the bandages on Keena's wounds.

"There, that about does it," Rachel says as she finishes securing Keena's bandages.

Leaning in for a hug, Keena tells Rachel, "Thanks girl."

Rachel, looking over at Shigeru standing in the doorway against the wall with his arms crossed says, "Okay, I'm gonna head up to the cabin and talk to Jon."

On her way out, she pats Shigeru on the shoulder.

Shigeru then moves over to Keena and sits where Rachel was a moment ago. He says, "Hey, how ya doin?"

Keena, looking down at her arm and then back up at Shigeru responds, "I'm okay. Still a tad shook up, but I'm fine."

There's a quick moment of silence, then she continues, "That was a good shot you pulled off."

Shigeru, nodding, chuckles and says, "Yeah, I suppose it was, wasn't it."

Keena goes on, "You know, you finally did it."

"Hmmm?" Shigeru asks.

Keena says, "You saved my life. You were worried about me saving you so many times, and now you've returned the favor."

Shigeru leans back, puts his hands up, and says, "What can I say? It was nothing."

Keena stands up, moves toward Shigeru, and sits across his lap. Wrapping one arm around his shoulders, she says, "Yes...it was."

Placing her right hand on his cheek, she leans in and passionately kisses him.

Chapter 24:

The KGB Remnant

A few more hours pass as the group continues their flight plan deep into Eurasia. Now relaxing once again, all four of our heroes are back in the center of the plane awaiting some news from the cockpit of their current location. Finally, the PA comes on. It's Sahib. He says, "This is captain Sahib Al-Nashmi. We're coming up on Chernobyl soon. I know this has been a rather turbulent flight, but I want to assure you, there are no more Gremlins on the plane. Al-Nashmi airlines, wants to thank you for your patience on this flight and hopes you enjoy the rest of your journey crushing the Cabal." The group all look at one another with joy and laughs.

After a while longer, the plane begins its descent down into the ruined lands outside of Chernobyl.

"Crazy to think how much in shambles this place still is after all this time," Rachel comments.

Jon adds, "Well this *was* the site of a nuclear meltdown after all. You can't just clean it up overnight."

Looking through the windshield of the plain, Sahib points out a spot for the pilot to land. The plane touches down in a small field just slightly out of sight of the wreckage and blown out buildings left over from the incident that took place several decades ago.

After coming to a stop, the pilot cuts the engine and Shigeru lowers the boarding steps. The crew gets out and looks around.

"It's almost too quiet," Rachel says.

The group looks around in the grassy field while waiting for Sahib to come down the stairwell. When he steps out, Jon asks, "Where to now?"

Sahib replies, "Hang on. They'll come to us."

A moment later, the group hears two vehicles heading in their direction. As they turn toward the sound, they see a canopied black military truck and a black SUV heading their way. After coming to a stop, the passenger of the SUV gets out. It's a gray haired Russian man wearing a black trench coat buckled in the front. The man smiles and says, "Good to see you again Sahib," in a very solid Russian accent.

Sahib shakes his hand and says, "Likewise Olaf." Turning to the others, he continues, "This is Olaf Kinski, former KGB agent and leader to the remnant section stationed here."

Introductions are made all around to the various members of the group.

Jon says, "We appreciate getting an audience from you. I hope we can make some sort of arrangement that can benefit our mutual cause."

"I'm certain of this," Olaf states, "Come; let us take shelter at our command center."

The group moves to get into the truck, leaving only Jon and Sahib to ride in the SUV with Olaf and his driver.

Jon asks, "What's the situation in North America currently?

Olaf responds, "The people and the resistant military have held off a successful occupation of the country but are facing a nearly unlimited supply of reinforcements from those replicates. If they are not stopped soon, then the country will be completely broken and the Cabal will move their forces into Europe and other nations around the world."

After a short drive, the convoy reaches another clearing and comes to a stop.

Jon then asks, "What's up? Are we getting out?"

Olaf replies, "KGB, former or not, still have their secrets.' He laughs for a moment, and then a square piece of the clearing moves back like a garage door opening sideways, with an incline leading down into ground. After the door opens, the vehicles begin driving down into the cavern. About 200 yards down, a vertical door opens as the entrance behind them closes, sealing off the sunlight. Entering the lower door, they find an underground base with steel walls and beams holding up the ceiling.

Looking around, Rachel says to Keena, "Finally we're in an underground base that *doesn't* belong to the enemy."

Coming to a stop, Jon sees about a dozen other trucks sitting in line in what appears to be a large garage. Russian workers are moving about, working on things, rolling tires across the ground, manning welders. Everyone seems to be hard at work. The group then gets out of their vehicles and follows Olaf through a door into a hall.

"I want to show you the main purpose of this facility, and my chief of operations here," Olaf says, as the group moves down the hall.

Coming to the doorway at the end of the hall, the next room is a large room with giant monitors high up on the wall displaying different map locations around the world. Men with digital clipboards are tending to them. In the center of the room are about twenty jet black variants of what appear to be drone planes. Olaf shouts something in Russian and a woman in a lab coat turns around and approaches the group. Jon is struck instantly. He notices the features of the woman. Of midsize build, the woman wearing a white lab coat and glasses has strawberry blonde hair, and is without doubt the woman Jon saw in his final vision when he drank Chief Crowfeather's memory water. Jon smiles as he realizes this is certainly a sign that they are still on the right track.

Once the woman reaches them, Olaf introduces her. "This is Dr. Katja Petrov. Doctor, these are our new friends I told you about, sent by our Arab comrades."

The timid looking doctor acknowledges the group with her eyes barely looking up from the ground in front of her.

"Katja is the daughter of the former Dr. Petrov who was the genius aeronautics engineer who served the beloved USSR," Olaf continues. "Unfortunately, Dr. Petrov passed away nearly two years ago. Katja has been filling her father's shoes and carrying his incredible work forward."

"And what work is that?" Jon asks.

Olaf turns and waves toward the planes the group noticed earlier. "Why the Berserker drones of course. While the Cabal used their secret facilities throughout the cold war for genetics research to develop those human replicates, our scientists focused on the most advanced computer-guided attack planes ever constructed."

Shigeru interrupts, "But other nations have drone planes too, especially the US."

Olaf continues, "The US of course has their predator drones as well, but they are insignificant compared to our Berserker drones. The Berserkers are impervious to being spotted on radar, can bypass any laser defense system, are equipped with precision targeting within five feet of the target, and have a nearly impenetrable shell casing and an advanced bunker busting weapon capable of erasing any underground structure from existence. We have just recently perfected them and are ready to strike as soon as we have a good target. That is why our interest was sparked when the Sheik told us you may have knowledge that could help us strike against the Cabal."

"Yes," Jon says. "Rachel and I have been to the HRT production facility ourselves and can point you straight to its coordinates."

"Brilliant!" exclaims Olaf. "This will stop the replicates dead in their tracks and allow your American comrades to succeed in flushing them and their controllers out."

"How are you going to carry out an attack?" Jon asks.

Olaf answers, "We'll have you plot the coordinates on our computers. Then we'll deploy our drones. The armament on the drones is more than powerful enough to destroy the facility."

"Great," Jon says enthusiastically. "I'll help right away."

"Good!" Olaf replies. "Katja, take them to the navigational computer and get those coordinates."

"Yes, Commander Kinski," Katja responds.

Katja takes Shigeru, Rachel, and Jon to the navigation computer and begins taking the information on the HRT facility from them. Keena and Sahib sit with the pilot and wait for the others to come back.

"Thank you for all of your help Sahib," Keena says. "We wouldn't know what to do without you."

"Don't mention it," Sahib replies. "I'm definitely no fan of the Cabal. I've studied their constituents for years, hoping to find a way to stop them."

Keena notes, "Yeah, unfortunately, I have a background *being* one of those constituents. But I believe I've finally redeemed myself."

Sahib says, "Yes, you certainly have. How are those wounds by the way?"

"Better," Keena answers.

After Jon and the others finish helping Dr. Petrov hone in the coordinates, he asks, "When do you strike?"

Olaf responds, "Tomorrow. That will be sufficient time to prep the drones and make sure everything is ready. I invite you to be my guests here to observe the attack. It will be the beginning of the end for the Cabal. Until then, I shall provide quarters here on base for you and your crew.

Inside Jon and Rachel's quarters, she asks, "Jon, how do you feel about all of this?"

Jon replies, "What do you mean?"

Rachel says, "I mean, being here, helping the KGB and all."

Jon says, "Rachel, we've heard horrible things about Arabs and Yakuza and they haven't turned out bad have they? And Keena isn't exactly too bad for a mobster. Besides Rach, I saw Katja in my vision after drinking the memory water. Apparently we're on the right track."

Rachel says, "You know I trust your judgment Jon. We've been over this. It's just that my intuition this time tells me something is amiss."

Jon, putting his arm around Rachel, comforts her saying, "It's okay. A lot has been confusing lately. I'll keep what you said in mind and we'll be fine."

Rachel nods. Then the two head off to bed.

The next day, the crew meets up down at the command center and finds the Berserker drones receiving their final preparations before launch. Olaf enters and shouts, "Good morning comrades! Today is the day of victory. Without their replication facility the Cabal will no longer be able to reinforce their troops. Dr. Petrov, prepare for launch."

Katja moves over to the main computer and opens a set of bay doors above where the drones are sitting. After she turns a few knobs, the 20 drone planes ignite and lift straight up slowly out of the bowels of the KGB remnant's secret base. Once about 50 feet off the ground, they jet off in unison forward.

"There they go," Shigeru says. "Off to destroy the HRT facility."

Keena adds, "Good riddance."

Rachel shakes her head and says, "I sure hope this works."

The group turns their attention to the large monitors. Some display maps, others display point of view footage of the drones en route to their target.

Olaf declares, "It is only a matter of time now. Katja, give us an approximate arrival time."

She responds, "Fifteen minutes and counting."

Jon exclaims, "Fifteen minutes!"

Olaf laughs, "I told you, state of the art aeronautics Mr. Peters."

The group waits and watches the monitors in near silence.

Finally, Katja says, "Three more minutes."

Shigeru asserts, "Here it goes."

Keena shakes her head, and says, "I'm more nervous now than I was going in to that lab in Wyoming."

The POV cameras on the drones begin showing the desert in New Mexico.

"One minute until rocket strike commander," Katja says.

"Good, they've slipped past all the laser defenses," Olaf notes.

"Bunker buster rockets firing in 5,4,3,2,1..." counts Katja.

A moment passes. Blips begin appearing on the monitors. One of the Russians stands up and shouts in his native tongue. Cheers go up all through the command center.

Shigeru sarcastically asks, "I take it that the attack worked?"

Olaf, happy as a lark, shouts, "Yes, our readouts show the facility has been obliterated!"

The whole group sighs in relief, realizing that the vast majority of what once threatened them has now been destroyed. With all the Russian partying around the room, Katja makes the order to return the drones to the base.

Olaf says to Jon, "You and your crew may stay here as long as necessary until things wind down in the Americas. I suspect the rebels will take care of the remaining threat in no time."

Jon, heady with joy, laughs and says, "I have to ask. At the height of the Cold War, why didn't the Soviet Union ever strike the West?"

Olaf replies, "Because, after intercontinental ballistic missiles were developed, the laser defense grid was put into place, effectively nulling out the technology. If any nuclear strikes were to happen, it would be because the Cabal allowed it." Chuckling, Olaf goes on, "Believe me; we would have attacked if we could."

As Olaf walks away, Jon is slightly disturbed by that last remark.

The next day, after a night of celebration, Olaf invites the group to stay and observe as the Russians plan their next strike against the Cabal. The group agrees.

After separating, Shigeru approaches Katja and asks, "I almost forgot, doctor, might you have parts for me to rebuild my broken satellite phone? I need it to contact my sources. Together we can end the Cabal for good."

Hesitating and reacting quite strangely, Katja frantically replies, "Ummm, well, may I see it?"

Shigeru withdraws the broken phone from his pocket and says, "I'm not too good with tech but if I had the parts maybe Keena could fix it."

Looking around the room, Katja reaches out and takes the phone, shoving it into the pocket of her lab coat.

"Let me fix it," she says. "It wouldn't be a good idea to let Olaf know you have this. He wouldn't be too happy with you having a satellite phone here in the base, for, uh, security purposes."

Shigeru, though thinking her behavior is a bit strange, lets her take it.

Several days pass until finally news hits that the last of the HRTs in America have been put down.

"When the base was destroyed, it must have knocked out the main signaling computer," Keena suggests. "If the remaining replicates couldn't receive commands then they would just begin moving aimlessly."

Olaf says, "Yes, and the United Nations will be meeting at the UN Building in New York for a summit. They are supposedly going to be investigating who was behind the deception. Ha!" Olaf scoffs. "As if they are not the ones. Mother Russia was foolish to have submitted our empire to the Cabal and joined the UN. They are probably just meeting to plan a counter attack against us. They have effectively decided our new target. The UN building."

Chapter 25:

HRTs Destroyed...Victory?

After their meeting with Olaf and the other Russians, the group meets in the hall outside their quarters and begins to talk.

Rachel asks, "Now that we've been successful in defeating the HRTs, what do you think is next?"

Keena answers, "Well, I guess the KGB are gonna go through with their strike and try to effectively dismantle the Cabal for good."

Jon says, "Hmmm, I'm not so sure about that."

"Huh?" Shigeru asks.

Jon explains, "Well, Rachel brought it to my attention the other day that something seemed amiss. Although I believe it was a solid move destroying the HRTs, I'm starting to concur with her feelings on that. Look guys, let's just watch out. It's not that I don't trust the Russians. It's just, things haven't been what we thought before."

The group agrees and Rachel, walking with Jon down the hall says, "I'm glad you're starting to be aware of what I felt." With her arm around his shoulder she rests her head against his arm.

Later, Katja arrives at Keena and Shigeru's room. When she knocks, Keena answers.

"I've finished repairing Shigeru's satellite phone," Katja says.

Shigeru, sitting on the bed, stands up enthusiastically to receive it and says, "Thank you!"

Katja reiterates, "Remember; don't let Commander Kinski know you have that. Tomorrow is the day of the summit and I wouldn't want him concerned with you when he's busy carrying out the next attack."

She then quickly turns around and heads down the hall. Keena shuts the door and says, "That was strange."

"Yeah," responds Shigeru. "She was acting like that the other day when I gave it to her. I'm going to contact my sources right away."

Keena says, "Great. I'll go grab Jon and Rachel."

Shigeru places his call and explains their circumstances. The correspondent on the line, sounding rather shocked, says, "Shigeru, what are they planning?"

When he tells about the strike on the UN building the next day, he is surprised by the response. Jon, Rachel, and Keena enter the room and shut the door just as Shigeru is receiving his orders.

The correspondent says, "Shigeru, whatever you do, you must not let them strike the UN."

"What? Why?" asks Shigeru, surprised.

The correspondent continues, "Those delegates meeting tomorrow, most of them are *not* members of the Cabal. Many of them aren't even their subordinates. They are real people like us trying to keep the peace. The KGB isn't part of the unified forces of light. The Russians who are housing you are *far* removed from the ones who served under and with Vladimir Lenin."

"What about the Arabs who helped us?" Shigeru asks.

"They aren't part of us either, but our sources show that they are friendly," the correspondent explains.

"Okay, so Sahib can still be trusted," Shigeru says.

"Yes, as far as I can tell," says the man on the phone. "Just do what you can to stop that attack. The KGB may have a mutual understanding with us, but they just aren't aware like we are of the true Cabal."

"Okay," says Shigeru with a deep sigh. "Goodbye."

Shigeru then turns with a depressed look, and updates the others.

"I knew something wasn't right," Rachel exclaims. "What are we going to do?"

"Well," Shigeru says. "We can go talk to Sahib. Maybe together we can talk the Russians down."

"I don't know," Jon adds. "Olaf is pretty dead set on his plan. It's worth a try though."

Following the discussion, the team goes to talk to Sahib and the Arab pilot.

After listening to the new information, Sahib says, "This is unfortunate, but we will petition it immediately to Olaf."

Down in the command center, the group approaches Olaf and urges him not to attack the building the next day.

Olaf shouts, "Nyet! I don't know where you... got your information," glaring at Katja as she looks down at the floor. "But I am certain that this is the proper course of action. You are my guests, and I value your presence. But I will not allow you to overstay your welcome," says Olaf with his index finger raised. "Now, no more of this. We commence the attack in the morning."

He turns and walks away.

The group, not knowing what to do, further discuss in their quarters how to stop the attack.

Rachel says, "I'd hate to say this, but I think we may have to sabotage the mission."

"What?" Jon asks. "How can we even do that?"

"I'm not sure," Rachel sighs.

Keena says, "Easy, I think I have a plan. But it's gonna require quick action, and we're gonna have to get out of here."

Sahib says, "Go on Keena."

She continues, "If the four of you can create a verbal distraction with Olaf, Shigeru and I might be able to disable a few of the drones. No drones, no mission."

"I'm in," Sahib says. "It may be the only way."

The next morning, just after final preparation for launch, Jon and the others minus Keena and Shigeru approach Olaf.

Olaf says, "I hope you have come to your senses and agree with this mission again."

"No, I'm sorry, but I can't allow this to happen," Jon says.

Sahib adds, "Neither can I."

Olaf turns around, "Sahib, you of all people should know what this facility has been built for and how much has been sacrificed to rectify this world. How can you oppose this like an infidel?"

Sahib responds, "I'm quite aware of all that, but I cannot allow the death of innocents."

"No more talk. Prepare for launch Dr. Petrov," barks Olaf.

"No, this can't happen," says Jon as he picks up an office chair and lops it right into one of the large monitors.

"You fool!" shouts Olaf. "Seize him guards!"

As he signals the guards he notices Keena and Shigeru moving down by the base of the drones. "What?!" Olaf screams. "Stop them!"

Keena and Shigeru draw their weapons and get into a firefight with the KGB guards. The Arab pilot pulls out his submachine gun and attempts to shoot at Olaf and his guards. Jon, Rachel, and Sahib take cover.

Keena and Shigeru, failing in their attempt to the drones, run toward a metal stairwell leading up to a small observation room. Running toward the stairwell as well, Jon and the others dodge fire from Olaf and his three guards. The other Russians are fleeing the command room. The Arab with his gun turns to fire, but before his gets a chance to fire straight he is hit by bullets coming from one of the guards. He drops to the floor dead. The others are now under the stairwell too, with only Keena and Shigeru to defend them.

"What now?' Jon asks.

Shigeru firing his treasured, gold plated pistol says, "I don't know. We didn't think this far."

Just then, the group notices three of the drone planes levitating.

"Shit, we're too late!" Rachel screams.

"Dammit!" Keena shouts.

Suddenly, one of the drones turns and fires a high caliber machine gun burst toward the guards, killing all of them, and leaving only Olaf behind his command platform. The group looks over to see Katja controlling the drones by computer. The other two drones begin firing at the still stationary planes on the hangar floor.

"Get up to the observation room!" shouts Katja.

The others waste no time. Once up the stairs, the group looks out the window to see Katja now running toward the stairwell herself, stepping over the fallen Arab's body. Once at the top of the stairs, Shigeru opens the door to let Katja in. The room below is in shambles.

"You have to get out of here," Katja says.

"Why are you helping us?" Jon asks.

"Because I believe you," Katja says. "My father was killed off by Commander Kinski when he tried rebelling against some of the KGB's methods. Olaf has kept me basically as a prisoner carrying on my father's work. Come, there is a hidden shaft up here that will take you to a small jet so you may escape."

"Come with us," Keena implores.

Katja hesitates then says, "Okay, but I must destroy what I've constructed first. There is an auxiliary control panel up here. I can set the bunker busters to explode here in the facility to vaporize any trace of this technology."

She then approaches the panel and starts a countdown.

"We must hurry," Katja declares. "Open the shaft and we'll go up to the escape hangar."

Suddenly, Olaf bursts through the door, pistol in hand. He has an injured arm from the attack downstairs. He shoots Katja in her back, dropping her to the floor. Shigeru fires back at Olaf, putting two in his chest and sending him over the stairwell.

Jon and Sahib rush down to hold Katja up.

She says, "Go, you don't have much time and I can't stop the timer now."

"No," Jon says. "You have to come with us. You have to escape this life of imprisonment you've lived."

"I already have," Katja replies. "And now I can die knowing that I've made a difference in the scheme of things."

Lying on the floor, bloody from her gunshot wounds, she dies.

"Come on," Keena says. "We better go like she said."

The team climbs up the shaft and finds the small black private jet. Sahib gets in the cockpit and starts the jet up. As the group flies away, an explosion encompasses the grounds that once housed the KGB remnant. Jon can't help but be reminded once again the words he heard before about certain souls slipping through the cracks of destiny. "Obvious examples were Dr. Katja Petrov and the Arab pilot," he thinks to himself. "But what about the others? Rachel has been proven to be more involved in the scheme of destiny. And what about Keena and Shigeru? Are they immune? Surely Shigeru has proven to be needed more after surviving the possession. But for how long? And what about Sahib?"

Just then, Sahib asks, "Where are we going? Back to Arabia?"

"No," Shigeru says. "I'll call my sources and tell them mission accomplished. Then we'll find out what to do next."

After Shigeru gets off the phone with his contacts, he tells the group the new plan.

"There's a lodge in the Swedish Alps that my sources referred us to," Shigeru explains. "We can take refuge there until we are contacted by the cell they are sending out to us."

Rachel asks, "Then what?"

Shigeru replies, "I'm not sure. They just said we should go there and wait. And that they had a proposition for us. We can land just a few miles down from the resort and walk our way to it."

Keena brightens up, "Resort?! Alright, this will be a change of pace."

Sahib asks, "Do you have the exact location to direct me?"

Shigeru answers, "Yes, I'll chart it right now. This plane has an excellent navigation computer."

The group, now heading toward the central countryside of Sweden, is unsure of their next move. Only time will tell what is in store for them there.

Chapter 26:

A Time for Rest and Relaxation

Sahib, flying the jet, says to the others, "We're coming just overhead of the coordinates you gave me."

The group looks out the window to see miles and miles of snow laden forests. A large clearing with a few trees comes into sight. At the center of the clearing is a large log built building, four stories high, with smoke puffing out of the chimney.

"Beautiful," Rachel says.

The jet passes over the large wooden resort and moves over the sea of trees.

Sahib says, "I'll land the jet in this soft spot up ahead. Thankfully the snow isn't deep enough to affect our landing pattern."

The jet comes down in an area just outside the forest, about three miles away from the resort.

As the group steps off the plane, Jon says, "So I guess now we walk and see what we find out."

Sahib says, "Good luck my friends. I can no longer follow you on your journey."

Rachel turns and asks, "Why not Sahib?"

He responds, "This has all been far too much for me. I'm glad to have helped and will do what I can for the cause in the future. But after what happened with the Russians, I can't bring myself to go any further."

The rest of the group gathers around for handshakes before letting him depart.

Keena asks, "Where will you go?"

"Back to Arabia," Sahib replies. "I need to update my people on all that has transpired."

"Besides," Sahib continues as he walks up the steps back into the jet. "I'll need to offer this jet as a replacement for all the damaged planes." Sahib laughs a little, then closes the door to the plane.

The group waves him off through the cockpit windshield as he flies off, leaving the group to head toward the resort.

Jon says, "Well, let's head on over."

The team of four now begins walking through the lightly snow dusted forest in the direction of the resort. The smoke from the chimney helps the group get their bearings on the direction they need to head.

"I just realized something," remarks Shigeru.

"What's that?" Jon asks.

Shigeru says, "My sources just said to come here. They didn't say what to do or anything. And we don't have any money so we can't just check into the resort hotel."

"Hmmm," Rachel says. "Well, maybe we can just go to the counter and ask if there's a forces of light special going on?"

The others chuckle a little.

"But seriously though. We should just go in and ask if someone's expecting us," Keena suggests.

Coming out of the woods, the team sees the full size of the resort. Four stories high, large patio decks around the premises, and a snowmobile corral out back with several guests riding them in and out.

Walking in the front door, the group looks out of place. They approach the front desk. A brightly blonde haired Swedish woman wearing suit pants and jacket behind the counter welcomes them.

Jon asks, "This might sound strange. But there wouldn't happen to be anyone waiting here for someone fitting our descriptions would there?"

The woman responds with her Scandinavian accent, "No, but I do have a deluxe reservation for four people fitting your description."

The group looks at each other slightly confused as the woman looks down at the computer monitor.

"Shigeru Iwata, Jon Peters, Rachel Lynn, and Keena Turoni?" the Swedish woman asks.

Excited, the group all nod their heads and agree.

"Great," says the woman at the counter. "I'll have you taken right up to your rooms."

The group is taken up to the fourth floor to a double suite. The rooms are connected and divided by a large door in the middle. Jon and Rachel choose the room to the right.

"We'll take this one, if that's okay with you guys?" Jon asks.

Shigeru responds, "That's fine with me."

Looking around the rooms, the group is in awe at the luxury. The rooms are equipped with king sized beds, wooden balconies, walk-in brick showers, big screen TV, a pool table in the right room and an arcade system in the left.

As they take in their surroundings, a bellhop comes to the door. When Jon answers, the man comes in with a complimentary cart. It contains two glass pitchers with white and chocolate milk, four glasses, a plate of large chocolate chip cookies, and a plastic gift card.

Jon thanks the man and sees him out of the door. Under the plastic gift card is a note.

He says, "Hey Shigeru, check this out."

The note reads, 'I've taken the liberty of setting you up at the resort until I finish my reconnaissance work. I understand that you have had a treacherous journey with few opportunities for relaxation. Please enjoy the resort stay until my arrival. I wish I could offer more, but a few days is all that you will be granted before our next move. P.S. The gift card is for the resort's department store, there is a $500 credit on it for you to get some new clothes. Signed, The Swede.'

Rachel says, "Wow Shigeru, this is almost too much. Almost."

Shigeru smiles and says, "Well, the forces of light are shooting for a better world. So they do what they can to make their agents feel comfortable when they can."

Keena, who hasn't waited a moment to crunch into those cookies, says, "I'm not complaining. I say we get down there and get to shopping so we can hurry up and get to relaxing."

Jon adds, "I second that."

Down in the department store, the girls split off and shop while Jon and Shigeru shop in the men's section.

Jon asks, "So who's the Swede anyway?"

Shigeru looking at some sweaters answers, "I don't really know. My sources just said he's a local agent in the area and he's supposed to talk to us when he gets here about the current Cabal situation."

Jon says, "Well apparently something serious is happening here if he's doing reconnaissance nearby."

Shigeru, choosing an outfit responds, "True."

That evening, Keena and Rachel decide to hit the Jacuzzi outside while Jon and Shigeru have some guy time. Bathing suit clad and wrapped in towels, Keena and Rachel step out on to one of the decks out back. The hot tub with steam rising from the water seems almost out of place with its snowy backdrop.

Keena says, "I never thought I'd be crazy enough to go outside with snow on the ground in a two piece."

Rachel, removing the towel and stepping into the hot water concurs, "Yeah, but that's a thing they like to do here, so when in Rome."

Keena steps in the water right after her. The two relax.

"Wow," Keena says. "This really ain't half bad."

"Yeah," says Rachel. She pauses a minute. "Can I ask you a question?"

Keena, with her head laid back and eyes closed says, "Shoot girl."

Rachel proceeds, "When this is all over, if it ever ends, what's gonna happen with you and Shigeru?"

Keena, opening her eyes and looking straight ahead, answers, "I'm not sure. I never thought things would have turned out the way they have since that first encounter with you guys in the alley, but I've come to see how much alike we are."

Rachel asks, "Do you love him?"

Keena replies, "Well yeah, but I don't know if that's enough when this fiasco is over. I mean seriously, think about it. Can an American black woman raised by Italian Mafia really work with a Japanese man who was sworn in to the Yakuza?"

Rachel says, "Keena, think of what day and age this is, race doesn't matter. And as far as the backgrounds go, you said it yourself; you have more in common than you thought. Look, when this is all over, I'll be here for you if you need help figuring all this out."

Keena responds, "I appreciate that Rachel. Ya know, don't worry about having been the damsel in distress before. I'm glad another woman is part of this group. I can only be tough bitch so much."

Rachel snickers a bit.

A moment passes, and then Keena asks, "What about you and Jon? Are you guys gonna go back the way you were before all this?"

"I sure hope not," Rachel says. "This whole deal brought me and Jon back together. If we went back to the way we were before, we'd be separate. I was stupid for throwing us away when I left for Greece, but I did need to get out there and have that experience. And Jon, he got rather stagnant after he graduated."

Keena says, "But if you hadn't gone, you would have never found that journal, and you and Jon would have never started this journey. This in turn led to me getting out of the mob. So in a way, I owe you more than Jon and Shigeru. It would definitely seem as if destiny has a hand in this."

Rachel says, "Yeah, I guess you're right. Hopefully when this is over, we'll have a more clear understanding of how things should be."

As the girls carry on, relaxing in the hot tub, Jon and Shigeru are upstairs playing pool in their suite. Shigeru, pool cue in one hand, takes a drink from his bottle of Redd's Apple Ale with the other. "Ah," he says. "That stuff is the best."

"Can I have one?" Jon asks after taking his next shot.

Shigeru, going over to the mini fridge says, "Sure, it's not like we're paying for it anyway."

He grabs a bottle and takes it to Jon. Shigeru leans in for his shot and asks, "If the forces of light ask you to join permanently, will you take them up?"

Jon answers, "Of course, I'm in this, and I know Rachel is too. After all we've been through so far, it can get much more dangerous."

"Let's hope not," Shigeru says. "I just wanted to make sure, because you really never signed up for all this. I mean, I'm not saying you can't handle it, cuz you have so far. I don't know what I'd do without your judgment."

Jon says, "Well, you wouldn't have had to go all around the world several times protecting me, that's for sure."

Shigeru smirks and says, "Don't worry about it. I knew what I was getting into the moment I found out the Cabal was sending that Shinobi after you guys."

Jon asks, "How do you know so much about them anyway? I mean, besides what your sources told you."

Shigeru replies, "Miyamoto Industries, who developed the Shinobis, have had it out for the Yakuza for a long time. Many years ago, a rival Yakuza clan to mine helped clear out the competition for Miyamoto. My clan, being linked to the forces of light, was ordered to try and stop its corporate takeover. My grandfather, who was the clan leader at the time, had his hands full and got overwhelmed. We had to back off. Years later, after reorganizing, I as a young Yakuza, was part of a task force that tried to take them down again. We failed miserably so we waited until the time to strike was right. That day has yet to come. Being so close to where the Cabal sent them to take you out, and having the knowledge I had about them, I was selected to be the one to retrieve you."

Jon says, "Wow, I had no idea. Maybe the time will be right soon. Maybe once things die down, I can return the favor for you saving my life by helping you take Miyamoto on."

Shigeru smiles and says, "Thanks Jon. I appreciate that."

Jon, taking a drink of the crisp Redd's Apple Ale says, "Damn! These really *are* good!"

Shigeru says, "See, I told you."

Chapter 27:

Enter the Swede

A couple of days pass and the group has gotten a great chance to recuperate after the recent turbulence. One night at dinner down in the dining hall of the resort, the group notices some commotion. A waiter brings a man with short thin hair and glasses over to the table. The man is wearing a striped sweater and appears to have just come in from outdoors. A snow storm is passing through the valley that evening so he has traces of snow on his clothes.

The man asks, "May I sit?"

Jon replies, "Of course."

The man sits down.

"Are you...?" Jon asks, before being interrupted by the man.

"The Swede," he says. "Yes. I'm sorry I can't reveal my real name to you, but it's for my own protection. Globally I am known as the Swede but unfortunately the workings of the Cabal have called me to my home country. You may call me SD, for short. I hope the accommodation I provided for you was sufficient."

Rachel says, "Oh yes, very much so."

Jon adds, "We can't thank you enough for it."

SD continues, "Good, now let's get down to business. The forces of light's high command, wants to make Jon and Rachel an offer. They've taken a particular notice to your successes in thwarting the Cabal. Escaping the education board and exposing Winston Drake was impressive. Surviving and stopping the human replicate threat was outstanding. And disposing the KGB remnant was the icing on the cake. Together with Shigeru, they would like to assign you to become a task force set to exploit various elements of the Cabal around the world. Right now, members of the Cabal are being exposed and overrun one at a time. Some, however, are too tough to take on by simple cells like myself. Will you accept this offer? The invitation is extended to Keena as well of course. After all, she was the one who killed Benjamin Washington wasn't she?"

Keena responds, "Yeah, that was me. Well guys, I'm in if you are."

Jon looks at Rachel. She nods to him. "Yeah, we're in," Jon says.

Shigeru says, "You know my answer. I'm already obligated."

SD enthusiastically says, "Great, this is wonderful. You will be given all the resources necessary for travel and accommodation. With this team in conjunction with our various cells and diplomats, the Cabal will surely crumble. Jon, with his amazing intuition and thinking skills will lead the group. Rachel with her ability to keep her cool will provide a level head to the team. Shigeru, with his cunning skills and knowledge will provide the force behind the team's operations backed up by Keena's electronics and computer skills and brash attitude to support the team, it all ties in perfectly. Your team has already existed for some time. Now you're just official and have the resources to really take it to them."

The group, excited, feels honored to be granted such prestige.

Jon says, "We accept. What's our first task?"

SD replies, "To help me. There is a real threat being manufactured right here in the mountains of Sweden and unfortunately the forces of light are spread too thin to aid me. I myself cut short another mission in Canada to investigate this threat. I arrived in the country shortly before you left Russia and requested assistance once my information was gathered."

Shigeru asks, "And what is this threat?"

SD pulls out a palm pilot and displays the image of man looking to be in his mid-40s.

"This is BjörnOlsen. He's a very low ranked member of the Cabal, who manufactures mechanized weaponry. His factory is just north of here. He hasn't had much of a prominent role in the Cabal's activities, but with the defeat of the HRTs we have reason to believe he could be a replacement threat."

"What makes you think that?" Rachel asks.

SD answers, "Just months before the replicates were deployed, we were investigating him and learned that his contract for military robotics manufacturing had expired and production was supposed to cease. We had planned to take the facility down, but stopped giving it attention because we realized the Cabal had something else in mind. We just didn't know what. The only problem is, several weeks after the contract was canceled and production had ceased, smoke started coming out of the factory again. No contracted workers returned to continue production, and we were too preoccupied with other moves against the Cabal to reinvestigate. Then the replicate threat appeared. But all the while, activity was still present at Olsen's facility. He himself hasn't been seen in months. He's very much your classical mad scientist these days, very reclusive."

"So what do you want us to do?" Jon asks.

"I could only do so much on my own," SD says. "I merely scoped the premises while I was up there these past few days. I need the four of you to come up with me to infiltrate the factory and find out what's really going on in there, and if possible, destroy anything that could become a serious threat to the world. Still interested in helping?"

Jon replies, "Of course, when do we leave?"

SD, smiling, pleased that he has the team's help, replies, "We leave tomorrow afternoon. By snowmobile. We should arrive just outside the production factory by nightfall."

The next day, SD takes the group out back and loads up on three snowmobiles. Leading the way, SD takes them north to the factory of BjörnOlsen. As they move through the beautiful landscape, our heroes can't help but appreciate the soft nature of the Swedish wilderness.

Just before the sun sets, SD says, "We should walk from here."

SD comments as the group comes to a stop, "As far as I can tell, he shouldn't have a way of knowing we're coming. In the two days I spent up here, I was never met with any resistance. However, I've never made it inside. The risk was too great for me to do it alone."

Shigeru, getting off the snowmobile after Keena says, "Well, that's what we're here for," cocking his gun and making sure the chamber is loaded.

After walking nearly a mile, the group beings to see smoke rising above the tree line, in the foreground of the setting sun.

SD notes, "We'll move a little bit farther. Then we'll wait until dark to get in through a window or something."

Scoping the premises from the edge of the woods and now under the cover of night, the group sees the full size of the factory. Rows of windows are at both ground and ceiling levels. The group spots a damaged window slightly out of view from the others that they think they can slip open.

Jon asks, "Should we move now?"

SD nods, and the group scurries out into the open area between the forest and the factory walls.

Once up to the window, Shigeru attempts leveraging it open. Successful, he hops through and is followed by Keena and SD. Jon comes through next and turns to give a hand to Rachel as she comes in.

Looking around the room, the group sees walls only about half as high as the room surrounding the interior. They hear the sound of a metal production line on the other side of the walls. Moving around the mid-sized walls quietly, the team is finally able to see what's making the noise.

Rachel exclaims, "My God!"

Large conveyor belts are running around the interior of the room. A mechanized assembly line is producing machines of war. The entire facility appears like an apocalyptic science fiction nightmare.

SD says, "I suggest we investigate further into the plant before attempting any sabotage."

Jon nods and says, "I agree. Let's move over there to that door and find out what's on the other side."

As the group approaches the double swinging door Jon pointed out, it starts to open. The group hurries to the walls on either side of the doors as to not be spotted by whatever is coming through. Jon and Rachel on one side and Shigeru, Keena, and SD on the other, they flatten themselves tightly against the wall.

Coming through the door are two bi-pedal walking robots. With rectangular bodies, the machines appear to have heavy machine guns for arms and two smaller gun barrels sticking out the front. On top, instead of some sort of head, the machines have a dome with a flashlight beaming around to the front of them.

Once the two robots are out of earshot, Jon comments, "These must be what they are building here."

SD responds, "Yeah, they must be acting as security too. Come on. Let's go through the doors before they come back."

The group then rushes in through the door into a long hallway. When they make it to the end of the hall, they step through cautiously to the next set of doors. Going through it, they find themselves in a very large room with a ledge running across the upper part of the far wall. The room is dark. Only moonlight from the upper windows shines through into the room.

Suddenly, a door opens up on the ledged level of the room. A man comes out with two more of the robots behind him. Jon and the others instantly recognize him as the mad scientist SD showed them in the picture. They have no time to hide.

Björn spots them immediately and says, "So I have intruders."

SD calls out to him, "Give it up Olsen. We're on to your operation here."

"Oh, you know of me?" Björn asks.

Jon interjects, "We know you are part of the Cabal and you've got some diabolical plan with these war droids you are building."

"Yes," Björn responds. "They are beautiful, aren't they? Machines are superior to humans in every way. The Cabal was foolish to rely on Ben T. and his human replicate program. I knew it wouldn't work from the moment it was suggested. Now he's dead and the program is obsolete. The Cabal has always put me on the back burner in favor of Ben T. and his genetics, then, on the other end of the spectrum with Miyamoto and his Cybernetic Shinobis. Sure, they make great assassins, but they can't be manufactured for large scale use like my Warbots can. When I replace the HRT program and the UN forces with my mechanized army, Miyamoto will be overshadowed and the Cabal will finally see me for what I am, a genius and a hero. There will be a dozen of these in every town around the world when production reaches its height."

Looking up at Olsen, Rachel says, "You're mad."

Björn Olsen responds, "Hmmm, maybe."

He turns and exits through the door he came in by. The two droids Olsen left behind walk over to the edge and open fire on the group. Realizing they are trapped, the group has no choice but to face the mechanical juggernauts.

Chapter 28:

In the Company of a Madman

Gunfire erupts all around them. The group runs for cover behind a stack of metal crates, unsure of how to escape the horrible machines.

Jon asks, "Now what do we do, SD?"

SD, pistol in hand answers, "I'm really not sure."

Keena, springing up from her cover, shouts, "I do, cover me."

She hands her gun to Jon and takes off running toward the wall beneath where the machines are standing. Jon, Shigeru, and SD pop up and shoot toward the droids just enough to draw some of their fire away from Keena.

Rachel shouts over the gunfire, "What is she doing?"

"I don't know," Shigeru says, ducking back behind the crates.

Keena, now against the wall looks to her left. She sees piping run up the wall to the top ledge. She scoots across the wall and attempts to climb the pipes.

Jon observes, "I see what she has in mind. Let's keep them from noticing her."

The team pops up once again to distract the robots as Keena scales the wall up to them. Once up top she runs back to a panel on the wall. The panel controls a magnetic lift running across the ceiling of the large room. Controlling the lift, she moves the crane directly over the droids and turns on the magnet. Just before the robots notice her and turn to fire, the magnet pulls them straight off the ground up to the base of the crane. Keena moves the crane, with the droids stuck underneath, to the center of the room. Releasing a lever, the crane's pulley drops. The large magnet then falls down toward the ground, crushing the droids underneath it. The rest of the team comes out from behind the crates.

Shigeru shouts, "Attagirl Keena."

Keena gives a salute and says, "Let me see if I can follow Olsen."

She tries the door, but it doesn't budge.

"It's locked," she yells down to the others.

SD says, "Let's try the door down here."

Rachel attempts to open it. "It's unlocked," she says.

After regrouping, the team moves into the next room in pursuit of Björn.

SD asks, "How are you on ammo?"

Keena answers, "I'm good."

Shigeru responds, "I got one clip left."

The team moves through a small hall past the doors and come to another door. They enter the room and find the ledge from the other room running across the wall with the windows up near the ceiling. Olsen is standing up on the ledge in front of a control panel with the moonlight to his back.

He shouts down, "Impressive, but you are far from stopping me. You all are going to participate in a test run of my newest product."

"Oh great," Jon says sarcastically.

Just then a large door on the other side of the warehouse opens up. With loud stomping, an enormous robot steps out into the moonlight. The group is in absolute awe at the size of the 30-foot tall metallic man.

Shaped like a Viking, and armed with a large battle-ax, the robot is a fierce and imposing sight.

"This is Hogarth," Olsen says. "He is an experimental machine, one of 300 more to be produced. He is not just an ordinary machine though. He is host of a wayward soul."

The group gasps, remembering the demon that possessed Shigeru several weeks earlier.

Olsen continues, "Giving bodies back to the wayward demons that remain on earth will really score me points with the Cabal. They will personally command my Warbot armies around the globe."

"You are mad!" shouts Rachel.

"That may be," Björn responds. "But I won't be of any concern to you much longer."

The mad scientist pushes a button on the control panel and Hogarth crouches before lunging toward the group swinging his metallic ax. The group scatters. Jon and Rachel run to the doors that they came through. Aiming their weapons, the others fire at Hogarth, but in vain.

When Jon opens the door he is shocked and closes the door quickly after seeing that the other two security droids the group saw earlier are heading down the hall toward the warehouse room. Turning back and seeing the group struggle with the large Viking robot, Jon gets an idea.

He says, "Rachel, run over to the others and help them distract that thing so that it faces away from this door."

"Okay," she says.

Rachel runs over past Hogarth and says, "Guys, come on. Let's get this guy to follow us this way. Jon's got a plan."

As the group distracts Hogarth, Jon opens the double doors back up. The two security droids walk into the room soon after. Jon begins running toward the giant robot, now facing the other members of the group. When the security droids see him they begin opening fire. Jon takes off and runs between Hogarth's legs. The spread of fire coming from the security bots clatters against his back, before ceasing. After taking considerable damage from the bottom of his waist up to the back of his neck, he turns around and faces the two droids. Running toward the two, Hogarth rears back his battle ax and in a swift swipe destroys both droids where they stand.

Before giving him a chance to turn around, Shigeru leaps up onto Hogarth's back. Once on, he attempts to fire his pistol into the exposed circuitry on the back of his neck. He pulls the trigger but nothing comes out.

"Damn, out of ammo," Shigeru thinks.

"Keena! Quick," he shouts, holding out his hand, signaling for her gun.

She tosses it up to him. Turning toward SD, Shigeru doesn't even have to ask. SD tosses his gun up to Shigeru as well. Now wielding two pistols, Shigeru shoots into the exposed insides of Hogarth's neck as he sways violently trying to shake Shigeru off. As the last shot is fired, Hogarth collapses to the ground, broken and defeated. A rush of air comes ripping out of the robot and flies outward toward an open window near the ceiling of the warehouse. The group realizes this is the wayward soul that was commanding the Viking android.

Shigeru, now getting back up to his feet with the help of Keena, turns his attention up to the ledge where Björn stands looking furious.

"Fools," Olsen says as he operates his control panel. "How dare you destroy my prototype? If I can't stop you, then I'll die with you. This facility is fitted with explosives. Enough to erase all my machines from existence in the event that someone attempts to take them from me. It will be more than sufficient to wipe all of you out."

Rachel shouts, "Shoot him!"

Shigeru says, "With what? We're all out of ammo."

As Björn is about to finish the self-destruct protocol, he bursts into maniacal laughter. The others watch helplessly. When the protocol is almost complete, Björn's laughter ceases abruptly. His body stiffens and he has a blank look on his face. The others look on, curious as to why the mad scientist is acting this way. Then suddenly he leans forward and falls over the balcony of the ledge, landing on the floor in front of the group. Out of his back a tomahawk is protruding from the top of his spinal column.

The confused team looks up to see a man standing in the moonlight from an open window up near the ceiling. The man is wearing glasses and light brown woodsman clothes along with moccasins on his feet. His face is covered in Native American war paint, and he has long black hair pulled into a ponytail.

Jon looks closely at the man and mutters, "Bear? Is that you?"

The man replies, "Indeed."

Keena asks, "Who?"

Rachel yells, "Bear, it is you!"

Bear, the man who led the group to Chief Crowfeather just under two months ago, leaps down to join the team. He walks over and retrieves his tomahawk from the lifeless back of Björn Olsen.

Bear says, "Chief Crowfeather felt that you could use some help. So he sent me personally. The united forces of light pointed me in this direction, so I came as quickly as I could. When I arrived I heard gunfire from this warehouse, so I proceeded with caution. I saw that open window when that spirit flew out of it."

Shigeru says, "Bear, you couldn't have come at a better time."

Bear smiles and says, "I'm pleased that you all are safe."

Keena says, "I still don't know who this is, but I'm grateful."

Jon assures Keena, "We'll explain it all later. Right now, I think we should finish rigging this place to blow and take off."

"Right," SD says.

After the explosion, the group watches the factory burn into the night. Everyone thanks Bear once again and just as silently as he had arrived, he disappears into the woods.

SD tells the team, "Let's go back to the resort. Tomorrow, I'll drive you all to Stockholm and you can fly anywhere you like."

Rachel asks, "But where will we go?"

Shigeru says, "Back to Japan."

The group turns their attention to him.

"I've decided that the threat posed here to SD's homeland is too similar to the threat to mine. It's a sign of my own personal destiny. I'm going to take down Miyamoto Industries."

Chapter 29:

New Enemies and Old Ghosts

After resting briefly back at the resort, SD takes the group to the airport in Stockholm and puts them on a Tokyo flight.

Before leaving, SD approaches Shigeru, shakes his hand and says, "Thank you my friend. I wish I could return the favor and come with you, but the forces of light need me here as a local contact."

Shigeru responds, "I understand, but thank you for the gesture."

The team then boards their commercial flight and is off to Tokyo.

During their flight, Rachel, after discovering the phone lines in North America have been restored, uses Shigeru's satellite phone to call her mother, still under the protection of the Order of the Square and Compass.

"Yes mom," Rachel says. "I've been through a lot, but I'm still okay. Yes, Shigeru is still with us. Mom, I just wanted to catch up with you. I know it's been a long time, but it's been chaotic. I'll call you again when we get to Japan. Okay mom. Love ya, bye."

Rachel turns to Jon in the seat next to her. "Mom says those guys in Evansville are taking good care of her, and that they were able to ride out the storm when martial law was declared."

"That's good," Jon says.

"I never thought I'd say this," Rachel says. "But I'm starting to like this role we've taken on."

"Hmmm?" Jon asks.

Rachel continues. "I mean, I know I don't do much physically but I'm glad to be a part of this group and what we're doing."

Jon replies. "I'm glad too."

Shigeru, returning to his seat next to Keena behind Jon and Rachel asks for his phone back.

"I'm gonna make sure some of my men are ready to pick us up when we land," he says.

A short time later, the plane lands in Tokyo and the team gets off. Three Yakuza are waiting for them and take them to a limo.

"Where we headed Shig?" asks Keena, who has never been in the East before.

Slightly embarrassed by his new nickname, he responds, "We're headed to a dojo here in the city. We'll base our operation against Miyamoto out of there."

Just then, Shigeru's satellite phone rings.

"Hello," he says.

A moment passes as he listens. Jon and Rachel, sitting across from Shigeru in the limo, begin to notice a look on his face.

"This can't be," Shigeru says. "Yes, I understand. We'll be at our utmost cautiousness. Thank you, goodbye." Shigeru hangs up.

"What's wrong?" Jon asks curiously.

Shigeru hesitates for a moment before answering, "My sources." He takes a deep breath before continuing. "They just reported to me that intelligence has received info that an assassin known only as The Drifter has been sent by the Cabal to eliminate us."

Rachel replies, "Well, so we've survived a lot worse. The replicates...robots...demons! How can one guy be worse than demons? I mean, we have all of your men here in Japan to protect us."

Shigeru with a very serious face responds, "You don't understand Rachel. This is not just some guy. The Drifter has never failed a mission. He has annihilated every hit that he has been contracted, including members of the forces of light that the Cabal has sent him after. No matter what, he has tracked them down. Even if he has to wait it out in order to get close to them, he finds a way."

Keena steps in, putting her hand on Shigeru's knee, "It's okay. We'll just have to keep our guard up. Besides, it will take him some time to get here if he even knows where we're at yet."

"You're right," Shigeru expresses. "And as long as destiny wills it, we can survive him."

The group then arrives at the dojo, which with its beautiful landscape is an excellent break from the gray consistency of the concrete jungle that is Tokyo.

Once in the house, the group sits down with various lieutenants of Shigeru's clan and some of their allies. Together, they begin devising a plan to take down Miyamoto Industries. Ultimately the decision is made to attack their labs and manufacturing facility on the other side of town.

Shigeru says, "Just like the Turoni family house and Olsen's plant in Sweden, our best course of action is to attack at night and swiftly. We'll need some heavy weapons because it won't just be security guards and other Yakuza. They'll have an unknown number of those Shinobis. We know they have at least three more, the ones we encountered in Chicago."

A man from another clan says, "We can provide a half-dozen grenade launchers for the attack."

Shigeru adds, "Yes, and the sticky bomb I used on the one we fought off before was somewhat effective, so we can use some of them as well."

"When are we going to do this?" Jon asks.

Shigeru replies, "The sooner the better. I say we do it the day after tomorrow. That should be plenty of time to gather resources, inform our men, and mobilize against them."

As the meeting comes to an end, Rachel asks Jon, "What role will you and I have in this mission?"

Jon answers, "If anything, we should go and just hang in the back and let the Yakuza deal with this matter. But we may be some support."

A day passes and the time comes for the strike against Miyamoto Industries. Before getting in the cars and heading to the labs, Shigeru meets with one of the Yakuza leaders. After carrying out a conversation with him in Japanese, Shigeru turns to Jon and Rachel.

"Look," he says. "You guys can sit this one out. I've just discovered we have nearly 50 men for this attack, and a lot of heavy arms."

Jon replies, "No, you know we should be there Shigeru. We'll stay in the back, but we have to go in case you could use us."

"Very well," Shigeru responds. "Let's load up and head out then."

Keena walks up with a tactical 12-gauge shotgun.

"I'll be using this on this mission," she says.

"Excellent," Shigeru exclaims with a smile.

The group gets into their vehicles and heads down to Miyamoto Industries.

As they stop just outside the gates, two guards approach the vehicles. Several Yakuza get out with assault rifles and detain the guards immediately.

After tying them up in their guard shack, the group opens the gate and the team of five dozen men enters the grounds. A group of Yakuza, hidden in the bushes, ambush two guards in a golf cart as they come around the corner. These two are tied up like the first set. When the strike team gets to the main building, they discover that a key code is required to open the door.

Jon suggests, "Why don't we get one of the guards to open it?"

"To hell with that," Shigeru replies as he draws his pistol.

He then takes aim and fires until the lock is broken.

Shigeru turns to Jon and says, "This *is* an assault after all," as the Yakuza charge into the lab.

Inside, the group is met with resistance from several more security guards armed with hand guns. A fire fight breaks out through the hallway. The surviving guards, severely outnumbered, retreat to a door around the corner of the hall. Dividing and conquering, the Yakuza spread throughout the facility. The heroes and a dozen Yakuza pursue the fleeing guards into the next room.

There, the guards are joined by several more guards in addition to some rival Yakuza who work for Miyamoto to help patrol the lab. Hiding behinds tables and cabinets, the Yakuza exchange fire with their enemies from across the room. Jon and Rachel hunker down near Shigeru and Keena. Jon, armed only with a small revolver realizes that it's time to use it. Lifting up just long enough to get a few shots off, Jon notices that the enemy is severely outnumbered. Finishing off the last few guards and Yakuza, the team rises up from their cover.

"Wow!" Rachel says. "This whole operation might be easier than we planned."

"It's never easier," Shigeru responds.

Just then, the red and blue Cybernetic Shinobi that kidnapped Rachel drops down from a panel in the ceiling. The Yakuza rush back for cover once again. Drawing their swords, the droids waste no time in slicing down the nearest Yakuza. Two of the men fire the grenade launchers, damaging the two droids severely. After dropping to the ground, the blue Shinobi gets back up, severely damaged. Keena, springing out from her cover, runs toward the robot firing the shotgun relentlessly. Finally, the droid drops for good. The team calms down and then moves on to the next room.

Moving through the facility, they come to the security room. The team stops to look at the surveillance cameras. On one screen they see members of their strike force in a crossfire with rival Yakuza outside in the company's garden. On another, the yellow Shinobi that attacked them in Chicago, firing Ninja stars from its wrists, is being torn apart by gunfire and grenades in a hallway somewhere in the facility.

Shigeru smiles and comments, "The day just might be ours after all."

Another camera shows a room that appears to be the storage department of the facility.

"Let's go there," Shigeru says. "That must be where they keep their inventory."

After finding the room's number below the security camera, the group heads toward the storage room. When they arrive, they find no resistance. Across the room is a ladder leading up to a platform with a door leading out of the platform.

Shigeru says, "These crates, lets rig the explosives here."

Members of the Yakuza begin setting explosives near all of the inventory doors. Just then, the door on the platform opens. A Japanese man with a gray moustache and glasses enters the room. He has two more Cybernetic Shinobis with him, one with pink and the other with orange markings.

Shigeru, moments before turning to fire, stops. He looks stunned.

"It can't be him," Shigeru says, shaking with fear.

The man says, "You shouldn't have come here Shigeru."

He waves his hand, signaling the Shinobis to attack, then turns and leaves the room. The Shinobis flip over the railing of the platform and engage the Yakuza at close range. Out of grenades, the group is being slaughtered. Keena aims her shotgun up to the pink Shinobi's face but before she can fire, it knocks the gun out of her hand then on to the floor next to the two surviving Yakuza. Shigeru is thrown against the wall by the orange Shinobi. Jon, trying to think quickly, notices the Shinobis are standing near the explosives that were placed by the men. He looks to his left and sees the detonator on the floor next to a fallen yakuza.

"Everyone down!" he shouts as he rolls for the detonator.

Throwing the switch the moment he has it in his hand, the two Shinobis are blown up as the room is rocked by the explosion.

After shaking off the debris, Jon pulls himself to his feet. He asks, "Shigeru, who was that man? Was that Miyamoto?"

"No Jon," Shigeru answers. "That was my father."

Chapter 30:

In Honor of Machiko

Running down the hall of the facility the group comes across two dead Yakuza.

"These are our men," Shigeru barks. "Come on, he must have gone this way."

The team comes to a door leading to the parking garage where they see Shigeru's father heading to a car. Turning to fire at them, the stray bullets cause the team to hide behind a supply truck. Shigeru begins yelling out in Japanese at his father. He yells something back, but the others don't know what's being said. After a heated fire fight, Shigeru's father makes a run for the car. Shigeru comes out and fires once more, this time, hitting his father in the back. He drops to the ground. The team runs up to see him. Shigeru turns him over, and holds his dying father up. In his last moments, he looks down and sees the gold plated gun that Shigeru's mother left for him.

"My son," he says. "You've honored me by carrying this with you all this time."

Shigeru says, "Yes father. I don't know why you walked out on us, but I always thought it was because you had to."

Shigeru's father replies, "I left because I thought the Cabal was unstoppable. I tried to convince your mother we were on the losing side, but she wouldn't listen. I never meant for her to die in the attack on the clan's headquarters. My son, listen, you must stop Miyamoto. He is in his penthouse on the top floor of the

Sagot building. I'm sorry son. I should have been there for you."

"I forgive you father," Shigeru declares, as his father dies in his arms.

Shigeru stands up.

"Come on," he says. "We have to stop Miyamoto before he leaves the city. He may already know of the attack here. Let this night see the redemption of Embo Iwata, and the vengeance of Machiko Iwata."

With victory at hand in Miyamoto Industries, the team, with a handful of Yakuza head to the Sagot building to stop its CEO before he can escape. Once they arrive, the team rushes up to the elevator and to the top floor. When they approach the door to the penthouse, Shigeru wastes no time kicking in the door with his father's gold plated gun in hand. The dark penthouse living room is quickly filled with motion from the agile guards awaiting them. Two gray medium-sized Shinobis jump out to engage Shigeru. Quickly he tosses two sticky bombs, one on each of their chests, disposing of them instantly. When the smoke clears, the others rush into the penthouse.

"He's not here," Shigeru says.

"No, but he was," Rachel says after finding an escape tube leading downstairs.

The team quickly jumps down the chute, discovering it leads to the parking garage. They are too late to stop him and Miyamoto speeds away in his jet black sports car. Jumping out of the way before being hit by the fleeing villain, Shigeru throws a small tracking device on the back of the car.

"Let's move," he says. "That device is only as good as long as he's in the car."

Racing through the streets of Tokyo, the team hurries as they track Miyamoto to a small personal jet hangar outside the city. Getting out of their cars, the group is accosted by the rival Yakuza clan working for Miyamoto. Shigeru, Keena, and the other men outgun the rivals quickly and run into the hangar with Jon and Rachel running close behind. Miyamoto runs toward a very high-tech looking personal jet. Trying to run as fast as he can, he trips and hits the ground. Just before Shigeru makes his way over to Miyamoto, he says something to him in Japanese. Miyamoto quickly reaches into his pocket and pulls out a tiny syringe and takes his own life with a lethal injection to the neck.

"What did he say?" Jon asks.

Shigeru answers, "You will never stop the Cabal."

Upon further investigation of the shiny personal jet with black tinted windows, the team discovers it is a very advanced craft built by Miyamoto Industries. On board, Jon finds a log written in Japanese. When Shigeru reads it, he begins to smile.

Rachel asks, "What is it?"

He replies, "This log shows the place where members of the Cabal go to meet for their energy gathering rituals."

Jon says, "Then we can stop them in their tracks."

'But it's not for a few weeks," Shigeru adds.

Jon shrugs his shoulders and says. "Then let's just rejoice in today's victory for the time being."

After returning to the dojo, the team makes their next plan to move against the Cabal. The TV is reporting that the ones behind the HRT crisis have been discovered.

The reporter on the TV is saying, "The masterminds behind this conspiracy have been brought to justice. Various corporate powerhouses have been exposed for plotting a US takeover. The plot entailed funding to the ring leader behind the conspiracy, Benjamin Thomas Washington, who created the replicate project. Washington was found and killed in his laboratory outside of Brooks Lake, Wyoming by US Army personnel."

The group looks at each other, all knowing very well that Washington was not the top of the totem pole in this conspiracy.

The reporter continues, "Reconstruction from the attack has fully commenced and Americans rest tonight, knowing the ones behind this are no longer at large."

Rachel snaps, "This is ridiculous. They're reporting it as if everything is over."

Shigeru reminds, "Just like when you were attacked at the hotel. Their media outlets report what they want the people to hear."

Jon adds, "They merely exposed the cohorts who were killed and threw under the bus those who were exposed."

The group decides that's enough propaganda for one night and decides to go to bed.

The next day, Shigeru says, "We have a few weeks before the next meeting that members of the Cabal will be attending. The log shows that it will take place at an old castle located in southwestern Germany. The land it sits on is government restricted land and is heavily forested. If we are to go to take on the Cabal, we'll have to do it on foot, so it will take a few days to even reach the castle. This place is pretty low key, so I don't think we have to worry about much security, just whatever they have at the castle."

Jon asks, "So what's the plan? Do we just hang out here for the next couple of weeks and then just sneak into the castle on the day of the ritual?"

Shigeru answers, "Well, it would be best to stay active against the Cabal in any way possible. I don't know what else we can do but wait."

Keena sits for a moment and thinks to herself. Then she says, "Wait a minute. I know something we can do to keep ourselves busy until the day of the ritual."

"Hmmm?" Shigeru asks.

Keena goes on, "When I was a teenager, Don Turoni took me on a business trip to Sicily, where the hierarchy of the Mafia resides. If we were to go there and take them out, it would spread confusion throughout the ranks of Mob Bosses around the world and their organization would fall."

Rachel says, "One less subordinate to the Cabal."

"Exactly," Keena agrees.

Jon asks, "Keena, are you sure you remember where the mobsters meet?"

Keena responds, "It's been a long time since I've been there, but I'm sure I can find it."

Shigeru says, "I'll get on the phone with my sources right now and let them know, they may be able to send some help on this mission."

After Shigeru places his call with his sources, the group makes plans to head to Sicily.

Chapter 31:

The Stranger

Several days later, a meeting takes place in the grand hall of a large mansion in Sicily. In attendance at this meeting are over a dozen high ranking officials of the Mafia, and a prestigious cardinal of the church.

"Are the shipments ready for delivery?" one mob boss asks another.

"They are, but it will take time to transport them. It hasn't been easy to get things into America since the crisis occurred," the other mobster replies.

"Cardinal, what is the Cabal doing to ensure continued business for us overseas?" the first mobster asks. "We are paying dearly for their mistake of using those failed human replicates."

Another mobster joins the conversation. "They can't possibly expect us to prosper as we did before now that access routes in and out of national borders are so tight," he says.

"Gentlemen, relax," Cardinal Buschetta says. "I assure you, the Cabal is well aware of all the problems your men are facing around the globe. Special access routes will soon be provided that will divert all traffic of goods around international security."

The disgruntled mobsters are slightly mollified. Suddenly, the door bursts open.

"Are the Cabal aware of us?" asks Keena as she and the others rush into the room.

Mobsters around the table start to stand up and draw their weapons. Keena and Shigeru shoot the first ones who make it to their feet. The others raise their hands in surrender. Another door opens on the other side of the room. Five armed men rush in.

The leader says with a thick Irish accent, "Okay Keena, the downstairs is all secure."

"Good job Nick," Keena says.

The Cardinal asks, "How? How did you know where to find about this place? Wait!"

The Cardinal looks closely at Keena.

"I know you," he says. "You're that girl Turoni kept with him."

"Yes, and I was his undoing too," she responds.

Shigeru says, "Nick here is the leader of the Dublin underground and is taking you back home with him for safe keeping until you all can be tried by the forces of light."

Absolutely shocked, Cardinal Buschetta and the gangsters are tied up and taken away.

After thanking Nick and the Dublin underground again for aiding in the capture of the leading mob officials, the team begins walking back out into the Sicilian countryside where the experimental jet built by Miyamoto is waiting for them.

Walking down the road as the sun rises, Jon says, "Well for once that was a very, very smooth operation."

"Yeah, you and Rachel didn't have to get your hands dirty at all," Keena notes jokingly.

The group laughs.

"Well, only a few more days until the ritual," Jon reminds the others. "I suppose we should head on up to Germany and find a way into that forest."

Rachel asks, "I wonder how many members of the Cabal are left, and how many there will be at the ritual?"

"In my vision, there are only about a dozen," Jon says. "This may be the same place that I witnessed it occurring."

Shigeru interjects, "Either way, we've been taking them down around the world at an exponential rate."

Just as the group is about to turn off the road to walk down the path leading to the jet, a car pulls up behind them. The group stops and turns around to see who it is. Six men get out of the car, drawing guns on the team. Shigeru, Keena, and Jon draw their guns immediately. Rachel steps behind Jon with her hands on his shoulders.

"Who are you?" Shigeru asks.

The last man to get out of the vehicle says, "Just ask Keena, she knows."

Keena gasps, "Giovanni?!"

"Who is this guy Keena?" Shigeru asks.

Keena replies, "It's Don Turoni's nephew. His mother was the Don's sister. I've had to work with him on several occasions in the past. How did you find me?"

Giovanni responds, "I knew that eventually you'd plot to take down the mob since you run with Yakuza scum now. So I came here to Sicily and waited for you to strike. Oh, and I'm the new Don of the Turoni family, so really I should thank you.

But I think I'll go ahead and act out revenge for my uncle just the same."

Before the gangsters can do anything else, Giovanni looks behind the team.

"Who the hell are you?" he shouts.

The team looks over their shoulders. About 20 yards back, they see a man wearing a western style duster and a rifle on his back. With the brim of his cowboy hat covering his eyes, the man just stands there in silence.

"Hey!" shouts Giovanni again. "I am talking to you. Who are you?"

The man looks up and says, "I am the one who adapts to the unknown."

Shigeru looks at the man more intently.

The man continues, "And I've grown underneath wandering stars."

Shigeru's jaw drops. "Oh no!" he says.

Jon looks at him wondering why he's so afraid.

The stranger continues, "I am by myself, but never alone."

Shigeru says to the group, "It's the, the, The Drifter!"

The man smiles and says, "Some call me a nomad or a vagabond, others a roamer or wanderer. You may call me what you will. But it doesn't change my purpose."

Giovanni, frustrated at the interruption, says, "That's it, I've heard enough. Kill him!"

Giovanni's men turn their weapons toward The Drifter and begin opening fire. Lightning fast, The Drifter lunges forward doing a barrel roll in midair, dodging all of the mobsters fire. Landing on his feet, The Drifter draws two six gun revolvers from holsters within his duster coat. Before the gangsters even realize they missed him, two of them are shot down by The Drifter. Jon and the others realize this scuffle is the perfect opportunity to escape. In unison, they dart to the right, down the path leading to their landed jet.

Running, Jon says, "Holy shit, that guy found us fast!"

Keena replies, "Yeah, thankfully Giovanni and his men came along."

Rachel suggests, "Bet you never thought you'd say that."

Keena responds, "His cockiness was good for something."

The team finally makes it to the jet. They hear a fire fight behind them. Boarding the jet, they take off immediately.

Flying over, they see the mobster's car and all their bodies strewn on the ground, including Giovanni's. The Drifter, just standing there, looks up and watches as his prey escapes their first encounter with him.

Now able to catch his breath, Shigeru, flying the jet says. "Well I suppose we should head to Germany, so we can begin finding a way into that castle."

Jon asks, "What about The Drifter?"

Shigeru replies, "That man is unstoppable. Only when we stop the Cabal will we not have to worry about him any more."

Rachel adds, "Yeah, no one to give orders, no orders to be followed."

After leaving Sicilian airspace, the group flies to a central region in Germany. Under the invisibility cloak provided by their experimental

Miyamoto Industries jet, the team is able to land in a clearing unnoticed by the Cabal.

"We're about 30 miles north of the entrance to the government land," Shigeru notes.

Rachel suggests, "Maybe we can hitch a ride to the edge of the forest.

Shigeru responds, "Yes, but we must be careful not to allude that we're going onto government land."

Jon says, "Okay, so we're just backpackers travelling through Europe then."

Shigeru replies, "Good idea."

When the group gets all of their camping gear together, they begin walking toward the main road that leads down to the forest.

After some time walking, a truck comes by and offers them a ride. The team loads up into the back of the truck and has the driver take them down to the dense forest's edge.

Chapter 32:

The Friendly Woodland Sprite

After thanking the truck driver for the ride, the team waits until no one can see them cross over the barbed wire fence with signs written in German telling civilians 'This is government land'.

Keena says, "Wow, after all we've been through, this mission has me the most anxious I've been yet."

Shigeru adds, "Well, we *are* going right for the heart of the Cabal here. And there's no telling what they have in this forest."

Jon asks, "How do we know there's no surveillance out here, or at the castle?"

Shigeru answers, "We don't. But it is highly unlikely that they would put much of anything technological out here that would give detection to their presence from overhead observation."

Rachel says, "All I know is that we made it this far as a team, and at least we have each other to count on."

The group continues into the forest and the farther they get away from the road, the darker it becomes.

After about a half hour of walking, the thick leafy branches overhead get so close together that light from the sun barely filters through.

Shigeru says, "Well, as dark as it already is, and it will be nightfall soon, we might as well go ahead and make camp using the little light we have."

Jon says, "I agree."

While the team prepares their camp, Keena starts to build a fire. Rachel sits down by her and says, "It's crazy how far we've come isn't it?"

Keena nods.

Rachel continues, "Do you think this could really be it if we were to catch the elite of the Cabal here?"

"I don't know," Keena says. "But it's definitely worth a try, right?"

"Yeah," answers Rachel.

The next day, the group rises bright and early. At least as bright as it could possibly be in the thick German forest.

Shigeru says, "Based on the coordinates from the jet's log, the castle should be due east from here. If we walk most of the day and rest this afternoon, we might be able to get to it late tonight.

Jon thinks to himself, "For being a sanctuary to the Cabal's dark rituals, this forest sure is nice and peaceful."

They walk the entire day, but begin to worry they are lost as late afternoon sets in.

"Dammit," Shigeru says. "At this rate, it will get dark and we may not make it to the castle in time. Or at all if we're lost."

Keena notes, "These woods never seem to end, they are so vast. We may never get out of here."

Jon suddenly notices a flicker of light just ahead of them.

"Look," he says.

"What is it?" Rachel asks.

"I don't know," Jon says. "But let's check it out."

The group walks over to the flickering light.

"It's like an orb, just floating against the wooded backdrop. Shigeru, do you know what this thing is?" Jon asks.

Shigeru, confused says, "I haven't a clue, guys."

Standing right in front of it, the team gets a better look at the small glowing orb.

Keena says, "No way! It's a tiny woman. A fairy?"

The group, stunned concurs.

"My God," Rachel says. "It is one."

"It looks like it wants us to follow it," Jon says.

"Are you sure we should?" Keena asks.

"What other option do we have?" Jon says. "I think we should. Think of it like this. With all of the evil things the Cabal has, *surely* something good is out there."

Reluctantly, Keena agrees with the others to follow the woodland sprite.

Nearly an hour passes. The group, still following the fairy, is getting tired of walking.

Shigeru says, "I trust your intuition Jon, but this little pixie is leading us on a wild goose chase."

Jon implores, "Hold on just a little longer. There has to be a reason for all of this."

The fairy starts picking up speed and gets out of sight of the group. Jon and the others start running to try and catch up to it before it goes completely out of sight. Then, just past the trees ahead, the team sees a road. The sides of the road are less dense with trees than the thick woods the group has become used to.

Shigeru says, "This must be the road that takes the members of the Cabal to the castle."

Keena says, "So by following it east, we should find it no problem then, right?"

Shigeru nods, "But we should stay off of it until dark, just in case someone comes across us. The ritual doesn't start until after midnight anyway."

The others agree and set up camp just out of view of the road so they can rest before they start trekking the rest of the way toward the castle.

After dark, the group prepares to move out. To lighten their load, they have left their camping gear just off the road. Stars are seen above in what is apparently a rather clear sky even though most of it is shielded from the team by trees. As they move down the road, fog begins to roll in slightly from the lower part of the woods onto the edge of the road.

Rachel, walking with her arms across her chest, notes, "This is getting kinda spooky now. I feel like we're in freakin Transylvania or something."

Jon says, "Yeah, no kiddin."

Although slightly spooked, the team is walking down the road rather leisurely. Shigeru and Keena are up ways from Jon and Rachel.

"What are we gonna do when we get to this castle Jon?" Rachel asks. "Will we even be able to get in? And if we do, how are we gonna stop the Cabal anyway? This all just seems so vague."

Jon, looking ahead while walking, acknowledges Rachel's concern.

"I know," he says. "But it's the best lead we've got."

Jon stops next to Rachel and looks toward her. She stops too.

"I know this has been a lot for you," Jon says to her. "I mean, you weren't exactly cut out for this lifestyle. Not that I was either though."

Rachel looks at Jon and says, "Really? Jon seriously, I don't need this damsel in distress stuff. I may not be a tough bitch like Keena, but I can handle myself in a lot of situations."

"Rachel," Jon says. "I didn't mean it like that."

Rachel crosses her arms again and starts walking forward as she continues speaking, "Really Jon, this is exactly the problem you had about me going to Greece."

Before Jon can respond, a large brown winged creature bursts from the trees to the left of the road and knocks Jon to the ground. Rachel turns around quickly, but the creature is already almost out of sight. Jon gets up and the two run to catch up to Shigeru and Keena. Before reaching them, they come across as small walking bridge in the road. The two run underneath it.

"What was that Jon?" Rachel asks.

Jon replies, "A bat-man!

"Bat-man?" she asks curiously. "You mean bat-man, as in the rich guy who lives in a mansion and fights crime by night?"

Jon says enthusiastically, "No, I mean bat-man as in its got wings and claws and sharp teeth and it's gonna get us!"

Right about then, Shigeru and Keena have walked back to see what's keeping Jon and Rachel.

"Shigeru!" Jon calls out in whisper. "Get down here."

Confused, Shigeru and Keena crouch near the ramp of the bridge to find out what's going on. Just then, the creature swoops by overhead, causing Shigeru to lose his balance and land on his rear. Keena hits the ground and crawls under the bridge with the others. Shigeru rolls over and does the same.

Underneath the bridge, Shigeru asks, "What the hell is going on?"

Jon says, "I don't know. Rachel and I stopped for a minute to talk and that thing just flew out and attacked me."

Just then, the group hears a thud above them on the bridge.

"Ssshhhh, it's up there," Jon says.

The group crouches in the underbelly of the bridge and listens as the creatures snarls and walks about above on the bridge. Just then, they hear another thud. A second one has landed on the bridge and is walking around. The team is stunned and doesn't know what to do. Just then, out in front of where the group is hiding, a third creature lands and starts walking around looking for them. The creature has sharp talons on its feet and stands about 6 feet tall. Brown with black shadings around its ears and wings, the creature looks more bat than man, having all of a bat's distinctive features.

As the group observes the creature's actions, they notice that it has no idea where they have gone to. Shigeru draws his pistol and begins to train it on the bat monster.

Jon whispers, "Wait!"

Shigeru says, "We might as well strike while they're distracted."

Jon continues, "Hang on a bit. I'm no zoologist, or cryptozoologist for that matter, but if they're anything like normal bats, they use sonar to seek out their pray."

"Huh?" Keena asks.

Jon goes on, "They don't hunt with sight, but with vibrational hearing."

Rachel exclaims, "That's right; when I was a kid in Southern Indiana, we would go out to the street at night and toss rocks in the air up to the tree line. It would make bats fly out and attack them."

Shigeru asks, "Okay, so how would that help us?"

Jon says, "Well as long as we're down here level with the ground, they can't hear our motions unless we are loud enough for them to pick up."

Keena suggests, "Maybe if we tossed rocks into the air, like Rachel said, it could confuse them enough for us to slip away."

Rachel says, "Yeah, but we don't know how many of them are out there. There's no telling how far we'd make it before running into more of them."

Just then, the other two bat-men hop down off the bridge next to the opening where the group is hiding. The creature's feet are just inches away from the team. Suddenly, all three of the creatures turn their attention back down the road from whence the team came.

Jon asks, "What are they doing?"

Keena says, "Look, they're leaving."

The three bat-men leap into the air and head down the road. A few moments pass, then a loud screech followed by gunshots is heard, then some more screeching.

Jon says, "Someone else is up there."

Silence falls again.

"What do we do now?" Rachel asks.

Then Keena says, "Listen. Someone's coming."

Down the road, out of the shadows, the team sees a man walking toward the bridge.

"Shit! It's The Drifter," Whispers Jon.

"Well he took care of the bats for us," Shigeru notes.

Rachel, shaken up, asks, "What if he finds us down here?"

Before anyone can answer, two more bat-men swoop down from the tree line on to The Drifter. Intercepting their attacks, he draws one of his revolvers and puts the creatures down without much effort. Opening his jacket up with one hand, he twirls the pistol and holsters it with the other. The Drifter, now only about 10 yards away from the bridge, stops and listens.

"What's he doing?" Keena asks, now with her gun ready in case they are discovered by The Drifter.

Just then, the group hears a sound behind them.

"Now what?" Rachel asks.

Jon recognizes that sound. "It sounds like...flapping."

The Drifter then crouches down in a defensive stance, drawing both pistols. The noise now louder than ever, can be heard descending onto the area surrounding the bridge. The Drifter opens fire into the air above the bridge as a swarm of the bat-men come into sight.

Jon says, "Come on. If we go now we can get away from The Drifter and the bats will be too busy going after him with all the commotion he's making."

Shigeru nods, "Right. Let's go."

The team stands up and runs out the back of the bridge in the opposite direction. About five bat-men have engaged The Drifter at close range. Running down the road, the team dodges bat-men flying past them in the direction of The Drifter, nearly hitting them as they pass. The group weaves in and out of the nearly three dozen bat like creatures swooping just overhead. Keena and Shigeru begin firing at the bats in an attempt to thin out their path. One of the creatures lands and makes a grab for Rachel. She screams as the monster grabs her by the shoulders. Jon rushes over and with one hand grabs Rachel by the arm and with the other, puts his snub nosed revolver to the bat-man's neck and fires. The creature jolts back and lets go of Rachel. Jon takes her under his arm and begins running to catch up with the other two. Aiming once more, Jon fires a shot at another beast, just before coming out of the swarm.

Looking back as the group continues down the road, Jon sees an overwhelming number of bats attacking the now out of sight Drifter. Not taking any chances, our heroes keep running so as to put as much distance between them and the threats they leave behind.

Chapter 33:

To the Heart of the Cabal and Into the Void

After running several miles down the road, the team finally stops to catch their breath. The screeches and gunshots from the fight can still be heard off in the distance.

Still catching his breath, Shigeru gasps, "Look. The castle."

The group turns their attention ahead to an area of the road no longer covered by the dense forest. A large clearing lies is ahead, with the castle at the center of it. Standing over four stories tall, the looming castle looks menacing underneath the starry night.

Shigeru says, "Come on, we better do this while The Drifter is still distracted."

Jon nods his head in agreement and the team moves forward to the small drawbridge over the moat at the castle's entrance.

"Well, this is it, Castle Richter," Jon says. "I suppose we go in and see what we find."

The group stands in front of the large open iron gate at the base of the old Germanic castle, unsure of what to expect once they enter.

Stepping into the dark castle, the team moves cautiously into the main hall. Once inside, they discover that torches line walls and the stairwell that leads up to the next floor.

Shigeru says, "I'm willing to bet that the Cabal will be meeting at the top of the main spire. It's a quarter after 11, so they will be starting the ritual soon."

The team makes their way up to the second floor. Once upstairs, they observe a maze of hallways that encompass the second level. Rich red carpets line the floor of the halls.

"Which way now?" Rachel asks.

Jon looks down one of the corridors.

"There's a door with a set of stairs down that hall," Jon says. "That's got to be the way."

The team looks down the hall to see a door with two large suits of armor facing inward on either side.

Keena asks, "How do you know that?"

Jon smirks. "There're torches lighting the way up," he says.

The team moves down the hall toward the door. Passing the imposing suits of armor, Rachel starts shaking nervously as she grips Jon's shoulder.

"I don't like this Jon," she declares.

"Relax," Jon says as the group passes by. "They're just suits of armor, it's not like they can hurt us."

No sooner than Jon finishes his statement, the two suits of armor come to life and lunge toward the team.

Falling back against the wall, Jon and Rachel dodge the swiping metallic hands of their attacker. The other haunted suit draws a sword and slashes at Shigeru as he reaches for his pistol. The second swipe knocks the gun out of his hand, and a third slash tears Shigeru's jacket. Keena, standing behind the suit attacking Shigeru, draws her pistol and fires at the ghostly armors back. With the clank of the bullets hitting and ricocheting off the armor, Keena realizes it's ineffective. Leaving Shigeru who is now down on the ground, the animated armor turns back toward Keena. It swings its sword, throwing her down to the ground, back against the wall. As the armor golem makes its way toward her, she fires again in an attempt to stop it. Running out of ammo, she drops the gun and leverages herself against the wall in order to kick the suit. Landing one foot on its chest, she kicks it with all her strength, knocking the suit of armor into pieces.

Meanwhile, the other suit has Rachel and Jon backed against the other wall. Jon pushes Rachel away as the armor bears down on him. Fighting from being crushed by its metal gauntlets, Jon is overpowered by the suit. Rachel, now on her feet, runs over and grabs the armor by the neck from behind. She crashes backward onto the ground, pulling the suit of armor with her. Now in pieces on the ground, the phantom suits of armor no longer pose a threat to the group.

"What were those things?" Keena asks.

Shigeru responds, "Must be some sort of haunting magic used by the Cabal to protect this castle."

Having overcome this recent attack, the group makes their way up to the next floor. Once upstairs, the team hears a noise.

"That sounds like a helicopter," Shigeru says.

Moving over to the window, the team sees a gated courtyard behind the castle. Two helicopters land side by side on a brightly lit helipad in the courtyard.

Jon says, "It's the Cabal. They're here. What time is it?"

Shigeru, looking at his watch, says, "Its 11:45."

Jon says, "Show time, the ritual will be starting soon. We need to get upstairs."

The team locates a staircase going up to the next floor and runs toward it in haste. Jon and Rachel, who are in the lead, reach the base of the steps. All of a sudden, a trapdoor opens beneath them, dropping them through. It closes immediately, leaving the others no time to react.

"Jon!" shouts Keena.

Shigeru too shouts, "Jon, Rachel. Are you guys all right?" as the two feel around the area of floor that swallowed Jon and Rachel.

A moment passes before Jon returns the call through the floor, "We're okay; it must have been some kind of booby trap to stop us from getting up there."

"Well, we can get past it now," shouts Shigeru.

"Go ahead without us. There's another staircase down here. It must be some kind of secret passage," Jon says.

"Are you sure?" Shigeru shouts back.

"Yeah," Jon replies. "We have to stop the Cabal at any cost."

"Okay, we'll see you up there," Shigeru says.

Moving up the stairs to the main spire, Shigeru and Keena prepare to complete their mission. Shigeru doesn't realize that the slash from the armor golem tore his jacket. As he runs, his satellite phone falls out onto the staircase. Too intent on stopping the Cabal, Shigeru doesn't even notice.

Finally, the duo reaches the top of the spiral staircase tunnel. They find a large door.

Shigeru looks at Keena and says, "Are you ready?"

Keena turns to him and says, "Whatever happens, I love you."

The two then draw their weapons and burst into the room. In the room, the two discover satanic decorations and dim lighting. In the middle of the room are a dozen men in black hooded cloaks starting their macabre fear gathering ritual. The men's faces are shrouded and cannot be seen. But the two realize that these men are members of the upper echelons of the Cabal. As the men turn to the intruders, Shigeru and Keena aim their pistols at them.

Shigeru says, "This ends today."

Before another moment passes, the shrouded men raise their hands and begin chanting. A rush of wind blows through the room. Shigeru and Keena open fire, dropping one of the veiled men to the ground. Lightning bolts begin streaking through the room, as a large black vortex opens up between the chanting men. Firing again, the duo's bullets are pulled straight into the void. With the wind picking up, sucking everything into the center of the vortex, Keena and Shigeru drop to the ground in order to avoid being pulled in. Helpless against the force of the wind, Shigeru and Keena grip each other in hopes to weigh one another down. Despite all their resistance, the two are pulled apart and cast off into the vortex. As the two disappear from sight into the abyss, the men stop their chant and the portal closes.

Meanwhile, down in the secret passage, Jon and Rachel sneak along the dark path in hopes of finding an exit. Coming up the steady incline of the cramped stairs, Jon and Rachel reach a dead end.

"Now what?" Rachel asks. "It's just a concrete wall."

"Hold on," Jon says. "There may be mechanism on the wall to open a hidden door."

Jon begins feeling around on the wall until finally a concrete brick slides inward. The wall cracks open.

"I love being an archaeologist," Jon says.

Rachel smiles at him as the two move through the passageway.

On the other side, the couple comes out from the secret passage into the same stairwell Keena and Shigeru took to get to the Cabal's ritual chambers. They waste no time heading up to assist the others.

As they run upstairs, Rachel notices something on the ground.

"Hey look," she says.

Picking it up, she realizes what it is. "It's Shigeru's satellite phone," Rachel notes as she hands it to Jon.

Jon says, "We can give it back to him later. Right now we just have to catch up with them."

Reaching the door of the ritual chambers the two burst in only to discover an empty room. No Shigeru, no Keena, no ritual. Confused, Jon looks around the room. In the corner, he discovers the injured man shot by Shigeru. The man is crawling toward an open floor panel.

Jon approaches, revolver drawn, and asks, "What happened here?"

The injured man laughs slyly. "It was a nice attempt to stop us," he says, "but the Cabal still will not be defeated so easily."

"Where're our friends?" Rachel asks sternly.

The man answers, "With our unlimited power, we opened a vortex to the nether world and sent your friends into oblivion."

"How can we get them back?" Jon asks.

"You can't," the man replies, "but sooner or later you'll join them in the abyss, if they last long enough for your arrival." The man laughs vilely.

"Oh yeah? Then I guess they'll see you in hell first," says Jon as he shoots the man mercilessly, finishing him off.

Rachel, a little shaken by Jon's reaction, says, "Come on, this panel must be the way out. We might still be able to catch up with the Cabal."

Jon puts his gun away and starts down the ladder found under the panel.

Once at the bottom, the two assess their surroundings. They find themselves in a large stable. Three limos are just driving away, exiting through the open barn door.

"That must be the other members of the Cabal leaving," Jon says.

The two then hear the helicopters taking off and flying away.

Standing alone in the stable, the two are confused as to what to do next. Then Rachel receives a jolt. "The Drifter!" she says. "Surely he's made it to the castle by now!"

Jon says, "You're right. We gotta get out of here."

Looking around, Jon notices an old World War II era motorcycle. The two approach it.

Rachel notes, "This thing can't possibly still work."

Jon says, "I don't know. It looks like it's been used recently."

Jon sits aboard the retro bike and begins to kickstart it. After a few tries, the engine turns over. Rachel hops on the back and they speed off out of the stable onto the road, leaving no chance for The Drifter to catch them.

As the two head down the road on the way out of the government protected land, Jon can't help but think. "Maybe Shigeru and Keena are just meant to fall through the cracks of destiny, just like many of the others we've come in contact with on this journey." Troubled by this, Jon continues driving out of the forest and back to the parked jet.

Once back at the jet, Rachel asks Jon, "Are you sure you can fly this thing Jon?"

Jon responds, "Yeah, it's really easy. Shigeru taught me how to do it in a flash. The controls on this thing are meant for anyone to be able to learn. And since it takes off from vertical propulsion, we don't have to worry about landing gear."

Rachel looks at Jon. "Do you think we can get them back?" she asks.

Jon sighs, "I don't know Rachel. But we're gonna try."

Rachel with tears in her eyes comes over to Jon and hugs him. "They've been the best companions we could ever ask for on this journey," she states. "I don't know if we can go on without them."

Jon holds Rachel, fighting back tears himself. "Come on," he says. "We better go before we're found."

The two then board the jet and take off.

Once in the air, Rachel asks, "Where do we go from here?"

Jon says, "I have a plan."

Holding up Shigeru's satellite phone, Jon explains, "I'm gonna contact Shigeru's sources and ask if they know anything at all that can help us."

After dialing the number, Jon awaits an answer.

The voice on the other end says, "Hello Shigeru, was the mission successful?"

Jon responds, "Negative, the mission failed."

The voice asks, "This isn't Shigeru, who is this?"

Jon hesitates then says, "This is Jon Peters. Shigeru isn't with us."

Chapter 34:

A Man Named Lao

Jon explains the events that just took place at the castle to the forces of light operator, and the conversation wraps up.

"I understand," Jon says. "Thank you. Goodbye."

Rachel sits across from Jon in the cockpit of the jet waiting for him to explain the plan.

Jon says, "There's a possibility to get them back."

"How?" Rachel asks.

Jon goes on, "Shigeru's sources told me that there is a group of mystics who have been hiding in Taiwan since the close of World War II. They may have knowledge on finding where Shigeru and Keena are and possibly how to get them back."

Rachel's eyes light up.

"They must be the Taoist priests Chief Crowfeather told us about," she says.

"Exactly," Jon replies. "We can only hope they can tell us what we need to know."

So, the two, alone for the first time since the beginning of this endeavor, head to Taiwan in hopes of getting the information needed to get their comrades back.

A few days later, after getting the coordinates from Shigeru's sources, Jon and Rachel touch down their high tech private jet at a secluded location in central Taiwan. Before even leaving the craft, through the windshield of the jet's cockpit, they see three modestly dressed Asian men approaching.

Rachel comments, "Well now, looks like they're certainly not afraid to welcome strangers."

Jon nods. "Let's go talk to them," he suggests.

The two lower the passenger ramp and exit the plane.

Once off the plane, one of the three men approaches, smiling from ear to ear.

"Greetings. My name is Lao," the man says. "We've been expecting you."

Jon, confused, looks over at Rachel to see an equal amount of bewilderment in her face.

"I'm sorry, expecting us, you say?" Jon cautiously asks. "You know who we are?"

The man calling himself Lao responds, "Well, not by name, but when one is in tune with one's surroundings to a certain degree, the arrival of guests can be sensed beforehand."

Jon and Rachel both try and take in what the man is saying.

Lao goes on to say, "It's been some time since we've had westerners as guests."

Rachel replies, "Oh forgive us. I'm Rachel and this is Jon."

Rachel slightly bows and offers Lao her hand in greeting. The man smiles even more graciously and accepts the handshake.

"So what brings you to us, Ms. Rachel, Mr. Jon?" Lao asks.

Jon answers, "We were directed here by allies of ours. They told us your people may be able to help us locate lost friends of ours."

"Ah!" Lao interrupts. "A friend in need is a friend indeed."

Jon, somewhat perplexed, smiles and agrees.

Lao continues, "We cannot show you the way to your friends. However, I believe we can show you the way to show you the way."

Jon absolutely confused at this point asks, "Is this a riddle?"

Rachel lightly slaps Jon on his chest with her knuckles and gives him a look.

"We are more than happy to receive any help offered," she replies.

Lao says, "Then come, back to our nature temple."

The two agree and follow Lao and his two Taoist companions.

On the way Jon asks the man, "How do you know English?"

Lao answers, "Years ago, I attended an international school in Hong Kong. It was a most pleasant experience."

Jon, still blown away by how chipper the Taoists seems to be, just shakes his head, smiles, and keeps following.

Finally, the group arrives at a large stone atrium, surrounded by well-maintained vegetation. Here they find over a dozen more modestly dressed Asian men, some gardening, some conversing. One man is sitting with a notepad and quill pen writing. The stone atrium appears to be surrounded by living quarters with the center being a place of communion.

Lao announces to the others in their native tongue that Jon and Rachel need help finding their lost partners. The men all the react to the news with as much excitement as Lao and the other two did when they first met Jon and Rachel.

Jon asks, "What is this place?"

Lao responds, "Well, for one, it is our home." He laughs then continues. "But, that's probably not what you were asking. This is our nature temple. It was established over half a century ago by fleeing priests from China. Those of us living here have dedicated ourselves to inner and outer peace. We act as priests to a local town and the surrounding countryside, offering everything from marriage counseling to financial advice. Sometimes, clear minds like ours can assess others whose situations are in dire straits. We are what you in the west might call, 'occupational therapists'."

Jon says, "Oh, I see."

Lao then says, "But enough about us. You are the ones in need."

Jon says, "Yes, what is it you can do to show us the way to the way, or whatever it was you said earlier?"

Lao replies, "Ah yes, the way. The way is the way to everything. Many study philosophy and ponder the way their entire life. Some sit and meditate on the way, and many have found it this way. Others seek the way outwardly. And it is possible to find the way like that as well. However, some seek the way at the expense of others."

Jon interjects, "Like the Cabal. Oh wait, I'm sorry; are you aware of the Cabal?"

Lao answers, "If you are referring to the ones who support the forces of darkness, then yes. It's a shame they fulfill their desires by the means in which they do. But they are way seers none the less as well. But again, we are off topic. You came here to find your friends."

"Yes," Rachel says. "And get them back if it's possible."

Lao smiles at Rachel and says, "By means of the Tao, all things are possible. I would like to invite you to partake in our local root leaf beverage tonight. It can grant you insights to your inner self and the unified consciousness."

Jon says, "Oh no. Memory water again?"

Lao reacts, "Memory water? If by that you mean the sacred water of Chief Crowfeather's tribe, then no."

Jon, in amazement that Lao knows of Chief Crowfeather asks, "You know of him?"

Lao responds, "*Of* him yes. I was just a boy when he visited the temple many years ago, but I am aware of his tribe. His journey was much like yours. It took him to and fro around the world, and for many years he refused to accept his role as the tribe's Chief. Until finally, he found what he was seeking and the seeking ceased."

Jon, interested, listens closely then returns his attention back to the root leaf, "So, if it's not like memory water, then what is it?"

Lao answers, "As I told you before, some seek through meditation the answers they want and this can take many years. But with the root leaf elixir, they can face their inner most selves and the universe from within, instantly. You will find your true self and the unified consciousness are but one thing. I warn you though. A person can only use the root leaf on occasion and in moderation. So whatever you have to ask the cosmos, you had better make it count. Too much exposure to the center of the universe will cause you to be engulfed by it and take you back into it from whence you came."

Jon says, "I understand. When can I take it?"

Lao answers, "Tonight."

That night, as the priests begin preparing the root leaf tonic for Jon's consumption, Rachel laughingly says, "It's not fair; you get to be the one that travels all the time."

Jon says, "Yeah, but I need you to take care of me again. After what happened last time I tried a psychotropic substance, there's no telling what might happen this time."

Rachel responds, "Awww, are you afraid you're going to need a 12-step program, Jon?" Rachel jokes in a pouty voice as she strokes the back of Jon's head.

Jon laughs and says, "Well, it looks like it's about time."

He points out that the Asian men are coming with a cup of the mystical elixir.

A man hands the cup to Jon and bows while smiling. Jon thanks him and stares at the liquid in the cup.

"Hmmm, smells kinda familiar," Jon notes.

Lao looks across the atrium center seating at Jon and says, "Good luck, Mr. Jon. May you find the answers you seek."

Jon holds up the cup in a toast and says, "Well, here's to psycho-holic slag." He drinks the liquid. "Oh wow," he says. "Tastes familiar too. That's like root beer. A really strong root beer." He chuckles. "A really *good* root beer.

He then takes another drink, but before he finishes, he faints and falls backward.

Chapter 35:

Jon's Inner Journey

Within moments of passing out, Jon wakes up, standing in what seems like an infinite room of nothing but white in all directions. There's a floor, but no ceiling or walls.

He says, "Well now, this *is* different than the memory water."

He then hears a familiar female voice. It's Rachel's voice. "Jon," the voice calls out.

"Huh?" Jon reacts. "Rachel?"

Just then, from out of the void comes Rachel.

Jon says, "Rachel, what are you doing here? Don't tell me you decided to drink the elixir too and are tripping with me now?"

"No Jon. I'm not really Rachel. I'm your higher self-coming to you as a guide that you would react positively to."

"Wow, really?" Jon asks.

"Yeah, really," Says Jon's higher self in the form of Rachel.

Jon laughs, "Well, you're just like Rachel."

The guide then says. "I'm going to show you some things before you can ask your question. Only by seeing these things will you raise your level of awareness enough to comprehend all of this and come out of it knowing it's not a dream. If you aren't able to sustain a certain level of awareness, your psyche won't process this experience on its way back into the world and you won't remember anything you've heard."

Jon, now serious, says, "Okay. Show me what I must see."

The guide raises her hand and suddenly, many different versions of Jon begin appearing in a circle around them.

Jon reacts, "Whoa! What's all this?"

The guide says, "These are various forms of yourself Jon. They make up the inner sanctum of your psyche. Think of them like your inner counsel in which decisions are made. You must take them all in and embrace their qualities and drawbacks in order to achieve unity. Only then can you consult the eternal source of the cosmos."

Jon, a little taken back asks, "Okay, how do I do that?"

The guide answers, "Simply turn around the room facing each one and take in what they represent."

"Alright then," Jon says.

He then turns and faces his first Doppelganger.

The other version of him says, "Jon, I'm your intellectual side. I'm the part of you that loves researching and teaching. Positively, I serve your instincts. Negatively, I overcrowd your mind and cause mental overload."

In no time at all, the apparition of Jon fades. Jon feels a jolt.

"Whoa! What happened?" Jon asks.

The guide responds, "You embraced your intellectual side and it is now brought to the forefront of your awareness."

Jon nods and turns to the next version of him.

This version says in a floaty voice, "Jon, I'm the part of you that is in love with Rachel. I help generate compassion in you, but my downfall is the reliance and dependency I can cause within."

The figure fades like the other and Jon feels another jolt.

"Hmmm, so far this hasn't been too bad."

The guide says, "Yes Jon, but those aspects of you are dominantly positive ones. Prepare yourself to face parts that you may have kept buried."

Jon turns and faces the third version of himself. This one is shaking frantically.

It mumbles, "I'm the version of you that's afraid Jon. Although at times I can help keep you in perspective, much of the time I block you from your true purpose."

The figure fades and Jon is jolted once again. This time, Jon breaks out into a frenzy.

"Oh my God. Oh my God!" he exclaims. "I'm finished. My career is over. My friends are gone. My parents are dead. I'm going to lose Rachel! Oh God!"

The guide then shouts, "Jon! Hold on. You must embrace *all* the aspects at once. Bring the first two to the forefront of your mind and the fear will be at bay."

A moment passes then Jon's anxiety subsides.

"Okay," Jon says calmly. "I'm in control again."

"Good," The guide responds. "Facing the others will be much easier for you now."

Moving on to the next one, Jon finds that this version of him is sitting with its head on its knees. It doesn't look up at him. Jon approaches it.

"Hey, what's wrong?" he says.

The Doppelganger looks up and in a dull voice says, "I represent depression in you Jon. Although I show the

240

humanity in you, I hold you back and prevent you from doing the projects you wish you would do."

Suddenly, the apparition morphs into a young preteen Jon sitting there.

Jon's inner child says, "We lost our parents Jon."

It starts to sniffle.

Jon leans down and holds the younger version of himself by the shoulders and says, "Hey, little Jon. It's okay. They may be gone, but look at who's new in our life. We have Rachel. And wonderful peers like Professor Gray. Oh! And friends like Keena and Shigeru. We have to get it together little Jon. To get them back. Together, we won't lose them like mom and dad."

Jon bends over and hugs his inner child. When he opens his eyes, the figure is gone and Jon stands up with a renewed resolve.

"Are you ready for the next one Jon?" the guide asks.

Jon, wiping a tear from his eye says, "Yes."

Turning to the next one, Jon notices the rage on its face.

"Okay, what do you represent?" he asks.

The figure responds angrily, "I'm the swelling anger within you Jon. I may come out only when you need it most, but I get the job done."

Jon asks, "Then what's your downfall?"

The angry Jon answers, "If I get too pissed off, I could become an absolute train wreck."

The figure fades like all the others and Jon feels the feelings he felt when Rachel was in trouble.

Turning over to the last apparition, Jon asks, "What could you possibly be?"

The final figure replies, "I'm an aspect of you that has yet to come out in your life Jon. I represent your sense of leadership. Part of me is connected to your intellectual side, like when you were teaching. And hints of me have come out through your loyalty to friends and your intuition."

Jon asks, "Okay, then what's your downfall?"

"My downfall is that you haven't really used me as a full aspect yet."

With these words, the apparition fades. Jon is left with only the Rachel look-alike guide standing behind him.

"How do you feel Jon?" she asks.

Jon ponders a moment then says, "Together."

The guide responds, "Good. Now you are ready to face the center of all that is."

Jon turns around to find the figure of Rachel gone. He looks around, but finds no one.

"Hello?" he calls out.

All of a sudden, a burst of wind, light, and electricity rushes from all directions into an enormous orb floating in front of Jon.

A bellowing voice then comes out of the orb, rippling sound waves past Jon.

"Hello Jon Peters," the voice says. "Congratulations for facing your inner self's counsel."

"Ummm, thank you," Jon says carefully.

"Do not be afraid Jon," the voice assures. "I am the center of all that is. The core of all creation."

Jon asks, "Are you God?"

The voice responds, "I am referenced by many. Some call me God, the Tao, the Great Spirit, the Force, the Q... I am that I am. I can influence destiny but never tamper. I neither control nor govern. Only create."

Jon, understanding, but blown away, asks, "Then you can help point me in the direction I need?"

The voice answers, "I already know what you seek. You seek the location of your friends."

"Yes, can you show me?" Jon asks eagerly.

A large rectangle then appears in mid air. Like a television screen, Jon is shown an image. The image is of Keena and Shigeru running through pure darkness, as if to escape something.

Jon, excited, says, "Then they are alive! So that's the nether world?"

The voice answers, "Yes. But they are in danger. Mortals from this world only can last so long in the nether world. The demons that inhabit it are fearsome. Shigeru and Keena have fared well because of their skill, but that won't be enough to keep them alive for much longer."

Jon assesses what he's been shown. Then he asks, "What can I do to get them back?"

The voice responds, "The only way to bring them back into this world is to open another portal to the nether."

Jon sighs, "But I can't do that. I'm not the Cabal. I don't know magic."

The voice says, "There is already a portal to the nether within the earth plane."

Jon asks, "How? Is it the Cabal's? Were they successful opening another vortex?"

The voice responds, "No. This portal was opened eons ago, by the ancients of your world.

Before the Cabal, when man studied all aspects of the universe. Then when demons found their way through, the ancients battled them off and sealed the vortex with an enchanted door that can only be opened from the side of the earth plane. The doorway has since been lost and forgotten."

Jon asks, "Where can I find it?"

The voice answers, "In the Himalayan Mountains, in a place where few dare to trek in modern times."

Jon's eyes light up, "Wait a minute. Is this portal the infamous doorway to the universe, Shambala?"

The voice responds, "It is one and the same. Go there and release your friends. When the door opens, they will know to go to it. But be sure to close the door before any demonic forces find their way through. Also, do not let anyone know the location of the door. If the Cabal finds it, they will use it for evil. Not even the demonic forces that they serve know the exact location of Shambala."

Jon asks curiously, "How will I know then?"

The voice tells Jon, "When you return to your craft, you will know. Your intuition will guide you. So it is willed by the way."

Jon smiles and says, "Thank you."

The ball of light that encompasses the voice begins to dissipate and Jon blacks out.

When Jon wakes up, he has a feeling of renewal in the presence of Rachel and the Taoists.

As he rises up, he asks, "How long was I out?"

Rachel, surprised, says, "You weren't. You fell back and then rose right back up."

Jon replies, "Huh? The memory water had me out for almost an hour. But hey! I know how to get the others back!"

Excited, Rachel shouts, "You do!"

Jon then explains his experience. When he tells Rachel about Shambala, she asks, "Is that the place I think it is? Didn't the Nazis send a task force to the Himalayas to find it?"

Jon says, "Yes, it's the same place. And we need to go right away because Shigeru and Keena won't be able to hang on much longer."

Lao, smiling, says, "Since you are going into very cold climate, we are more than glad to provide you with warm clothes."

Rachel replies, "Thank you, Lao."

Jon seconds Rachel, "Yes Lao, you've been more help than we ever could have imagined."

After gathering supplies for their journey, Jon and Rachel say their goodbyes to their newfound friends. With haste, the two fly off toward the Himalayan Mountains.

Chapter 36:

The Doorway to the Universe

Flying over the mountains, Rachel asks, "How do you know where exactly we're going?"

Jon replies, "I *don't* know. That voice just told me my intuition would show me where. My awareness has been sharpened greatly since coming out of that experience. I think this is an example of divine intervention."

Surveying the mountainscape through the windshield of the jet, Jon looks as if he knows precisely where they should land.

"Over there," Jon says, pointing outward. "That's the spot Rach."

Rachel looks down to see a flat spot on the edge of a mountain cliff.

"Alight," she says. "I guess we'll be walking from there then."

Jon lowers the plane down to the clearing. The two suit up and begin their trek into the snowy ranges of the Himalayas.

Suddenly, Jon says, "Hey, go take a look up ahead for me. I have something I wanna check out on the jet before we head out."

Rachel replies, "Okay," then heads over to the edge opposite the cliff side the jet is parked on.

Looking down below, she sees what appears to be a snow covered path going through a ravine. After bundling herself a little tighter, she takes a look through her binoculars to get a better look. Through the scope of the binoculars, she confirms that it is in fact a path. Just before taking down the binoculars from her eyes, she sees something move quickly through the sights. Rachel looks through the binoculars again to see what it was. She looks around, but there is nothing. Turning back toward the jet, she goes to tell Jon about the path. Seeing that he still hasn't come out of the jet, she calls out to him as she approaches, "Jon, are you ready yet?"

Jon comes down the loading ramp and closes it on the way out.

"Yeah, sorry, I just had to take care of something," he says.

Rachel goes on to say, "I think I spotted a path. If you're right about this being the place, then it could lead to Shambala."

Jon responds enthusiastically, "Great! Let's get going then."

The two head down to the path Rachel saw down in the ravine.

As the two walk on, Rachel says, "Ya know, when I was looking down here, I could have sworn I saw something move."

Jon suggests, "Hmmm, maybe there's wildlife up here."

Rachel responds, "I don't know about that. I mean, what could live up here at this altitude?"

Just then a large, white furry creature lunges out and attacks the two, throwing them back off of their feet. Standing over eight feet tall, the large hairy monster lets out a death curdling roar. Jon reaches for his pistol. The beast crouches down toward them and begins swinging its arms at the couple lying on the ground. Jon fires several rounds into the chest of the creature. Finally, it drops to the ground and ceases to roar.

Panting, Rachel brings herself back up to her feet. "My God Jon!" she says after she catches her breath. "I think that thing is a Yeti!"

Jon takes a closer look. The creature has large paws with claws and sharp teeth.

"I think you're right Rachel," he says. "Given the circumstances we are currently in, it's no surprise. But this just adds to the unlimited list of enormous discoveries that could be made public if not for impending threat to the state of the world."

Rachel nods and says, "At least we have heard about the Yeti. I don't know *what* in the world those bat-men were."

Moving on up the path, the two reach another cliff side.

Jon sighs and says, "Well, I guess we just have to follow it around and continue the way we were going."

The couple continues walking around the mountain with only a few feet between them and the edge. Rachel looks down and away quickly out of fear of falling. Finally, the two come around the corner to a more open area. The edge is still within sight. But opposite it, the mountainside has a very large cave entrance.

Rachel asks, "Jon, what do you think? Could that be the entrance?"

Jon answers, "I have a feeling it is. Let's go check it out."

Before they can reach the mouth of the cave, a second Yeti rushes out from inside, wailing and flailing its arms around. Jon reaches for his pistol once again, but the beast knocks it out of his hands with its intense slashing. Jon and Rachel run to the edge of the mountain.

There is an endless drop below them. The Yeti moves slowly toward them. Rachel puts her arms around Jon as the creature looms over them. Jon looks back and notices a small ledge just below the cliff side.

Jon says to Rachel, "Hold on and trust me."

As the Yeti makes its final charge toward the couple, they fall backward off the edge in each other's arms. Landing on the tiny ledge, the couple is safe out of the creature's grasp. Losing its balance from the charge, the Yeti falls off the edge hitting its foot on the small ledge Jon and Rachel landed on. The monster's roar can be heard fading into silence as it drops off the mountain.

Getting back on to their feet, Jon and Rachel climb their way back up to the larger ledge. Jon retrieves his revolver before the two proceed back into the cave.

Not too far inside the cave entrance, Jon and Rachel see an enormous wooden door at the end of the tunnel. Red, with gold trim, the door is sealed with wooden planks securing large metal clamps. Off to the side, the two see a pulley system supported by scaffolding.

Jon says, "That must be how to open the door."

As the two begin rotating the gears to the pulley, Rachel asks Jon, "How are Shigeru and Keena going to know where the door is once we open it?"

Jon answers, "I'm not sure. The voice just told me they'd know how to find it and to shut it once they come through so nothing else gets out."

With the planks now lifted, Jon and Rachel go to open the door.

Jon looks over at Rachel and asks, "Are you ready?"

She responds, "I'm here ain't I?"

The two open the large double set of doors. Inside, they see what seems like infinite darkness. Suddenly, they hear footsteps running toward them through the darkness inside. Shigeru and Keena come running out into the light.

"Shigeru, Keena!" shouts Rachel.

Before Jon even suggests it, Shigeru and Keena begin shutting the doors. Rachel and Jon run back over to the pulley gears to close the locks. Just as they come down, a loud thud is heard on the other side. It is as if something is trying to get through.

"What happened in there?" Jon asks.

Shigeru, nearly out of breath, responds, "You don't wanna know. It was a living nightmare in that place."

Keena adds, "Yeah, I don't know how we survived. We only have about a clip's worth of ammo left each."

Rachel asks, "How did you know where the door was?"

"A fairy," Shigeru replies. "Like the one we saw in the forest. It came to us and told us it could take us to the way out and that you'd be coming to open it. It didn't explain how it knew."

Jon smiles and says, "Divine intervention."

"Huh?" Shigeru asks.

"Never mind, we'll explain later," Jon says. "Right now we need to get out of here. You guys aren't dressed for this place. Good thing we're parked not far from here."

As the newly reunited team starts out of the cave, two more Yetis run in from the entrance. Jon, Keena, and

Shigeru draw their weapons and fire at the beasts until they drop.

"I'm out," Shigeru declares, looking at his empty gun.

Keena says, "Me too."

Jon adds, "That's it for me too."

Shigeru notes, "Jeez, I don't know if it's worse out here or in there. Hopefully we can get back to the jet before something else happens."

Moving quickly back down the path, the team tries to get back to the jet before nightfall and the cold gets to Keena and Shigeru.

After climbing up to the cliff side the jet is parked on, Jon says, "Okay guys, it's just around the corner of this mountain."

The group walks around the rock wall, but before taking another step, they come to a halt at the sight of what's awaiting them. Between them and their jet parked near the edge of the mountain, a man is standing, awaiting the team's return. The man is none other than The Drifter. Not bothering to reach for their weapons due to lack of ammo, the team just stands there speechless.

The Drifter takes a few steps toward them and says, "Well now, not in any rush to leave are ya?"

With his hands in the pockets of his duster, The Drifter doesn't bother arming himself.

"Judging by the fact that you are not shooting at me, I'll take it you all are unarmed," he says.

Jon asks, "Why do you have to do this?"

251

"Have to?" The Drifter repeats. "I don't *have* to do anything. Need to? Maybe. Want to. Now that's more my style."

The Drifter starts pacing around very slowly while talking, and the team just looks on and listens.

"Twice ya'll have escaped me by distraction. People have gotten away from me before. But I always catch up to them eventually. No one escapes me. It doesn't seem like there's much way out here to distract me from ya'll this time, does it?"

The Drifter stops and looks at the group.

"I tell you what." he says. "Since ya'll have given me a real run for my money, and you're unarmed, I'm gonna turn around, and give you to the count of three before I draw my six guns and finish my mission."

The Drifter turns and takes a few steps back toward the jet, stopping about seven feet away from it. He then begins counting, "One!"

Jon notices how close to the jet he's standing.

"Two!" The Drifter counts.

Jon then reaches into his pocket and pulls a small cylinder out. Just before The Drifter finishes his count, Jon depresses a button the cylinder and says, "Three."

*BOOM! *

The jet explodes into a massive fireball, rocking the mountain and throwing The Drifter on to his back. The blast causes the cliff side to collapse off of the mountain, taking the destroyed jet and The Drifter down with it. The others lower their arms from protecting their faces in time to see the edge fall straight down the mountainside.

Shigeru asks, "Whoa! What was that Jon?"

Jon shows him the device in his hand and says, "It's a self-destruct protocol detonator for the jet. I read about it in the computer after I turned the text translator

252

on. My intuition told me that something might try and get between us and the jet, so I grabbed it in case I was right."

Rachel says, "So that's what you were doing when I was looking down at the ravine."

Jon replies, "Uh Huh."

"Why didn't you tell me?" Rachel inquires.

Jon replies, "I didn't want you to be alarmed. Hell, it could have just been my mind playing tricks on me."

The group all shares a laugh. Then Keena says, "Okay guys, The Drifter's gone, but now how the hell are we gonna get out of here? I'm already starting to freeze."

Jon smiles and says, "Ah Ha!"

Reaching into his pocket, Jon pulls out Shigeru's satellite phone and hands it back to him saying, "I believe this is yours, my friend."

Shigeru smiles and takes it back. "Thanks Jon. With this, we can call for a ride." Shigeru goes on to say, "We can't thank you enough guys. Not only did you save us, but you two showed that you can handle things by yourselves when necessary."

Shigeru then calls his sources and the team waits for a helicopter to be sent out.

Chapter 37:

Sister and Brother Down Under

After being picked up by a Chinook helicopter provided by the forces of light, the group reflects on their most recent endeavors. Shigeru then makes contact with his sources to learn the team's next move.

Shigeru, getting off the phone, says, "Okay, gotcha, Goodbye. Okay, guys. Here's the deal. This chopper was sent out from a very strong resistance group in Australia, known as the Sydney Underground."

Keena cuts in, "Like the Dublin Underground?"

"Yes," Shigeru says. "Except, more organized and with larger numbers. The high command of the unified forces of light is devising a plan, even as we speak, to strike at the Cabal one last time. Because of our recent accomplishments, they want us to help execute it."

Shigeru looks at the others with a smirk on his face, "They want us to come to headquarters to meet with them." He goes on, "I myself have never been there before."

Jon says, "So I guess this mission is of the utmost importance then."

Shigeru nods.

Rachel asks, "Where are the headquarters located?"

Shigeru responds, "I don't know. But we're not going there yet. They need more time to strategize against the Cabal. In the meantime, they want us to help the Sydney Underground with a mission. Afterwards, they will take us to the headquarters."

Jon asks, "So now we go to Australia?"

"Yes," Shigeru says. "They'll debrief us on the mission when we arrive."

So flying down from the Himalayan Mountains, the team makes their way to Sydney, Australia, to make their next move against the forces of the Cabal.

Once they have landed in Sydney, the group is taken to a warehouse on the coast where they meet the leaders of the Sydney Underground. Bill and Layla, brother and sister, have run the Sydney Underground since its unification. Their father, who made connections with the forces of light just after the Vietnam War, was killed several years ago by an assassin sent by the Cabal.

Bill says, "Glad to have you all aboard. We've heard you've been making some serious waves in our struggle against the Cabal."

Jon replies, "Yes, we came very close to stopping several of their members last week in Germany. Although we didn't stop them, we did eliminate one of them and disrupted their fear gathering ritual."

Layla, smiling, says, "You are just the type of blokes we're looking for then."

Rachel asks, "What exactly is it you need us for anyway?"

Layla asks, "Are you familiar with the techno pop sensation, Alice Malice?"

Rachel, with a confused look on her face, responds, "Yeah, the slutty acting party girl who can't decide on a hairstyle and changes outfits every ten feet. What does she have to do with anything?"

Layla answers, "Come with us to the office and I'll explain on the way."

So the group follows Bill and Layla to the warehouse office and on the way, they are filled in on the pop star's mysterious involvement.

Layla continues, "Alice Malice is one of the highest agents in the Cabal's brainwashing programs. From her appearance and through her music videos, she provides subliminal hypnotic suggestions to her fans. The small suggestions affect the brain on a subconscious level and cause fear and confusion to be the dominant activity. This is why many young girls who follow pop stars engage in depraved behavior long before their adolescent minds should even be able to understand things. It also fuels adult men with pedophiliac tendencies to act upon their thoughts. In a nutshell, Alice Malice and many other pop stars start a chain reaction through the masses to help encourage the fear that the Cabal thrives on. Our plan is to expose her to the world to help tear down some of these blinding walls they've put up."

Rachel asks, "But how can we expose her?"

The group arrives at the door to the office and walks in. Inside is a projector, prepped to screen some clips for the team.

Bill says, "Come in, sit down. We have some things to show you."

The group sits down and begins watching a clip. It's a music video for one of Alice Malice's hit songs. In the video, she's stark naked in the bathtub with a large butcher knife. She slits her throat while singing and blood begins spraying violently all over the room. It runs down her body and fills the bathwater bright red. The camera pans around and blood, spraying from her neck, hits the lens of the camera.

Jon comments, "Whoa! Death Metal bands don't even get like this."

Bill chuckles and says, "Death Metal bands aren't widely affecting the world population at a subconscious level like she is either."

Layla says, "We've obtained secret records of Alice Malice's programing. To a large extent, she's not even fully aware of what she's doing. I suspect the same of most other pop stars."

Bill begins rolling the next reel. The team watches as they see Alice from her early teens go from a talented contest winner, singing songs that were popular in her youth, to her own personal programing sessions. There is also documentation of the social engineering sound bites that were put into her album tracks.

Next on the reel, the group is shown footage of Dark Occult magic users planning the themes of her music videos.

Rachel notes, "It's a shame. Her music isn't half bad either. Too bad she's puppeteered by the most evil congregation to have ever existed."

Jon says, "Impressive. It's all here. Everything needed to expose her. But how are we going to get it out? Are you planning to take over a television syndication?"

Bill responds, "No, even better."

Layla turns the lights back on and explains. "Because of the reconstruction effort in America, FEMA has put on a benefit tour to help send relief aid. The first and one of the largest tour dates is scheduled next week, here in Sydney."

Keena interjects, "I get it, we're gonna crash that concert and expose her right on stage aren't we?"

Bill says, "Bingo."

Shigeru asks, "That show is going to be massive. Do we have the manpower to pull a job like that off?"

Bill replies, "Listen here mate. Layla and I have nearly 40 available members of the underground here in Sydney alone that can help pull this off. With your help, we can make it happen."

Jon claps his hands and says, "Sounds great. What's the plan?"

Bill answers, "We still have to work a few kinks out. But now that we know we have your help, we can pull the rest of the plan together in the next day or so. Right now, you all need to rest. I understand it's been quite rough for you the last few weeks."

Rachel responds, "The last several months have been very rough."

After settling into their tiny bunk rooms at the far end of the warehouse, Rachel rolls over in bed to face the door to the room.

Jon turns toward Rachel's back and puts his arm around her. "Rachel," he says. "I know it's been rough, but you do deserve credit for hanging in this long. I couldn't possibly have made it this far without you. You've truly been my motivation to keep going."

Rachel sighs and says, "I know Jon. I just wish there was more I could do physically to help take down the Cabal. It seems like when all the action is going on, I just hang in the background. I mean, what if something happened to you? I feel like it would be partly my fault for not doing anything."

Jon laughs and says, "What about that suit of armor back at the castle? You took that thing down, and it was about to get me."

Rachel, now with a few tears in her eyes, laughs a little too and turns to face Jon in the tiny bunk they share. "I love you Jon. When this is all over, I think we're gonna be just fine this time around."

Jon replies, "I love you too Rachel. I just hope this is all over soon."

The next night, the team is called back to the office to review the plan with Bill, Layla, and various other members of the Sydney underground. Bill displays a map of the concert site on the projector.

"The concert is an outdoors one of course," Bill instructs. "The main stage is located here. In the back are four sound towers. Now if we can pull this off, hundreds of thousands of people present will be exposed. And the televised showing will reach millions. Within a few days, billions."

Jon asks, "What if the Cabal pulls the plug on the feed? They control the media, so how do we know we'll be able to stay live?"

Bill responds, "Good question. A van with our best hackers will be parked just outside the venue. They can access the controls to all the transmitters and satellites around the world. Since it will be broadcast by multiple media outlets, they can keep a few running if the Cabal manages to have any shut down. Also, a squad of about a half a dozen men will be outside the van to prevent them from being subdued."

Jon and Shigeru look at each other and nod in agreement.

Bill continues, "Moving right along. We have nearly two dozen men who will be strategically placed as concert security through the venue. So the physical take over and securing of the premises should be rather smooth. In each of the four sound towers, I'm placing a man to observe the crowd to warn us of any surprises. When we enter from the rear of the stage and the front entrance, we'll have about 10 men to help keep people from exiting through the main gate. Backstage, Layla and I will take a squad to detain the stage crew. Keena, you and a handful of our boys will secure the stage and keep the audience at bay from there. Shigeru, your job will be to capture and hold Alice Malice. I can't stress enough the importance of getting her."

Shigeru nods understandingly.

Bill goes on, "Jon, because of your history and charisma, your job will be to go out on stage and present the information to the world. You can go armed, but your primary focus should be educating the people."

Jon agrees, "Right, I can handle that, no problem."

Rachel chimes in, "Well, what about me? Is there anything I can do?"

Bill replies, "Don't worry Rachel, we didn't forget you. Your job will be as vital as Jon and Shigeru's. Here, in the center of the audience standing area is a projector and lighting building." Bill points to a square near the center of the map. "It can only be accessed by tunnel, going under the crowd. The entrance is back stage, so you'll be going in with the rest of us. I'm sending you with four of my best men to secure the projector. From there you will replace Alice's concert reel with our footage of her expose'."

Jon says, "Everything sounds, fine. So show time is in four days?"

Bill responds, "Right, if we pull this off, it could be the change in the tide of people's minds for good, and the Cabal will have less grasp over them than they've have had in nearly a century."

Chapter 38:

The Fame Monster

The morning of Alice Malice's relief concert arrives. Just before the teams ready themselves prior to heading out, Layla approaches the group with a radio for Rachel.

Layla says, "We will be communicating by code names via these walkie-talkies. Bill is Mother Goose. Our man in the van is Black Canary. The head of the team out front is Blue Jay. The four men on the towers are Bird's Eye 1 ,2, 3, and 4. And you're Hummingbird, Rachel. Since we'll be within earshot of Jon and the others on stage, they won't need a radio. Keep chatter to a minimum once we commence, but give us a progress report."

Rachel looks at the radio and nods. "Right," she says.

Bill walks in and claps his hands. "Alright everyone," he says. "Let's move out. We've got a Horror Queen to take down today."

The team loads up into their vans and head out.

On the road, Bill says, "We won't strike until near the end of Alice's first song. The crowd will be fully fired up by then. Security that's not our guys will be busy, so no one will notice our infiltration."

Arriving at the back of the concert site, the team can already hear the roar of thousands of Alice's fans shouting as they wait for the show to begin.

Layla hands Bill the walkie-talkie and he says, "Mother Goose to Black Canary, is everything in place?"

A moment passes, then the man in the hackers van responds, "This is Black Canary; all is quiet on the western front."

Bill calls again, "Mother Goose to Blue Jay, prepare to secure the main gate."

The man responds, "This is Blue Jay, operation underway."

Layla says, "Alright everyone, let's move."

The team gets out of the van and begins making their way to the gate behind the stage. Two security guards approach; nodding to Bill they open the gate and let the group in.

Just before they reach the steps, the radio goes off. "Mother Goose, this is Bird's Eye 3, Alice is taking the stage now."

Bill responds, "Copy that Bird's Eye 3."

A moment later, the crowd is heard cheering and clapping as the intro to Alice Malice's first song comes on.

Now out on stage, Alice waves to her fans on the sunny South Pacific day that may very well be her final concert. Wearing what looks like a black one piece bathing suit with silver lightning bolts down the side, her voluptuous figure is enough to drive anyone observing her go wild. Her snowy white hair falls sleekly down to the sides of her arms and her shoulder blades. She has black, blue, and silver eye shadow painted from her eyes up to her brow. She is bare from her hips down to her ankles with black leather shoes covering her feet.

Out on stage with the mic in her hand, Alice Malice begins her first song.

Backstage the team starts rounding up and detaining the stage crew. Bill locates the access panel to the tunnel over to the projector building. "Down here Rachel," he says.

Rachel runs over with the reel in hand.

Jon shouts, "Wait!"

Rachel turns around. Jon kisses her and wishes her luck. She responds, "You too Jon." Then she descends into the tunnel with the four Sydney underground elite assigned to her.

Bill closes the tunnel entrance and says, "Okay, Layla is securing the sound board so we can keep the show going to continue the facade that everything is normal. As soon as we hear from Rachel, you guys will take the stage." Bill grabs his radio and says, "Black Canary, this is Mother Goose, commence hack."

"Aye Aye, Mother Goose," the man responds.

Bill nods and says, "Only a matter of time now."

Rachel and the men making their way down through the tunnel encounter a staff member. The elite members overpower and tie him up in the tunnel before continuing forward. Finally, they reach the door to the projector room. The men burst through the door and secure the conductors in the room. The men begin tying up the controllers while Rachel preps the projector. Once everything is in place, she grabs her radio. "Mother Goose, this is Hummingbird," she says. "We're ready here."

Bill looks at the others and pulls the radio up to his mouth. He replies, "Good job Hummingbird, watch for our signal to begin the reel."

Looking out on the stage, Rachel sees Alice moving around like a wild animal, flaunting herself amorously to the crowd. As she finishes her hit song, the others prepare to storm the stage. She sings, "I stab your heart, you stab my back. Its love and feelings that we all lack.

You've given your all, I've driven you off. Now it's me you see, all full of glee. It's been my pleasure here, watching you bleed."

Bill now gives Jon and the others the signal to make their move. Like a flash, Keena and five members of the underground run past Alice to the edge of the stage, weapons drawn and aimed at the crowd.

Alice exclaims, "What the hell is going on?!"

Shigeru follows quickly and grabs Alice by the arm. He pulls her in close to his side and presses his gun to her temple. She struggles at first but soon gives in. Jon walks out on the stage with his revolver in one hand. Approaching Shigeru and the detained pop star, he takes the microphone from her hand. The crowd, confused, starts booing, and various screams are heard throughout the audience.

Jon says, "Listen up everyone. This is all a masquerade. Alice Malice is a part of a massive deception. You have all been warped.

Most of the crowd starts listening.

Jon goes on to say, "We have evidence here to show you the truth."

Rachel takes that as the signal and begins rolling the reel, exposing the subliminal programing of the Cabal's brainwashing engineers. As the people watch, their anger turns to cheers. The people start clapping, and shouting, "Yeah! Yeah!"

Confused, the team on stage begin looking at one another.

Keena shouts, "What's going on Jon?"

Jon replies, "They're so warped, they think this is part of the show."

Shigeru says, "Everyone's so used to her depravity. They think this is another stunt of hers."

Alice begins to smile, "Ah! I live for their applause. They love me and my magnificent talent," she gloats.

Shigeru yanks Alice in closer and cocks his gun. "Can it lady," he says.

The short petite pop star stands only about five foot four and is towered over by the six foot two Japanese man.

The video continues, and gets to a part that shows Alice's unwillingness to commit heinous acts willingly. She is shown going through a process of being brainwashed and then being rebranded to be a more fitting pop star. Alice looks at the video in surprise and awe as if she was unaware of how she was treated. She mutters, "No. It can't be. No!" She cries.

Jon gazes at her, noting she is in genuine pain on realizing her hidden past. Jon shakes himself out of it and turns his attention back to the crowd once the video stops. "You must see now," he says. "This is not part of the show. This is your reality being altered by dark powers."

Backstage Bill radios to the men in the sound towers. "Bird's Eyes, this is Mother Goose. Check in and give a report on your observations."

The radio responds, "This is Bird's Eye 4, everything's secure here."

Then the next man answers, "Bird's Eye 3, all clear."

And then, "Bird's Eye 1 here, everything looks under control."

The radio is silent. Bill waits for another response. Nothing.

Bill speaks into the walkie-talkie again. "Bird's Eye 2, what is your report?"

No answer.

"Bird's Eye 2, this is Mother Goose, why aren't you responding?" he asks again.

Bill looks at Layla and says, "Something's wrong."

Chapter 39:

An Unlikely Fan

Jon, still talking to the crowd, has gotten their undivided attention again, "Everyone, not just you here, but everyone at home. Around the world, we are being manipulated by a monolithic and ruthless conspiracy. Its hierarchy relies on covert means for expanding its sphere of influence. It uses infiltration instead of invasion for its conquests, subversion via corporate power instead of elections, and intimidation instead of free choice."

Rachel watches from the view of the projection room, as the crowd continues to listen. Then suddenly, a gunshot is heard. A bullet strikes one of the lighting rigs above the stage. The stage light comes crashing down next to Jon, interrupting his speech. The crowd screams and hunkers down, but no one can leave because of the Sydney Underground's blockade of the gates. Everyone backstage is shocked.

"What happened?" Bill shouts. "Where'd that shot come from?"

One of the men on stage turns up and aims his gun at the second sound tower and fires but is hit and killed by another shot.

Jon quickly looks up at the tower. As his eyes travel upward, he sees the missing member of the underground with his throat slit, hanging by one leg from the tower by a cable. Looking up further, in the nest of the tower, he sees a man with bright yellow sunglasses and a cowboy hat holding a scoped rifle.

Jon murmurs, "The Drifter, it can't be."

Bill, from backstage, radios, "Bird's Eyes 1, 3, and 4. Remove the threat from tower number two, immediately!"

Before the men can even react, The Drifter, with his rifle still trained on the stage, leaning over the balcony, draws one of his six guns from his coat with his left hand. Aiming under his right arm, he fires two shots, taking out the men in towers 3 and 4. Extending his arm outward to the left, he fires again, eliminating the man in the first tower. Never taking his eyes off the scope, he twirls his six gun and drops it back into the holster within his jacket.

Jon steps closer to Shigeru, still gripping Alice Malice. Keena at the edge of the stage backs up as well. The other men soon follow.

Jon shouts, "Drifter, wait!"

The Drifter, with his sights trained on Jon shouts down back to him, "And why should I do that?!"

Jon shouts, "Because! We have Alice!"

Shigeru joins in shouting, "You may wanna ask your employers if it's okay to let her die here today with us!"

The Drifter shouts back, "I ask no one! What does it matter to me if she dies?! I can shoot right through her and take you out with her, Yakuza!"

Jon responds, "That may be so. But she's one of the Cabal's greatest assets! They may not be too happy about you letting her die!"

The Drifter, discouraged, snarls and says, "Argh! Okay, what's your offer?!"

Jon says, "If you let us go, we'll leave her here. You can always hunt us another day! But to end it badly today will surely piss the Cabal off!"

Looking from backstage, Bill gets a better look at The Drifter.

"Wait a minute," he says.

Layla asks, "What is it Bill?"

Bill answers, "That's the bastard that killed Dad!"

Before Layla can respond, Bill runs out on stage, gun in hand."

Layla shouts, "Bill, no, wait!"

Out on stage, Bill fires up toward The Drifter's location. The first few shots miss, but the third grazes the top of his rifle anchored left forearm. The Drifter turns his aim over to Bill and shoots him in the left shoulder, dropping him to the stage floor.

"No!!!" Layla screams, before rushing out to the stage to help him.

Rachel says, "Oh my God! Let's go. We have to help them."

She and the four elite underground men leave the projector and run down the tunnel back toward the stage.

The Drifter, looking at the brother and sister on stage says, "Hey! I know you two! You're the brats belonging to that Aussie rebel I killed some years back!"

Bill lying back, holding his wound, shouts, "You should have killed *us* back then too!"

The Drifter laughs and says, "I didn't wanna waste my bullets on teenaged weaklings."

Just then a helicopter flies over and from its loudspeaker, a voice addresses them, "This is the Australian Defense Force! Cease and desist your activities now! Lay down your arms and await apprehension by our ground forces! You are all enemies of the state!"

Rachel and the others have now made it out on stage.

"Now what Jon?" she says.

Jon thinks for a moment, and then says, "I have a plan. Layla, give me the radio." Jon grabs it from her and begins talking. "Black Canary, abandon your post, the mission has changed. Blue Jay, open the gates and let everyone out, mix in with the rushing crowd to escape the military."

Keena says, "Good thinking Jon. The chaos of the crowd should shroud our escape."

The Drifter looks outward toward the encroaching army outside and says, "Damn!" Throwing his rifle over his shoulder, he grabs a rope on a pulley and slides down into the fleeing crowd.

Shigeru, noticing that The Drifter has disappeared into the audience, throws Alice Malice down to the ground and runs over to help Layla and Keena pick up Bill and escape through the backstage.

Jon says, "Okay, here's the deal. Let's get to the vehicles and split up. If anyone feels as though they're being followed, divert off route until you can shake 'em before coming back to the warehouse."

As people trample and fight their way out the front, the stage crew, now released by the underground, runs wildly across stage to escape as well.

Keena, Layla, and Shigeru help Bill get to the van out back while the other members of the Sydney Underground rush to their vehicles.

Alice Malice sits crying on the edge of the stage, perplexed by the events that have just transpired and the horrid truth she just learned about her past. Just when she's about to give up, someone stands over her and offers their hand to her. Alice, with mascara running down her face looks up to see Rachel kneeling down to her with her hand out.

Rachel says, "Hey, come with us. It's okay. The world we wanna make has a place for you in it too."

Alice sniffles and replies, "Really, even after all the hell I've caused?"

Rachel smiles and says, "The new world can't exist without part of the old one. Besides, you were manipulated and deceived, just like all of us."

Jon looks back across the stage and shouts, "Rachel, come on, we've *got* to go!"

Alice looks up and reaches out to take Rachel's hand.

"Thank you," she says.

The two rush off backstage and escape with the others.

After returning to the warehouse used by the Sydney Underground, the team regroups and celebrates a long awaited victory. Champagne bottles are popped and joyous commotion is heard all through the warehouse. Bill approaches Jon and Rachel, with his shoulder bandaged and his arm in a sling and says, "Thank you both, without you, Shigeru, and Keena, we couldn't have pulled this off. This is the first major victory we've had against the Cabal. The number of people woken up by this must be huge."

Rachel adds, "Yes, and those who weren't woken up have now been seeded with the concept of their controllers' existence."

Just then, Layla emerges from the crowd of celebrating rebels. She approaches them and says, "I owe you Jon. Not just for your efforts against the Cabal but also for saving my brother."

Bill concurs, saying, "Yes, I am thankful you saved my life, but I wish we could have killed that son of a bitch for what he did."

Jon smiles and says, "You're welcome, but that man is an unstoppable force, and it is by destiny's hand alone that he didn't kill all of us."

Rachel smirks and looks at Jon with pride. She thinks to herself, "Jon has changed, but it's for the good. He truly believes in something now."

She then turns to Layla and says, "I want to go check on Alice. Will you come with me? She needs the care of women right now."

Layla answers, "Sure. She has been through just as much as all of us. Only in a different way."

The two walk off as Bill and Jon move over to the others enjoying the party.

Entering the same office where the team was told just days earlier about the plan to expose Alice Malice, Layla and Rachel find the former pop star sitting at the desk.

Alice, wearing a rain jacket provided by her rescuers over her stage outfit, is sitting with her head down on a desk. Her arms are wrapped around her head, covering her face. Sobbing at the thought of her wasted past, she doesn't even acknowledge the door of the office opening. Rachel and Layla sit down on either side of her to try and comfort the broken woman. Alice lifts her head up and looks at the two.

"Why are you being so nice to me?" Alice asks.

Rachel replies, "It's like I told you, the new world will need remnants of the old to be able to go on."

Layla adds, "Right, and you yourself have been just as much a victim as all of us. The Cabal has fed off of all of our fears and you were manipulated to help spread that fear. It's not your fault."

Alice's sobbing starts to subside a little.

Rachel says, "Today is the beginning of a new life for you Alice."

Alice looks at them with a frown and says, "Alice, Bluh! Alice Malice isn't even my name. My real name is Allison Mallory."

Rachel responds, "Well, you can be that again. All the Cabal did is temper and mold the talent you have for their own gain."

Layla nods in agreement with Rachel.

Alice sits up with new resolve and says. "You're right. From this day forward, I will dedicate myself and all that I am to solving the world's problems, not adding to them."

The other women smile at their success in aiding the torn woman and musical artist formerly known as Alice Malice.

Back at the party, Jon and Bill find Keena and Shigeru conversing with several other members of the Underground. The two turn their attention to the approaching men.

Shigeru says, "Jon, I don't know how we've done it, but that's four times we've survived The Drifter. Our luck is about out."

Jon says, "Yes, and it's only a matter of time before he finds this hideout."

Bill interjects, "No worries. Our boys have plenty of places to disperse to."

Shigeru asks Bill, "When will we be leaving to the forces of light headquarters?"

Bill answers, "We can head out tomorrow. Layla and I will personally take you there."

Keena asks, "Where is it anyway? And how will we be getting there?"

"By submarine," Bill replies. "Departing from the bay. It's just southeast of the Australian mainland, parallel west of New Zealand and east of Tasmania."

Jon asks, "Is it an island?"

Bill smiles and says enigmatically, "You'll see."

Chapter 40:

Under the Sea

The following day, the crews of the Sydney underground prepare to head out and abandon their compound in the Sydney bay warehouse.

The newly restored Allison Mallory approaches the team one last time to thank them. The former illustrious pop star looks like a new woman wearing typical street clothes, no makeup, and her hair pulled up.

She says, "I just wanted one more time to thank you for freeing me."

Jon responds by saying, "You are more than welcome. I wasn't sure if you were going to survive that operation, much less leave with us."

Shigeru and says, "Yeah, and I'm sorry I had to be as rough with you as I was, but I'm glad you made a turn around."

Keena adds, "I'm sorry I couldn't get to know you better, but I hope you'll be okay here with the underground."

Allison answers by saying, "I'll be fine. I'm sure they'll take care of me at their base in the Northern Territory."

Rachel hugs her and says, "Oh, I'm so glad you're feeling better today."

Allison tells the group, "Good luck to you all on the rest of your journey."

She is then helped aboard a supply truck and leaves the warehouse.

Bill and Layla come to the group and ask if they are ready to go. Once prepared, the team is taken to a boathouse on the bay side of the warehouse. Down in the lower levels, they board a small submarine with a large glass dome at its bow. The team, along with Bill, Layla, and a sub pilot, begin to depart from the Australian continent. With the fully exposed front of the sub, the team is able to see the wonders of the sea as they go deeper and deeper into the Pacific Ocean.

Bill begins to explain, "When the forces of light started to unify in the early eighties, our father was part of a small resistance force here in Australia. Little did he know at the time but a much larger resistance already existed in Australia. They were the most organized rebellion to the Cabal in the modern world. When his small resistance merged with the existing one, our father was in charge of protecting the location of its main base. He and his men acted as a fence between the high command and the many cells and units around the world as a way of stopping any infiltration."

Keena says, "Compartmentalization, just like the Cabal uses with its many sub secret societies and organizations."

Layla responds, "Precisely. The unified forces of light could never be too careful."

Bill continues, "However, several years ago, the Cabal pinpointed our father as the fence. That's when they sent The Drifter after him. I'll never forget that night. The three of us battled him, but obviously our father didn't survive and we were left to carry on with his activities. Just before his death, high command began constructing an underwater facility to escape the Cabal from their search on land."

Jon questions, "So that's where we're going, an underwater base?"

Bill answers, "Yes. It's been the home of the high command for nearly a decade now."

Shigeru adds, "I've been receiving information and taking orders from the unified force for years. I've always known they had cells and people in different positions around the world, but I had no clue they had anything like this."

Bill laughs and says, "Good, then we've been doing a good job of keeping it secret."

After some length of time maneuvering through the seemingly endless depths of the ocean, a gleaming light appears in the distance. As the sub gets closer and closer, the yellow light gets brighter and brighter. Finally, a large glass dome in the middle of the sea floor comes into sight.

Jon says, "My God, it looks like a small town in there."

Layla notes, "About 140 people live down here."

The group looks on in awe.

The bottom levels of the dome have walls blocking the view from outside. The middle level looks like one big glass wall surrounding a single room, allowing the inhabitants to observe the ocean from within. The top and smallest level appears to have walls with normal sized windows for viewing. Outside the dome, several submarines, like the one the group are in, are circling the underwater base as if protecting it.

A voice comes over the radio saying, "We have you on our screen. What is your cargo and purpose?"

Bill reaches for the radio, "This is Low Flying Buzzard Hawk. I'm here on a special mission with specific orders from high command."

A moment passes before the voice returns to the radio, "Aye, Aye Buzzard Hawk, you have clearance to land in docking bay 5."

The sub then passes the other patrolling submarines and heads toward the base of the underwater dome. A large rectangular door near the bottom with a number 5 on it begins to open. The pilot steers the sub into the docking bay. Once inside, the door closes again. Water in the bay begins draining out of the room until about two-thirds of the way drained, leaving the sub level with a small dock leading to a doorway into the facility. Two guards come out to the dock and wait for the team to exit their sub.

Once out, the team is escorted down the hall to a large freight elevator.

Bill says, "Well, its time you finally met the unified forces of light's high command."

Jon and Rachel, nervous, look at each other as a way of preparing themselves for the unknown.

Once the elevator stops, the door opens and the team finds themselves at the center of the underwater facility. It is a large open room, the size of a football field, with people scurrying about. Technical crews, butlers, maids, men with suits, etc., are all seen. Through the glass, the patrol subs can be seen slowly moving around the dome, with the beams of their lights shining through the darkness of the sea.

Bill says, "Okay, allow me introduce you to high command."

Nervous and unsure what to expect, Jon and the others have reached an entirely new level of their unfolding journey.

Chapter 41:

High Command Revealed!

As the team follows Bill and Layla, they see five individuals standing side by side. The man to the far left is wearing a classical suit and has a sharp moustache and pointy beard, like that of a conquistador. To his right is a young woman with long blonde hair and an elegant pink dress. Next to her is a rather rugged looking man wearing a military-like outfit with curly jawbone length hair and a goatee. To his right, is a younger looking man with glasses and short light brown hair. And finally, the man on the far right looks to be in his late forties and is wearing a dark black suit with a comb over haircut.

Bill and Layla take a small respectable bow and introduce the team.

"We've brought them here without a problem," Layla says. "Let me introduce them."

She points to the group one at a time and says, "This is Jon Peters, Rachel Lynn, Shigeru Iwata, and Keena Turoni."

The Elite looking group of rebels to the Cabal nod to the team.

"We'll leave the high command's introductions to themselves," Bill says as he waves his hand to the man on the far left.

The man steps forward, and with a rolling Spanish accent says, "I am Francisco Delgado. I have been a prominent member of the forces of light since I was ousted from my position. In the mid nineteen nineties, I was a UN delegate who was making much headway on the drug crisis in my country."

Jon interrupts, "Wait, I remember reading about you. I read that you committed suicide."

Francisco replies, "I was about to blow the lid on some very shady activity brought on by my own government. An attempt was made on my life. So I faked my own death. It was at this point I discovered the newly emerging unified forces of light."

Jon nods in acknowledgment as the team turns their attention to the beautiful woman in the pink dress.

The woman begins by saying with a slightly off Australian accent, "Greetings, and thank you for coming here. I am Princess Romina of the Richter family line. My father was leader of the unified forces of light until his death a few years ago. I have been acting in his place ever since."

Jon thinks for a moment, then makes a connection with the family name the woman has given.

"Hold on a second," he says. "Your name is German, and wasn't Richter the name of the castle we traced the members of the Cabal to?" says Jon as he looks to Rachel and the others for confirmation.

Princess Romina responds, "Excellent, you truly are a solver of mysteries, Jon Peters. My family line was royalty in Germany in the middle ages. The Richters didn't see eye to eye with many of the harsh monarchies that were in the norm those days. By the time the Concert of Europe came about, any royal families who were not subordinate were overthrown. The Richters were exiled, like many others, by the British Empire to Australia. We were effectively written out of history."

Jon, with a look of awe, says, "So the Cabal must have been using your family's home, Castle Richter, for their fear gathering rituals because of its remoteness and lack of evidence about its existence."

Romina nods with a sad look.

Jon goes on to say, "But we all felt a sense of peace in the area surrounding the castle."

Shigeru adds, "Yes, and there was that fairy that helped us."

Princess Romina answers, "The woodland sprites in the area must still reside there. Our family was friendly to good natured creatures and that's partly why the Cabal wanted us gone. They didn't want anyone of prominence to be around to reveal that such things existed once they took them out of the mainstream. Your discovery of the Cabal's location and my family's home partially influenced our calling of you here today."

Rachel asks, "So how did your family line survive to this day?"

Romina replies, "When they were taken to the Penal Colony of Australia, they were looked to as a beacon of hope in their settlement."

Francisco adds, "After some time, the Richters became a figurehead of a better future. When the unified force of light was assembled, they remained a symbol for those who knew about and opposed the Cabal."

Princess Romina smiles and says, "Well enough about me, allow me to introduce the next member of our merry band." She waves over to the rough looking man standing to her right. He smiles as she introduces him. "This is Commander Todd Owens. He is in charge of our Special Forces operations and personally heads security for high command. Todd, do you want to say anything to our new friends?" Romina asks.

Todd steps forward and crosses his arms. He takes a deep breath and with a western Kentucky accent says,

"It would seem you all are pretty good at fuckin shit up for the Cabal. You're all okay in my book." Then he steps back.

The Princess follows up by saying, "Please forgive Todd for his rather unorthodox approach to things. He really is very good at what he does."

Todd says, "Alright, alright, I guess I can tell 'em a little about myself. I was a Staff Sergeant in the United States Army during Operation Desert Storm. When my squad came across some things in Iraq that seemed a little shady, we decided it was best we expose them. Well, that didn't exactly go too far up the chain of command. Navy Seals were sent in to eradicate us. Only I and three others from my squad survived their assault. We bailed out of the country. Several months later, we were picked up by the Richters and asked to form a special team of covert operations. When the next Iraqi war rolled around, I offered to help out since I knew the country so well. The so called 'coalition of the willing' claimed Iraq had WMDs and mobile weapons facilities running up and down the highways of the countryside. It was all bullshit. UN forces, in collaboration with the Cabal, were bringing weapons into the country. They were going to plant them and blame it on the Iraqis. I formed a team that went out there, knocked out the unit that was taking them in, and discarded the munitions before they could be exposed."

Shigeru smiles and says, "That was you! You were behind all of that."

Looking at Jon and Rachel, Shigeru says, "That's the operation I told you about when I first met you guys."

Todd smirks and says, "Glad my reputation precedes me."

The next man in the line steps forward.

The man with glasses introduces himself, "My name is Chris Green. I worked in NATO Intelligence until I discovered some of the things they were up to in East Asia and North Africa. Being in intelligence, I was slightly aware of the unified forces of light. Rather than them finding me, the way they did with Francisco and Todd, I went looking for them. After they took me in, I reformed their very ragtag intelligence team."

Shigeru says, "Your voice sounds very similar."

Chris responds, "That's because we have spoken several times before, Shigeru. In addition to intelligence, I'm director of the call center here at this facility. My team of eight and I make contact with the many cells we have around the world. I'm also the one who took your call Jon, when Keena and Shigeru went missing."

Jon responds, "Wow! I'm amazed at how organized all of this is."

Francisco interjects, "Yes. It wasn't always this way, but we are at our height."

Princess Romina adds, "Francisco and I have been the main decision makers on what moves to make against the Cabal. But Todd and Chris work very closely with us on these decisions. When Bill and Layla's father was aiding our union with the various resistance groups around the world, my father decided it best to keep high command all in one place and make it very secret. That's how this facility came to be."

Francisco says, "That's how we became so organized and compartmentalized."

Princess Romina proceeds to introduce the last man, "Which brings us to the reason we requested you be brought here." She motions to the man in the suit on the far right. "The Cabal has made a critical error and the time to strike is now," Romina notes. "Several weeks ago, this man turned himself in to us. This is Lucis Wendell. He was a very high ranking member of the Cabal until he realized his folly."

The team is dumbfounded at this latest introduction.

"Lucis," Romina says. "I'll let you explain why you are here."

The man steps forward and says, "I can understand your being alarmed by my past. I hope that my presence here will bring redemption to my former follies. I was raised the son of an American businessman and a British Duchess. The Cabal was all I ever knew until a few weeks ago. On a business trip to India, I was exposed to the harshness of the Cabal's actions. Something stuck with me after seeing child labor and cruelty in my sweatshops. It was topped off when a young boy fell down running out in from of my limo. I got out to scold him, but he was thin and weak and awoke in me the empathy I lacked as a member of the Cabal. That's when I decided to put myself in a position where I could be picked up by the unified forces of light. They were aiding the exposure of many of our ranks these past few months. I understand you all had your part in that. Several were killed in the uprising in America, a few hundred through indictment by the higher members like myself. We would throw anyone under the bus in order to protect ourselves. Dozens more of us were exposed and eliminated around the world."

Romina says, "Lucis has revealed to us that the surviving members of the Cabal have discovered an ancient temple, and I mean ancient, in the Pacific Ocean east of Papua New Guinea. The once fabled continent of Lemuria has only its highest points above water, the most famous being Easter Island. The island discovered by the Cabal, Mu, contains a temple that was used by the

Lemurians to bring demonic forces into this world. Realizing their mistake, the shamans of the continent banded together and used magic to flood the land and destroy the demons. Because of our efforts, the Cabal has been forced to resort to using this temple once again. Your exposure of Alice Malice has only hastened this. Their grip has loosened and they have no army or machinery to occupy the world from a physical perspective."

Lucis adds, "Only about 400 members of the Cabal remain and they will be at the temple all at the same time in an attempt to open a gateway to the nether world."

Romina goes on to say, "In a vain effort to engage us and our many cells around the world with what little agents they have left, the Cabal won't have much to defend against an attack on the temple. However, with 400 members and whatever defense they *will* have, Todd's team won't be enough to subdue them."

Francisco says, "That's where you come in."

Keena interjects, "I hate to be the bearer of bad news, but as bad ass as we may be, the four of us won't be a significant enough addition to Todd's team."

Shigeru adds, "She's right. You'll need a small army to be able to pull it off."

Romina responds, "We understand. We aren't expecting you to do it alone. We want you, combined with Jon's persuasive skills as a speaker to amass that small army you suggest."

Jon asks, "But how?" If we were to do it publicly, then the Cabal would know what we were up to."

Romina continues, "There is an island, in the Atlantic Ocean, off the coast of South America. It's called the Island of the Amazons. It's a matriarchal society of women who were upset with a world run by men. They have much angst against the Cabal. They are the most elite physical grouping of persons in the world and their jungle tactics would make them perfect in the environment on Mu. Will you accept this mission and help crush the Cabal once and for all, Jon Peters?" the Princess asks.

Jon looks at the others. All three of them nod in agreement.

"Yes," he says. "We'll do it."

After accepting the new mission to quell the Cabal once and for all by the unified forces of light, Jon proceeds to ask a question.

"How will we get to the island?" he asks. "Our jet was destroyed."

Romina answers, "We'll arrange transportation for you."

Just then, the room trembles slightly. The group all looks to the left and notices a horrible sight. One of the patrol submarines outside has exploded. The shockwave from it rippled through the water and shook the facility.

"What happened?!" shouts Rachel.

Todd steps forward and yells, "We're under attack! Something's out there!"

Chapter 42:

To Fight and Run Away

Looking closer, Jon and the others notice the silhouettes of dozens of human-like figures treading in the water. Over half a dozen of them attack the next nearest patrol sub. The group moves closer to the glass wall to better assess the situation.

Having a difficult time making out the figures, Romina asks, "Who's out there?"

Suddenly, one of the unknown assailants slams into the glass in front of her. Romina screams and stumbles back at the sight of the horrid creature.

Appearing to be a man in form, the monster is covered in scales and has gills. Its hands are webbed and its feet are almost like flippers, wadding in the water. It has bulbous eyes, with a haunting, soulless gaze.

Lucis yells, "Gill-men!"

The others turn their attention to him.

He goes on to say, "They're gill-men. Amphibious demons unleashed by the Cabal. They've used them before but not in such quantity."

Todd responds, "Dammit! They must have traced us here when we picked you up."

By this time, the dozens of gilled creatures have swarmed the sub patrols all around the underwater base. The creature that slammed into the window moments earlier begins attacking again, and after several hits the glass starts to slightly crack.

Francisco says, "Come on, we must evacuate."

Other creatures, now up on the glass around the dome, begin attacking to try and break their way into the facility.

Bill says to Layla, "I'll get Romina and the rest of high command out on our sub. You go with the others to make sure they get out."

"Right," Layla responds.

Romina interjects, "Wait. Todd. Go with them. Make sure they get out. They're our best shot at ending all of this."

Todd agrees and the group begins moving toward the exits.

In the chaos of the attack, the crewman and staff begin taking up arms and prepare to engage the monsters that have infiltrated the facility from its lower levels. Just as they approach one of the exits, the doors open from the other side, releasing several of the creatures into the main room. Gunfire breaks out from the armed facility security as the gilled monsters rush them.

Realizing this way is no good, Shigeru draws his pistol and says, "We've got to find another way out."

Bill shouts, "This way!" He gestures at another exit.

Before they can reach the doors, a mob of the creatures surrounds the group. Todd and Keena, now with pistols in hand, join Shigeru in gunning the creatures down. Without warning, one of the amphibious monsters springs out agilely and grabs Lucis. As Lucis scuffles with the creature, it opens its mouth and sprays a steaming black ink all over him. Upon contact the ink burns through his skin like some sort of acid. Lucis, now screaming, begins to dissolve. Still alive, his face melts into a skeletal morbid sight. Todd turns and fires his gun at the gill-man's head, killing it. It is too late to save Lucis, and he falls to the ground and dies.

Todd looks down at his lifeless body, melted face, and upper body, and says. "Damn! I've failed him."

Romina consoles him, "It's okay Todd, there's nothing you could have done. Now we've got to get out of here."

The group runs out through the exit and down the outer hallway to the escape subs. The two fleeing teams then split up and head to their individual subs resting in ports parallel to one another.

Just before reaching the entrance to the port containing the sub Layla is leading them to, an explosion occurs overhead, knocking Jon and Todd back against the wall. Todd, who has taken the brunt of the hit, remains lying on his back as Jon gets up. Jon rushes over to Todd and kneels down to help him up.

Jon asks, "Todd, are you okay?"

Todd sits up looking angry and responds, "Motherfucker, I've been shot twice! Desert Storm vet!"

Back on his feet, he and Jon head into the room where the others are preparing to board the sub.

Rachel looks back to reassure herself that Jon is okay and has made it in before following Layla and the others aboard.

Once in the sub, Layla presses the controls that open the bay doors. The group heads out into the ocean, leaving the facility in shambles behind them. Several of the gilled creatures swim toward the sub as they exit the bay.

Layla, who is at the controls, aims the joysticks forward and fires several small torpedoes that hit two of the monsters. They explode and are eliminated.

Once out into the deep blue, several other subs can be seen fleeing as well. Some of the subs are under attack and bursting into pieces before sinking to the depths. Finally, the group gets clear of all the chaos.

Todd, pistol still in one hand, looks dejected and says, "I really wish I could have done something for Lucis."

Jon says, "There was no way you could have. Those things struck so quickly and you were wrapped up fighting the other ones off."

Todd sighs. "Yeah," he says. "But it just bothers me, cuz I felt obligated to him. When he came to us seeking asylum, I personally swore to make sure he'd be safe from the Cabal's clutches. I know what it's like to be someone who once did the bidding of the Cabal and had to take refuge because I didn't see eye to eye with them."

Todd looks back at Keena and continues, "Keena knows what that's like too. That's why I'm taking his loss so hard."

Keena nods.

Shigeru asks Layla, "Where are we going to now?"

Layla, steering the sub, answers, "The survivors all know the escape protocol to meet at a set location in New Zealand. There are supplies, housing, and transportation there."

Taking all the most recent events in, Jon leans back in his chair and takes a deep breath. Rachel puts her hand on his shoulder and the two share a moment of acknowledgment looking at each other as the undersea vessel moves on toward New Zealand.

Arriving in a bay off the Northeast coast of New Zealand, our heroes' submarine resurfaces. Once in shallow enough water, Layla opens the top hatch, and the group climbs out. The beautiful land down under is enjoying a sunny day, a refreshing change from the terrible experience in the slimy deep the night before.

Now on the shore, Rachel asks, "Okay, now what? How do we find the others?"

Todd answers, "The rendezvous point isn't far. It's just inland a little ways from here."

Jon remarks, "I hope the others escaped okay. There was a lot of carnage down there."

Shigeru turns and points down the bay a little way. "Look!" he shouts. "Another sub!"

Sure enough a second sub is on the other side of the bay with its hatch open.

Todd smiles and says, "Well, at least someone else besides us escaped. And I'm willing to bet that if one sub did, then so did another. Come on."

Todd then proceeds to lead the team inward toward the secret location, in which everyone is hoping survivors will be met.

Chapter 43:

The Great Southern Trendkill

Trekking through the beautiful coastal area of New Zealand, the team finally arrives at the rendezvous point where they find Bill and the other members of the high command. A few dozen other members of the underwater facilities crew and staff are there as well.

Romina greets the group. "Thank goodness!" she says. "I wasn't sure if anyone was going to survive that attack."

Jon replies, "We were worried too. Now how do we know the Cabal won't track us here too?" he asks.

Francisco says, "We don't. In fact, they most certainly will. Romina and I have decided that it would be best if we threw ourselves to the wind."

Keena asks, "What do you mean?"

Francisco answers, "We need to scatter ourselves around the world to throw off the Cabal. They are already spread thin trying to root out our many agents and cells. Looking for us will become a priority, so by staying on the move, we will distract them further."

Romina adds, "I will stay with Francisco, Chris and his team will stay together so they can continue contact with our agents, and Todd will go to assemble his strike team for the attack on the temple, while you go to the Amazons."

Bill asks, "What about Layla and me? Do you need us any further?"

Romina smiles at the brother and sister, noticing Bill's shoulder wound from his encounter with The Drifter and Layla's fatigue from worrying about whether her only family left will make it.

"Go back to Australia," she says to the siblings' surprise. "You've done all you can for us and Jon's team. Keep the Sydney Underground together and do what you can for them in these most critical hours."

Francisco interjects, "She's right. You've done all you can. And if our plan fails and we are captured, the only ones left to stand against the Cabal will be movements like yours."

Bill and Layla agree and seem to have something like relief in their eyes at the news of their discharge.

Shigeru now asks, "That is all well and good. But how are we supposed to do anything from here? We're basically in the middle of nowhere and all we have are a few battered submarines."

Romina laughs a little and says, "Why Shigeru, haven't you learned by now that we're more prepared than that."

Shigeru looks slightly surprised. Romina and Todd go over to the edge of the clearing and move the shrubbery out of the way for the others to see. Underneath the cover of the very tall trees in the dense forest, the team sees over a dozen airplanes all being prepped by crewmen.

Romina explains, "The planes will be ready shortly. I'm assigning Todd to personally escort you to the Island of the Amazons before gathering his strike team."

Francisco adds, "We are just waiting for one more person to arrive."

Jon, confused, asks, "Huh? Someone else?"

Romina say, "I've called in someone special to go with you to the island. We can't just send you in alone. The Amazonians can be quite hostile, especially toward men. And we felt it best that someone with more terrain experience than Shigeru and Keena be there to protect you. I'd send Todd, but we need him to prepare for the assault. So you're getting the next best thing," Romina says with a smile as she looks at Todd who smiles back.

Jon asks, "Who then?"

Before the Princess can respond, the group hears a sound like that of a jet, heading their way. Down from above the tree line, a man in battle fatigues riding a rocket-powered hang glider soars down toward the group. The glider lands and the twenty-something man with slick black hair unclamps himself from the helm of what looks like a space age piece of technology.

Kneeling down and bowing his head, the man says with a distinctive, Texan accent, "I came as quickly as I could, Your Highness."

Romina replies, "Your timing is impeccable, Captain. We were just about to tell the team about you."

The man comes to his feet and looks over toward the group.

Romina continues, "Everyone, please allow me to introduce you to Captain Rex Anselmo Abbott, Former United States Army Ranger, and elite member of Todd's Special Forces. He, like Todd, came across some rather startling things on a mission and decided to opt out of his rank in the Rangers and join up with us."

Todd comes over and puts his hand on Rex's shoulder. "Rex is the absolute best we've got. Well, besides me, but I'm startin to get too old for all this. He's still young and able. He's a regular cowboy from hell, driven too. Ain't that right?"

Rex responds, "Far beyond driven sir."

Romina says, "Let me introduce the team, Captain Abbott."

Going around the lineup, Romina introduces everyone one by one. "This is Jon peters, Rachel Lynn, Keena Turoni, and Shigeru Iwata."

The Captain, shaking hands with everyone, takes Rachel's hand and kisses it, saying, "Well, what have we here?"

Rachel smiles and almost looks star-struck at the respectable military man. Jon comes to stand beside Rachel, not amused at the Captain's advances.

Realizing that Rachel is with Jon, Rex replies, "You sir, have a lovely Yankee rose here."

"Thank you," Jon says, still taken back by Rex's abrasiveness.

Rachel chuckles and says, "Why Captain, you certainly are flattering."

Rex says, "Please, all of you. Call me Rex. I prefer keeping formal and personal names separate. So call me Rex or Captain Abbott, never the other way around."

"Okay, Rex!" Rachel says smiling. "I trust your reputation will be enough to back us up on anything we encounter on this mission."

Rex replies, "Until I pass the cemetery gates, the Cabal can just keep on sendin things my way."

Jon sarcastically responds, "Well now, let's just hope that's not anytime soon then."

Rachel nudges Jon in protest at his remark.

Romina says, "Well now. Are all of you ready to commence the plan?"

Shigeru comes up next to Jon, who is still staring down Rex, and says, "Yes ma'am. I'm sure Jon is just as eager as I am to get things moving."

Jon turns and steps away slightly. "Yes," he says. "We can leave anytime."

Princess Romina declares, "Good. Then let this be the final action against the Cabal and all the damage they have done to this world."

Bill and Layla give a word of thanks one last time to Jon and company for all they have done to help them.

After saying their goodbyes, the alliance against the Cabal spread off to the corners of the earth as Jon and his comrades prepare to visit the Island of the Amazons in hopes to amass them as an army.

Chapter 44:

The Island of the Amazons

Flying at a high altitude over the Atlantic Ocean near South America, a small plane is about to drop off the last great hope to save the world from demonic ruin.

Talking loud so as to be heard over the sound of the propellers and wind rushing by, Jon shouts to Todd, "I didn't realize you were gonna have us jump out of the plane!"

Todd shouts back, "Sorry, but due to lack of time and the risk of a confrontation with the Amazons, we gotta keep moving. I have a team to assemble remember?"

Jon yells back, "Yeah, but I've never done this before and neither have the others!"

Todd shouts, "I know, that's why we strapped you and Rachel together, same for Shigeru and Keena! Besides, Rex here has jumped hundreds of times. He'll be out there to make sure you're okay!"

Jon glances at Rex, finishing adjustments to his jumpsuit and gear. Rex gives a little salute to Jon.

Jon shouts back to Todd, "Yeah! I feel real safe!"

"We're about to go over the island now!" says Todd, as he opens the door the rest of the way before Captain Abbott moves out to the edge to jump.

Turning around to face the others, Rex blows a small kiss to Rachel before back flipping out of the plane.

Shigeru, with Keena strapped to his back steps up next to the others and says to Jon, "It's okay man! We'll be alright! Just go with it!"

Then without much hesitation, Shigeru and Keena make their leap.

Moving out to the edge with Rachel, eyes closed and strapped to him and gripping him tightly around his waist, Jon asks Todd, "Now how do you do this again?!"

Todd answers, showing Jon his pull cord, "What you do is! Ya take this sum bitch right here, and ya jerk that sucker back! Then let go and that'll open your chute!"

Jon, taken back by Todd's unusual way of explaining how it works, halfheartedly says, "Okay! Here we go, I guess!"

Out on the edge, right as Jon and Rachel are about to make their jump, Todd gives them a little push. Dropping down from the aircraft, Jon and Rachel scream. First in fear, then in excitement.

Jon, smiling, looks back at Rachel to see that she is enjoying it as well. With the vastness of the ocean before them below and the blue sky above with their escort plane puttering away, the couple are actually enjoying the free fall.

Catching up to the others, they all begin descending together to the island below. Rex swims his way a little closer to the others and gives the signal that it's time to open the parachutes. With a great whiplash, Rex's chute opens and he drifts up above the others. Next, Keena and Shigeru open their parachute. Jon, smirking as he recollects Todd's unconventional directions, pulls his and Rachel's cord. Their parachute opens without a hitch and they float elegantly down to the tropical surface.

Landing just a few feet from each other, the group touches down in a mess of tropical island vegetation. Jon sits up with Rachel still strapped to his back. Looking around, they see Shigeru and Keena doing the same.

Rex, in his pile of brush, sits up and says, "Well, we made it. Now we just gotta find these Amazon women."

Seeing the trees rustling around them in all directions, Shigeru responds, "I don't think that's going to be a problem Captain."

Encompassing full circle around them, dozens of women come out of the forest wearing very scanty loincloths. Some of the women hold staffs, others don spears and some have bows and arrows trained on the team.

Starting with Rex, each member of the team raises their hands in surrender.

One of the women who has long, waist length blonde hair, steps forward.

Holding a Bowie Knife, the woman says, "Who are you and what are you doing here?"

Rachel, who has just detached her jumpsuit from Jon's, nudges him and whispers, "Jon, that's your cue."

Jon hops to attention. "Right," he says.

Coming to his feet, he raises his hands higher and begins to explain. "My name is Jon Peters. I'm here with my friends to invite you to join an alliance that could mean the end of a great threat to this world."

The woman, not seeming impressed by Jon's introduction, moves closer with the large blade and responds, "What makes you think we want to align ourselves with the likes of *men*?"

Keena, rolling her eyes back and sighing, says, "Awesome. Off to a good start."

Jon looks back at Keena, then back to the Amazon woman with the large knife. He starts again. "Okay...maybe if you understood the circumstances of this alliance, and the symbiotic relationship we share in this world..."

Before Jon can continue, Shigeru interrupts, "Jon. It's not working. Let me give this a try." Shigeru stands up and says very bluntly, "Look. The planet is under a serious threat, and if you don't help us..."

Just then, one of the women standing near Shigeru takes his feet right out from under him with her staff. Knocking his breath right out from him, Shigeru lands on his back as several of the women shake their spears toward him.

The blonde woman with the Bowie Knife aggressively shakes it toward him saying, "We don't allow *men* to tell us what to do and not do!"

Right about this time, Rex speaks up. With his suave Texas accent, he says smoothly, "Okay, my turn."

The women turn their attention to him.

"Okay darling," he says. "Here's what's shakin."

Jon rolls his eyes and gasps.

Rex goes on to say, "We got ourselves a little ole common enemy. And if we work together, instead of against one another, maybe we can do something about it."

Jon interjects, "I don't think that's a good idea, Captain Abbott."

Rex pays no attention to Jon and asks, "What do you think sugar?"

Awkward silence fills the jungle.

The women with the bows cock them back in a very, to the point, manner. Rex gets the point and shuts his mouth.

About 20 minutes later, the three men find themselves being carried through the jungle, roped under the belly of logs.

Rachel and Keena, walking behind the group, are asked by Shigeru, "How come we got tied up and you two get to walk?"

The blonde Amazon answers, "You three *men* are the ones who spoke out of turn. These women held their tongues. Although they are not being punished for your crimes, they are still trespassers like you. Once back at our village, we will discuss your purpose here and determine whether you will be freed or punished."

After traveling for some time, the group arrives in the Amazon village. A series of huts covered in vegetation are seen all over. To Jon's surprise, the village is one of the most culturally diverse places he has ever seen. Women of all colors and nationalities are seen. White, black, Asian, Arab, etc.

When the caravan stops, the men are cut down from the tree limbs they have been carried on. Rubbing at the rope marks from his wrists, Jon gets to his feet.

The blonde woman approaches and says, "You are permitted to walk freely, because I assure you, you won't be escaping. However, we are keeping your weapons for now. By the way, forgive me for my informal introduction. My name is Cheryl."

After finally being placed at some level of comfort among the Amazons, the group begins pitching their story.

Sitting in a circle around prominent members of the tribe, Jon inquires, "What's the population of your village?"

Cheryl answers, "Living in this village are about 350 Amazons. But, around the island, in various villages and huts, we number in the thousands."

Jon is shocked and he thinks to himself, "Wow, this number seems to be much more than even the high command thought."

Cheryl asks, "What could you possibly need us for out in your world?"

Jon responds, "As you are probably aware, there are certain powers controlling this world. We know them as the Cabal."

Cheryl adds, "Yes, all of us here are well aware of this group that has helped push a man's world upon society. In the past century, no group has been more anti progressive than they. The inhabitants of this island are strong women, both mentally and physically, who were fed up with the way they were thought of less out in this man's world. So they came here, where they could be the dominant ones. We no longer have the need for that world and we have our own now. Which is exactly why I ask you again, what could you possibly need us for out there?"

Shigeru interjects, "Jon, I don't think it's going to work. They are so anti-male that they can't possibly see the bigger picture."

Cheryl turns to Shigeru and says, "We don't hate men. We just realize how superior we really are to them."

Rex stands up and says, "Oh, really now? That's an awful big presumption. Ya know, to say that *all* of you are superior to *all* of us."

Cheryl says, "Okay Captain Abbott. If you're supposed to be the best of the best when it comes to men, why not have a little friendly competition with the best of the best in our world?"

303

Rex smirks and says, "Alright, I'm game."

Cheryl looks over her left shoulder and shouts, "Li Lu!"

A small built Asian woman runs up to Cheryl's side.

"Li Lu here was a Chinese gymnast," she says. "For her size, she is in peak physical condition. She wasn't treated fairly in the man's world because of jealousy. So she joined us. How about, the first one to hit the ground loses?" Cheryl asks.

Rex answers with a little chuckle, "Well sure."

The two walk to an open area off away from the sitting area. Standing about 15 feet from one another, the two prepare for combat.

After a moment of stare down, Cheryl shouts, "Begin!"

Without hesitation, Li Lu starts handspringing toward Rex. Rex has his guard up as he attempts to catch her in midair. When her legs come down on Rex's shoulders, he attempts to throw her, but she simply swings her way around his neck and launches herself behind him, turning him slightly and throwing him off balance.

Rex regains his balance and says, "Lucky start."

This time Rex takes the charge. He swings violently at her, but her amazing agility protects her from each blow. Finally, she runs up toward Rex, putting her hands on his shoulders and projecting herself upward. Spreading her legs, she hops over his head like he's an Olympic balancing board. On her way down, she catches the sides of his head with her thighs. Overpowering him, she brings Rex down on his back and handsprings herself into a flip, landing perfectly on her feet. The others are in absolute awe. Claps and applause erupt from the Amazonian women. Rachel and Keena can't help but clap along with them.

Cheryl turns back to Jon and says, "Well. Now that that is taken care of, you may go on with your explanation."

Rex dusts himself off and goes back to his seat next to Shigeru.

Jon continues, "In a nutshell, our allies have devised a plan to stop this Cabal once and for all. It could mean the end of the tyranny that has caused the centuries old suppression and segregation you were talking about. We were sent here to discuss an alliance with you to see this through. You see, we don't have an army. But we realize the might of your tribe, and humbly request that you aid us in this final struggle."

Cheryl says, "Hmmm, ending the tyranny of the outside world does interest us. What can you tell us of this plan?"

Jon replies, "There is an island on the other side of the world, where the whole of the Cabal is meeting all at once at an ancient temple. Our plan is to strike them and eliminate them all in one fell swoop. Being that you specialize in jungle warfare and you have the numbers, we would need you to engage the temple head on, while our strike team penetrates the inner sanctum."

Cheryl, with an interested look on her face, thinks a moment.

Jon goes on to say, "I feel it's only fair to warn you though, that many Amazonians will likely be killed in the conflict. But it will serve the greater good of all people."

After a few more moments of thinking, Cheryl says, "Although I am leader of the Amazons, we are a democracy here. I must admit, the thrill alone interests me, but I cannot make a decision without consulting the other sisters. I'd like to ask you to relax and enjoy yourselves here until we make our decision."

Jon nods, smiles, and says, "Thank you. That's good enough for now."

Chapter 45:

A Decision is Made

Sitting around a campfire, Jon and Rachel discuss the situation with each other.

Rachel says, "Jon I think you handled that as well as you could have, given the audience you had. High command really made good judgment sending you here."

Jon replies, "Yeah, but it didn't help having that hellbound southerner get all cocky with them."

Rachel smiles and says, "I think Rex means well, he just doesn't know how to approach certain situations."

Jon looks at Rachel and says, "Uh, he blew you a kiss."

Rachel laughs a little. "Jon. Don't worry. I'm not going for him or anything. I just think he means well and is good at what he does. Otherwise, they wouldn't have sent him with us."

Jon says, "I don't know. I think he's arrogant."

Rachel answers, "That may be, but I don't want you worried about me being interested in him. It's you I want."

She leans in to kiss him just before being interrupted by Shigeru and Keena approaching.

"Guys," Shigeru says. "The tribe is about ready to make a decision."

Back in front of Cheryl and various other members of the neo-feminist tribe of Amazonians, Jon and the others wait for their answer to whether the Amazons will aid the forces of light in the final conflict with the Cabal.

Cheryl calls out, "Jon Peters. We have discussed your proposition for us, and we have nearly unanimously found it quite attractive."

Jon and the others rejoice as they receive the news they were hoping for. But before they can fully celebrate, Cheryl chimes in with another declaration.

"However," she says. "We have found you to be an unfit leader for us in this expedition."

Jon, a little confused, asks, "Who then? The forces of light high command felt it was best I come here with my team to try and convince you to ally with us, then lead you into the temple."

Cheryl answers, "Convince us, you have, Jon Peters. But lead us, you are incapable."

Rex then speaks up, "I get it. They want me to lead the fight."

Jon looks over at Rex and rolls his eyes. "Oh, please," Jon snaps.

Cheryl replies, "Captain Abbott is not fit either, and neither the Yakuza."

Rex and Jon both look confused now.

Cheryl says, "No *man* is fit to lead the Amazons into battle. Although, if one of your women were to pass some skills tests, we would consider allowing them." Jon and Shigeru look at the girls. Keena and Rachel with a look of surprise on their faces, stand stunned at the proposal.

Jon turns back and asks, "What are the skills tests?"

Cheryl answers, "Training with our greatest warriors, followed by a triathlon, then a final test of good faith to prove one's self to the tribe."

Shigeru turns to Keena and asks, "Okay, Keena. Do you think you're up for it?"

Keena responds, "Of course, I'll do what I have to, to make this alliance happen."

She looks to Jon.

Jon nods to her, and then turns back toward Cheryl. "Okay," he says. Keena will accept the challenge to earn leadership."

Just then, Rachel interjects, "So will I."

The group turns to Rachel.

"What?!" Jon exclaims.

Rachel responds, "I have to. It will double our chances of succeeding in this."

Shigeru turns to Rachel and says, "Rachel. Come on. Ya know I love ya girl. But Keena's got this, really."

Rachel replies, "Shigeru, I know what I'm doing. I can't always be the damsel in distress. This is an opportunity where I can really help this team, more than I've been able to in this entire endeavor."

She looks back at Jon.

"Shigeru's right Rach," Jon states. "Keena has it under control. You don't have any business risking yourself like that."

"No!" Rachel cries. "I'm doing this Jon! I'm going to prove once and for all that Keena is not the only bad ass chick in this group who can take care of herself."

She looks at Keena.

Keena says, "I don't have a problem with it Rachel."

Jon asks one more time, "Are you sure about this Rachel?"

She answers, nearly with tears in her eyes, "Yes Jon. Trust me."

Jon nods his head in detached agreement, "Okay," he says. "I will."

Cheryl reenters the conversation with, "Okay. The two of you will compete then. Both of you can achieve tribe status from these trials. But only one of you will be granted leadership. I warn you. The trials can get very dangerous."

Keena and Rachel both nod in acknowledgment, unsure of exactly what awaits them.

Starting the very next morning, on a sandy beach just, just off from where the group landed in their parachutes, Jon, Shigeru, and Rex stand off as Keena and Rachel are initiated into the rites of the Amazons.

They are still in their modern-day clothes and appear quite different from the other women who are scantily clad in their brown and green loincloths.

Standing side by side, the two accept the challenge with an oath to do their best to serve the tribe and achieve victory in their trials in the name of all women. Soon after, the women are taken separately to learn some basic combat out on the sandy dunes of the beach. Each is assigned a different member of the tribe from whom to learn different skills. Staff combat, balance, agility, then finally, evasion.

After several hours of basic practice, the two are told they are ready to take their training into the jungle. There they will learn to use their surroundings to their advantage. Realizing the girls are on their own from here, the guys go back to the village and discuss the course of the coming weeks.

Rex starts by saying, "I hope they can get what they want out of those two quick. We've got less than three weeks before the attack begins. I don't wanna leave Commander Owens hanging."

Shigeru replies, "Don't worry. Keena will give them what they want."

Jon stares off into space before turning to the others and saying, "Yeah, I just hope Rachel can hang with it."

Shigeru, placing his hand on Jon's shoulder says, "Hey man. Don't worry. You know Rachel's just trying to prove her worth to us. She'll do what it takes."

Rex adds, "You're a lucky man, Mr. Peters. Rachel seems to be one hell of a woman. And I see why she'd go for a man like you, given the way you carry yourself in front of a crowd. I know you may not have really liked the way I came on when we first met. But I hope you can forgive and forget."

Jon smiles at Rex. "Yes Captain Abbott. I think we can start over new given the circumstances."

Chapter 46:

Every Woman for Herself

Several days pass before the training party returns to the village. Jon and the others go out to the edge of town to greet them and see how the training has come along. Cheryl meets them along the way saying, "Well, today's the day. You'll find out how your women fared out there working closely with ours."

Jon asks, "Do you think your people gave it their all teaching them your ways?"

Cheryl responds, "I'll tell you this much. Surely they made women out of them."

Now at the edge of town, the group looks on as the party of staff carrying Amazon warriors enters. Jon and Shigeru look around the group and at first don't see Keena or Rachel. But just then, the two realize something. They are standing right in front of them.

No longer wearing the modern clothes they had at the beginning of their training, Rachel and Keena are now dressed in the same revealing outfits the Amazons are wearing. Jon is star-struck at the sight of Rachel's bare feet and milk white legs going all the way up to the curvature of her voluptuous hips. Her bare midriff is seen just below her only slightly draped cleavage. Her long black hair hangs down her back and appears to be wild like the newfound fire in her eyes.

Shigeru is also compelled to look on at Keena in an all new light. Like Rachel, her body is sweat drenched, with her petite figure barely covered by the jungle garb she has on, that leaves little to the imagination. Her curly ebony hair is pulled back behind an olive drab cloth that acts as a bandana.

The two men almost need their tongues rolled back into their mouths before they can bring themselves to speak. In the background, Rex is having almost the same issues, with his eyes nearly popping out of his head as well.

Cheryl breaks the silence by saying, "Well Evie, how did they do?"

Evie, the lead trainer, with long dark hair nearly down to her thighs answers, "They did very well, both of them. They are ready for the triathlon."

Jon and Shigeru give out a shout and go over to congratulate their partners.

Jon says, "This is wonderful. But how could you possibly have come so far in just a little over six days."

Cheryl answers for her, "Jon. Six days in this jungle with our women is equivalent to nearly six months training in an air conditioned gym out there in your world. You'll find they are quite ready for whatever we have for them during the triathlon tomorrow."

Walking back to Jon and Rachel's lodging, he asks her, "So, how was it out there?"

Rachel, with a bright look, answers, "Jon, the only word that comes to mind when trying to describe what I experienced after the fourth day with the women is...vitality!"

Jon, shocked by the sight of Rachel's eyes getting big as she answers, responds with, "I'll take that as a good thing then."

Rachel replies, "Yes, I'm sure I can pass their tests tomorrow."

Jon says, "Good. Just make sure you get enough rest tonight."

Holding the door to their hut open for her, Jon can't help but size Rachel up one more time as she enters.

The following day, the two women prepare for their side-by-side triathlon.

Standing at the edge of a densely forested area, Cheryl announces the first test. "Accuracy will be your first trial today. Your skills with a bow will be tested. This should show whether or not you have the sharp eye of an Amazon."

Stepping up first, with bow in hand, Keena takes an aiming stance. Up in the trees are several women with wooden bull's eyes, strapped with ropes.

On Cheryl's signal to begin, one of the roped bull's eyes drops. Without hesitation, Keena fires an arrow, hitting nearly dead center as the target swings limply. A moment later, two more targets swing down inward toward each other. One at a time, Keena fires arrows into the center of each one. A second passes, when all of a sudden; a boulder strapped on ropes flies toward Keena from behind. She ducks and rolls to the right just before it hits her and fires an arrow into the target tied to the back of it. Afterwards, another target drops from the trees, and like clockwork, she hits that one as well. With no more targets falling, Keena stands at ease. Applause erupts from the crowd of women as well as from Keena's comrades.

Next up is Rachel. As she stands there bow in hand, she starts to shake slightly. Then she realizes how much she's learned, and why she's made it as far as she has — destiny. Just then, two targets fall. She hits each with an arrow, though not as accurately as Keena's. A third target swings from left to right. She hits this one dead on. Then from her left, a boulder swings down, like the one aimed at Keena. Rachel rolls forward, only to be distracted by a second boulder swinging from her right. Nearly clipping her, the boulder swipes by as she ducks down very low to the ground. Catching her balance, she fires an arrow at the back of the first boulder, then swings around to hit the second. Success! Rachel, like Keena, has passed the first test.

Later on, near midday, the group treks up to a cliff where a waterfall crashes into a ravine. In front of the waterfall, a large wooden pole lies across the canyon. Smoothed out, the pole seems to be sturdily placed there intentionally for this test.

Cheryl shouts slightly over the raging waters of the falls, "For the second test, you will be tested on balance! Simply cross the ravine."

Shigeru looks at Jon and Rex. "Doesn't seem so bad," he says.

Keena steps up to the edge of the narrow pole first and begins taking her first few steps. She starts slowly; putting one foot in front of the other, then gradually picks up speed. About halfway across the pole, Keena brings herself up to a steady stride. Then suddenly, several Amazon women show themselves from behind the waterfall and fire rocks from slingshots toward Keena. Several of the rocks pelt her, throwing off her balance slightly. She slows herself to a lesser speed and does her best to avoid the rocks. Now nearing the other side, she picks up speed again and lunges over to land once again. Assessing her bruises, Keena relishes in the success of passing the second test.

Now up to the base of the pole is Rachel. Aware of the women hidden in the falls, Rachel doesn't start out with great speed like Keena, but rather slowly steps out to the ledge. Looking down, she realizes that the fall may or may not kill her, but the rapids below are not something she wants to deal with. After creeping several feet out on to the pole, the slingshots begin firing at her. Dodging the first few because of her awareness and expectancy of them coming, Rachel prepares for a chance to make a break for it. After the second volley, only some of the rocks hit her. Upon impact, she gives a slight grunt, and then takes off running toward the other side. When more rocks come as she's running, several more hit her, throwing off her balance greatly. Only 10 feet from the edge, she slips and falls. Just as Jon cringes in fear that he has lost Rachel, she grabs the pole and hoists herself under the belly of it. Holding steady, she begins to shimmy herself to the other side. Jon and Shigeru cheer for her. Just then, the slingshot fire picks back up, hitting her in the arms, legs, and ribcage. Yet Rachel continues moving forward until she finally reaches the edge. On the other side, Keena helps lift Rachel up to the upper ledge. Though bruised worse than Keena, Rachel manages to pull off the victory she strove so hard to achieve.

A few hours later, out on the very beach where Keena and Rachel were sworn in to the Amazonian way just a week earlier, the two await their final test. Cheryl stands in front of the two women and says, "Now the time has come for your third and final skill test of the triathlon, Combat Strength. Each of you will face off against an Amazon warrior. The rules are the same as the exhibition between Captain Abbott and Li-Lu. The first one to land on her back loses. You will each be armed only with staffs. Since Keena has gone first on both of the other trials, why not change it up and start with Rachel this time."

Rachel, looking down, receives a jolt and looks up quickly in response to Cheryl's suggestion. She nods in agreement and takes up a staff.

Cheryl smiles and says, "Very good, your opponent will be Evie."

Rachel is slightly surprised. Evie, aside from leading the training party, is the very trainer who taught her how to handle a staff this past week.

Evie, staff in hand, steps up and prepares to engage Rachel. Rachel, starting with a basic defensive stance stands there slightly frightened at her opposition. After Cheryl gives them the signal to start, the two erupt into melee combat. The sound of clattering wood is heard all around the beach, nearly drowning out the sound of the crashing waves. Rachel, holding her own against the far superior skilled Evie, is doing all but making contact with her. Though she has blocked every hit, Rachel has yet to attempt an offensive. After several more minutes of the two going round and round, staffs smacking against each other, Evie steps back and says, "Rachel, come on now, remember your training."

The two recommence in the same old tiresome cat and mouse battle. Another moment passes. Then Evie stops once again and shouts, "Rachel! We trained you better than this!"

Again, the fight resumes much the same. Finally, Evie stops once more and says, "Dammit Rachel. Why aren't you attacking?"

Before finishing her sentence, Rachel swipes the staff behind Evie's legs, dropping her straight down to the ground. Shocked, the other Amazons, as well as Jon and company, gasp. Rachel leans in to help Evie back up as Cheryl asks. "Amazing, how did you do that so easily?"

Rachel, smiling responds, "Well, after training with Evie, I realized how stern she could get. So I figured if I just did nothing but defend myself, it would irritate her and leave an opening for me."

Jon smiles and says to himself, "Attagirl Rach."

After several moments of applause and congratulations, Cheryl addresses the group again. "Rachel has all but proven herself to be an Amazon. Her only task remaining is her sign of good faith. But now the final test for Keena is about to commence. Keena, are you ready for combat?"

Keena eagerly and determined nods her head and says, "Yes, I am."

Cheryl says, "Good, your opponent...is me."

Keena, unsure if she can compete against the leader of the Amazons, thinks of her odds. "Really, it's no different than Rachel versus Evie," she thinks. "I went into that jungle a tough bitch to start. No offense to Rachel, but she was very malleable going in. Her wits plus the skills she picked up from the training, is what won her fight. They expect more from me, so they sent the top dog to be my challenge."

Looking over at the Amazon tribe leader, Keena awaits the signal to begin.

Evie, standing in front of the two, shouts, "Begin!"

With zero time wasted, Keena and Cheryl explode into ferocious combat. Keena holds back none, and as the fight goes on in its first few moments, Cheryl realizes she can't hold back either. This fight is not like Rachel's at all. Blows are contacting skin repeatedly and without reservation. Keena, realizing that Cheryl has done this thing hundreds of times before, calculates that her best chance of winning is to do something unexpected.

After exchanging several more blows, Keena acts upon her instincts. She stops attacking and with one hand, puts the staff down into the sand and turns toward Shigeru. Shigeru, confused by Keena's action, just looks at her. Looking as though she's about to break down and cry she says to him, "Shigeru, I can't go on."

Cheryl, commencing her attack, attempts to knock Keena's legs out from under her. As she swings her staff, Keena spins around counterclockwise grabbing her staff out of the sand on the way around and smacks it straight into the back of Cheryl's skull. The shocking blow brings her straight to her knees. Then after a moment of haziness, she falls flat forward, making Keena the victor.

Later that night, as Cheryl recovers from the head trauma she received in the fight, she congratulates the ladies. "You two are more than well on your way to becoming Amazons. Only a final task remains. And you may start it tomorrow. Each of you will set out across the island, and will attempt to bring back something as sign of good faith to the tribe. It is merely a simple token of appreciation for being accepted among us. There is no wrong answer, but you will know what the right item will be when you find it. Due to the special circumstances, we will make the finder of the rarest item brought back, the declared leader of the Amazons in this escapade you have asked us to participate in."

The two realizing the seriousness of this final task, and what it means to the tribe, accept the challenge and spend the rest of the evening with their men relaxing before the dawn. The next day will decide the course of how the final stand with the Cabal will go.

Chapter 47:

To the Ends of the Earth

The next day, the group meets with Cheryl and other members of the tribe on the outskirts of town.

Cheryl gives one final declaration before sending them on their final quest. "You two have made the Amazons proud and will surely be accepted among us, though only one of you will be permitted to lead us in the name of your allies against the Cabal. Remember, don't fret over what to bring back to us, just realize it will come to you when the time is right and you will know. Now, without further ado, you may begin your final test."

Rachel turns to Keena standing next to her and says, "Good luck."

Keena nods and responds, "You too, girl."

The two then split up and walk off into the wilderness.

Jon, proud at the fact that Rachel is finding herself, smiles as he sees her disappear into the jungle. Upon returning to the village, Rex approaches him.

"Jon, I need to talk to you about something," he says.

Jon asks, "What is it?"

Rex replies, "Jon, I know that high command thinks highly of your intuition on certain matters. Well, to some extent I have great intuition too. It's partly what's made me who I am. And it's gotten me out of a lot of predicaments. I don't know if you've felt something strange, but something seems amiss."

Jon, looking at Captain Abbott, asks, "What do you mean?"

Rex answers, "What I mean is, ever since the day the girls came back from their training, I've felt something odd, like something is out of place. Or something is out there. Ya know, in the wilderness. Not something that's supposed to be."

Jon says, "I'm not sure if I sense anything strange. I mean, this whole place is rather strange."

Rex says, "It's okay if you don't. But I do feel something out of place. I'm going on a hike out there to see what I stumble across. If the Amazons ask where I went, just tell them I went sightseeing and will return."

Jon nods his head and says, "Okay."

Right before Rex walks away, Jon extends his hand to him and says, "Good luck, Captain Abbott. I hope you don't find anything out there."

Rex smirks and shakes Jon's hand as he says, "Neither do I."

After Rex walks off into the jungle, Shigeru comes up to Jon and asks, "Where's Rex heading?"

Jon says, "I don't know. He said he felt something strange out there and wanted to go see it for himself. I didn't sense anything at first, but now it has me wondering."

Shigeru stands there for a minute looking off into the jungle with Jon, and then says, "Hmmm. Well, let's go get something to eat buddy. We can discuss our girls' new outfits."

Up the trail, Keena starts looking around for anything that catches her eye. She eventually finds herself in a valley where there are several Amazon women working on a large garden.

As she approaches, one of the women stops working and says, "You must be one of the new women here on the island."

Keena answers, "Yes, I'm on my final quest of seeking something as tribute to the tribe."

The woman says, "So your instinct brought you this way, I see."

Keena replies, "I guess. But I really don't know what I'm looking for."

The woman says, "Well, maybe you don't have to know."

Just then, Keena hears a terrible screech coming from over the hill in the distance.

"What was that?" she asks.

The Amazon woman replies, "That was a Dragon Vulture."

"A Dragon Vulture?" Keena asks, confused.

The woman continues, "It's a large predatory bird that is indigenous only to this island. Though very rare, they are still a great threat to Amazons who come across them alone."

Keena says under her breath, "Hmmm, rare huh?"

The woman says, "Oh, thinking of going after one are you? Well if you are you must be *very* careful. Even experienced Amazon warriors have fallen against them alone."

Keena responds, "Well, like you all keep saying. Let my instinct lead me."

Keena then heads out in the direction she heard the bird screech.

Just up over the hill, she finds herself overlooking a canyon with a wooden bridge across it. She decides to head the way the path leads and crosses the bridge.

Once on the other side, she finds a rocky spiral path leading narrowly up the side of the mountain she's on. Continuing upward, she finds herself going higher and higher. Finally, the path leads her to a cliff with an indention in the mountain. Nearly at the top, she realizes she may very well be at one of the highest points on the whole island.

Looking around, she starts to feel disappointed. "No Dragon Vultures," she thinks to herself.

Then she realizes she is standing in a giant nest. The entire cliff is covered in tall brown grass. Before she can react, she feels a rush of wind, and the biggest bird she's ever seen comes flapping down to the edge of the cliff. Its long brown feathers are ruffled in anger at her presence. After all, she is an intruder to the bird's home. The enormous bird, with a beak large enough to snap Keena's neck, squeals at her in a rage.

Keena, armed only with her staff and a small knife given to her by the Amazons, takes up a stance against the bird. Walking in a circle around each other, Keena holds her defensive pose until the bird strikes first. When it does, she bats it off with the staff. Holding it with both hands, she swings at it, offensively. Opening its wingspan up further, Keena realizes the bird's true size. The bird strikes again, and Keena puts her staff between her and the Dragon Vultures open mouth, catching it when it bites down. The bird holds the staff in its mouth for a moment, then bites down, snapping the staff in two. Keena, shocked by the bird's immense jaw strength, steps back.

Looking down, she sees a piece of her broken staff lying on the ground, now a giant splinter. Without hesitating, she makes a run for it, dodging the bird's next attack on the way down. Once she grabs the large makeshift spear, she rolls underneath the bird's right wing. While under it, she makes a quick decision to spike the sharp piece of wood into its wing. The bird lets out a painful screech.

Now behind the bird, Keena takes out her knife and jumps onto its back. Wasting no time at all, she stabs the bird at any opening she sees as it sways around trying to throw her off. Finally, the bird collapses from blood loss.

Keena, covered in blood and ruffled feathers, jumps off the birds' back. Realizing she's won, she begins to smile before sawing off the bird's head as a prize to bring back to the tribe.

Meanwhile, on the other side of the island, Rex wanders through a semi dense forested area. Unsure what it is he expects to find, he unsheathes the combat knife he managed to keep hidden from the Amazons.

Walking slowly through the forest, he hears only the sounds of nature and sees only the green of the vegetation and the sunlight filtering down through the trees.

Up ahead, Rex hears the sound of what seems to be twigs snapping. He thinks to himself, "That can only mean one thing. Footsteps."

Holding his knife in a position of readiness, he walks on to find out what made the sound. But when he reaches the spot where he heard the sound, he finds nothing. Sighing, Rex, almost disappointedly, turns around. To his surprise, someone is standing just 20 yards in front of him.

With his signature brown cowboy hat, boots, and duster jacket, the man is none other than The Drifter.

Rex, almost immediately realizing who it is, says, "Well now. I knew someone was out here. But I didn't think it would be you."

The Drifter looks up and says. "Know me, do you?"

Rex answers, "Only by reputation, of course."

The Drifter responds, "Well, then you must certainly know my track record, and that no one who has ever stood up against me has survived my fury."

Rex laughs a little and says, "Well, that's because you've never had me at the other end. Besides, I've got some friends that seem to have done a good job of evading you."

The Drifter replies, "They will be dealt with soon enough. But your cocky attitude has me interested for the moment."

Rex says, "Interested in your demise?"

The Drifter snarls back at him, "Your arrogance blinds you!"

"That may be," Rex quips. "But I ask you please; just give us five minutes alone to see who is the most fucking hostile cowboy around."

The Drifter smirks and says, "I'd gladly oblige, but I'm afraid you brought a knife to a gunfight."

Rex says, "Yeah, that would be a problem. As much as I'd like to have a good old fashioned pistol duel at the count of three, I'm afraid the Amazons have left me handicapped. I know you can shoot, and shoot damn good. Hell, so can I. But what do ya say we handle this thing a little rawer? Ya up for a real fight?"

The Drifter laughs and says, "Hardly a difference. I should be fair and at least let you keep your knife."

Rex responds, "No, I won't use it. Just as long as you don't go drawin barrels on me."

The Drifter says, "Okay. Bring it on."

The two modern-day cowboys prepare to brawl.

Captain Abbott sheaths his knife, and rushes The Drifter, fists swinging. Dodging left and right, The Drifter proves a difficult target to be hit by Rex. Finally, he makes contact, but The Drifter shakes it off and returns with an equally powerful hit. Rex shakes it off, but not as quickly as The Drifter shook off his hit.

The two break out into full-on melee frenzy. There in the quiet peaceful woods, the two most elite men in the world duke it out.

Dodging a strike, Rex causes The Drifter to hit a tree, splitting the bark into pieces. The Drifter retaliates by roundhouse kicking Rex straight across the jaw, bloodying his face. Rex, a little dizzy, puts his fists up and attempts another attack. This time, The Drifter catches his punch in midair with one hand and swings at him with the other, sending him spiraling sideways. Rex recovers again and lunges at the mercenary once more. He makes contact a few times, but is then repulsed by The Drifter's intense reflexes. The Drifter swings and lands one right across Rex's face again, bloodying it even more. Again he strikes, cracking his jaw. The again, he brutally bashes his knuckles into Captain Abbott's cheek, knocking several teeth loose.

Bloody, bruised, and semi delirious, Rex backs away from The Drifter and nearly out of breath says, "You have no idea who I am. Do you?"

He hastily reaches for his knife, but before he can attack, The Drifter reaches into his jacket and with a quick motion, lashes out with a bullwhip, snapping the blade from Rex's hand. He swings again, wrapping the lasso around Rex's left arm and pulls him toward him, bringing Rex to his knees. Bloody and teary eyed, Rex kneels before The Drifter as he leans down toward him.

The Drifter says, "You are Captain Abbott of Razor's Edge Special Forces unit. I know all about you. You were my next target after dealing with that other vermin you came here with. But I'm satisfied dealing with you now."

Rex responds, "You'll wish you never followed them here."

The Drifter smiles and says, "Oh, I already do."

Then he draws one of his revolvers from inside his coat and executes Rex with a gunshot to the head.

Back at the village, Jon goes to Shigeru and says, "Something's wrong. Rex should have come back by now."

Shigeru says, "I agree. What should we do?"

Jon replies, "I say we get a party together and look for him."

Just then, the two hear cheering. When they investigate the source of it, they find that Keena has returned to the village with the feathers and skull of the Dragon Vulture.

Cheryl, amazed at Keena's gift, welcomes her.

"Amazing," she says. "You have truly earned the right to be called an Amazon."

Cheryl speaks up so everyone around can hear her, "Let it be known that on this day Keena Turoni is officially an Amazon warrior!"

Roars of cheers erupt all around at the declaration.

Keena, muddied and slightly ratty looking, asks the guys, "I take it I made it back before Rachel?"

Jon answers, "Yes, but I'm worried about Captain Abbott too. He left shortly after you two did, saying he was just going on a scouting hike, but hasn't come back yet."

Keena responds, "Psshhh! That redneck's probably playin 'Cowboys and Indians' in the woods by himself."

Shigeru says, "Just the same, maybe we should go look for him. Jon's intuition has been correct in the past."

Jon sighs and says, "Yeah, and I am worried about Rachel too."

Keena consoles Jon, saying, "Jon. Don't worry. Something changed in Rachel out there in the jungle last week. She may not be like me or the majority of these women. But she has courage. She's doing this for you, and for us. To prove she can be of help to us. Rachel will be fine."

Jon replies, "Okay. But that still doesn't change the fact that something seems out of place with Rex."

Keena says, "Alright, let me change out of this jungle garb and clean up. Then we'll see where he's at."

About a half an hour later, Keena returns, cleaned up and back in the 21st century clothes she arrived at the island in.

Now toting her pistol once more, she is ready to help the others search for Captain Abbott. She learns that Cheryl and a band of about a dozen Amazons have agreed to help her, Jon, and Shigeru search for Rex.

Cheryl says, "Okay. Our best trackers can help us find Captain Abbott in no time. You say he left through the jungle this way, Jon?"

Jon nods.

The party then proceeds on the trail Rex took to leave the village.

Sometime later, the search party makes their way into the same lightly forested area where Rex and The Drifter had their bout. One of the trackers says, "There! Look ahead!"

Jon looks up, only to see a body lying on the grassy path, between the trees. Everyone rushes over to it.

Shocked, they discover it is the beaten and shot lifeless remains of Captain Abbot.

Jon murmurs, "He was right. There was someone here who was a danger to us."

Shigeru corrects Jon, "Someone who *is* a danger to us."

Cheryl says, "My trackers have picked up a faint trail of whoever did this. There's not much here but it appears as though Captain Abbott's killer went in that direction."

She points and continues to say, "There is a small village that way; maybe they've encountered whoever did this."

Jon and the others agree to head to the village.

Chapter 48:

Rachel Survive!

Just a few miles from the village, the group hears gunshots break out. Everyone starts running toward the depths of the jungle where the noise came from.

After several more shots are heard, Jon comments, "What's going on? Is there an army here to stop us?"

Just then the gunshots stop.

A moment later, another shot is heard, then one more a few seconds later. Then silence again. Finally the group arrives at the small village. Bodies of Amazon women, weapons in hand, are strewn everywhere. The entire group is stunned.

Cheryl asks, "Who could have done this? And how could they defeat Amazon women so easily? There were over 30 women in this village."

One of the Amazon women says to Cheryl, "Look ma'am, this one was killed by strangulation, and these by blade."

Jon notes, "Someone snuck up on them and picked them off until the attacked was discovered, that's when the gunshots broke out."

Shigeru then comments, "But seriously, who could have done this?"

Suddenly a voice snarls from above, "Oh come on, surely you could have figured it out by now."

It's The Drifter, standing in a tree above them.

As they look up at him, he hops down to the ground not far in front of them. Shigeru and Keena attempt to shoot him, but as soon as they draw their weapons, The Drifter draws one of his signature six guns. With one hand holding the gun and pulling the trigger and the his left hand batting down the hammer of the revolver, he fires two quick shots, knocking the guns right from the couple's hands. One of the Amazon women attempts to cartwheel toward The Drifter, but with a third bat of his hand on the revolver hammer, he guns her down. A second Amazon standing near the back of the group draws back her bow and arrow in another attempt to kill The Drifter. The arrow fires, but with lightning fast reflexes, he catches it in midair, just before it impacts his chest. Jon, not nearly as fast of a draw as Keena and Shigeru, doesn't even attempt to reach for his pistol.

Now with both revolvers in hand The Drifter holds the group hostage.

"Well, well," he says. "Looks like I caught up to ya'll again. And here on the fabled Island of the Amazons too. Ya know. I have to admit. It's pretty impressive to try and gather the Amazons as an army against the Cabal. But what good is an army up against a one-man army like myself. Now they may give me a real challenge after all. I think once I'm finished with all of you, I'll use the remaining Amazons as a sport, since after I finish you; most of the real challenges for me in this world will be gone."

Jon asks, "How did you know we were amassing them as an army against the Cabal?"

The Drifter answers, "I arrived shortly after you did. I wanted to see what I was up against since there were so many inhabitants on the island. So I stood back and watched for a bit." He motions toward Keena and says, "I saw that little black beauty there and the other little girl training out in the jungle. By the way, where is that pretty thing at anyway?"

The group remains silent.

The Drifter goes on saying, "Oh yeah, that's right. She has to prove herself on her own to the tribe. Maybe I'll just go get her first."

Jon lunges forward but stops to finish listening to The Drifter.

"Well," he says. "I may be stupid here for not finishing you off while I got the chance this time. But I can't resist the opportunity to get a little good sport in with the last remaining threat to the Cabal. After all, I took care of Captain Abbott easily enough."

The group cringes.

Jon shouts, "The Cabal will not go on forever! If not us, then someone else will stop them!"

The Drifter breathes heavily and says, "I once thought as you do, Jon Peters."

Stepping back with both pistols still drawn on the group, The Drifter moves toward the tree line. He makes one last remark before leaving. "I'm gonna find that sweet girl, and I'm gonna kill her. Maybe that will light a fire under your ass to give me some real competition."

He then darts off into the jungle.

Several Amazon women start to run after him, but Cheryl says, "Stop. Don't pursue him. He'll kill us all."

The women halt.

Jon says hastily, "Well, we can't just let him kill Rachel."

Cheryl hopelessly replies, "It's too late Jon. A man like that can't be stopped. And he may be right about the Cabal. If they have a single man like him, they are invincible on the large scale."

332

Jon sternly says, "Wait a God damn minute! What happened to all that Amazon warrior might stuff? And what about your obligation to fellow sisters? Where'd that go huh?"

Cheryl begins to listen up.

Jon continues, "Rachel has practically made it through your trials, and Keena already has. They played by your rules. You can't tell me you're suddenly going to abandon your oath now!"

Cheryl responds, "You're right. Now is the time more than ever to prove our worth among men. By stopping him, we would be stopping the most elite man in the world and that would put women as a superior gender on the map forever! Quick, let's go. His tracks are light and well masked, but we can find him. If Rachel can just survive long enough, we can get there before it's too late for her."

The Amazon women start out in their mission to hunt down The Drifter, the most formidable mercenary in the world.

On the way out, Shigeru says to Jon, "You did it, man."

Jon responds, "Did what?"

Shigeru answers, "You convinced the Amazons to join us. Just like high command thought you could."

Jon smiles as Keena puts her hand on his shoulder and agrees. The group then moves out in hopes of catching up to The Drifter before he gets to Rachel.

Up a ways, on the steady incline of a nearby mountain, Rachel is walking along still looking for her tribute to the tribe, unaware of what has transpired.

Rachel thinks to herself, "What the hell am I gonna bring back? I wonder if Keena has found something yet.

Come on Rachel, you can do this. Keena may be stronger and wittier than me, but surely I'm intellectually smarter. I can figure something out."

Just then, she hears something behind her.

Looking back down the grassy, tree covered hill, she sees nothing. Turning back to look up the hill ahead of her, she is startled by a familiar voice.

"Hello Rachel," The Drifter says.

Scared, she braces her staff tightly.

"My, my, looks like you've toughened up a little bit. And that outfit. Wooo! You are a doll," He continues.

Rachel, shaking, asks with a quiver in her voice, "What are you doing here?"

The Drifter responds, "I'm here to finish my job and now that I've taken care of Captain Abbott, you're next sweetheart."

Rachel shocked at what she just heard, thinks to herself, "Oh no, he killed Rex. He really is unstoppable."

The Drifter draws out one of his six guns and says, "Hate to end this so quickly, but I got deadlines to meet."

Rachel shouts, "Wait!"

The Drifter stops to hear her out.

She continues, "It's really that easy for you, isn't it. You can just shoot me and it's over. I don't have a gun, and even if I did, I couldn't out shoot you. No one probably can. But can't I get a shot at fighting you hand to hand. I mean, I've been doing all this training. At least let me die knowing I tried."

The Drifter smirks, puts his revolver back into his coat, and says. "Okay sugar. Show me what you got."

Rachel stands there a moment and thinks, "Okay Rachel. This is it. Fight or die. Wait. Fight or die. That IS it. I've never looked at it like that. I truly realize that I am going to die today, so there has never been a time more for me to give it my all. I'm not keeping archives in Greece anymore. I'm going to die."

The Drifter says, "Ummm, okay, I can draw my peacemaker out again if you're not gonna make a move."

Without responding verbally, Rachel just lunges toward The Drifter, swinging her staff. The blow lands right across his shoulder, knocking him sideways.

Rubbing his left shoulder and triceps, he says, "Damn! You're feistier than I thought you'd be."

Then he swings out toward her landing a closed hand punch right across Rachel's sweet feminine face.

After recovering from the blow, she attacks several more times with the staff, each time either missing or only lightly grazing him.

Retaliating, The Drifter lands several more hits, bruising Rachel even further.

Not afraid to die, she takes the blows and returns them, busting The Drifter square in the nose. He steps back to discover his nose bleeding lightly.

Aggressively, he kicks Rachel in the gut sending her tumbling several feet down the hill. Running up on her, he attempts to stomp her into the dirt. She braces herself and hops up to intercept his colliding body with her open palms. The two hit the ground and roll.

Getting to her feet first, Rachel tries kicking a mud hole in The Drifter's stomach, but he hops up and grabs her by the throat, choking her.

Fighting and gasping for air, the scantily clad beauty grips The Drifter's wrists to loosen his grasp. Finally, she hikes up her knee, striking him between the legs. He loosens his clutch, allowing for her to fall down to the ground and roll back toward her staff.

Way down the mountain, the group is hurrying, yet fighting against the incline. The would-be rescuers are rushing to try and make it to Rachel in hopes of saving her.

Keena, running, shouts, "I sure hope we make it in time."

Shigeru notes, "All Rachel has to do is survive."

Cheryl responds, "The girl's at least good enough to do that."

Jon thinks to himself as he hustles up the low mountain terrain, "Come on Rachel. Just hang on a little bit."

Now with the staff in hand again, Rachel takes a defensive stance. The Drifter, sick and tired of her unexpected evasiveness, has a change of tone and draws his pistols. As the shots crack off from both barrels, Rachel falls backward, dodging the initial barrage of fire.

Landing on her back, she slides down the grassy slope of the hill, staff still in hand. The Drifter's bullets whiz overhead, barely missing her. Just before lowering his fire to hit her, both revolvers run out of ammo. Continuing her slide toward him, Rachel points her staff toward his chest like a medieval joust. In a vain attempt to stop the hit, The Drifter casts aside both guns and tries to block the staff. Hitting him in the chest, the two fall even farther back down the slope together.

Getting up first this time, The Drifter reaches for his bull whip and lashes it around Rachel's staff, yanking it from her hands. As the staff is yanked out of her hands, she rushes The Drifter like a football player, landing her palms and head into his chest, between the lapels of his duster jacket.

Closing his fist, The Drifter punches Rachel across the side of her right eyebrow, throwing her off of him. Standing back up, he kicks her hard in the ribs, cracking them, then lassos the whip around her neck and pulls her up to her knees. Stooped before him, Rachel is being choked to death by the ruthless menace. The Drifter pulls her in closer as he strangles her to death. Grasping the edge of the rope around her neck, Rachel feels the life leaving her body. The Drifter laughs as he watches the beaten and bruised apple of Jon's eye slowly pass away. Rachel is pulled in closer to The Drifter's body, knowing she is about to die. The Drifter laughs even more, and then abruptly stops. His expression suddenly freezes, as if time has stopped. His grip loosens and Rachel falls back onto the ground as she recovers from the near fatality.

Looking down, The Drifter realizes that he has been stabbed in the gut and is bleeding horrendously. He notices the forgotten knife of Captain Abbott's that he took after killing him, is stuck in his gut, with Rachel's hand at the other end of it. Rachel, while being throttled, reached into his jacket and grabbed the knife while he was distracted by his own maniacal laughing.

Not saying another word, The Drifter falls back, drenched in his own blood and passes away on the hillside.

Farther down the hill, the group hears the gunshots The Drifter fired at Rachel and starts panicking.

"Oh no," cries Cheryl. "We may be too late!"

Jon says angrily, "No! Rachel! I can't let you die. Not today."

As the group continues upward toward the gunshots they heard minutes earlier, they see a figure ahead of them. Stopping to see who it is, they begin to make the figure out.

Limping down the hill, bruised, bloodied, and holding her cracked ribs with one hand, is Rachel. Still wearing her revealing jungle clothes, she is using her staff as a sort of walking stick. Noticing the others below, she lets go of her ribs with her right hand and holds up an object. It's the brown cowboy hat of the infamous Drifter, as a symbol of victory and tribute to the tribe of the Amazons. The others are shocked at the sight. Rachel, who was just a simple historical reference worker earlier this year, defeated a man deemed by many to be invincible, and she did it mostly with her wit. Jon and the others rush over to her, realizing she is bruised pretty badly.

Nearly speechless, Jon just simply wraps his arms around Rachel and kisses her. She embraces his love fully and is all but quick to let go of him. She then turns to see Cheryl and the other Amazon women kneeling with their fingers interlocked together, in a sort of praying fashion at her.

Cheryl says, "Rachel, we are indebted to you. Your tribute is more than worthy of being accepted as an Amazon. It is enough for us to call you leader."

Rachel, stunned, responds, "Are you sure? What about Keena?"

Keena answers, "My tribute was fairly impressive, but I could have never stopped The Drifter."

Cheryl stands and says, "Yes. Men like him, with hardened hearts are not stopped easily. Before coming here to the island, I was married. My husband was a women's martial arts manager. I was to be the next big thing. He promised me everything on my way to the top. Then one day, when I didn't accept his order to be passed around like a cheap thrill to his colleagues, he promised to ruin me. He had one of my fights rigged, my opponent was allowed to get away with throwing powder in my eyes and she had a piece of metal under her closed fist. The ref called no penalties. Soon after, I left him and was denied opportunity after opportunity. He was just a low ranking member of the Cabal. But still, that Faustian fraternity requires hardened hearts to keep it running. The Drifter had the same kind of heart. He would have surely wiped out all of our people. Now I ask again. Will you lead us, Rachel Lynn?"

Rachel looks at the others, then the Amazons, then back to Cheryl.

"Yes," she says. "I will lead us to victory, once and for all."

Chapter 49:

The Last Hurrah

Far out at sea, on the other side of the world, an island in the Pacific Ocean not occupied in millennia has been fortified by a secret force created by the Cabal. The large stone monuments and buildings litter the island that was once part of a massive continent.

Among this vast array of stone buildings is a defense force consisting of reanimated corpses of various soldiers from around the world, fitted with red and silver battle gear and metallic face masks. These warriors, who were commissioned by the Cabal, are the ultimate mix of modern technology and necromancy, a blend of ancient alchemy and science. Supplies and machine gun nests surround the main temple on the island as a means of supporting these undead abominations.

Unbeknownst to the surviving members of the Cabal, who have gathered here on this day, Rachel, who in the weeks prior has become an Amazon Warrior and defeated one of their most valuable assets, The Drifter; is now present on the island. Leading a task force consisting of over 1800 Amazon Warrior women, and accompanied by her friends, Rachel, barely recovered from her wounds, has chosen to continue donning the revealing jungle outfit of the Amazons as a symbol of leadership. Keena, however, has fitted herself with black shorts and tank top as well as a pair of black combat boots and leather gloves. Jon and Shigeru, who has sacrificed his usual brightly colored bell bottom pants and club jacket, are now wearing flak jackets and cargo pants. This is a new look for Jon and is far different than the casual male dress clothes he taught his class in.

The small army is nestled on the outskirts of the island after making an amphibious landing via canoes provided by the inhabitants of New Guinea the night before.

Looking through binoculars, Jon sees several of the undead troops patrolling up over a ledge on the perimeter. He comments, "Okay, so intelligence says there are about 500 of them, correct?"

Shigeru answers, "Yes."

Jon further asks, "And there are about 400 members of the Cabal in there, right?"

Shigeru again answers, "Yes."

Jon says, "Well, with us, and Todd's crew, that makes nearly 2,000 of us against less than 1,000 of them. This should be a cinch."

Cheryl cuts in and says, "Maybe, but with them being as fortified as they are and as heavily armed, it may also take everything we've got to penetrate their lines. As you said before, many Amazons may be killed. Cunning warriors we are, but we can only dodge so many bullets."

Keena adds, "Which is why Todd's Special Forces team arriving is of utmost importance. We'll need him to make absolutely sure no members of the Cabal escape while the Amazons keep those things out there at bay."

Jon says, "I only hope they make it in time. We haven't heard a word from him."

Shigeru throws his hands up and says, "Guys, relax. They'll be here. When I talked to Chris on the phone, he assured me that Todd and the other members of Razor's Edge always get the job done."

Changing the subject, Cheryl says to Rachel, "It's interesting; Mu is a lot like the Island of the Amazons.

Other than the temples here, the environment is quite similar. It's almost as if it were destiny for us to help do this."

Rachel responds to Cheryl's observation with one of her own, "We've all learned a lot about destiny lately."

Minutes later, Cheryl approaches Jon and says, "If your people don't get here soon, we're going to have to commence this attack without them. We'll lose the element of surprise if the Cabal's scouts discover us."

As Jon contemplates the problem, of Todd's group not being present, Rachel steps in.

"Now," she says firmly. "Let's do it now."

The others, amazed at Rachel's command presence, nod in agreement.

The Amazons, all in place strategically around the encamped undead troops protecting the temple, prepare to strike.

Just above the team, on a stone ledge, two scouts walk by. As their backs turn, Rachel, Cheryl, and several other Amazons spring up and attack them.

Rachel shouts on their way up the ledge, "Attack!"

From all over the jungle surroundings, Amazonian women rise to the heavily armed mechanized enemy. Arrows and thrown spears soon fill the air. Gunfire is returned soon after. With the element of surprise, our heroes start the attack off right. Running out into the chaos of battle, Jon, Keena, and Shigeru now join the fight as well.

Deep inside the confines of the temple, the large cache of the Cabal are preparing for their summoning ritual.

The large room appears to be like a stadium, with seating on all four sides of the inner sanctum to seat the over 400 present members of the Cabal. The members all hear the clatter of gunfire and battle cries of the Amazon women outside.

One member asks, "Are we safe here? No one was supposed to know about this island!"

A high ranking general of the United States Army and member of the Cabal, replies, "Not to worry gentlemen. Our elite undead defense force has been invented by the greatest minds in military and occult thought." Gesturing over to a slimy looking scientist type, with a white lab coat and glasses, and a dark, macabre looking chap with a cloak, the general says, "Fire and Ice together can be quite a destructive force."

Fire, the scientist, states, "Yes, combining the archaic knowledge of old, with current research in genetics has been most successful."

Ice, the dark man with the cloak adds, "No need to fear. Necromancy has never been so effective in all of history, until the Fire and Ice program was started."

The general continues, "If we had only put more into that project, rather than Ben T.'s HRT program, the tables would not have turned on us as they have."

The other members of the Cabal nod and murmur in agreement, to the General's comfort.

Meanwhile, outside, the battle is fierce. The intimidating mechanized army of undead clash with the beautiful but skilled Amazon warriors.

Side by side under cover, Keena says to Jon, "Jon! This is a blood bath! We may have the numbers, but they are just too advanced for us to engage like this!"

Jon responds, "We need to get in that temple and stop the Cabal directly. No Cabal. No opposition."

Shigeru, now crouching next to them asks, "So what's your suggestion?"

Jon answers, "Well, if we can manage to get into the temple with a dozen or so of the Amazonians, we should be able to stop them no problem. The battle will just continue as a diversion like we planned."

Keena asserts, "Yeah, but that plan involved Todd and his men."

Jon replies, "We'll just have to improvise. I'll go tell Rachel."

With gunfire and commotion all around, Jon makes a run toward Rachel's position.

At the jungle's edge, Rachel and several Amazon archers battle from under the cover of vegetation. Several dead Amazon women lie near their position.

Jon arrives by her side and says, "Rachel, I need you to lure those things out into the jungle. With victory on their minds, they'll follow suit, and we can make our way into the temple to take out the Cabal."

Rachel responds, "Just the three of you?!"

Jon says, "Maybe you could spare a dozen or so Amazonians to help us."

She answers, "I'll see what I can do."

Jon nods and runs back to Shigeru and Keena.

Several minutes of firefight later, Rachel calls out to the other women to retreat into the jungle.

In the chaos of their retreat, Jon sees Cheryl and over a dozen Amazon women run to cover behind them. Jon, Keena, and Shigeru restrain their fire in an effort to mask their presence from the enemy as they pursue the other Amazon warriors.

Cheryl and the other women sneak their way over to Jon and the others.

Cheryl says, "What's your plan?"

Jon replies, "The back area of the temple will be relatively undefended, especially now that Rachel has retreated. The enemy will be busy chasing after them. If we can knock out what remaining defense they have, we can scale the wall and enter the temple."

Cheryl replies, "Alright, I'm not happy that your so-called unified forces of light didn't follow up with their end of the agreement. But you all have proven yourself to me. We'll see this through until the day is ours. Just know that we will be quite reluctant to work with them in the future."

Jon answers, "Understood."

The team then skirts silently around the undead troopers who are running toward the jungle and finds a low stone wall with only a handful of guards and a single machine gun nest protecting it. Swiftly, Evie, the very same Amazon woman who helped train Keena and Rachel, signals two archers to eliminate the two undead that are manning the machine gun nest. Confused, the other three soldiers look up to see what is going on. Before they even realize what has happened, a mob of women swarm them from all sides and clear the area to scale the wall.

Inside the temple, as the Cabal gets their dark ritual of sorcery underway, a large monitor on the wall comes on. On the monitor, fragments of the battle can be seen in the background, and one of the faceless undead soldiers stands in front of the camera.

The General asks, "What is the situation?"

Behind the shroud of the masked trooper, a metallic raspy voice answers, "It's over, Commander. The rebels have been defeated and the last of them are fleeing into the jungle. We've sustained heavy loses, but have enough to engage them and finish them off."

The general replies, "Good. Eradicate them. Let none of them leave this island."

The screen shuts off, and the attention in the room goes back to the ritual.

In the upper levels, the team has made their way into the room where the Cabal is holding their ritual. Looking down, they see what looks like a small concert of people chanting and looking toward the center of the room.

Shigeru says, "Jeez, we couldn't have timed this any closer, could we?"

Just as the words leave his mouth, a small dark portal begins opening at the center of the arena-like room.

Jon replies, "No, we couldn't have."

Keena, distressed, asks Jon, "Now what do we do?"

Jon thinks a moment and says, "There's nothing we can do except finish this."

Jon takes off running down the slope below toward the center of the room, pistol drawn. He makes it halfway down before even a few members of the Cabal notice him. Down near the edge of the portal, he holds his gun out with both hands and yells, "Stop!"

Keena, running with the others down toward him shouts, "Jon! Look out!"

Jon turns around and sees something start to protrude from the portal. A large, red, lizard-like creature with yellow eyes and a forked tongue is making its way from the nether world into this one. Jon turns and fires.

346

The monster drops dead, but more silhouettes begin making their way through. The others, now by Jon's side, prepare to combat this ancient evil. As more of the creatures come into the earth's plane, the Amazon women brace themselves for action.

Cheryl says, "I don't think we can last long against what's coming through."

Jon says, "I'm so sorry, Cheryl."

Just then, gunshots are heard from above. The group looks up, and to their surprise, they see several people coming down via zip lines from the opening at the top of the temple.

Shigeru smiles and then shouts, "It's Todd! And Razor's Edge!"

Sure enough, Todd and the other 16 elite members of his Razor's Edge Special Forces Unit are descending down to their aid, firing on members of the Cabal who have taken up arms themselves, and the demons who are making their way in. Three members of the unit run to the edge of the portal and, gun first, step in halfway to fire at anything they see.

Todd stands next to Jon and says, "Sorry we're running late. Damn Cabal shot down our first plane, had to get a new one."

Cheryl standing on the other side of him responds, "I was beginning to worry, but all that matters now is that you're here and we can end this."

Suddenly, five of the undead troops come rushing in and join in the fire fight. Several members of Todd's team are taken out. The squad defending the portal entrance is pushed back as several demons force their way in. Much of the chanting has stopped due to members of the Cabal rushing to take up arms, but the portal is still open. With only nine of the Amazon women left, and eleven members of Razor's Edge, the group's numbers are dwindling.

Just when all hope seems lost, the doors of the temple burst open and Rachel, along with hundreds of Amazon women, rush into the main room. The portal closes as the chanting ceases and a feminist massacre of the elite Cabal, begins.

Rachel, looking around, sees Jon and smiles. She starts to run toward him and as he starts to go to her, he is hit by a shot in the back of his left shoulder.

Rachel screams, "Jon! No!"

Behind him is a member of the Cabal, holding a tactical 12 gauge shotgun.

Cheryl, turning to see what has happened, notices the man.

"Ralph?" she questions as she realizes it is her former husband.

The man looks at her and gasps, "Cheryl?"

Without a second thought, Cheryl flings her signature Bowie Knife right into his chest.

Rachel, now at Jon's side, starts crying, "Jon, please hang on!"

Jon, lying on his back, and short of breath replies, "Rachel. You did it. Now you're no longer the damsel in distress you hated being."

Tears flowing down her face, Rachel says, "But I can't go on without you. Please don't die on me."

Jon, no longer able to respond, closes his eyes in Rachel's arms. The others stand by and look on as the army of Amazon women sweep the temple, ridding the world once and for all of the once invincible Cabal.

Chapter 50:

Hindsight is 20/20

Five weeks later, on the rooftop of a hotel resort in Morocco, a summit is underway. This gathering, held by Francisco and Romina, is to bring members of the forces of light to the public, with non-Cabalist leaders and heads of industry from around the world to create a new system.

Rachel, with longing in her eyes, stares out at the beautiful Moroccan landscape. She has traded in her Amazon clothing for a white sweater.

After a moment, she hears a voice behind her say, "You always have romanticized the desert."

She turns and sees the most amazing sight in the world. Jon, the love of her life, nearly recovered from his wounds. She turns to kiss him and be held in his arms. The two stand on the balcony and look out for a moment before being interrupted. It's Shigeru and Keena.

Shigeru says, "Hey, Jon! Good to see you standin up."

Jon turns to shake hands and hug him.

Shigeru continues, "You're lookin a lot better than you did last week."

Jon smiles and says, "I feel a lot better too."

Keena interrupts, "All right guys, we gotta cut this short. The inauguration is about to start, and we can't be late for our award ceremony."

The group then heads off to a large stage area surrounded by thousands of onlookers and television cameras. Seated near the front, Jon and Rachel are put next to Cheryl, who opted out of wearing a formal outfit and stuck with her Amazon clothing. She and the other Amazon women present have been the center of attraction today.

After greeting Keena and Rachel, Cheryl asks, "Rachel, I have to ask you one more time. Are you sure you don't want to come back to the Island of the Amazons and lead us?"

Rachel responds, "Cheryl, I can't. My place is with Jon. I already took one opportunity over him before, and destiny showed me that I was wrong. Besides, you are fit to be their leader far more than I could ever hope to be."

Cheryl smiles and says, "Okay, but you and Keena both will be Amazons until the day you die. Just know this."

Keena replies, "We do, and we consider it an honor that we will never forget."

A moment later, Francisco takes the stage and approaches the microphone.

"Ladies and Gentlemen," he says as the crowd falls silent. "Today, we embark on a new vision of world order. Not a new world order as many have sought to construct in the past, but one that is based on principle. In recent times, we have seen the destruction caused by such orders. The lying, cheating, stealing, coveting, and overt covering up of the Cabal is no more. Many great individuals banded together to stop this great evil. Many of them were sacrificed at the altar of democracy. In the wake of their efforts, we have designed a new system to be installed as a replacement for the old. A democratic congress of men and women made for the people, by the people. This new governing body will be overseen by a constitutional monarchy. Not one of dictatorship or tyranny, but of dignity and morale. This leader has been chosen by a unanimous vote over the past weeks delegation. May I present to you, Princess Romina, the last of the Richter family line."

The crowd bursts into cheers and applause as Romina makes her way out onto the stage.

Blonde and stunning, she seems almost unreal in comparison to the dark suited leadership that has been seen in recent times before her.

Francisco says to Romina, "As Prime Minister of the new governing body, I ask you. Do you accept the title of Queen, and will you rule justly unlike those before you?"

Romina nods and turns toward the audience, "Yes, I do."

The crowd again breaks out into applause.

Romina goes on to say, "In my first act as Queen, I wish to properly thank four individuals who just one year ago were living their daily lives, and who unknowingly affected what was going on behind the curtain. Like many of you, they had relationship problems, work problems, family problems, and just plain problems. Destiny itself, though a journal by a man named Cyrus Methena, brought these four together, and because of them, we are standing here today. People, we owe a great debt of gratitude to these men and women. Please take the stage."

Romina then motions to the group to come up.

As they approach, Todd comes forward with four medals and hands them to Romina.

On the far right of the line of recipients is Keena. Romina takes the first medal and drapes it around her neck.

She then addresses her, "Keena Turoni, your valiant efforts in supporting this group has been more than worthy of note. You followed them around the world and aided them with every quest they took on. Without any reason or gain, you put your life in harm's way for them. You greatly contributed to taking down several branches of the mighty Cabal. Thank you for all you have done."

Keena bows as Romina moves on to Shigeru.

Draping his medal over his neck, Romina says, "Shigeru Iwata, your faith and dedication to your clan has affected the entire outcome of this conflict. You defended two westerners whom you had never met, to the point of nearly your own demise. You overcame a demonic entity and saved the others from similar forces. Without you, this team would have been eliminated before it was even formed. I thank you sincerely."

Shigeru nods and says, "Thank you, ma'am."

Romina then moves over to Rachel.

"Rachel Lynn," she says. "Your contribution has been limitless. You found and sent the journal of Cyrus Methena to the one person you knew could make sense of it. You then followed him around the world and made sure that the information was used to its fullest. You held the sensibility of the team together with your level head. And in the most notable show of courage, you defeated the most dangerous man to have ever walked the earth. This qualified you to be leader of the Amazons and with that leadership you took down the very core of the Cabal. I thank you, and as far as I am concerned, you are *my* Queen."

Rachel accepts and wipes a tear from her eye as Romina moves over to Jon.

Not putting the medal over Jon's neck first like she did with the others, Romina says, "Jon Peters, your very name should be written on my crown. I cannot put your value into words. Before all of this, you broke the rules and saw through the smokescreen veil of the Cabal. You followed the journal from Greece to Cameroon. You accepted a challenge from the system itself. Faced with death on numerous occasions, you never gave up. When the time called, you saved your woman, you saved your friends, and you saved the world. You are the master of your field, and an inspiration to us all. Rachel is lucky to have you as a mate."

She then places the medal over his head and kisses him on the cheek.

"Thank you, Jon Peters. I thank all of you," she says looking down the line at the others.

The crowd begins roaring and cheering the group of heroes before them. Jon is stunned at the reaction. He turns to the others and says, "Wow, I never would have got an ovation like this teaching archaeology, that's for sure."

When the applause dies down, Romina says, "Now I would like everyone to stand and honor several notable heroes who died in their efforts to stop the Cabal. These, of course, are not all of those who gave their lives, but they are worthy of mention on this day."

The sun, now nearly set, has left the open air stage dark. The stage lights dim and spotlights turn on to showcase more than three dozen portraits across the stage behind the group. The team turns around to view them with everyone else.

Among the pictures are several familiar faces. Katja Petrov, Rex Anselmo Abbott, Emily Morgan, Lucis Wendell, Jeff and Bridgette Carls, and to Shigeru's surprise, Embo Iwata. Shigeru, amazed at seeing his father's picture up there with the others, stands there stunned. Jon walks up and puts his hand on Shigeru's shoulder.

"I told 'em to put him up there Shig," Jon says. "They asked who we think should be honored. So along with the others, I suggested him."

Shigeru, with tears streaming down his face says, "Thank you, my friend."

After a moment of silence, Chris Green of the unified forces of light approaches the microphone. A groovy techno beat accompanies him as he says, "Now everyone, without further ado, a song from the artist formerly known as Alice Malice."

The group, shocked, looks over to see Allison take the stage. She has a new and squeaky clean look. She sings the new song that she wrote just for this event. It deals with overcoming the odds. During a break in the singing, she runs over to the others.

"I just wanted to thank you all again," she says. "From now on, I'm going to use my talent constructively."

Rachel says, "Wow. Good for you. I knew you weren't all bad."

As the catchy tune sets in, the team prepares to party the night away.

The following morning, the group meets on the desert plain, at a small airport.

Shigeru says, "Well, that must be our flight."

A plane comes taxiing down the runway toward the team.

Romina and Francisco approach the group.

"Jon, your plane will be ready momentarily," Romina says. "We have a familiar face who will be taking you back to the US."

"Who?" Jon asks.

Just then, a small jet that seems familiar makes its way down the runway. Getting off the plane is the face to match it.

Jon exclaims, "Sahib?!"

It is Sahib, flying the very jet they used to escape Chernobyl.

"What are you doing here?" Jon asks.

Sahib responds, "I was requested by The Sheik to fly him in for the summit. While I was here, they assigned me to fly you and Rachel to the US. No gremlins this time, I promise."

Everyone bursts into laughter.

Shigeru asks, "So what is it they got you doing, anyway?"

Jon answers, "Well, my old colleague, Professor Gray, started up a new board to reform the education system the right way. He wants me to come back and head the whole thing up. Looks like I'll be doing what I love after all. What about you? I can't convince you to come with us?"

Shigeru replies, "Nah, me and Keena are gonna head back to Japan, reform the Yakuza clan, and maintain some order."

Jon nods his head and says, "You do well my friend."

Shigeru responds, "You too."

The two shake hands and hug.

Keena says to Rachel, "Come here girl," and they hug as well.

Jon turns to Keena and says, "Take care of him. I think you're the only one who can."

Keena smiles and says, "I will," as she hugs Jon.

Shigeru moves over to Rachel.

"Well," he says. "I'm gonna miss you, little lady."

Rachel hugs him and says, "I'm gonna miss you too Shig."

After all the hugs and goodbyes are exchanged, Shigeru and Keena board their plane. The two then fly off, while the others wave at them from the Moroccan desert landing strip.

Jon turns to Rachel and says, "I suppose it's time we went too."

Rachel asks, "Pick up where we left off?"

Jon chuckles and says, "I sure hope not."

Rachel's jaw drops.

"Uhh!" she says.

Jon redeems himself with, "I thought we'd stay together this time."

Rachel replies, "Me too."

Jon adds, "I thought maybe with marriage."

Rachel smiles as the two follow Sahib aboard the plane.

Waving goodbye to Romina and Francisco, the two set out to their new life in the brave new world they helped launch, starting over, never to be corrupted by the likes of the Cabal again...

...Or is it?

Afterword

I hope you enjoyed reading *Glimmer in the Ashes* as much as I enjoyed writing it. If you would like more information on the fascinating world I created, I'd like to invite you to converse with me on my website *www.dsnewman.com*. Be sure to sign up for my mailing list there so you can be updated about my next book, *Way of the Drifter*. It's a prequel that tells the story of "The Drifter" character from this book. Also, be on the lookout for this book's sequel, *Ashes Rekindled*. You can also Like me on Facebook, Follow me on Twitter, and Review me on Goodreads. Thank you for reading; I look forward to hearing from you!

Acknowledgments

First off, I want to thank all the readers who purchased this book. It's because of you that I will continue to create.

I'd like to thank my friend Scott Tipton for bullshitting with me in D.C. last year. The entire basis of this book wouldn't exist without you.

I want to say thank you to Amanda Demigod for designing this awesome book cover.

Thank you to my friend Matthew Crum who helped temper my ideas in the early stages of this book.

Thank you to Nandita Naik for doing an excellent job editing. I've gained a whole new perspective and confidence in my writing due to her.

Thank you to my girlfriend Liz, who was not only my first reader, but a huge supporter of mine through most of the process of creating this book.

Thank you to my boss, Romina York, for having such a beautiful name that inspired the name of a character in this story.

Thank you to my friend Hanan, whose maiden name, Al-Nashmi, was used in the story.

Thank you to my Mother for inspiring the name of Keena.

Thank you to Cheryl for just having the name Cheryl when I just needed a name to use.

Acknowledgments

(Continued)

Thank you to DJ KAPKOM for having an excellent Greek surname that inspired Cyrus Methena.

Thank you to Morgan Webber and Todd Lancaster, two people who I know in real life that helped inspire characters based on them.

Also, thank you to MillerCoors Legal Department, for giving me permission to use Redd's Apple Ale, their delicious beverage, in my story.

And a special thanks to Pantera, for inspiring the character Captain Rex Anslemo Abbott, and the countless other inspirations for characters and themes throughout the book.

Meet the Author

D.S. Newman is an Independent Author currently residing in Southern Indiana, although he is a traveller at heart. He draws many of his influences from a wide range of his favorite fiction, such as, Star Wars, Comic Books, Video Games, Anime, and his own imagination. He is also a History buff and a lover of music.

Connect with him at:
www.dsnewman.com